The Man on the Coffeehouse Floor

GERRY DONOHUE

Copyright © 2023 Gerry Donohue
All rights reserved

CHAPTER 1

Don't cross the thin blue line. That's the only inviolable rule. It's not about right or wrong, or legal or illegal. It's about Loyalty, with a capital L. Loyalty to the Department. Loyalty to the badge. And above all, Loyalty to your fellow officers. Stay true, and you can do just about anything you want . . . right up to the edge of that line.

Including, apparently, murder.

Six months before, someone was killing young black men in the drug trade. It was an unfortunately common occurrence in D.C., and the Metropolitan Police Department treated it that way, even though the killings bore no resemblance to the typical drug-trade murders. Rather than a drive-by shooting with a 9mm on full auto, these were execution-style homicides: a single bullet behind the right ear.

As the body count rose, however, the pressure on City Hall became too heavy, and the MPD threw some bodies at the investigation, including Detective First Class Martin Kinsale. Rather than trolling the drug-trade angle, he followed his own line of enquiry, which eventually led him inside the Department. As an eighteen-year veteran of the force, he'd known that bringing down a killer cop would spur repercussions from his fellow officers, but he'd figured they would be short-term and sporadic.

He'd been wrong.

The case blew up in the local press, dominating the front page of The Washington Post for three weeks, with Kinsale featured prominently in the narrative. Within the Department, it was bad enough that Kinsale had hunted down a fellow officer, but bringing public disdain down on the badge was unforgivable. Instantly, he was toxic, and everyone in the Department from the cadets at the Academy to the former chief wanted him gone. In fact, Kinsale was the reason that Francis X. Broughton had very quickly become the ex-chief.

Given Kinsale's sudden high profile and long and distinguished record, firing him was impossible, so the Department did what bureaucracies have done since the first form needed to be stamped. They put him, metaphorically speaking, in the back of the bottom drawer. Once all the internal investigations had wrapped up and The Post had latched onto a new scandal—a homophobic Congressman found in flagrante delicto in a men's room at the Tampa Convention Center—the Department reassigned Kinsale from Homicide to the Second District.

Within the Department, officers in the Second District were nicknamed "squirrel chasers" because crime was almost non-existent in the city's affluent northwestern neighborhoods. The Second was where old detectives went to play out the string, incompetent detectives went to hide, and lazy detectives went to nap. And as is so often the case with human nature, these pariahs punished Kinsale even more. Beyond reporting for rollcall at the beginning of his shifts and signing out at the end of the day, they made sure that Kinsale had nothing to do. He wasn't even allowed to make coffee.

Just to rankle the bastards, Kinsale resolved to obediently serve out his punishment. For the first time in years, he started showing up on time. He sat at his empty desk in the farthest corner of the squad room, watching the others do what he'd done for so long.

As the weeks passed with no end in sight, however, Kinsale found it increasingly difficult to control his mounting fury. So, after three months, he accepted that not even Lazarus would be able to climb out of the grave they'd dug for him, and he searched to find a friendlier place to wait out the months until he hit his twenty years.

He settled on The Laughing Dog Coffeehouse on Chesapeake Street, just off Wisconsin Avenue in the Tenleytown neighborhood. It was more than a mile from the Second stationhouse, and there were two Starbucks and a McDonalds in between, so it wasn't a regular cop stop. Occupying the first floor of a hundred-year-old rowhouse, The Dog had a comfortable vibe, with its high, tin ceiling and worn plank flooring. Local artists displayed their work on the exposed brick walls, and the corkboard by the front door was feathered with hand-written notices and faded business cards.

The service counter ran along the length of one wall. At the far end, a swinging door led to the small kitchen. Five two-person tables lined the opposite wall, and in the front window was a large round table. Early on, Kinsale had staked claim to the last table along the wall. It gave him an unimpeded view of the place and behind him was the short corridor to the restrooms and the back door.

Mostly, he read the days away. He had a long list of books that he'd always planned to read but had never found the time. Now that he had time in spades, he was working his way down the list. His current selection was Tim Pat Coogan's The IRA, but it was a dry, tough slog, so when he saw Lucy

Thayer heading his way, he laid the book on the tabletop to let her know that he was up for an interruption. Thayer owned The Dog, and over the past few months they'd become friendly. Sometimes when business was slow, she'd bring over a couple of coffees, and they'd pass a few minutes.

She was wearing her work outfit today, a black apron with a drawing of a white dog laughing at the moon over a tight white T-shirt and faded jeans. Tall and lithe, she had caramel-colored skin, short hair with a fade on the sides, and dimples that accentuated her smile. Today, though, she wasn't smiling.

Rather than sit, she placed his coffee in front of him and then leaned against the kitchen wall, her eyes flitting between him and the front of the café. "That's a hefty tome you've got there, Martin." She was trying to sound casual, but he could hear the strain in her voice.

When she next looked away, he followed her gaze. There were six other people in the coffeehouse. Rennie Esposito was behind the counter. A chemical engineering student at American University, he'd started working part-time at The Dog a couple of weeks before. He was a good kid, and Kinsale enjoyed their brief conversations when he went up to the counter to order.

Two men and one woman were working singularly at tables along the wall. Kinsale had developed a nodding acquaintance with the woman, who always took the first table, and one of the men, who regularly sat at the middle one and always faced away from the front door. He'd never seen the other man.

At the front table, two men were deep in a conversation. One was a well-dressed, older, white man. Even at a distance, Kinsale could see he was having difficulty with the late morning sun streaming through the big window. Sweat glistened on his sallow, fleshy face, and his breath was rapid and shallow as he leaned in and talked stridently across the table. His companion was a young black man. He was small and slight and had an awkward diffidence about him. Although he was listening to the old man, he was pressed into the back of his chair, looking like someone who'd sat down next to a Scientologist and was too polite to get up and leave.

"Sorry, what did you say?" Thayer asked, turning back to Kinsale.

"I didn't say anything."

"Sorry." She shook her head. "I've got something on my mind. How's the book?"

He tucked the flyleaf over the page he'd been reading, closed the book, and asked, "What's going on?"

"Going on?" Her gaze drifted again to the front, and she had to pull it back.

"Yeah, you seem distracted."

"Distracted? I'm not—" She took a deep breath and then pointed to the young man at the front table. "That's my brother Chris. Chris Dowling."

"He can't be your brother—he's a kid. He can't be more than..."

"He's older than he looks." She smiled like she'd said it before. "He's only twelve years younger than I am."

"That makes him, what, seventeen?"

Thayer managed a light laugh. "Don't I wish. No, he's almost ... Let's just say that he's in his late twenties."

Kinsale was pleased that she hadn't wanted to tell him her age. Not for the first time, he thought that if she weren't married... "So, what's up? Is something going on with him?"

"Up? No, nothing. It's just that I haven't seen him in a while."

"He's visiting from out of town?"

"No, he lives here. He's an instructor at the Georgetown Academy."

Kinsale was both surprised and impressed. The Georgetown Academy was the most prestigious private boys' school in a city full of prestigious private boys' schools. Dowling didn't appear to have the age, bearing, maturity—or skin color—that Kinsale thought would have been prerequisites for teaching the sons of the global elite.

His sister had obviously seen that reaction before as well. "He's very bright," she said. "Also, he's an old boy."

"Old boy?"

"An alumnus."

"Your brother went to the Georgetown Academy?"

"On scholarship."

"Where did you go?"

"Cardozo."

Cardozo was a fair-to-middling high school in the less-than-fair-to-middling D.C. public school system. "That doesn't seem fair."

"Like I said, he's the smart one."

"Who's the old guy?"

She shrugged. "I don't know."

After eighteen years of working the streets, Kinsale was adept at spotting a lie, and she'd just told him one. He wondered why she would feel that need. It wasn't as if they had a relationship beyond The Dog. And if it was because he was with the MPD, what were the two men up to?

He gave her a doubting look, but she'd already turned away. He focused again on the man talking to her brother. Part of the problem was his clothes. In his gray flannel pants, button-down shirt, blue blazer, and a self-consciously colorful bowtie, he was overdressed for D.C. at the end of April. Kinsale watched him pull a handkerchief out of his pants pocket and rub it across his forehead to keep the sweat out of his eyes.

Thayer pushed away from the wall and said, "I better get back to it."

As she headed back to the counter, her brother stood and went to meet her. They talked with their heads just inches apart. She was obviously upset, speaking in a rapid hush. After a tense pause, she turned on her heels, went behind the counter, and pushed through the kitchen door. Before it had stopped swinging, she returned and dropped two pills into her brother's outstretched palm. He gave her an apologetic smile and asked for something more. She fixed him with a long glare and then made an exaggerated show of getting him a glass of water.

Dowling took the water and the pills back to the table and placed them in front of the old man. He dropped the pills into the water, which immediately became cloudy and began to effervesce. He waited until the pills had dissolved and then drank down the water. The effort seemed to tire him out, because he sat back and closed his eyes.

Kinsale went back to reading, but he had trouble concentrating on his book. He could not focus, his mind stuck in a groove of speculation about why she'd lied to him.

An anguished cry split the silence in the coffeehouse, followed a moment later, by a chair crashing to the floor.

Looking up, Kinsale saw Dowling standing with one hand over his mouth and his eyes wide with shock. His upended chair lay behind him. His companion was splayed face-first on the tabletop, liquid dripping out from under him onto the floor. At first Kinsale thought it was coffee, but then he saw the yellowish tint and thickish consistency.

The man's right arm dropped from the table and hung loosely under him. And then with an awful inevitability, his body began to slide off the edge. The fingers on his right hand bent limply when they touched the wood planking. And then a moment later, his body toppled over and crashed to the floor. He made no move to protect himself, and his head landed with a sickening smack. A few seconds later, the empty water glass rolled off the table, landed next to him, and shattered.

CHAPTER 2

Dowling stumbled back until he was pressed against the front window. His eyes were wide and unblinking and locked on the body on the floor. For a long moment, everyone remained as still as a photograph, and then the man whom Kinsale didn't know leaped out of his chair, scooped up his laptop and papers in one fluid motion, and raced out the door. The two regulars rose to get a better look but stayed where they were. And behind the counter, Rennie Esposito looked to Lucy Thayer for guidance.

Kinsale leaped up, his legs hitting the underside of the table and knocking his book onto the floor. He stepped over it at a run and reached the prone man in a half-dozen steps. Kicking away the shards of the broken glass, he kneeled, grabbed the back of the man's blazer in clenched fists, and flipped him over. A sickly sour smell filled the air. Kinsale gagged at the back of his throat. The dripping liquid he'd seen was a viscous, mustard-yellow vomit, and it was plastered across the old man's chest and was slick on his face and in his hair.

Kinsale wrestled with the bowtie, his hands slipping on the puke-wet knot, but it finally loosened. He grabbed on either side of the shirt placket and ripped it apart. Buttons flew into the air like teeth in a bar fight, and the man's pale, flaccid skin sagged on either side of his hairless chest. Kinsale felt for a pulse on the neck but got nothing.

Sensing Dowling inching closer, he looked up. The young man's gaze was fixed on the prone body with a mix of morbid curiosity and mortal horror. Kinsale was about to tell him to move back, but then Thayer appeared and draped an arm around her brother's shoulders.

"Is he dead?" she asked, her voice a hush.

"Get back," Kinsale growled. "I need space."

Instead, she leaned forward to get a closer look, as if to make sure the man was dead.

"Lucy, please!" He was exasperated.

Only then did she move back, pulling her brother with her.

"And call 911," Kinsale called after her.

He wiped what he could off the man's face and pried open his mouth. Seeing nothing blocking the airway, he sealed the man's nose with his left hand, tilted back the head, and blew into the mouth. The acrid taste of vomit curdled in his throat. After breathing into the mouth for a second time, he saw that the man's lungs were still not working on their own. Placing one hand in the center of the chest and bracing it with the other, he pumped several times rapidly. Again, he checked for signs of life and still found none.

Kinsale began the CPR cycle of two breaths followed by thirty chest compressions. He quickly got over any queasiness, ignoring the smell of bile and the sheen of vomit smeared across the man's face. He concentrated on the task at hand. Breathe. Breathe. Pump, pump, pump...

After several minutes, Kinsale started to have difficulty breathing himself. He stopped for a moment and tried to take a deep breath, but his lungs felt like they were lined with plastic. He went back to the CPR but could no longer maintain the rhythm. He lost track of the number of compressions and then couldn't decide whether to guess what it was or to start over. And then he couldn't remember what he'd decided. Soon he was gasping for air again, and when he paused to rest, a wave of vertigo swept over him.

"Does anyone here know CPR?" he asked. When no one responded, he looked over at Dowling. "You're a teacher. Don't they require that you know how to do it?"

Dowling blanched at the suggestion, and his sister pulled him to her. "No, Martin, he doesn't know how."

That was the second lie she'd told him in less than half an hour, but he couldn't worry about that now. He went back to trying to revive the man. He tried not to think about how tired he was or how muzzy his head had become because there was no stopping until the EMTs arrived. He wondered if Thayer had called them and then couldn't remember if he'd asked her to.

He cursed himself for not attending the Department's annual CPR refresher courses. They were mandatory but so were a lot of things that he didn't do. Anyway, the technique was straightforward, and he was sure he was doing it right. But if he were, why was he having such difficulty?

Suddenly, strong hands gripped his shoulders and pulled at him. He fought against the sudden force and whipped his head around to see who was trying to stop him from helping the old man. A broad, black woman in a dark blue uniform was tugging at him and saying something, but he couldn't hear her because of the roaring in his ears. She wrenched at him, but he continued to resist, although he no longer knew why. He couldn't remember what he was doing. She yanked again, and this time he felt himself lifting away from the body.

Darkness edged into his vision. He watched the floor race towards his face, and then everything went black.

Kinsale meandered back to consciousness. After a while, he remembered where he was and what had happened, but only when he felt someone touch his shoulder did he open his eyes. The woman was kneeling over him and checking his pulse.

"You hyperventilated," she said. "That can happen when you don't do CPR right. You'll be all right if you just lie here for a while."

That's what he did. He watched the woman and her partner bundle the body onto a gurney and strap it down. The other EMT was a wiry black man with a small mustache and two studs in his left earlobe. When they were done, she held open the front door while her partner guided the gurney through.

She returned to Kinsale and squatted down. "We're taking him to Sibley," she said.

"How's it look?"

She shook her head. "If it looked good, I wouldn't be talking to you right now. How do you feel?"

"A lot better. I just needed a few minutes."

"I'll need your information." She took out a small pad and pen from her breast pocket.

"Why?"

"Because you were treating the patient, and I ended up treating you."

Kinsale gave her his name. "I'm with MPD."

She looked up from writing and smirked but stayed quiet out of professional courtesy.

"Take it easy for a few days," she advised, and then she stood and left.

When the door swung shut behind her, an unnatural silence settled over the Dog. Everyone remained rooted in place, uncertain what to do next. Kinsale would have been happy to lie on the floor for the rest of the morning, but he needed to clean himself off. The skin on his face and hands felt tight with dried vomit, and his shirt was beyond saving. And now that the adrenaline in his system had ebbed, his sense of smell had returned with a vengeance.

He pushed himself to his feet and began a wobbly trek to the bathroom.

CHAPTER 3

When Kinsale returned ten minutes later, only the two siblings remained. They were sitting close together at the front table. She had one leg tucked under the other and looked as tense as an addict. He was staring out the window, looking detached, which under the circumstances, struck Kinsale as odd.

As he approached, he saw that someone had mopped up the mess. He wished he'd been as successful. Trying to clean the vomit stains from his shirt, he'd only made it wetter and more yellow. On the table were three glasses of water and a well-worn black-leather, three-ring day planner. Kinsale sat down across from them, picked up the closest glass of water, and drained it.

"I figured you could use that," Thayer said. "You looked totally spent. In fact, you still don't look too good."

"They never mentioned how exhausting that could be."

Her eyes widened. "You've never done CPR before?"

"If I had, I probably wouldn't have keeled over next to the victim."

"What do you think happened?" she asked.

"The EMT said I hyperventilated."

"To him, I mean." She gestured toward the spot on the floor where the man had lain.

"I don't know. Heart attack? Stroke? Something like that."

"That's the first time I've ever seen anyone…"

"It's always hard," Kinsale said. "Especially when it's someone you know."

Thayer winced and looked down.

"Come on, Lucy," Kinsale said. "You knew him."

He could see that she wanted to continue her denial, but she was smart enough not to. "I knew who he was," she admitted and then added, "but I'd never seen him until today."

"Who was he?"

"James Kennedy. He was one of Chris's teachers when he was at the Academy."

"And?"

"And he was in town for the day. They were catching up."

Kinsale turned to Dowling. The young man hadn't moved. He appeared to be unaware that they were talking about him. Or that they were there at all. "Mr. Dowling?"

"Can't it wait?" Thayer reached across and put a hand on Kinsale's forearm. "After what just happened."

"It would be best if I talked with him now."

"But he's—"

"A man is dead."

"From a heart attack or a stroke. You said so yourself."

"Lucy, I need to talk to your brother."

"He didn't—"

"Lucy," Kinsale talked over her. "The Department investigates any unexplained death. Some get more attention than others. This one probably won't require much, but they'll still send a team down here to talk to you and your brother. Maybe Rennie too. And maybe they'll track down your other customers and talk to them. I think I can shortcut all that. I talk with you two right now, write up a preliminary report, and maybe the whole thing goes away by the end of the day."

That wasn't true, but he figured it was fair play given her earlier deceptions. Kennedy's death appeared to be by natural causes. That's probably all it was. Each day on average about fifteen people died in D.C., and almost all of them passed due to natural causes. The Department might send a car around for a death that occurred outside of a medical setting, but more often than not it wouldn't.

There remained, though, the fact that she'd lied to him—twice—and he needed to know why.

"I can talk to him, Luce," Dowling said in a small voice.

His sister glared at her brother, but he ignored her, continuing to stare out the window. She clicked her tongue in annoyance and sat back with her arms folded. "Might as well get it over with then."

Kinsale thought she was being overprotective, but he could see how Dowling would bring about such behavior. He asked him, "Do you want coffee or anything?"

"Tea would be nice."

Kinsale glanced at Thayer. Again, she clicked her tongue, but she stood. "You wait until I get back before talking," she commanded.

"Fair enough," Kinsale agreed, but once she was behind the counter, he said, "Some sister you've got there."

"The best."

"I haven't seen you in here before."

"I don't come too often. In fact, I think this is the first time I've been here since, probably, January."

"That's just about when I started coming here. End of January."

"Closer to the beginning."

"You don't like the coffee?" Kinsale asked. "Or the tea?"

"I spend most of my time at the Academy," he said and then seemed to fade out of the conversation. They remained quiet until Thayer returned.

She put the tea in front of her brother and then pulled her chair even closer to him. There was no mistaking that it was now them against Kinsale, which intrigued him.

"I'm Detective Martin Kinsale with the Metropolitan Police Department," he said to Dowling. "I would like to ask you a few questions about what happened today. Is that okay?"

Dowling nodded, and Kinsale asked him to describe what he'd seen.

Dowling picked up his tea, and after a moment, started speaking into the cup. "We were just talking, and then suddenly Jim froze. In mid-sentence. His eyes became very wide and...and I think he was scared. He started to retch, and then he vomited onto the table. Twice, I think. He looked at it like he didn't understand what was happening. And then he just collapsed. I stood up and then you..."

"Can we go back before that? How did you two come to be here?"

Dowling carefully set the cup on the table and his eyes rested there. "He was an old instructor of mine. From the Academy. He was in town for the day. We decided to have coffee together."

"He called you?"

Dowling nodded.

"When?"

"Yesterday afternoon. Around three or so."

"What did he say?"

"That he was coming to town, and he would love to see me."

"Where was he calling from?"

"I don't know." Dowling rotated the cup a quarter-turn on the tabletop. "He lived in Michigan."

"Do you know where?"

"In Midland. He taught at the Midland Military Institute."

"So, it was just two private school teachers having a cup of coffee and catching up on old times?"

The description appeared to please Dowling, and he nodded.

"I've got to tell you, Chris, it didn't look like that at all. I was sitting back there," Kinsale turned and pointed to his table. "I had a clear view of the two of you and it looked to me like Kennedy was agitated, maybe even upset. And you... Well, you were basically recoiling from him."

"Martin, that's not fair," Thayer said. "Chris was—"

"Really? It looked like that?" For the first time, Dowling looked at Kinsale. His large eyes were the same dark color as his sister's. "Jim was a passionate man, maybe even a little...extravagant. I think that's what you saw."

Dowling was a better liar than his sister. It helped that he was slight and had an air of innocence, but he was also practiced at it. And now Kinsale had to wonder why both siblings felt the need to lie to him.

"I'll say again that it didn't look like that from my vantage point," Kinsale said.

"I can't help what it looked like. We were just talking."

"There's no issue if you're having an argument with someone, and their heart gives out," Kinsale said.

"We weren't having an argument," Dowling said, his mouth forming a pout.

Kinsale turned to Thayer. "You gave your brother some pills for Kennedy."

Thayer wasn't ready for the question, and she fumbled for an answer. "I... They were Alka-Seltzer. Chris said Kennedy wasn't feeling well."

Kinsale looked back at Dowling. "And you gave them to Kennedy?"

"Yes. Lucy gave them to me, and I gave them to him."

"Did Kennedy have anything with him?"

"Like what?" Dowling asked.

"A briefcase, a bag, a coat?"

"No."

"What about this?" Kinsale gestured towards the black-leather day planner.

"It's mine." Dowling pulled it to him.

"I hope it didn't get puked on."

"It'll be okay. There's nothing important in it."

"Mind if I take a look?" Kinsale extended a hand.

"I'd rather you didn't." Dowling pressed down on the binder. "It contains confidential student information."

"You just told me that there was nothing important in it."

"I meant that there was nothing important regarding Jim's death."

Dowling's hands on top of the notepad-sized planner looked like a child's, and Kinsale could have easily pushed them aside. In other instances, he might have done so, but Thayer's presence stopped him. He didn't want to believe that she—and by extension, her brother—would be involved in anything untoward, and he was willing to give them the benefit of the doubt until proved otherwise.

"I've got what I needed." He pushed back in his chair. "I'll write this up this afternoon. I don't see it going any farther."

Thayer let out a relieved sigh, as if she'd been holding her breath since Kinsale had sat down.

"How can I get in touch with you if I need to?" Kinsale asked Dowling.

"I live at the Academy." He pulled out his wallet and handed over a business card. "I'm a residence advisor."

"One last thing," Kinsale said to Thayer as he stood. "Earlier, you told me you didn't know who Kennedy was. Why?"

"I thought it was him, but I wasn't sure," she said. "Like I told you, I'd never actually seen him."

Kinsale nodded like he believed her answer and then went back to his table to retrieve the Coogan book. He could feel Thayer's gaze on him the entire time, but as he walked to the front door, she was looking down at her phone.

And Dowling had gone back to staring out the window.

CHAPTER 4

Kinsale's twenty-year-old black BMW 328 was parked directly across the street from the Dog. In the half-minute it took him to reach it, he came to two conclusions. First, that Kennedy's death was more than just a heart attack. And second, that for now, he would keep his suspicions to himself.

Even in the moment, he knew he was being foolish. He had nothing tangible that pointed to it being more than a heart attack, just the seemingly inconsequential lies the siblings had told him. Except, lies were never inconsequential.

And if his suspicion about Kennedy's death turned out to be correct, failing to make it official was a dangerous path to follow. The Department was eager to latch onto any reason to get rid of him, and if they learned that he was pursuing his own investigation, he would hand it to them. In fact, he could break the case, and they would probably still bring him up on charges.

But, if he reported his concerns to Captain Gregory Scott, who commanded the Second District detectives, the file would immediately be turned over to his old colleagues in the Homicide Branch, and he would go back to doing nothing. That was untenable. He'd tried to fool himself into thinking that he could survive—even enjoy—spending his days drinking coffee and reading books, but in truth he was killing himself as much as he was killing time.

He left the car door ajar to give the black-leather interior some time to cool down and then opened the trunk, where he kept an overnight bag. He pulled out a clean shirt. It had been in the bag for a few months and had an old-car odor, but that was preferable to Kennedy's sour-smelling puke. He took off the stained shirt and put on the clean one. He balled up the old one, stuffed it into a nearby trashcan, and then climbed into his car and headed for Sibley Hospital.

Sibley touted itself as the best hospital in the city. It was certainly the most established. If a patient's blood had even the slightest tint of blue, they went to Sibley, if only because they couldn't bear to tell their social circle that they'd gone elsewhere. Inside, though, it was like every other hospital. The emergency room waiting area had the institutional pallor of beige linoleum, pastel walls and furniture, and fluorescent lighting that flattened out the shadows, and it smelled as if someone had spilled a barrel of disinfectant and then gone on break.

A middle-aged Asian nurse with a broad, flat face and flower-patterned scrubs sat behind the reception desk. Two people were in line ahead of Kinsale—a young girl holding her right arm close to her body like she was carrying a baby bird and an older woman who smelled musty and was carrying three overflowing reusable grocery bags. After a brief conversation with the girl, the nurse picked up the phone, said a few words, and an instant later, a tall black nurse in pale blue scrubs and hot-pink tennis shoes came through the automatic door that led to the examination area. After a moment's consultation, he gently led the teenager back through the still-open door. Only then did Kinsale notice that the girl's elbow was bent in the wrong direction.

The older woman shuffled forward and launched into a strident monologue in a low voice. Whatever ailed her couldn't have been too serious, though, because the nurse immediately directed her towards the waiting room chairs. The woman tried to argue, but the nurse was having none of it and pointed towards the chairs. The woman sulked away.

Kinsale stepped up, flashed his shield, and said he needed to talk to someone about James Kennedy. The nurse wordlessly motioned for him to sit next to the old lady and picked up the phone.

There were about two dozen people in various stages of discomfort spread around the waiting room, and most of them eyed Kinsale as he sat down, trying to discern if whatever ailed him might push him ahead of them.

After about ten minutes, a young doctor in a seriously starched lab coat came through the automatic doors, surveyed the waiting throng, and walked over to Kinsale. He was smallish and palish and had a receding hairline that he tried to disguise by combing over thin wisps of hair. He had a beige folder under his left arm and a clear plastic bag in his right hand.

"Detective?" He had the pinched voice of the self-consciously busy. "I'm Dr. Pederson. You're here about James Kennedy?"

Kinsale stood and extended his hand. Instead of shaking it, Pederson dropped the plastic bag into it. Kinsale lifted it up and turned it around. It held a black billfold, a hotel key sleeve, a cell phone, some car keys, a tank watch with a black leather band, a stained handkerchief, and some change. "These would be his?"

Pederson opened the file and read out loud, "Mr. Kennedy was pronounced dead at 12:07 p.m. on April 30."

"Cause?"

"Preliminarily, myocardial infarction."

"A heart attack," Kinsale said.

Pederson nodded.

"Were there any signs of a pre-existing condition?"

"Are you kidding?" Pederson asked with the exasperation of the overworked and underappreciated. "He was a sixty-four-year-old man."

"Were there any signs of a pre-existing condition?" Kinsale asked again.

Instead of answering, Pederson swept his left arm across the room. "What would you say? There are twenty-five, thirty people waiting out here. We're probably working with half again as many inside. With two doctors. Two! And this is the quietest it's been all day."

Seeing that his words were having no impact, Pederson stopped. He gave Kinsale a put-upon look and opened the file again. "He was a drinker, probably heavy, and was a smoker, or at least he had been and for quite a while. He was overweight and probably hypertensive. So, yes, there were signs of pre-existing conditions. He was dead when EMTs rolled him in, was probably dead before they reached him. We called the morgue, and honestly, I haven't thought about him since."

"Think about him now," Kinsale said. "Take a minute."

"I just told you that I don't have a minute."

"Sure, you do."

Pederson looked ready to argue, but then his shoulders sagged. "What do you want me to think about?"

"Anything that comes to mind. Anything out of the ordinary."

Pederson made a show of reading through the file. Kinsale doubted he was making much of an effort, but then the doctor's eyes took on a quizzical look. "It's probably nothing."

"But?"

"You don't usually see such violent emesis with an MI."

"Emesis?"

"Vomiting. It happens but not like that."

"What could account for the elm . . . vomiting?" Kinsale asked.

"If it were a massive event, the body might react that way," he said, but he didn't sound convinced.

"Could he have taken something that would cause a heart attack? Something that would also have made him throw up?"

"What do you mean?"

"He took some Alka-Seltzer a few minutes before."

Pederson shook his head. "That would have the opposite effect."

"What if it were some other type of pill?"

"It would depend on the pills, wouldn't it?"

"What type of pill would do that?"

"That's outside my purview, Detective," he said. "If the Medical Examiner decides to do an autopsy, maybe they'll find something, but don't get ahead of yourself. Like I said, this was a sixty-four-year-old man."

CHAPTER 5

The Second District station was a bunker-like, two-story building on Idaho Avenue—drab concrete slab walls, a flat roof, and tall, narrow windows. There was even a line of what looked like bullet pockmarks at the southeast corner of the building, but they were just flaws in the concrete.

Kinsale parked in the lot behind the stationhouse and went in through the officers' entrance. The duty sergeant made a point of ignoring him. He joined two uniformed officers on the elevator. They acknowledged him, but that was likely because they didn't recognize him, given how little time he put in at the Second.

He crossed the second-floor hallway and pushed through the double glass doors into the detectives' bullpen. It was a large, open space with two-dozen-or-so desks laid out in back-to-back pairs. The room smelled of second-hand smoke, beer sweat, and a lack of ambition. Four glass-walled offices faced the bullpen along a long wall. The three detective sergeants had spaces about as wide as a queen-sized bed, and Captain Scott had the corner office. Kinsale glanced in and saw that he was on the phone.

The squad secretary Royale Moon gave him a playful double-take. She was built like a linebacker but carried herself like that was sexy, and so it was. She dressed in bright, form-fitting clothes and squeezed her feet into impossibly tight shoes. Today, her eyes were blue under doe-like lashes. "Your shift ain't nowhere near done, Martin," she said. "What are you doin' back so early?"

Kinsale perched on the edge of her desk. "Believe it or not, I actually have some work to do. Of course, it took a guy dropping dead right in front of me."

"Some people get all the luck." Moon didn't approve of Kinsale's being ostracized and refused to participate.

"You've got to figure I'm due."

"Was it the man in the coffee shop up on Chesapeake Street?"

"How did you know about that?"

"EMS called in about twenty minutes ago. They said the officer on the scene had a little prob—" Her face lit up with delight. "That was you."

Kinsale felt the blood rush to his face. "I think I hyperventilated."

"That's what they said." She leaned back in her office chair, filling it like over-leavened bread. "They said you passed out."

"I got a little woozy."

"They said you passed out on the floor. They called to make sure you were okay."

He stood. "I'm fine. I'd better go and write it up."

"You be careful," she called after him. "You have any problems, you let me know. I'll show you the right way to do mouth-to-mouth."

Moon had an infectious laugh, and Kinsale couldn't help smiling as he made his way to his desk. He passed eight of his colleagues on the way, but not one of them looked up. His desk was the only single in the pen. In the back and flush against the west-facing window, it appeared to be a prime spot. It was anything but. During a cold snap in early February, frost had formed on the inside of the window, and now, even though the official start of summer was more than a month-and-a-half away, the afternoon sun radiated through the pane like it was a magnifying glass. For now, the small fan he'd brought into the office sufficed. Come July and August, he'd need something more industrial.

Two hours later, he hit the print icon on his computer and walked across to the printer. The day shift was winding down, so most of the detectives were back at the station, standing around and talking while they waited to clock out. He had to pass several of them, and they stood stolidly in place, forcing him to step around. Not for the first time, Kinsale acknowledged the fact that no one held a grudge like a cop.

He stayed by the printer and reread the report. He liked how close he came to saying that there were questions regarding Kennedy's death without spelling them out. No one was going to read the report too closely at this point, but if the shit hit the fan later, he could at least use it as cover.

Crossing over to the corner office, he knocked on Scott's open door. The Captain was working on his computer, typing with his two index fingers and maintaining an impressively fast pace. Every few seconds he would look at the monitor to track his progress.

Kinsale had a couple of years on Scott. They'd never worked together, but he'd long known him by reputation. Scott was the type of partner that every detective wanted. When it came down to the details of a case, he was unrelenting. Most detectives weren't willing to put in the work to track down every lead, but in the end, that's how most cases got closed. Scott's case files always bulged two or three times bigger than anyone else's—probably four times bigger than Kinsale's—and he routinely had one of the highest clearance rates in the Department. So, of course, the Big Hats had pulled him off the streets and stuck him behind a desk. To his credit, Scott took to it. Commanding the Second detectives was certainly just the first rung up the ladder to the Fifth Floor.

Scott favored high-collared dress shirts and narrow ties. Today's shirt was a light violet, and his gray tie had a subtle pattern. When he looked up and saw Kinsale at his door, he grimaced.

"Captain, can I have a minute?"

Scott considered his answer before gesturing to one of his visitor's chairs. Kinsale sat and laid his report on the edge of the desk.

"Had a guy die from a heart attack in front of me today."

"Where was that?"

"The Laughing Dog."

"You've been spending some time there."

"I like it," Kinsale said. "Anyway—"

"ID?"

"James Kennedy. From Midland, Michigan. He was sixty-four years old."

Scott picked up his Styrofoam coffee cup and looked disappointed when he saw it was empty. He tossed it in the trash can and motioned for Kinsale to continue.

"He was likely dead before he hit the floor. EMTs took him to Sibley. ER doc pronounced him dead at 12:07."

Scott gestured toward the report. "You wrote it up?"

"Thought I might as well get it started." Kinsale nudged the pages across the desk.

Scott picked them up and scanned them. "Did you call Kennedy's doctor?"

"I wanted to find out how you want to play it. I can clean up the loose ends. Or maybe you want to want to assign it to someone else?"

Kinsale had actually come to like Scott since arriving at the Second. Of course, he'd iced out Kinsale like everyone else, because he was MPD blue to his DNA. Still, Kinsale had the sense that he didn't like it, even though the Captain never gave him any indication of that.

Scott studied Kinsale for a moment and then flipped back and forth between the two-page report. "You think it was a heart attack?"

"Looks that way."

"I asked what you think."

Kinsale didn't hesitate. "I think it was a heart attack."

Scott nodded and pointed at the bottom of the first sheet. "What's this about him puking?

"The doctor said it was unusual for someone to throw up like that during a heart attack, but it was probably because it was so severe."

Scott turned over the second sheet to see if there was anything on the back. "Everything here?"

"Everything."

Kinsale could see that Scott wasn't convinced. He still had his detective instincts, and he sensed something wasn't right. Although he didn't need a good reason to take Kennedy away from Kinsale, he was enough of a leader to want one. "Okay," he said finally. "You finish it up. Call his doctor. Track down his immediate family or leave that to the Midland PD. Check in with the ME tomorrow to see if they're going to do an autopsy."

"Do you want me to start a file on this?" Kinsale asked. A file meant a case number, and that meant he would be in the system as the investigating detective.

"Not right now. Let's wait to see if they do an autopsy."

Kinsale stood and headed out. "Do you want me to shut the door."

"No," Scott said. "And Martin."

Kinsale turned around. Scott waited a beat and then said, "Why don't you sign up for a CPR refresher course?"

CHAPTER 6

Kinsale was halfway back to his desk when Brian Magner stepped into his path. On the far side of fifty, with a soft belly and a disappointed face, Magner was the quintessential Second District detective. He'd been taking it easy for so long that he thought it was in his job description.

"Did you finally turn in your papers?" Magner asked. Other detectives were watching, and he was playing to the crowd.

"Nah." Kinsale made an exaggerated show of avoiding the other man's bulk, raising his hands while slipping to the side. "The Captain was just thinking that since I don't have anything to do and you don't do a god-damn thing, maybe we should partner up."

A couple of guys sniggered, and Magner shut them down with a malevolent stare. He wasn't popular in the squad but was senior enough that detectives needed to stay on his good side. Turning back to Kinsale, he growled between clenched teeth, "You're done. Toast. Gone. You just don't know it yet."

Kinsale kept moving. Magner was just barking, and Kinsale wasn't going to let him spoil this moment, because for the first time in the past six months, he felt good. The Job had always demanded so much from him, and he'd happily given everything to it. In so doing, though, he'd shed a lot of his outside life, and what he'd lost no longer felt recoverable. Since being assigned to the Second, he'd awakened each morning to see an empty shell staring back at him in the mirror. Eventually, if he didn't break the cycle, he wouldn't want to look in the mirror. Or even wake up.

The late afternoon sun had continued to bake his desk while he was in Scott's office, so Kinsale turned on the small fan to move the air around. He input Kennedy's driver's license information into the Michigan DMV database and within a few seconds had the dead man's vitals.

There were two listed phone numbers. He opened his bottom desk drawer, where he'd put the plastic bag of Kennedy's effects, and pulled out the cellphone. He tried to open it, but it was password protected. He called the first number from the database and the cellphone rang. He cancelled the call and tried the second number. It rang six times before clicking over to voicemail. "Thank you for calling." Kennedy's voice sounded old and self-important. "I cannot come to the telephone at this time. Please leave a message after the tone, and I will return your call as soon as possible." Kinsale hung up without leaving a message, because Kennedy wouldn't be returning any calls, and he'd learned what he needed to know. The message was all about "I." The old man had lived alone.

Next, he went online and found the website of the Midland Military Institute. He called the 800 number at the bottom of the page and a woman answered on the second ring. He identified himself as an MPD detective and told her, "One of your teachers, James Kennedy, has taken seriously ill here, and we're trying to reach his doctor and relatives."

"Mr. Kennedy?" She sounded shocked. "Will he be all right?"

Until Kinsale talked to a relative, Kennedy's condition would have to be grave rather than terminal. "We don't know, but we need to talk to both his doctor and his family."

"Well, I know he isn't married."

"Any relatives? Brother? Sister?"

"I don't know."

"Could you look it up?"

"The office is closed."

"But it's four o'clock there," Kinsale said, checking the time in the corner of his computer screen. "You're on Central Time, aren't you?"

"No, Eastern. It's just gone five, but our office hours are 8:30 to 4:30."

"You're there," he pointed out.

"I'm one of the night operators."

"Why does a school need a night operator?"

"The Institute has more than 260 boarding students. We have staff on duty at all times."

"But no one in the office?"

"No one, sir."

Kinsale tried a different tack. "What health insurance does the school provide to employees?"

She hesitated. "Excuse me?"

"What insurer does the school use. If you tell me that, I can contact them and find out about Mr. Kennedy's doctor."

"I am not . . . I get my insurance through my husband. I don't know what coverage the Institute provides.

"Does your husband also work the night shift?"

"Sometimes. He's in the Coast Guard."

"There's Coast Guard in Michigan?"

"We're only twenty minutes from Lake Huron," she said. "Maybe you should talk to the Commandant? I'm sure he could answer your questions."

Kinsale breathed out heavily. "Sure. Is he in the office?"

"No."

"What's his number?"

"Oh, I couldn't possibly give that out, but he checks his messages frequently. I could put you through to his voicemail."

"That'd be great," he said. "And thanks for your time."

"My pleasure," she said and put him through. After listening to Commandant Philip Shelvey's message, Kinsale repeated the story he'd told the night operator and asked him to call.

His last call for the day was to the Midland Police Department. He explained to the desk sergeant who he was and why he was calling and was put through to Detective Leslie Ridenour.

"So, it was just a heart attack?" she asked.

"That's where we are right now. The issue is whether we leave it at that or put him on the ME's dance card."

"But it was a heart attack?"

"Yes, but . . . I just wanted to let your department know, as a courtesy."

"We appreciate that. Thanks. I'll log it," she said and disconnected.

Kinsale stayed at his desk for another hour, inputting notes, organizing his thoughts, and planning out next steps. He didn't need to, but he hadn't enjoyed himself so much in a long, long time.

CHAPTER 7

Kinsale lived in a large, green clapboard house on the corner of Rock Creek Church Road and Fifth Street. It had once been the home of the city's most successful dry-cleaning dynasty, but since then, it had gone through several owners and had finally been sub-divided into a two-up, two-down condominium. He had a one-bedroom unit on the second floor. The building was in a quiet residential neighborhood, although Fifth Street carried a lot of morning, rush-hour traffic. Fortunately, his apartment was on the opposite side, so he rarely noticed it.

He'd been home only a couple of minutes when there was a knock on his door. Opening it, he found his friend and downstairs neighbor Manny Oturos holding four Coronas laced between the fingers of his upraised right hand.

"You shuffled in late today," Oturos said as he sidled past and headed for the refrigerator. "I thought I was going to have to start without you."

For several years, Oturos and Kinsale had shared a happy hour once or twice each week, but since Kinsale had been assigned to the Second, it had become an almost nightly ritual. "I was busy," he said.

Oturos stopped in mid-stride and spun around. "No way. They finally caved?"

"Not exactly. A guy died of a heart attack at that coffeehouse where I've been spending my time. Right in front of me. I'm looking into it."

Oturos digested the news as he put two of the beers in the refrigerator, opened the other two, and returned to the living room. "Man, you are scraping the bottom of the barrel if you're investigating a heart attack."

He handed one of the beers to Kinsale and dropped onto the couch. Kinsale sat in the reading chair. "If it were anything more, Scott would have whisked it away from me without a second thought. And, anyway, I've got the feeling that there may be more to it than just a heart attack."

"What you're saying is you hope there's more to it, and . . ." Oturos thought it through. "You're not telling anybody on the force because you want to have the chance to solve it, if it really is something."

"Yeah, although when you put it like that, it sounds kind of pathetic."

"I'm not judging, Martin; you know that. They've backed you into a corner. Whatever you gotta do to get out seems like fair play to me."

Over the past months, Kinsale had come to look forward to the calming effect of their nightly beers, but even more, he appreciated Oturos's friendship. "What about you?" he asked. "How was your day?"

"There's a pharmaceutical sales meeting at the hotel." A smile spread across Oturos's face. "Let me tell you. You've never seen so many beautiful young people in one place. Women and men. And don't they know it too? The money they spend on clothes and hair products in a year. Maybe I should get into that."

Oturos leased the gift shop at the Hyatt Hotel near the D.C. Convention Center. He was a Cuban American. His parents had brought him to Florida when he was a child, and he'd worked a succession of hard-labor jobs, climbing the ladder one rung at a time, until he'd finally acquired his own business.

"Did they give you any free samples?" Kinsale asked.

"I'm going to assume you're talking about the pharmaceuticals, and no, they didn't."

Their conversation wandered around after that, and they were halfway through their second bottles when Kinsale's phone rang. He recognized the Midland area code from the calls he'd made earlier in the day. "This is work," he said. "I don't know how long I'll be."

"No worries." Oturos stood and headed for the door. "Good to see you with your nose to the grindstone."

Kinsale waited for the door to close to pick up. "Detective Martin Kinsale."

"Yeah, this is Lieutenant Ralph Wingate. I'm with Midland PD SIS. I'm calling about James Kennedy."

Any relaxing effect from the beers instantly dissipated. Special Investigative Squads in police departments around the country had a variety of duties, but Kinsale doubted any of them involved following up on an old man dying of a heart attack halfway across the country. And even if that were in the Midland SIS's purview, they wouldn't be calling him after hours to talk about it.

"I thought we could have a little chat," Wingate said.

"Are you still on shift?"

"I came back in after Detective Ridenour called me."

"He was somebody then."

"Oh, yeah. A scumbag of the first order. In fact, we'd issued an arrest warrant for him just this morning. He was part of a ring of pedophiles. We rolled up the others, but he'd already done a runner."

"Not for long."

"Long enough," Wingate snapped. "I've got two guys trying to figure out how he got the word."

"Was this one of those internet things? Kiddie porn and all that?"

"If only. This was five pervs picking off schoolboys. Looks like it had been going on for years." Wingate paused. "Tell me about today."

Kinsale understood now why Thayer and Dowling had lied to him, but he wondered whether Dowling shared the old man's predilections or had been a victim. Based on his personality and his sister's behavior, it was almost certainly the latter, but . . .

It took about two minutes for Kinsale to take Wingate through the events of the day. The Midland detective was quiet for about half as long again, and then asked, "Why do I have the feeling that there's more to this than just a heart attack?"

"I don't know."

"Maybe because you do, too."

"It certainly looked like a heart attack to me, Lieutenant," Kinsale said carefully. "One minute he was sitting at the table, and the next he was face-down on the floor."

"But?"

"What are the odds that somebody keels over from a heart attack? Even if they are an unhealthy old man. Pretty small, right? And then what are the odds that a child molester running from a warrant dies from natural causes that same day? That's got to be infinitesimal. When you put those two together . . ."

"Are you guys going to do an autopsy?"

"Still up in the air. I need to track down his doctor to find out if he had any pre-existing conditions, like a diseased heart or—"

"Oh, this guy had a diseased heart," Wingate said.

"Sounds like."

"I'd appreciate you going ahead with the autopsy regardless. I can have an official request sent over to you first thing in the morning."

That was the last thing Kinsale needed. The moment Scott got the request, he'd pull Kinsale off the case.

"Send it my attention," he said and recited his email address.

"What time do you think you could get back to me with the results?"

"We should have the preliminaries by the end of the day. I'll sit in on it and let you know."

"You're going to sit in?" Wingate's tone was mocking. "For an old guy who died of a heart attack?"

"An old pervert," Kinsale corrected.

CHAPTER 8

True to his word, Wingate sent the autopsy request to Kinsale just after eight the next morning. Kinsale forwarded the email to the Medical Examiner's office along with his copy of the incident report and then called to approve the request.

"What's the file number?" asked the man on the other end of the line.

"I'm in my car right now," Kinsale said from his dining table. "I'll be at the autopsy. I'll bring it then."

"We need it beforehand."

"No, you don't. You'd prefer to have it beforehand, but it's not required. I'll show up early and give it to you then."

Getting no response, Kinsale asked, "What times do you have available?"

"There's an opening on the schedule at 10:00."

"Lock it in. I'll be there at 9:45."

Kinsale then called Kennedy's home number again, on the off chance that he did live with someone. He hung up when the call went through to voicemail and then punched in the number for the Midland Military Institute.

"I telephoned your office this morning," Commandant Shelvey said when Kinsale's call was put through. "I left a message."

"I appreciate that. I'm on appointments outside the office this morning, so I thought I'd try to reach you between times."

"How's Jim?"

"I haven't heard anything yet this morning. I'm trying to track down his doctor."

"Yes, you mentioned that in your message. I have his personnel file here. His doctor is Fred Dunstag. I have his number." He read it off and Kinsale added it to the call log in his notebook.

"Did Kennedy have a history of heart problems?"

"Did?" Shelvey asked.

Kinsale ignored the question. "Does his personnel file list any relatives?"

Shelvey let the silence lengthen, but Kinsale waited him out. "No," he said finally. "We ask for an emergency contact. Jim listed the school."

"Okay then, Commandant, Mr. Kennedy died yesterday afternoon of an apparent heart attack."

"I'd feared as much." Shelvey let out a long sigh. "What a tragedy."

"I didn't say anything earlier because in these circumstances we inform relatives first."

"Of course."

"Did he live alone?"

"As far as I know."

"Do you know that the Midland Police Department issued an arrest warrant for Mr. Kennedy yesterday?"

"I . . . There was an article on the Chronicle website yesterday afternoon."

"But you knew before that, didn't you?"

Shelvey didn't answer right away. Kinsale wasn't surprised. The school faced difficult times ahead. Kennedy had likely sexually abused some of the students, but even if he hadn't, the school would be hard-pressed to explain to parents how it had allowed an alleged child molester on the faculty. "The police came by yesterday morning looking for Jim."

"And?"

"He'd gone home sick the day before. He told the provost that he'd probably be out the rest of the week."

"I'm assuming the police explained the charges."

"Yes, they told me. And I told them that I found it hard to believe."

"Do you still feel that way?"

"Yes," Shelvey said stiffly. "Jim had been with us for eleven years, without even the faintest whisper of scandal." He paused. "Of course, we can't control what our instructors do away from the . . ."

"He was a teacher at a boy's school," Kinsale interjected. "You don't think there might be a connection."

"We are taking steps to explore that . . . possibility."

Shelvey sounded like he'd already talked to the school's lawyers, which probably explained his lack of empathy. Rather than focusing on how to atone for the damage, he was already concentrating on how to contain it.

Kinsale's next call was to Dr. Dunstag, whose receptionist told him the doctor had a strict policy of not interrupting patients' appointments for phone calls. Kinsale explained that he was with the MPD and needed to talk to the doctor immediately, but she held firm. Finally, he told her that one of the doctor's patients had died, and the ME was going to cut him up into little pieces on the autopsy table unless the doctor advised otherwise.

Dunstag came on the line thirty seconds later. Kinsale broke the news about Kennedy and then asked about his health history.

"James was a sixty-four-year-old man who'd spent most of his life smoking and drinking." Dunstag's voice was cracked and soft around the edges, creating a picture in Kinsale's mind straight out of a Norman Rockwell painting.

"Any specific problems?"

"Certainly."

"Serious?"

"If you're asking me if it is possible that James had a heart attack, then the answer is yes."

"Are you surprised that he did?"

"Detective, after all these years, I am more surprised by the strength of the human body than its frailty."

Kinsale wasn't sure what Dunstag's answer was, so he asked again. This time the doctor said, "No."

"What health issues did he have?"

"He had stable angina, continued to poison his liver at a dangerous rate, the onset of emphysema, which finally convinced him to stop smoking, and chronic sciatica, although that wasn't bothering him so much the last time that he was here."

"When was that?"

"About a month ago."

"Why did he come to see you?"

"He typically came in about every three months."

"Was he on medication?"

"Of course."

"Which ones?"

"It's a long list. I'd have to consult his file."

"Later," Kinsale said. "Doctor, did you hear that there was an arrest warrant out for Kennedy?"

"I did."

"What do you think about that?"

Kinsale's phone buzzed. He looked at the screen and saw that someone was calling him from his building's front door. He walked over to the window.

"I am dismayed," the doctor said, "if the allegations are correct. Horrified."

"Are you surprised by the allegations?"

"Detective . . ."

Kinsale looked down to the front stoop and saw a tall, angular woman with a mane of unruly auburn hair and a large brown leather bag over her left shoulder.

"I appreciate your time, doctor," he said.

"Are you going to proceed with the autopsy?"

"Do you see any reason not to?"

"No, I don't suppose I do."

Kinsale hung up, flipped over to the other call, and hit '9', which unlocked the front door to the apartment building.

Stepping back, he checked his reflection in the window. He was a little disappointed. The months of inactivity at the Dog had taken their toll. He'd had no reason to stop being active when the Department ostracized him, but he had, and now for the first time, he could see the impact. His face was fuller, and his body looked softer. He took a deep breath to pull in his stomach and went to open the door.

"Morning," he said as Trish Lewis topped the stairs. She still looked good, wearing a sleeveless ivory silk blouse and black slacks. Her trademark big sunglasses were pushed above her forehead, keeping her riot of red hair off her face.

Her green eyes crinkled in a smile. "You've let your hair go."

"Among other things." They embraced briefly, and then he stepped aside to let her into the apartment. She looked around as if to refamiliarize herself with the surroundings and then sat on the couch. She put her bag next to her.

They had enjoyed an intense, but short-lived, fling several months before. She'd been a society reporter for The Washington Post and helped him out on a murder case. He'd given her an exclusive on the case, and that had propelled her onto the crime desk at the newspaper, which then made any sort of romantic relationship between the two of them untenable. They'd tried to maintain a professional relationship, but when Kinsale got on the wrong side of the Department and ended up sitting on his thumbs at The Dog, he'd pulled back. She'd called him several times early on, but he'd let her calls go through to voicemail and then deleted them. Eventually she'd stopped calling.

"Coffee?" he asked.

"That'd be great."

"Still just sweetener?"

"If you have any."

"All I have is sugar."

"Then no."

He poured her a cup and brought it over. He sat down across from her. "So, it's been a while."

"It certainly has."

"To what do I owe the pleasure?"

"For the first time in six months, your name popped up in my alerts?"

He cocked his head in surprise. "Really? How so?"

"A James Kennedy died at a coffee shop up in Tenleytown."

"Seriously? I mean I was there when he died, but that's about the extent of it."

She smiled devilishly and sipped her coffee.

"Okay," he asked, "how did my name come up?"

"EMT report."

"You track paramedic reports?"

"I have an alert for your name. When it came up, I called the paramedic, and she told me that you were there and had performed CPR."

"That's about as far as it goes. There really isn't a story for you."

"I didn't really think there was."

He studied her, remembering how much he'd enjoyed their time together and wondering why they hadn't tried harder to… Why he hadn't tried harder to keep it going. "It's good to see you, great even, and I'd be happy to spend the rest of the morning catching up over coffee, but…"

"Why am I here?"

He nodded, and she said, "Maybe I just came by to see how you were."

"You could have done that any time in the past six months."

"I tried, but you shut me out."

Recognizing a bad conversational path for him, Kinsale said, "I'm doing well. You?"

Rather than answering, she asked, "You're not going in today?"

"I have an appointment."

"From what I've heard, you don't have too many of those these days."

Kinsale had been worried that Lewis had learned about Kennedy's crimes in Midland and was already pursuing the story, but realizing that she wanted to talk about him and the MPD, he relaxed. "Actually, I've been pretty busy lately."

"Really?" Her look was knowing. "That's not what I've heard."

"What have you heard?"

"That you've been put out to pasture. It wasn't enough to send you to the Second District, where writing a parking ticket counts as a major bust, but they've closed you out completely. They want you to quit, and if you don't, they're going to bore you to death."

She was smiling, almost laughing, letting him know they were on the same side, just like old times.

"I'll be the first to admit that police work can be slow sometimes, and the Second is not exactly on the front lines, but whoever you've been talking to . . . well, frankly, they're full of shit."

"It hasn't been just one person and they haven't been shy about enjoying your situation. But, okay, if every single one of my sources is full of shit, why have you been spending every day at that coffee place?"

She'd caught him by surprise and looked pleased.

"I'm staking out Wilson High School," he said. The school was a block away from the coffeehouse. "Trying to crack a truancy ring."

"That's pretty funny, Martin. I'll be sure to pass that lead on to our education editor." She leaned forward. "What I want to do is write about a detective who took on the Metropolitan Police Department and is now being quietly, and illegally, punished."

"That makes one of us."

"Come on, Martin." She set her coffee cup on the table. "Why not talk about it? Not only would they have to put you back on duty, but you could probably take them to court."

"If I knew what you were talking about, or more to the point, if you knew what you were talking about, I still wouldn't have anything to say."

"Then can you explain why one of the best homicide detectives in the city has been invisible for half a year, and why, when he finally does re-emerge, it's because in the middle of the morning, he was having a leisurely cup of coffee at a coffee bar that is in no way walking distance from his stationhouse and an old man dies of . . . What did he die from?"

"Heart attack."

"That makes it even worse," she said, flailing her hands in frustration.

They were quiet and then he said, "I've missed you."

She looked annoyed that he was changing the subject but then softened. "The invitation was always there."

He nodded. "You're looking good."

"You, on the other hand. Too many lattes?"

He accepted the jibe. "How's work? I see your byline pretty regularly now."

"Not on the front page, though. I'm lucky to get the front of Metro."

"Politics sucks all the air out of the room in this town," he said. "And The Post likes to think it's a national paper. No one in Podunk, Iowa wants to read about somebody getting shot in Logan Circle."

"Still . . ."

"It's better than covering embassy receptions."

"Oh, yeah," she agreed. "What about you? I know, I know, you've been working hard, but what about the rest?"

"Going well. A little quiet, but that's okay."

"How's Manny?"

"Still griping about hotel guests and the women in his life, although usually in the opposite order."

"Tell him I said hi." She stood and picked up her bag.

"Maybe we could grab a drink some time," he said before he could stop himself.

"Maybe."

"Is that a yes or a no?"

She grinned. "It's a maybe."

"Where does that leave me?"

"Wondering," she said and turned to go. "I'm off to the Second. Will I see you there?"

"You're really going to pursue this story?"

"It's my job. Will I see you there?"

Kinsale shook his head. "I have that appointment."

"Right." Sarcasm dripped off the word like maple syrup. "Your appointment."

CHAPTER 9

The D.C. Medical Examiner's office was in a government building on E Street SW. The building housed multiple agencies, but Kinsale only ever went to the fifth floor for autopsies or down to the basement where the scientists and technicians in the Department of Forensic Sciences plied their trade. Arriving at 10:15, he considered going down to say hello to Duane Engler, who headed forensics, but opted not to. They hadn't talked in six months, and Kinsale missed their byplay, but he knew it wouldn't do Engler any good to be seen talking with him.

Also, he was already sufficiently late for the autopsy.

The ME's offices on the fifth floor looked like an outpatient medical facility, with a reception area with ferns, padded furniture, and a receptionist in a lab coat behind the desk. She looked to be in her early thirties, with tightly braided hair and designer nails. The edge of a tattoo peaked out over the top button of her blouse.

Kinsale flashed his shield and told her he was there for the Kennedy autopsy. She checked her computer screen. "Says here we still need the file number."

"Really?" Kinsale asked, sounding upset. "My Captain said he was sending that over. Are you sure it's not here?"

"Yes, I'm sure."

"Look, I'm already late as it is. How about I get that number for you immediately after?"

She shrugged and checked her screen. "Room 5208."

He started towards the examination rooms. "Who's the pathologist?"

She checked the screen again. "Dr. Armistead."

He didn't know Armistead, but that wasn't surprising. With the exception of the Chief Medical Examiner, who was just an administrator, pathologists cycled through the facility faster than a lot of the corpses.

As he walked down the brightly lit hallway, he wondered how Captain Scott would react when Trish Lewis started asking him questions about the blackballing. Scott's first thought would likely be that Kinsale put her up to it, but he was fairly certain that the Captain would realize that didn't make any sense. Bringing in The Post would seal Kinsale's fate, because the newspaper and the Department had long had what could only be described as a hate-hate relationship. The question, though, remained. What would Scott do after accepting that Kinsale hadn't sicced Lewis on him? It would be very easy to blame Kinsale anyway, recognizing that would be the fastest way to get rid of him.

Outside Room 5208, Kinsale buttoned up his jacket in anticipation of the lower temperatures inside and pushed through the door.

A short, middle-aged black woman stood a few feet inside the door, struggling to pull a surgeon's gown over a lime-green cardigan sweater. Her grip on the ends of the sweater sleeves made it difficult for her to get a hold on the gown. The tip of her tongue was poking between her lips as she battled with grim determination.

Kinsale stepped behind her, grasped the back ends of the gown, and yanked them towards the middle. The gown slid into place over the cardigan. The woman twisted around, gave Kinsale an arch look, and then begrudgingly nodded. "Thanks, I don't usually have that much trouble," she said in a gravelly voice.

"Dr. Armistead, I presume?"

She nodded again.

"I'm Detective Martin Kinsale."

"You're late."

"Am I? It looks like you haven't started yet."

"We were waiting for you, but I finally decided we couldn't wait any longer."

"I guess it worked out then."

"Get suited up," she said and turned away.

A technician was arranging instruments on a waist-high, stainless steel roller tray next to the examination table upon which Kennedy lay. The old man's doughy body looked milky blue in the bright light.

"So, you think there's something to this?" she asked when Kinsale approached the table.

"Hard to say. I happened to be a few tables away at the time the guy keeled over, so—"

"That was you?" Her eyes went wide behind her face shield.

"What was me?"

"The one who . . ." She closed her eyes and mimicked fainting backwards. Dumbfounded, he asked, "How do you know about that?"

She couldn't hold back a barking laugh. "They were talking about it when

I was getting breakfast."

Kinsale shook his head, both at his sudden notoriety and the thought of eating breakfast in this place.

"Are you okay now?" she asked.

He started to get annoyed but then saw the twinkle in her eye. "My self-respect is on life support, but everything else is okay."

"Glad to hear it. Let's get started."

For Kinsale, MEs were a breed apart. He'd known a few dozen of them over the years. Some he'd met only once; a few had stayed on the job long enough to build a rapport. To a person, he'd found them to be scientists who relentlessly pursued the truth, but something about them always seemed a little off. Or maybe it was just him. He couldn't understand what would lead someone into the field. It seemed to be a cold, dirty, smelly, repetitive job. Of course, he recognized that they probably thought the same about his line of work.

"First one of the day?" he asked.

"Second; the first one was a ninety-one-year-old female who died in her sleep."

"This one won't be much different. The doctor at Sibley said he died of a heart attack."

"Pays the same whether it's easy or hard." She picked up a buff-colored file from the roller table and opened it. After a moment's reading, she said, "It looks pretty straightforward. As it stands, I'm going to skip the toxicology. If I see something during the exam, I may decide to put in for it. If I do, though, you'll have to wait for the final determination."

Kinsale needed the toxicology. If Kennedy had been murdered, that's likely where the evidence lay. "I saw him take a couple of pills a few minutes before he died."

Armistead looked at him and then back at the file. She flipped back and forth between the two pages. "It doesn't say anything about that in here."

"I didn't include it."

"Why not?"

"At the time, it didn't seem relevant."

She gave him a sidelong glance. "How could a man ingesting unknown pills minutes before he died not seem relevant?"

She was right, and that's why he'd left it out. "I know the person who gave them to him. She said they were Alka-Seltzer."

"It still should have been in here."

"Point taken. I apologize."

"Looks like we're going to have to run the blood after all, Cyrus," she said to the assistant.

From the initial Y-incision to open up the chest and abdomen to expose the rib cage and vital organs to the sawing off of the front top quarter of the skull to remove the brain, Kinsale had always found autopsies to be dehumanizing. It was like watching a butcher process a cow, except deep down, there was the knowledge that one day that cow might be him.

Some detectives enjoyed watching the pathologists do their work, while others made a point of not eating for several hours beforehand. Early on, Kinsale had developed a system to get through the process. He concentrated on the pathologist rather than what they were doing. He would watch their facial expressions and listen to the steady drone of their voice as they described their findings into the overhead microphone. When the pathologist would tell him to look at something, he would narrow his focus as tightly as possible, look where they were pointing, and then return to watching them. He hadn't spewed yet.

"Look here, Detective," Armistead said when she was well into the task. Dutifully, he looked as she poked around in the cavity. "This wasn't a healthy man," she said. "His heart had been starved of oxygen for I don't know how long."

"So, it was a heart attack?"

"At the moment, I'm comfortable with that. As to the cause, it could have been any of a half-dozen mechanisms."

She continued to cut away at the body and he continued to watch her. She worked steadily with a remarkable degree of concentration. "Looks like the Alka Seltzer completely dissolved," she said.

He glanced down at the table and immediately wished he hadn't. Kennedy's stomach was spread open in front of him like a Scottish buffet. He had to force the bile back down his throat. He looked away. "Nothing there?"

He could hear her stirring around in the stomach like it was a stew. "I didn't expect to see anything. We'll sluice it, but don't get your hopes up."

"We need to confirm that that's what they were."

"That'll come in the bloodwork."

Ten minutes later, she said, "Okay, so there's no hemorrhaging in the brain."

This time, he didn't look. "What does that mean?"

"It wasn't a stroke."

"Definitely a heart attack, then."

"Appears to be."

"That's what you're going with?"

"Until I get the toxicology."

"How long is that taking these days?"

"Recently it's been anywhere from forty-eight hours to two weeks, depending on how busy the lab is."

That worked for Kinsale. He needed to keep the determination of cause of death open for as long as he could because if the toxicology showed that

Kennedy had been murdered, Scott would yank the case away from him.

"You're going to leave it open until then?"

"I just said I…" She paused to stop her irritation from getting the better of her. "Tell you what, detective. I'll be done here soon. It's just procedure at this point. Why don't you let me finish up and then we can talk in my office?"

As much as Kinsale wanted a definitive answer on the timing, even more he wanted to get away from the gore on the table. "I'll be in the hall."

She came out twenty minutes later with the file tucked under her right arm and signaled for him to follow her down the hall. She'd stripped off the surgeon's gown but was still wearing the green cardigan over a set of light-blue scrubs.

She opened the door to the stairwell and went up one flight. Her office was the first on the left. The nameplate read Dr. Caroline Armistead. She pushed open the door, and Kinsale was immediately hit by a wave of stale cigarette smoke. D.C. had a strict ordinance prohibiting smoking in any government or commercial building, but Armistead apparently hadn't gotten the memo. Two steps inside her office, she pulled out a packet of Camels and a disposable lighter from one of the cardigan pockets and lit up.

He looked around the office. The furniture was standard government issue, and she'd made no effort to personalize it. Except for the large, overflowing ashtray.

"Take a seat." She pointed to one of the visitor chairs as she stepped around her desk. "Preliminarily," she said as she sat down, "I'm ruling myocardial infarction, but as I told you several times, and you should know anyway, I can't make the final determination until I get the bloodwork back."

"Just so you know, Kennedy had stable angina."

"What's up with you, detective?" she growled in frustration. "That wasn't in your report."

He held up his hands. "This one's not on me. I only talked to Kennedy's doctor in Midland this morning."

"Still, you could have said something during the examination." She picked up a pen. "Anything else?"

"His doctor said he was taking a laundry list of prescription meds."

"That'll delay things. I'll need to know what he was taking. Do you have his doctor's number?"

He opened his notebook, flipped to the call log, and read off Dunstag's number.

"I'll try to call him this afternoon," she said as she wrote it down.

"Why don't we call him now?"

She stubbed out her cigarette in the ashtray and looked at her watch. "I was hoping to grab some lunch before my next exam."

Kinsale couldn't imagine eating so soon after seeing Kennedy's exposed stomach and doubted he'd be able to eat for the rest of the day. "It won't take a minute, and it'll save us both a lot of time."

"It'll definitely take more than a minute," she countered. "And while I could see how it might save you some time, I don't really see what I have to gain."

"Just a couple of minutes then."

She stared at him and then leaned forward and pushed the speaker button on her desk phone. As she punched in the phone number, she lit up another cigarette.

Dunstag wasn't with a patient, so he came on the line quickly. After going through the results of the autopsy, Armistead asked him about Kennedy's prescription history.

"James was taking Isordil for angina," he said.

"Other prescriptions?"

"Certainly, if you'll give me a moment, I'll get his file."

While they waited, Kinsale asked, "Did they tell you when you took the job that you're not allowed to smoke in District office buildings?"

"I'm from D.C."

"Yet . . ."

"First time they told me I couldn't, I told them I would, or they could find another pathologist. You don't do this job without having some blowback." She held up the cigarette. "This is mine."

"And they let you get away with that?"

"Haven't heard a word since. And that was three months ago."

Dunstag came back on the line and immediately began reciting a string of prescriptions. Armistead grabbed a yellow legal pad and started writing. When Dunstag finished, she ran the back of the pen over the list. "Glucophage? He was diabetic?"

"Borderline," Dunstag said. "We'd been managing it for a few years. Or at least I was trying to manage it. Jim wasn't the most cooperative patient."

"Doctor, would you mind emailing that list to me?"

"Not at all."

She reeled off her email address and then Kinsale recited his.

After she hung up, Kinsale pointed to the scribbles on the yellow pad. "That's a lot of drugs."

She sucked on the cigarette as she looked down at the pad. "It looks like a lot, but most of them are fairly common for a man his age. He was definitely taking more than most, but not so much as to raise a red flag."

"His being dead, though, does."

"Does what?"

"Raise a red flag."

CHAPTER 10

"Two gentlemen here to see you," Royale Moon said as Kinsale came into the squad room an hour later. He looked over at the hard-backed wooden bench reserved for visitors and saw Bill Thayer and Chris Dowling. "But the Captain wants to see you first. ASAP."

Thayer stood as Kinsale approached, while Dowling stayed seated and stared straight ahead as if he could see through the walls and out to the horizon.

"Detective Kinsale," Thayer said. He was slightly shorter than Kinsale and much slimmer, with darker skin than his wife. He sported a small goatee that was sprinkled with gray. "I'm Bill Thayer."

Kinsale had seen him several times over the past months at the coffeehouse, dropping by to talk to his wife or to help out when she was short-staffed.

"Good to finally meet you," Kinsale said. "I've seen you at Lucy's place."

"Do you have some time? Chris and I would like to talk to you about what happened yesterday."

"Great, but could you give me a couple of minutes? I just need to make a report to my Captain."

"Certainly, we appreciate any time you can spare."

Kinsale glanced over at Dowling as he turned away. The young man hadn't moved.

Scott was on the phone and signaled for Kinsale to wait. When he hung up a minute later, he gestured for Kinsale to come into his office and to shut the door.

"I wanted to fill you in on the autopsy."

"Right, the autopsy." Scott leaned back in his chair. "And?"

"ME is leaving cause of death open for right now."

"Why is that?"

"No big deal. The guy definitely died of a heart attack, but he was on so many prescription meds that she can't say what caused it until she gets the toxicology."

"Seems like a lot of trouble and expense for an old guy who definitely died of a heart attack," Scott said.

Scott's tone put Kinsale instantly on guard. "Just being thorough."

"Or maybe the fact that the Midland Michigan PD had a warrant out on Kennedy for being at the center of a bunch of fucking perverts molesting young boys suggests that there may be more to his death than a heart attack?"

Kinsale hadn't seen that coming and needed some time to sort out his response, so he said, "Wingate sent the autopsy request to you too."

Scott slid forward in his chair and placed his forearms on the desktop. "He sent it to your old pals at the Homicide Branch. They forwarded it to me, wanting to know why they hadn't been informed. I had to call Midland and sound like an idiot to find out what was going on."

"I wanted to make sure it—"

"Shut up, Martin," Scott snapped. "I'm in no mood to listen to your crap."

"Captain, I—"

"I thought I'd do you a favor. Let you stretch your legs a little bit. And you instantly start . . ."

"I—"

Scott talked over him. "This time you went too far. Internal Affairs has opened a new file. Or more likely, just dusted off the old one. Except you couldn't even toe the line long enough for any dust to settle."

Kinsale waited for Scott to say something more, but he'd settled into a seething silence. Kinsale said, "I hardly screwed up. I only found out about Kennedy last night. After hours. I figured we should go ahead with the autopsy, and then I would lay it out for you and let you decide what you wanted to do."

"Except you came in here and told me that Kennedy died of a heart attack," Scott said. "Didn't say a word about Midland."

Scott put up his hand to stop Kinsale from speaking again. "I'm not interested in a damn thing you have to say. Homicide has the Kennedy file now, and Magner and Collison will be assisting here. And this afternoon, I have a call with the Chief in . . ." He looked at the lower right corner of his computer monitor. "Seven minutes in which I have to explain to her why I let you out of your cage."

Kinsale opened his mouth to speak but Scott waved him off. "Go back to your desk or go to that coffee shop or go home, for all I care." He picked up a piece of paper from his desk and started reading it. "IAD will be calling you soon enough and then you'll be their headache."

Kinsale doubted the Internal Affairs Division could do anything to him.

Blackballing wasn't official policy and was blatantly illegal, and Scott had given him the file. All he'd done was follow through on the Midland PD's request for an autopsy. Still, dealing with IAD was going to be time-consuming and a hassle, and it would get in his way.

"That's it, then?" Kinsale asked.

"Are you still here?" Scott didn't look up.

Kinsale left the office and returned to the front of the squad room. Thayer stood again, and Dowling continued to look like he was in a trance. "Sorry, that took so long," Kinsale said. "Chain of command and all that."

"Do you have time now?"

"I do, but I noticed that our conference room is being used, and I could really use a coffee."

"Okay?" Thayer looked puzzled.

"There's a Starbucks up on Wisconsin Avenue." Kinsale smiled. "I promise not to tell Lucy that you visited the Evil Empire."

"I'm actually a little addicted to their Frappuccinos."

Thayer reached down and helped Dowling up, and then guided him into the elevator lobby.

Under his breath, Kinsale asked, "Is he on something?"

"Yes, but he has a prescription. He had a rough night last night, so we gave him a Xanax this morning to take the edge off."

He looked like he'd taken more than one, but Kinsale didn't say anything. He led them out of the station and up Idaho Avenue. Dowling lagged behind, and several times Kinsale and Thayer had to slow their pace to keep from distancing him.

When they reached the Starbucks, Kinsale asked Dowling if he wanted anything to drink, but he didn't respond. Thayer said a green tea would be fine for him, and he would like a venti Frappuccino. He reached for his wallet, but Kinsale waved him off and went inside to order. When he came back outside, the two men were at one of the sidewalk tables, sitting across from each other like strangers. The leather planner lay on the tabletop in front of Dowling.

"How's Lucy doing?" Kinsale asked as he sat down.

"She's still pretty shook up," Thayer said. "She went in this morning, but she was on the fence about whether to open or not."

"Bill, before we go any farther," Kinsale said. "You're a lawyer, aren't you?"

"I am, but it's real estate law. This situation is way out of my area of expertise."

"I understand that, but if you're here as your brother-in-law's lawyer, that totally changes this conversation."

Thayer shook his head. "Nothing like that. I'm here as family, for moral support. Chris doesn't need a lawyer. It was all just a misunderstanding."

Kinsale wasn't so sure. With Homicide taking the file, their situation was about to become a lot more complicated. Turning to Dowling, he asked, "Why don't you tell me about this misunderstanding?"

The young man had angled his seat away from the other two and was staring across the street. It appeared that he hadn't heard Kinsale's question, but then, still avoiding their gaze, he said in a small voice, "I'm not sure where to start."

"Start with yesterday," Kinsale said.

Dowling shook his head in slow-motion frustration. "That doesn't explain anything."

"Then start where you want."

Dowling went quiet again, but Kinsale was willing to wait. There was no point in pushing him. He would start when he was ready. Thayer, on the other hand, leaned in to speak to his brother-in-law, but Kinsale gestured for him not to. "It's okay, Bill, let him take his time." He took a sip of his coffee and then said, "Whenever you're ready, Chris."

Dowling relaxed a little. He fiddled with the tea bag in his cup, pulling it out and wrapping the strings around the stir stick to squeeze it out. After stirring the tea in lazy circles, he took a sip and then put down the cup.

"That's not mine," he said, pointing to the small three-ring binder. "It was Jim's day planner."

"I figured as much."

"I told you it was mine because . . ."

He lapsed into silence again, so Kinsale said, "Maybe this will help. I've been in contact with the police department in Midland. They told me they'd issued a warrant for Kennedy on a series of sexual molestation charges."

Dowling shuddered, and Thayer immediately reached across the table and put a comforting hand on his arm. Dowling recoiled like it burned, and Thayer pulled his hand away.

He was halfway through his tea before he spoke again. "Jim molested me when I was a student at the Georgetown Academy." He cracked a small smile, although Kinsale doubted he was aware of it. "It took me ten years of therapy to come to some sort of terms with it, but now, it's all come back like it was yesterday."

Kennedy's name hadn't been in the system when Kinsale had run it through the night before. "You didn't report him?"

"I did." Dowling sounded like it hurt to speak.

"He's not in the system."

"Maybe I can explain," Thayer said.

Kinsale didn't want him to. He preferred to hear the story from Dowling, but at the pace he was telling it, they'd be old men themselves before he finished.

"I knew Chris peripherally at the time," Bill said and then hesitated. "I . . .

Now I can see Chris' dilemma. I'm not sure where to start. It's kind of a delicate situation."

"Did you know Kennedy?"

"No."

"How did you know Chris?"

"As Chris told you, he attended the Academy. My father was the headmaster."

"Did you go to the Academy?"

"No, I went to Upper Canada College in Toronto."

"That's kind of odd, isn't it?" Kinsale asked. "Your father was the headmaster of one of the best schools in the country, and you didn't go there."

"I was already in Canada when my father was appointed to the position. I loved it there and didn't want to leave."

Kinsale gestured for him to continue.

"This is where it gets . . ."

"Delicate?"

"Yes, delicate," Thayer said and then shrugged. "I might as well dive into the deep end."

"Might as well."

"Okay, so this was seventeen years ago," Thayer said. "At the time, my father was the first black headmaster in the Academy's history and one of only a handful of black headmasters in the top tier of preparatory schools in the country. Less than a handful, really."

He seemed to expect a response, so Kinsale said, "That's impressive."

"At the same time, Chris was one of the few black students at the Academy. My father was trying to bring in more minority students, but he had to move slowly."

"Your father hushed up the incident," Kinsale said, jumping ahead. "Chris reported it and your father made sure it went no further."

Up to that point, Thayer had been speaking deliberately, searching for just the right words. Now he talked rapidly, the words bumping into each other as they tumbled out. "You have to understand. If he'd reported it, it would have effectively ended any chance of minorities leading these institutions for another generation. Or to even attend them. The establishment was looking for any excuse."

"It also would have destroyed your father's career."

"That's true. I don't deny that." Thayer's hands were clenched tightly together in front of him. "If he would have been the only casualty, my father would have called in the police immediately, but there were larger issues at stake." He gestured with his clasped hands toward Dowling. "Chris understood that."

Kinsale turned to Dowling. From the young man's expression, it appeared he wasn't paying them any attention, but Kinsale could see the glint of tears at the edges of his eyes. He asked, "How old were you, Chris?"

"Twelve."

Kinsale doubted that a twelve-year-old boy could understand the larger issues at stake and didn't see why he should have had to. "The Midland PD has an arrest warrant out for Kennedy because he and bunch of other twisted fucks have been molesting boys for several years at the school where he was teaching. Who knows how many boys he assaulted since your father decided to push this one under the rug?"

"He hardly pushed it under the rug," Thayer protested. "My father confronted Kennedy immediately after he learned of his . . . transgression."

"Crime," Kinsale corrected.

Thayer winced but nodded. "Yes, crime," he said. "My father forced Kennedy to resign and warned him that he could never have any contact whatsoever with Chris. He told him that if he ever harmed another boy, he would report him to the authorities regardless of the consequences."

"Warned?" Kinsale spat out. "Consequences? What the—"

"If all this had happened today, of course, my father would have acted differently." Thayer's face was rigid now, the words struggling to escape his clenched jaw. "I am certain of that. Today we understand what a heinous crime it is, and we know that sexual predators will continue to prey on the young unless they are stopped. My father didn't know that then. If he had realized that Kennedy would continue—"

"What did your father think Kennedy would do?"

"I can't speak for him, but I am certain that he believed that the threat of exposure would be more than enough to stop Kennedy."

"Or push him farther underground," Kinsale countered.

"Today we know that," Thayer conceded. "But at the time, my father was working without that understanding."

Thayer's rationalizations rankled Kinsale. What adult of any time period didn't know that sexual deviants were deviants for life? They'd been killed throughout history largely because that was the only way to be sure they wouldn't do it again. People couldn't turn off their sex drive, even if they wanted to, and nobody ever really wanted to. He took a breath to calm himself and then asked, "What do you think of all this, Chris?"

"He—"

Kinsale raised his hand and cut off Thayer. "I want to hear from Chris."

Thayer bristled but didn't argue. Again, Kinsale asked Dowling what he was thinking.

"What Bill said is basically what happened." He spoke so quietly that Kinsale had to replay the words in his head to make sure he'd heard him.

"What about the decision to let Kennedy walk?"

He breathed in deeply and blew out the air slowly. "I don't really remember. I wasn't in a position to have much of a say in that decision."

"What about your parents?"

"They . . . They thought it was the right decision." It all became too much for Dowling. His head dropped, and a sob shook his narrow shoulders.

"They understood the situation," Thayer said, unable to hold back. "If they'd reported it, Chris would have been forced out of the Academy, one way or another. What happened had already happened. Kennedy was gone. They needed to think about Chris's future."

Kinsale recognized it would have been a dreadful decision. Either option was bad, yet he was shocked that Thayer couldn't see that his father and Dowling's parents had made the worse one.

"I'm sure your father explained the bigger issues to them," Kinsale said to Thayer. His mocking tone riled, but the lawyer was smart enough to swallow any retort.

Kinsale turned to Dowling, "You stayed at the Academy?"

Dowling raised his head. His eyes were red, and his cheeks were wet. "Jim was gone, and nobody else knew."

"And now you teach there? After what happened?"

"Headmaster Thayer offered me the position." He slumped down again, and his movements were becoming increasingly lethargic, as if his systems were shutting down. "I talked it over with my parents and Lucy and my psychiatrist. They thought it would be a good idea, and it has been."

"Is your father still the headmaster?" Kinsale asked Thayer.

"No." Still angry, Thayer clipped the word. "He retired four years ago."

"Does he live in the area?"

"He lives in a retirement community in Silver Spring."

"Which one?"

"It's called Hawthorn. It's off Cherry Hill Road."

Kinsale turned back to Dowling. "Did you and the headmaster ever talk about what happened?"

Dowling shook his head.

"He never asked how you were doing?"

"Naturally, my father has taken a special interest in Chris's progress," Thayer interjected. "He is thrilled at how well Chris is doing. He says he's a natural with students."

Kinsale ignored Thayer and asked Dowling, "Were you in touch with Kennedy?"

"No." He recoiled from the thought. "Never. Not until he called me on Tuesday."

"Out of the blue?"

Dowling nodded dismally.

"Why did you agree to meet him?"

It was the obvious question but appeared to catch Dowling by surprise.

He looked at Kinsale with a furrowed brow, as if he needed to give the question some real thought. When nothing occurred, he glanced at Thayer, but his brother-in-law just hitched his shoulders.

"I can't really explain it," Dowling said finally. "He said he was in trouble, and he asked me to meet him. It just seemed like the right thing to do."

"You're going to need to do better than that," Kinsale said. "After what he did to you and not seeing him for fifteen years—"

"Seventeen."

"After all that, why didn't you tell him to go to hell and hang up?"

Kinsale watched Dowling struggle with the question. Perhaps he didn't like being pressed so hard. Or maybe he didn't like having to face the answer. "Sometimes you just have to do what's right," he mumbled.

"How could that be right? The man molested you."

"He needed my help. He'd swallowed his pride to call me and ask for it. I couldn't really say no."

"I'm sorry, Chris, but I'm having trouble getting my head around this."

Dowling looked down at his empty cup. Thayer stood up. "Can I get you another, Chris?"

Dowling held out his cup. "Black tea this time, please. With milk and sugar."

"Anything for you, detective?"

Kinsale shook his head, and Thayer headed inside, tossing his empty plastic cup in the trashcan by the door.

"I like a lot of milk in my tea," Dowling said. "Lucy jokes that it's more like lukewarm milk with tea flavoring."

Dowling was trying to change the subject. Normally, Kinsale wouldn't let that happen. He would keep pushing until he had what he needed, but he followed his instincts and backed off.

They waited in silence. When Thayer returned, he was carrying two large cups. He set one in front of Dowling and took a sip from the other as he sat down. "I love Lucy's coffee—don't get me wrong," he said. "But there's something about the kick from a cup of Starbucks. You have no doubt that you're drinking coffee."

His brother-in-law's reappearance had a calming effect on Dowling, and Kinsale let the moment linger. Then he said, "Tell me about yesterday. What happened?"

"Jim was there when I came in," Dowling said. "Lucy was waiting on him. She didn't know who he was, but when she saw him turn and hug me, she—"

"He hugged you?"

Kinsale's disbelief unsettled Dowling, and he pleaded, "You have to understand. I . . ."

"It's okay, Chris." Kinsale raised his hands in apology. "That was my fault.

You don't have to explain. Just tell me what happened."

"I'd spent the night at Lucy and Bill's house because I was so . . . bothered, and she was adamant that I shouldn't meet Jim."

"But you did."

"As I said, I felt it was the right thing to do." Dowling drank some of his tea. "Anyway, when he hugged me, Lucy was furious."

"Why did you meet him at The Dog? Why not meet someplace where you wouldn't be shoving Kennedy in her face?"

"He wanted to meet elsewhere. At Café Milano on Capitol Hill, but Lucy wouldn't have it. She said that if I was adamant about meeting him, she would have to be there."

"How did Kennedy react to the change?"

"I sent him a text and he replied with a thumbs-up emoji."

"You said earlier that Kennedy said he needed your help. What did he want?"

"He told me that the Midland police were about to issue a warrant for his arrest." Dowling gave Kinsale a challenging look. "He said that the charges were spurious."

Kinsale motioned for Dowling to continue.

"Jim said that he hadn't . . ." Dowling scrounged for the right word. "Hadn't been . . . involved since he left the Academy. He said that he'd lost the urge because our . . . because our relationship had meant so much to him. When it ended, it ended that aspect of his life."

"How did he explain the charges?"

"He said that he knew men who continued to follow that . . . lifestyle." Dowling was searching for the blandest euphemisms he could find, and being an academic, he was finding them. "Over the years, he'd told them about him and me. When the police infiltrated their group, these men turned on him to protect themselves."

Kinsale couldn't tell if Dowling believed what he was saying, or if he so fervently wanted to believe it that it was self-fulfilling. This was not an uncommon reaction among the sexually molested. They needed to believe there was something more to their nightmare than just exploitation and domination. They wanted to hear that their molester loved them, wanted to believe that he wasn't actually an awful person. And even seventeen years later, an experienced predator like Kennedy would have known how to play on all those emotions.

"What did he ask you to do?"

"He asked to borrow some money," Dowling said. "He needed to get out of the country. He wanted to go to Venezuela."

"But if he was innocent . . ."

"Innocence doesn't matter with charges like these." Dowling sounded like he was reciting the words, making Kinsale wonder if Kennedy hadn't delivered the same speech to him. "Once he was tarred with that brush, his career and his life were ruined. He had no choice but to leave."

Kinsale pushed down the urge to reach across the table, grab Dowling by the lapels, and shake some sense into him. It was difficult to listen to him defend the man who had wreaked such destruction in his life. No one could say what Dowling might have become, but the man sitting across the table was a pale reflection of that potential. Kinsale glanced at Thayer. He was looking at the younger man with hooded eyes, as if he'd long ago reconciled himself to these tortured, emotional contradictions.

"When I saw the two of you talking at the Dog, Kennedy didn't look well," Kinsale said. "Was he already feeling ill when you got there, or did it come on afterwards?"

Dowling looked relieved that Kinsale had moved on from his relationship with Kennedy. "I noticed it fairly soon after we sat down," he said, but then shook his head. "But now that I think about it, he didn't look that good when I arrived. I thought he was having trouble dealing with the heat. He was sweating and breathing heavily, and it definitely got worse as we were talking. I told him we could get together at another time, but he insisted on staying. Then he developed a splitting headache and started to feel nauseous."

"Did you consider taking him to the hospital?"

"I suggested that, but he said he just needed something. Lucy gave me the Alka-Seltzer, and I gave them to him. He didn't get any better, though."

"Are you sure those pills were Alka-Seltzer?"

"What do you mean?" Dowling asked, but an instant later, Kinsale's implication dawned on both his brother-in-law and him.

"It's a simple question. Could the pills have been something else?"

Thayer leaped to his feet, sending his chair skidding back several feet. "That's ridiculous."

"I agree," Kinsale said, motioning for him to sit down.

But Thayer remained standing. The anger radiated off him, and he was vibrating with the urge to hit out. Kinsale's calm demeanor, however, denied him the impetus. After several tense seconds, he spun around and retrieved the chair. Sitting down next to Dowling, he folded his arms tightly across his chest and glared at Kinsale like he'd killed his dog.

Kinsale turned back to Dowling. "What were you two talking about at the end?"

"He was telling me about his plans to live in Venezuela. He told me I should come and visit." He added quickly, "I wouldn't have gone."

Kinsale wasn't so sure, but he kept his doubts to himself. He realized that he was keeping a lot of doubts to himself in this case, and that bothered him. The key to any successful investigation came from laying out the facts and the suppositions and then subjecting them to the bright light of objectivity. Only then could he see what remained and what melted away. The more that he let Dowling off the hook, the more the darkness crept in around the edges, and the less sense everything made.

"And then he vomited, slumped onto the table, and fell to the floor," Dowling continued. "I remember watching his glass roll off the tabletop and shatter. I don't remember much after that."

Kinsale had forgotten about the glass. When he'd returned from the bathroom the day before, it was gone. Someone had mopped the floor, and he'd only thought about the puddle of vomit. What had happened to the pieces of glass?

They settled into a strained silence. Kinsale replayed the conversation in his head to see if there was anything that he'd missed. When nothing occurred, he asked, "Is there anything more that you think I should know?"

He looked first to the lawyer, who was holding onto his anger and shook his head like it was an effort. Dowling appeared to be totally spent and was staring at the tabletop with unfocused eyes.

"I really appreciate the two of you meeting with me," Kinsale said as he stood. "It was the right thing to do, and you've cleared up a lot of questions." He picked up the planner. "And thanks for bringing this."

"So, that's it then?" Thayer asked. "Case closed? We won't be bothered anymore?"

Kinsale could have eased Thayer's concerns, but he wasn't feeling in a charitable mood. "I think that train has left the station."

CHAPTER 11

Royale Moon gave Kinsale an arch look when he returned to the squad room. "Back so soon?"

"I forgot something."

"Forgot to lay low and take your medicine, that's what you forgot," she said and extended a piece of paper to him. "I was going to hold onto this until tomorrow, but here you are."

"What is it?"

"Homicide detective wants to talk to you."

Kinsale hesitated and then took the sheet. It was yet another complication. He'd hoped, given their strained relationship, that the homicide detectives would hold off talking to him for a while, but that had always been unlikely. Not only had he been the investigating detective, but he was also a witness. Looking at the paper, he didn't recognize the name, but he knew there'd been a shakeup in Homicide in the wake of his departure. Dalvin Harewood must have been some of the new blood.

He thanked Moon and headed for his desk. The squad room was empty except for a pair of detectives, Audrey Guilford and Hugh Yates, who were talking quietly across their desks. Scott's door was closed, and the blinds were drawn. Maybe he was still having that conversation with the Chief. If that were the case, Kinsale wanted to be gone before it ended.

He retrieved the bag of Kennedy's effects from the bottom drawer, and then carried it and the day planner to the printer and spent the next five minutes copying each of the two-dozen-or-so double-side pages. At one point, he noticed Guilford and Yates were no longer talking and could feel their eyes on his back, but he ignored them, and sure enough after a few seconds, they became bored and resumed their conversation.

He took a less direct route to leave the squad room, taking him past Brian Magner's desk. The stack of active case files on Magner's desk was at least a foot tall. It was a perverse badge of honor with the old detective that he had the biggest backlog of open cases. Kinsale glanced around. Moon had her back to him, and Guilford and Yates appeared to have forgotten about him, so he grabbed the top case file, mouthed the number several times to memorize it, and then stuffed the file into the middle of the stack.

Again, he felt that he was being watched. He looked over and saw Guilford staring at him. They'd hardly shared any words since Kinsale had arrived at the Second. Early on, she'd called him a "cock-sucking turncoat,", and he didn't think that was a good foundation for a friendship. She eyed him now with suspicion, likely wondering why Kinsale was on that side of the squad room, but then her apathy once again got the better of her, and she turned away. Kinsale headed for the door.

"Remember everything now?" Moon asked.

"Everything." When he reached the elevator lobby, Kinsale pulled out his notebook and wrote down the file number.

He waited until he was driving to call Homicide. He wasn't surprised when Jessica Dent answered. She was the bureaucratic equivalent of a granite plinth. Everything in Homicide had flowed around her for as long as anyone could remember. She hadn't liked Kinsale from the start and their relationship had gone downhill from there.

"Detective Dalvin Harewood, please," he said.

"Who's calling?"

"Detective Martin Kinsale."

"Kin . . ." After a long pause, she said with a sneer, "I'll put you through."

Harewood came on the line and said, "I understand you had the file."

"There actually wasn't a file," Kinsale said. "We were working under the assumption that it was natural causes."

"What about the Midland warrant?"

"We only learned about that last night."

"At which point you should have turned it over to us."

"Who's your partner?" Kinsale asked.

"Excuse me."

Kinsale repeated the question.

"Why are you asking?"

"I used to work in the squad."

"I heard."

"And I was wondering if I know your partner," Kinsale said. "How long have you been there?"

"Let's get back to the issue at hand," Harewood said. "We need to talk."

"Okay."

"When can you come down here?"

"Harewood," Kinsale said, "Regardless of who your partner is, I'm sure you know that I am persona non grata down there."

Harewood hesitated. "Okay, we can do it at the . . . Where are you now? The Second?"

Even with the noise coming through his car window, Kinsale had no trouble picking up on the derision in Harewood's voice.

"How about this? Have you been to the scene?"

"The coffee place? Heading that way later."

"Why don't we meet up there, then? Say, in a couple of hours?"

"1:00?"

"That works." Kinsale smiled as he ended the call. Harewood was obviously new to the game. He shouldn't have let Kinsale push him around like that, but then Kinsale was an old hand at pushing.

He parked across the street from The Laughing Dog five minutes later. Stepping out onto the sidewalk, he pulled Kennedy's rental car keys from the evidence bag and pressed the panic button. Instantly the horn and lights erupted on an electric-blue Ford Fusion about fifty feet down Chesapeake Street. He hit the unlock button to cut the clamor and walked down to the car. Tucked under the driver's side windshield wiper were two parking tickets. Kinsale wondered idly if the rental car company would try to hold Kennedy responsible for tickets written after his death.

He pulled on a pair of latex gloves and opened the driver's side door. It was hot and suffocating inside, and he waited a moment before climbing in. The rental agreement was tucked in the driver's door compartment, and he saw that Kennedy had rented the car on Tuesday night. When he'd taken the car, it had 2,654 miles on it. Kinsale inserted the key into the ignition to turn on the electrical system. The odometer read 2,716, so since his arrival, Kennedy had driven 62 miles. The trip from Baltimore/Washington International Airport into the city would account for about 40 of those, which didn't leave a lot of mileage for other activities.

Checking the rental agreement again, Kinsale saw that Kennedy had planned to return the car on Saturday morning. He folded the pages and put them back where he'd found them. He opened the ashtray. It was empty. In the glove compartment, he found the owner's manual and emergency instructions from the rental car company.

He moved to the backseat. It was clean, and when he tried to search under the front seats, there was so much seat adjustment machinery that he couldn't push in his hand past the first knuckle. He climbed out and walked around to the back of the car. There was nothing in the trunk but the spare tire and the equipment to mount it. Maybe Duane Engler and his crime scene team could find something in the vehicle, but Kinsale was done.

He walked across to The Dog. It was dark inside, and a "Closed" sign hung in the door. He peered through the glass and saw Lucy standing behind the counter. He knocked lightly, and she turned towards the door. She started to wave him off but then recognized him. He saw a look of not so much dismay as sadness cross her face, but then she took a resolute breath and came over and opened the door. Turning away immediately, she dropped into the closest chair. He sat across from her and asked, "How're you doing?"

Her face was taut, and her eyes were grim. "I'm still pretty messed up. I can't get my head around it."

"That's totally normal. It's tough to see someone die in front of you, but you have to realize there's nothing you could have done."

"You don't understand," she said, and the corners of her mouth formed a brittle smile. "I wouldn't have done anything even if I could have. I'm glad he died. And I'm glad that I saw him die because now I know for sure that he's dead."

Kinsale did understand. Over the years, he'd encountered dozens of people who'd done the world a favor by dying. And many more who should have.

"I feel terrible for feeling this way," she went on. "For the past seventeen years, I've hated that man. Hated him more than anyone. And I've wished he was dead." Her eyes vibrated now with passion. "I've wished a thousand times that he would die a horrible death for what he did to Chris. You can't imagine . . ." She shook her head. "It doesn't matter. Whatever he did, I should be sad that he died. I want to be sad. I just can't. And that, well, that makes me sad."

He wanted to tell her something to relieve some of her anguish, but he knew nothing he could say would make a difference, so he said, "I talked with Chris and Bill this morning."

"Bill and I spent a lot of time last night convincing him to tell you about Kennedy. It would be horrible if after all that man did to him, Chris was thought to be involved in his death."

"So, you think he was killed?"

His question knocked her back, and she fumbled for an answer. "No... I mean, I don't... Why..." She stopped and took a deep breath. "It was a heart attack, right?"

"That's what it looks like, but the Medical Examiner is holding off on a final determination until she gets his bloodwork back."

She hesitated, not wanting to know the answer, but finally she asked, "Do you think he was murdered?"

"At first I would have said no, but then you and Chris were so evasive yesterday, I began to wonder."

"But," she said, spreading her hands wide, "now you know why."

"Now I do, but—"

"But what?"

"But then I talked to the Midland police department, and they had a warrant out for Kennedy. Suddenly his death feels a little bit too coincidental."

She studied him. "I thought you were on leave or something."

"Or something."

"Then why are you here."

"Because I was on the scene. My captain asked me to tie up the few loose ends."

"Loose ends?"

"Two things." He pointed to the line of tables along the wall. "First, those people who are always working here, the man and the woman. Do you know who they are?"

"The woman is Marnie, and the guy is Tony. Marnie is, I think, some kind of a musician, and Tony has something to do with software or consulting. He's always talking on his phone."

"Do they pay with a credit card?"

"Tony does and Marnie may have."

"You may need to pull those receipts."

She nodded as if that wouldn't be a problem. "What's the second thing?"

"Kennedy knocked a glass off the table when he collapsed. It shattered on the floor. When I came back from the bathroom, it had been cleaned it up."

"Rennie swept it up."

"Do you know where he put the pieces?"

"In the trash can."

"Where's that?"

She pointed towards the counter. "Right under there, but it's empty. I have a cleaner come in every night. She puts all the trash in the dumpster out back."

"When are your trash pickups?"

"Pickup," she said. "Just the one. On Fridays."

He groaned, and her eyes widened as she realized what he needed to do. He tried to tell himself that he was lucky that the trash hadn't already been picked up. If it had been, he would have had no hope of finding the glass pieces. On the other hand, the coffeehouse's garbage had been rotting in the dumpster for six days. And with daytime temperatures having pushed into the high eighties several times during the week, plus the rising humidity, the inside of the dumpster would be like an industrial petri dish.

"I've got some HAZMAT coveralls in the trunk," he said. "I'm going to put them on and then go dumpster diving. First off, though, do I have your permission to look in your dumpster?"

She smirked. "Of course."

The coveralls were made out of Tyvek, a plastic material that homebuilders wrapped around new homes to prevent air infiltration. He also wore a Tyvek cap and booties and three pairs of skin-tight evidence gloves layered one over the other. He managed to stuff a couple of evidence bags between two of the layers.

By the time he'd climbed through the hatch into the dumpster, he was already soaked in sweat. Inside, the temperature was at least twenty degrees hotter, and throat-thickening decay hung in the dead-still air. Flies and other insects—some he'd never seen before—buzzed around in a feeding frenzy.

He should have slit open each of the two-dozen-or-so green plastic trash bags and sifted carefully through the contents, but that wasn't going to happen. He wasn't going to last five minutes in this particular circle of hell, so he just ripped open the sides of the bags and upended the festering contents around his feet. Within a couple of minutes, everything in the dumpster, including him, was covered in oily clumps of wet coffee grounds. Having eaten lunch at the Dog for most of the past few months, he recognized a lot of the sandwich pieces, and he doubted that he'd be able to order any of them again.

He found the first glass piece in the fifth bag. He would have missed it, but it was wedged point first into the butt-end of a piece of focaccia that landed on his left foot. He pulled out the narrow shard and slipped it into one of the evidence bags. He wanted to give up the search at that point, rationalizing that he only needed a single piece, but he forced himself to continue. Rifling through the rest of the detritus in that trash bag, he found eight additional pieces, including the bottom of the glass, which was intact. He added them to the evidence bag and then clambered headfirst out of the hatch.

He stripped off the protective clothing like it was bee infested, bundled it into a ball, and tossed it back into the dumpster. The Department required that officers turn in their used Tyvek suits to be cleaned and reissued, but he hadn't signed out the suit in the first place.

His shirt was soaked through, and he'd forgotten to replace the spare that he'd used the day before, so he went back into the Dog hoping that the Tyvek had at least kept the smell at bay. He couldn't tell for himself, though, because the stink of curdled milk, spoiling meat, and old coffee was spackled to the inside of his nose.

"How awful was it?" Lucy asked from behind the counter.

"That was about as uncomfortable as I've ever been, but I found most of the glass." He had a horrible thought. "At least I hope it's the right glass. I should have asked before I went in there."

"Don't worry," she soothed. "That was the only broken glass this week."

"That's a relief. I'm not sure I could have gone back in there."

"Don't you have technicians whose job it is to do that sort of thing?"

He shrugged. "I was here."

"Can I get you anything?"

"I'll take a glass of water."

As she turned to get it for him, he asked, "How long are you going to stay closed?"

"I don't know. I can't imagine anyone is in a hurry to have a latte in a place where someone just died. And I can't say I blame them."

"This too shall pass."

"I guess." She put the glass on the counter, watched him drink it down, and then asked, "Will you be coming back?"

He wasn't ready to tell her that he wouldn't be. Regardless of what happened with the case, he was done whiling away the hours at The Laughing Dog. Kennedy's death had sparked his will to live again, and he had no intention of backsliding now. "In my line of work, I've gotten used to drinking coffee around dead people," he said and headed out.

He waited for twenty minutes—his old car's anemic air conditioning system struggling to keep the mid-day heat at bay—and at 1:06, a white Chevrolet Malibu pulled up in front of the coffeehouse.

He got out and walked over to the other car. The driver's side door opened and out climbed a tall, well-built black man with a shaved head, aviator sunglasses, bow tie, and seersucker suit.

"Detective Harewood?" Kinsale asked.

"Kinsale?" Harewood looked him up and down like he doubted it.

"I am." Kinsale extended a hand and Harewood shook it. "Good to meet you."

The Malibu's passenger side door opened, and Alan Casey stepped out. Kinsale and Casey had been partners for more than six years but had fallen out during the previous year over a couple of cases. It had been a messy divorce and had contributed to his being banished from Homicide and shuffled off to the Second.

Casey looked across the top of the car to see Kinsale's reaction to his appearance, but Kinsale had been expecting him. On the phone call, when Harewood had avoided naming his partner, Kinsale figured that he'd been told not to, and Casey was the only homicide detective who would bother to do that.

"Alan," Kinsale said.

Casey scowled and came around the front of the Malibu. As usual, he was dressed to impress, sporting a gray pinstripe suit, blood-red tie, and spit-shined black wingtips. "You look like crap, Martin," he said.

In his still-damp shirt and wrinkled pants, Kinsale couldn't disagree. "It's been a busy day."

"In the Second?" Casey asked. "Did you get a call about someone having flowers stolen from their garden?"

"Something like that," Kinsale said and turned to Harewood. "That's the coffeehouse right there. That's where Kennedy died."

Harewood looked to Casey for guidance on how to proceed. Not getting any, he said, "I figured that. Should we go inside to do this?"

"If you don't mind, I'd prefer to do it out here. After we're done, you can go in and talk to the owner yourselves, without me getting in the way."

"Suit yourself," Harewood said. "Can we at least find some shade?"

They moved under the branches of a large street tree. Kinsale took them through the timeline, from his first noticing Kennedy and Dowling to Scott pulling him off the case a few hours ago. It didn't take long because he omitted a lot, including his talk earlier in the day with Bill Thayer and Chris Dowling and his recent dumpster dive.

"Shouldn't have had the file in the first place," Casey growled when Kinsale finished.

"Why not? I'm a detective."

Casey started to respond but then thought better of it and said, "When you found out about Kennedy in Michigan, you should have brought us in right then."

"Maybe, but it was late, and we already had the autopsy scheduled for the next morning, so I figured I'd wait until the results to take it to my captain."

"The way I hear it, Scott took it to you."

Kinsale wasn't surprised that Casey had heard about the dressing down. There were a lot of rivalries and cliques within the Department, but everyone could find common ground against the blackballed. Again, he turned to Harewood. "Do you need anything more from me?"

Harewood flipped through the pages in his notebook. "You have Kennedy's effects?"

"Oh, right. They're in my car. I'll go get them."

As he opened his car door, Kinsale glanced back to see that Harewood and Casey had remained in the shade under the tree. He pulled Kennedy's rental car keys out of his pocket, rubbed them against his pants leg to wipe away his fingerprints, opened the evidence bag, and dropped them in. Then he removed Kennedy's hotel room key card from the bag and put it in the glove compartment along with the bag of glass shards and the copied pages of Kennedy's planner.

He walked back and handed the bag and the original planner to Harewood. The young detective lifted the bag up to eye level and turned it around. He said, "There's car keys in here."

"Really?" Kinsale raised a surprised eyebrow. "I hadn't gotten that far."

CHAPTER 12

The Department had a well-documented procedure for searching a hotel room. No fewer than two officers would meet with the hotel manager to explain the circumstances. They would gain permission to enter the room and establish a perimeter. The officers would enter the room only to ensure that there was no immediate need for action. They then would secure the site until the forensic technicians arrived. The procedure had proved over time to be the best method for protecting the evidence chain.

That wasn't how Kinsale preferred to do it. He liked to search a room alone. He used the silence to get the feel for the room and the occupant. When there was another detective with him, they tended to talk, saying things like, "We should probably wait until the Crime Scene guys get here."

Also, in recent years, hotel managers had become increasingly reluctant to allow access to their guest rooms. They would stall while they put in a call to the home office, which would call the lawyers, which would usually result in needing a search warrant, which would require going in front of a judge, which would invariably take several hours.

Kinsale was alone and anonymous as he walked through the front doors of the Windermere Hotel on New Jersey Avenue. It was one of the many boutique hotels around Capitol Hill that catered to the out-of-town lobbyists and CEOs who came to Washington, D.C. to help Congressmen and Senators calibrate the exact relationship between campaign contributions and voting records. The lobby was small and elegant, with a white marble floor, dark-wood wainscoting, a hot-tub-sized chandelier, and a curved staircase leading to the second-floor meeting rooms. He walked past the registration desk to the bank of elevators. Sporting a suit jacket and a loosened tie, Kinsale looked like a lobbyist returning to his room after a long day of buying influence.

The plastic hotel key card didn't have a room number on it. That was both for economy and security. The desk clerk could easily code a new key for a guest who lost theirs, eliminating the need to maintain a supply of dedicated keys. And without a number, anyone who stole the key would have no idea which hotel room it opened. If all Kinsale had were Kennedy's room key, he would have had no way to know which room—or even which hotel--to search, but Kennedy had kept his key in the small folder that he'd received at check-in. On one side of the folder was a picture of the hotel, and on the other was the number 304 written with a chisel-tipped black magic marker.

He took the elevator to the third floor. A short hallway extended to his left and right. The small brass plaque on the facing wall informed him that rooms 300-304 were to his left. The thick, patterned carpet dulled any sound as he walked that way. When he reached Kennedy's door, he slipped the card into the slot and went in.

Standing with his back to the shut door, he took in the room. What it lacked in size, it more than compensated with opulence. The brocaded wallpaper had a Celtic pattern of gold and white, matching the heavy curtains over the window. The queen-sized bed had a carved wooden headboard with a padded suede-leather center panel. There was a small, elegant desk along the other wall and a ceiling-high wardrobe that likely housed the television. The tiny bathroom to his right was all mirrors and marble.

Pulling on a pair of latex gloves, he began to search. He soon realized that Kennedy hadn't spent much time in the room. All the surfaces were clean. Nothing had fallen on the floor. Kennedy hadn't emptied out his pockets or thrown anything in the trash can. On top of the leather desk blotter lay his plane ticket. He was scheduled to fly back to Midland on Sunday evening. Kinsale recalled, however, that he was going to return his rental car on Saturday morning. Likely, the flight to Caracas left then.

In the top drawer of the wardrobe, he found two pairs each of carefully folded black pants, oxford-blue boxers—also folded—and black socks. In the closet across from the bathroom were three white shirts on hangars and a small pile of dirty clothes.

So much for Kinsale's method. He'd been in the room for ten minutes and hadn't learned a thing.

The bathroom had more to share. Six prescription bottles stood in a line in front of Kennedy's black leather travel kit. He used his cellphone to take a picture of each bottle label. Under the sink, he found a wood-handled plunger and a single small white plastic bottle with no label. He picked it up and shook it. The contents rattled loudly. Unscrewing the cap, he spilled out a few pills into his palm. They were blue and diamond shaped. Stamped on one side was "Pfizer" and on the other was "VGR-100." He smiled at the thought that maybe there was some small dose of cosmic justice after all. Not even Kennedy's twisted sexual desires were enough for him to get it up without some chemical assistance. Putting the pills back in the bottle, he shut the cabinet door. Two minutes later, he was out of the hotel room and heading down the hall.

The reception desk was empty when he came off the elevator. There was a dark wood box on the counter with a brass plaque that read "Room Keys." He dropped Kennedy's key in the slot as he passed.

It was a quick drive across the National Mall back to the government building on E Street SW. He parked on the street, grabbed the bag with the glass pieces from the glove compartment, and headed inside. This time, rather than ride the elevator up to the Medical Examiner's offices, he took the steps down to the Department of Forensic Sciences. He walked past the brightly lit labs to Duane Engler's office at the far end.

The city's chief crime scene scientist looked up from his computer when Kinsale came through the door. "Back from the dead," he said with a smile.

"Been a while, Duane." They shook hands, and Kinsale sat in one of the visitor chairs. "How have you been?"

"Life's been a lot quieter since you dropped off the grid, but our fair city's citizens have nevertheless managed to keep me busy. You?"

"Tanned and rested."

"Heard you had some trouble yesterday." Engler smiled as cupped his hands together and mimicked a CPR compression.

"Did I miss the article in The Post?" Kinsale asked. "How does everyone know about that?"

"Come on. Your fellow officers are reveling in it."

"You too, apparently."

"Nah, just happy to yank your chain," Engler said, pushing his black, heavy-rimmed glasses down his nose and looking over the top. He was a tall, thin man who'd long ago flouted the onset of male pattern baldness by shaving his head.

"Consider it yanked."

"Seeing as you had six months to drop by and say hi, but didn't, I'm guessing this isn't a social call."

"I figured it wouldn't do your career any good if the Fifth Floor learned that you and I were talking."

"Yet here you are."

Kinsale acknowledged the point. "No, it's not a social call." He lifted the evidence bag. "I need to have this examined."

Engler raised an eyebrow. "You're on a case."

"Not . . . exactly."

"How . . . not exactly?"

"Not at all."

"Who is?"

"Alan and his new partner, Dalvin Harewood."

Engler nodded. "That makes it interesting."

"It has its moments."

"So, what's in the bag?"

Kinsale gave him yet another abridged version of the story. This time he focused on the broken glass, the nightly trash removal, the dumpster dive, and talking with Casey and Harewood but left out his recent hotel visit.

"Why didn't you turn this over to Alan?"

"This is my case."

"But it's not, is it," Engler said.

"Alan isn't going to close it."

"Why do you say that?"

"Because I have to believe it," Kinsale said, the truth slipping out in an unguarded moment. "Look, we're not even sure it's a homicide, and if it is, it's an old creep who ruined a bunch of young men's lives and finally got what was coming to him. No one is going to put too much effort into it, least of all Alan."

"And you're going to?"

"I have a light schedule this week?"

Engler studied him. "You're playing a dangerous game here, Martin."

"What's new?"

"You're asking me to play it with you."

"I have a little cover for you," Kinsale said. "It's not much, but it may be enough."

"Cover?"

Kinsale pulled out his notebook and flipped to the page where he'd written down the file number from Magner's desk. "This is an open file in the Second." He read off the number. "You can use it to run the tests. If the shit hits the fan, you can fairly tell them that I gave you that file number."

"No one is going to believe that."

"Believing something and proving it are two totally different things. They'll be pissed off at you for a while, but you're pretty much indispensable."

"Not too long ago," Engler said as he reached for the bag, "I thought you were too."

CHAPTER 13

Kinsale headed home. He still had some work to do but couldn't do it at the Second. Everyone in the squad room would be watching him, and they'd go running to IAD if he as much as logged onto the system.

He headed north on 7th Street, which turned into Georgia Avenue at Florida Avenue. He'd just crossed through the intersection when his phone rang. It was Duane Engler.

"Don't tell me you've got the test results already," he said.

"You'll never guess who just called me."

"Who?"

"Your old partner, asking if I'd talked to you."

"You've got to be kidding me," Kinsale snarled, the months of frustration getting the better of him. "Doesn't Alan have more important things to do?"

"Apparently not."

"What did you tell him?"

"I asked him regarding what, and he said the Kennedy file, and thanks to your second-grade subterfuge, I could honestly say no."

"So, not so second-grade."

"He also asked me to send a tech up to that coffee place."

"Not much point. It's been more than 24 hours, and they had cleaners in last night."

"You never know."

"You might also want to look into the Windermere Hotel."

"Why is that?"

Rather than answer, Kinsale asked if the glass pieces were already in the lab.

"As we speak. I'll call you when we're done."

Walking into his condo, Kinsale stripped as he headed for the bathroom and climbed into the shower. The smell from his time in the dumpster had long since dissipated, but he needed to wash away the memory.

Afterwards, he made some coffee and considered making a late lunch, but the thought of food still curdled in his stomach. He carried the coffee to the couch and called Wingate in Midland.

"I was wondering if I was going to hear from you again," Wingate said.

"Why is that? The autopsy was just today."

"I'm not talking about the autopsy. Your Captain Scott let me know in no uncertain terms that you were playing off the reservation."

"That was just a misunderstanding."

"Really? Because he had no idea what I was talking about when he called me this morning."

"That's because I hadn't had the chance to brief him. You and I talked last night, and the autopsy was first thing this morning. I laid it out for him afterwards." Kinsale paused for effect. "It's all good now."

"If I call him now?"

"He'd tell you the same."

The line was quiet for ten seconds. "Are you still on the case?"

"Nope. We handed it over to Homicide."

"So, Kennedy was done?" He sounded hopeful.

"We're leaning that way."

"Why?"

"Mainly because of the circumstances—sexual molester goes on the run and returns to his first hunting ground."

"What do you mean?"

Kinsale told Wingate about the Georgetown Academy and Dowling.

"Do you like Dowling for it?"

"I don't, but it's early days."

"What did your ME determine as the cause of death?"

"Heart attack, but as to why, she's holding off until she gets the toxicology."

"What are you thinking?"

"It could be some kind of drug interaction. We searched his hotel room. The guy was a walking pharmacy."

"An overdose? You said a minute ago you were leaning towards homicide."

"I said, could be."

After another pause, Wingate asked what they found in Kennedy's room.

"He stays in top-tier hotels, he's neat, and he travels light."

"I could have told you that yesterday."

"How about that he travels with a big bottle of Viagra?"

"That's something new. I'm not sure it's relevant, but I'm glad to hear it."

"I had the same take," Kinsale said. "I found his plane ticket. He was scheduled to Midland on Sunday morning."

"Not a chance in hell," Wingate snorted. "That's standard operating procedure when you're on the run. We wait around until Sunday morning, planning to grab him as he comes off the plane, but he's on his way to Brazil or—"

"Venezuela."

"Yeah, or Venezuela."

"No, it was Venezuela. He told Dowling that's where he was going."

"For someone who doesn't have the file anymore, you certainly seem to be up on it."

"Just taking a professional interest."

"Where does your professional interest take you from here?"

"Me? Nowhere, but I would guess that our guys are working the premise that one of his victims killed him. There are undoubtedly more than Dowling."

"We're trying to get a tally here," Wingate said. "But as you might guess, a lot of boys—and their parents—are hesitant to come forward about something like this."

"Give it time."

"I know, but I really want to nail these guys."

"Did you find out who tipped off Kennedy?"

"You won't fucking believe it," Wingate said. "It was the chief himself. He's got designs on the mayor's office, and he wanted to make sure that he got all the credit for the bust, so he gave an exclusive to a local TV reporter. He told her to keep it quiet until we'd rolled them all up, but it turns out that a friend of hers has a kid at the Institute. She warned her friend, who then confronted Kennedy right off. He went home sick and was on the next plane out of here."

"Save us from the politicians."

"Amen, brother."

"You can expect a call from one of our guys, Alan Casey or Dalvin Harewood. I'm kind of surprised they haven't called already."

"I'll be waiting for it," Wingate said and hung up.

Kinsale remained on the couch for a few minutes, his thoughts meandering from the details of the conversation to whether it was too early to have a beer. He decided it wasn't and fetched one from the refrigerator. He carried the bottle over to the couch, set it on the coffee table, and picked up the photocopy of Kennedy's planner.

The first several pages were permanent, a mostly alphabetized list of contacts. Kennedy had written the name and phone number of each of them, followed in varying degrees of completion by email and home addresses, other phone numbers, and the occasional piece of additional information, such as "Suzanne's brother-in-law." He'd left room between the entries to insert a new contact in the correct alphabetical order, but his system had broken down for numerous letters, especially M and S. Kinsale gave the list a quick perusal. Most of the contacts lived in Michigan, but a few were from other states. None, though, came from the D.C. area.

Following the list was a single sheet that listed Kennedy's passwords to several dozen websites, none of which were incriminating.

Next came Kennedy's calendar. These pages were preformatted with a thick black line down the middle. On the left-side was an hour-by-hour appointment calendar, and on the right side was space for notes. In the upper outside corner of each page was a blank box for the day's date. The pages in the calendar ran from March 26 through April 30, which fell on the day Kennedy died. There were six blank pages at the back.

Kinsale flipped through the calendar pages. Kennedy's days had been filled with classes and appointments, and he made notes in a small, neat handwriting. His final entries were on Tuesday, April 29. The left-side of the page looked like all the others, starting with a phone meeting with Doris Willoughby at 8:00 in the morning and followed by blocked-out class periods and a reminder to call Snider's garage during lunch to make an appointment for an oil change. He planned to have dinner with Paul Portman at Molasses at 7:00.

The notes side of the page had a completely different character. Gone was the almost calligraphic handwriting from the previous pages. In big block letters, he'd written the information for his flight that evening to D.C., which he'd then boxed. Next came the information for the rental car. And near the bottom of the page, he'd written five pairs of capital letters, followed by phone numbers:

BT 301-XXX-XXXX

CD 202-XXX-XXXX

LF 202-XXX-XXXX

RC 301-XXX-XXXX

EH 703-~~XXX-XXXX~~

XXX-XXXX

The first number had a Maryland area code, the next two were in D.C., the fourth was another Maryland number, and the final one was a Virginia number, although Kennedy had crossed it out and written another number below.

The BT in front of the first number was almost certainly Bernard Thayer. His son had said that his father lived in Maryland.

Checking the business card that Chris Dowling had given him the day before confirmed that his cellphone was the second number. The other initials meant nothing to him.

He wrote down all of them in the call log just as they appeared in Kennedy's planner and then called LF. A man answered after the second ring. "This is Larry."

"Hi, Larry. This is Detective Martin Kinsale with the Metropolitan Police Department."

"Is something wrong? My mother . . ."

"Everything is fine. Nothing to worry about," Kinsale said. "Can I get your last name?"

"Farber. What's happened?"

Kinsale ignored the question. "Do you know James Kennedy?"

"U . . . umm," Farber stammered. "I don't think so. Why?"

"We found your name and phone number is his day planner. Are you sure you don't know him?"

"Oh, Mr. Kennedy. I wasn't thinking back far enough. He was a teacher when I was in high school."

"Did you see him yesterday morning?"

Farber went quiet. As the silence stretched out, Kinsale could almost hear the gears in the man's brain grinding as he wrestled with whether to lie. Finally, in a resigned voice, he said, "Yeah, I did."

"I'd like to come by and talk to you about him."

"Why?"

"He died of a heart attack yesterday."

Farber emitted a noise that sounded like a strangled laugh. "You're kidding."

"Why would I kid about something like that, Mr. Farber?"

"I didn't mean it like that," he said quickly and then asked, "Why do you want to talk to me?"

"We're looking into the details of his death. I'm following up with everyone who met with him while he was in the city."

"Hold on. You're saying he was murdered?"

"That's still open."

"We met, but I don't know anything about him dying. I just told you that."

"We still need to talk," Kinsale said.

"Now?"

"It's getting late. How about tomorrow morning? You can come to the station, or we can grab a cup of coffee someplace convenient to you."

"I work in Georgetown. How about Helene's?"

"Eleven?"

"I'll be there," Farber said and hung up.

The next call went much faster. RC in Maryland was Randall Chamberlain, and he freely admitted to knowing Kennedy and to having met with him the day before. Kinsale scheduled to meet him at 1:00 p.m. at his house in Potomac, the mansion-filled suburb northwest of the city.

Kinsale called the second Virginia number first, adding the area code, but it just rang and rang. He then tried the crossed-out number. After the first ring, a recorded voice came on the line and told him the number was not in service. If he'd still been in the good graces of the Department, Kinsale could have found out within a couple of minutes who had those numbers, but being on the outside, it would require a little more effort.

He returned to the top of the list and called the Maryland number.

"Hello," a man answered in the middle of the third ring.

"Mr. Thayer?"

"Yes?"

Kinsale introduced himself and then asked, "Do you know James Kennedy?"

"Don't you mean 'did' I know Jim?"

"How did you hear?"

"My son called me last night."

"Did you meet with Kennedy yesterday."

"We were supposed to meet this morning."

"Did he say why he wanted to meet with you?"

"No," Thayer said. "He told me we had important things to discuss, and I responded that nothing in the world was that important, but he was very insistent, so I eventually agreed."

"We need to talk."

"Why?"

"I need to find out about Kennedy."

"I just told you the full extent of our conversation."

"Regardless."

"I hadn't seen the man in at least ten years, probably fifteen."

"What time tomorrow would work?"

Thayer chuckled. "Not an easy man to put off, are you?"

"I wouldn't get very far in this job if I were. Tomorrow?"

"I have a full day tomorrow. Would Monday work?

Kinsale didn't want to wait, but having no official capacity, he couldn't afford to push, so they agreed on 10:00 on Monday.

"Before you go," Kinsale said, "do you know anyone with the initials EH?"

"EH?"

"I think he was a student at the Academy when Kennedy taught there."

"Nobody comes to mind," Thayer said, "but then my memory isn't what it used to be."

CHAPTER 14

Before heading out the next morning, Kinsale called Dontay Blalock. A detective in the Fifth District, Blalock and his partner Jeff Evans had helped him on a couple of his cases, including the last one that had ended with Kinsale being blackballed. Blalock and Evans had survived the episode unscathed because by the time the IAD bloodhounds came sniffing around, Kinsale had covered their tracks.

"Martin Kinsale," Blalock said. "I wasn't sure I'd ever hear from you again."

"Wasn't sure or hoped you wouldn't?"

"Little of both."

"How're you doing, Dontay?"

"Same old, same old. Another day, another dollar," Blalock said. "I hear you been getting a suntan up in the Second."

"Trying to keep busy."

"Is that why you're calling?"

"I need a favor."

"You have to be the last person in the world I can afford to do a favor for," Blalock said. "I'd be better off helping that fat-ass North Korean dictator."

"Probably," Kinsale agreed.

They were silent for a while, and then Blalock said, "Never had a chance to thank you for keeping me and Jeff outta your mess."

"It wouldn't have been fair. You guys were just backing me up."

"It'd be enough for the Fifth Floor."

"True."

Blalock said finally. "What do you need?"

"Can you run a couple of phone numbers for me."

"You can't do that yourself?"

"They've got me locked down pretty good."

"What are the numbers for?"

"A file I'm working."

"You just said they got you locked down."

"There's locked down, and then there's locked down."

"What's that supposed to mean?"

"Did you hear about that detective who passed out giving CPR to a dead guy up in Tenleytown?"

"In passing."

"That was me."

"That was you?" Blalock struggled to keep from laughing.

"So, I've got some skin in the game."

"Yeah, but . . ."

"And something about it just doesn't feel right."

"What doesn't feel right about it?"

"At first, I felt like the people on the scene were hiding something," Kinsale said. "Turns out they were, and they can explain it away, but I don't know, it just keeps smelling like three-day-old fish."

This time, the silence seemed to stretch into the next dimension before Blalock said, "Gimme the numbers?"

Kinsale read off the two Virginia numbers.

"I'll text them to you. Best not to do this through official channels."

Kinsale arrived at Helene's Café a couple of minutes early. Like so many places in Georgetown, it was squeezed into what had once been a rowhouse. There was just enough space for the small counter, and six two-person tables. Three of the tables were open, so Kinsale got a cup of coffee and sat at the one closest to the door.

Farber arrived fifteen minutes late. He was a big man, a couple of inches taller than Kinsale and at least fifty pounds heavier. His face had an alcohol flush, and his thick neck overhung his shirt collar. His suit was well cut, but he wore it shabbily.

"Can I get you a coffee?" Kinsale offered as Farber sat down.

"No thanks." His face was set in a petulant glare. "Can we just get this over with?"

"Fair enough. What do you do for a living?"

"I'm a CPA."

"Where do you work?"

Farber crossed his arms. He probably intended the gesture to be aggressive, and given his bulk it should have been, but it didn't come off. "I thought you wanted to talk about Jim Kennedy."

"We need to get the preliminaries out of the way first."

"Fine," he spat out. "I work for the Eugene Farber Trust."

"Your family?"

"My grandfather."

"Do you run it?"

"My mother is the trustee."

"Do you like it?"

"Yeah, I guess, but what does that have to do with anything?"

"I'm just trying to get a sense of who you are."

"Can we just focus on Kennedy?"

"Okay," Kinsale said, opening his notebook. "Let's start at the beginning. You were at the Georgetown Academy when Kennedy taught there?"

"Yeah.

"The whole time you were there."

"He was gone before I graduated.

"Did you know Chris Dowling?"

"Dowling?" Farber's eyes shifted into the past. "The black kid? Yeah, I remember him. Small, a couple of years behind me."

"Kennedy sexually molested him."

Farber tried to look shocked. "I can't believe it."

"Why is that?" Kinsale asked. "He molested you, too."

"What are you talking about?" Farber surged out of the chair. "Where do you come off saying something like that?"

The patrons at the other tables looked over in alarm, but Kinsale remained calm, and after a couple of seconds, Farber's fury fizzled like a spent sparkler. He dropped back down into his seat.

"Kennedy had an arrest warrant for sexual molestation in Midland, Michigan. He came here to get some cash from his previous victims so he could hightail it to Venezuela. We know he called several men whom he molested and met with at least one, who confirmed that he did. He called and met with you."

"He wanted some investment advice." Farber jutted his jaw stubbornly.

"No, he didn't," Kinsale said. "He told you that the charges against him were trumped up and that you'd always meant the most to him and that he really needed you now to help him escape."

Farber pressed his hands onto the table, and his eyes flared. "That's what you think he said? That's what you think he said?"

Kinsale nodded.

"How fucking wrong can you be?" Farber flailed his arms, and he sat back in the chair.

Again, Farber's histrionics were attracting attention, and Kinsale said in a low voice. "Listen, Larry, you—"

"He threatened to reveal everything unless I gave him money." Farber's face was screwed into a nasty grimace. "There were no false charges or me meaning anything to him. It was straight-up blackmail. I give him $100,000 or he turns himself in and tells everybody every single thing that he . . ."

Farber's anger overwhelmed him now. He couldn't get the words out. He stood up and staggered backwards, crashing into the wall behind him and sending his chair clattering across the floor. "If you want to talk to me again," he sputtered, "call my lawyer." He turned and stormed out.

Kinsale watched him go, dazed by the sudden force of the man's anger. He hadn't thought Farber had it in him. Even after all these years, what Kennedy had done to these young men was like a raw wound.

A while later, Kinsale navigated out of Georgetown and then drove north along the Potomac River to meet with Randall Chamberlain. In the late morning, traffic out of the city was light, and he made better time than he expected, so he stopped in Potomac Village for lunch before continuing to the appointment.

Just short of one o'clock, he pulled into Chamberlain's half-circle cobblestone driveway, parking a respectful distance behind a late-model silver Aston Martin and a timeless chocolate-brown Bentley convertible. The house was like so many in and around Potomac, new, huge, and ostentatious. And even though it had plenty of architectural flourishes, including two-story columns flanking the arched front door and no fewer than five gables across the roofline, it had no character beyond flaunting the wealth of its owners.

A butler answered the door. Or Kinsale figured he was a butler, as he was wearing a formal black jacket with tails, a bowtie, and gray-and-black striped pants. Kinsale told him he had an appointment with Randall Chamberlain. The butler nodded and directed him to follow him down the broad central hallway towards the back of the house.

Kinsale's phone buzzed. He glanced at the screen and saw that Blalock had sent him a text. He'd run both phone numbers. The first was out of service and had last been issued to Ernest Haslett, and the second belonged to Lee Simms in Arlington, which was across the Potomac River from D.C.

The butler led him through a set of oversized French doors onto a flagstone terrace. Chamberlain was sitting under a wood-ribbed umbrella at a round table by a large swimming pool. Even at a distance, Kinsale could see that he was drunk. Or stoned. Or both. He was lounging in the chair so languidly that it seemed at any moment he might flow off the edge and into the pool. He grinned when he saw them and waved them over. The butler stopped at a respectful distance and recited Kinsale's name in the slightest of English accents.

"Sit down, sit down," Chamberlain insisted, gesturing vaguely at the other seven chairs around the table. "Can White get you anything?"

Kinsale sat down and said to White, "Coffee, if you have it."

"Certainly, sir," White said with a small bow. He turned to Chamberlain. "Anything for you, sir?"

"Another of these." Chamberlain held up a full Margarita glass with a lime slice and salt ringing the rim. "And maybe you can have Mrs. Wade throw together a sandwich." Chamberlain turned to Kinsale. "Do you want a sandwich?"

Kinsale shook his head, and White went back into the house.

"So, you're here about Jim," Chamberlain said. "What do you want to know?"

Chamberlain looked to be in his early thirties. He was tall and towheaded with a narrow face that was fleshing out from indolence and too much alcohol. He was wearing an oxford blue shirt unbuttoned halfway down his pale chest, frayed and faded khaki shorts, and aviator sunglasses.

"You were a student of Kennedy's?"

"Not actually."

"You weren't?"

"Nope."

"Did you go to the Georgetown Academy?"

He took a long sip of his drink. "But I never had Jim as a teacher."

"How did you know him?"

"Ernie Haslett introduced us."

"Do you have a current number for Haslett? The number I have is out of service."

"Yeah, Ernie has a lot of trouble with the phone company." Chamberlain picked up his cellphone and started to look. "What number do you have?"

Kinsale flipped the pages in his notebook to the call log and read out the number that was out-of-service.

"Doesn't ring a bell," Chamberlain said and then giggled drunkenly at his joke. He took another long sip and then looked again at his phone. When he found Haslett's number, he recited it. Kinsale added it to the call log.

"That number is probably one Ernie had before the one I just gave you. Like I said, he's always had a lot of trouble with the phone company."

"Why is that?"

"Ernie isn't the best at paying bills on time. Or at all." Chamberlain finished off his drink and looked around for White. Distracted, he said, "After a while, the phone company just cuts him off, so he has to go to a new one. He's probably on his second cycle by now."

"When was the last time you talked with him?"

He shrugged. "A couple of weeks. A few months. Maybe longer."

"Do you know Lee Simms?"

Chamberlain considered the question for a moment and then shook his head. "Who is he? Or is he a she?"

"I don't know. They have one of Haslett's older numbers now."

"Maybe Ernie's gotten to the point where the phone companies won't take him anymore. Could be a friend fronting for him."

White appeared carrying a silver tray with a fresh Margarita and Kinsale's coffee. He set down the tray and placed an empty bone china cup and saucer in front of Kinsale. He poured out the coffee from a silver pot, set out a sugar bowl and cream pitcher, and lined up a silver teaspoon at an exact right angle to the table's edge. He picked up Chamberlain's empty glass and put down the new drink. "Your sandwich will be ready momentarily, sir."

"You said Haslett introduced you to Kennedy?" Kinsale asked when White was out of earshot.

He had to wait as Chamberlain knocked back half of his drink and then relished the effect. "Yeah. We were friends, and he and Jim were friends."

"And Larry Farber?"

Chamberlain arched an eyebrow. "You know Larry?"

"I talked with him this morning. Kennedy reached out to him as well."

Chamberlain remained silent as he digested the information.

"What did you mean when you said Haslett and Kennedy were friends?"

Chamberlain chuckled. "You know what I mean."

"I do?"

"Kennedy liked to fuck little boys. He was fucking Ernie, and he asked him if he had any friends. Ernie thought of me." He raised his glass. "Cheers."

Kinsale thought Chamberlain's casual affability bordered on the pathological. "Haslett was being molested by Kennedy, and he brought you into it? He doesn't sound like much of a friend."

"We were like thirteen-years-old, man. What did we know?"

"Still . . ."

He waved away Kinsale's objection with a flick of his wrist. "That's water under the bridge. Or semen up the ass. Whatever the correct term should be."

Kinsale could see why Chamberlain needed to stay permanently lubricated. His light-hearted facade was a thin and brittle shield. If he actually faced up to his past, it would likely crumble and take him with it. "Water under the bridge works for me."

Chamberlain extended both arms with his palms up, as if he were giving a gift.

"So, Kennedy molested you?"

"Oh yeah," Chamberlain said without even a flinch. "For three or four months. Then my parents sent me away."

"They found out?" Kinsale sensed an opening.

"No, but I was acting out. Drinking, drugs . . ."

"At thirteen?"

"I was precocious." Chamberlain slurred his way through the three-syllable word. "They sent me to Choate, but it didn't help."

"Did they ever find out about Kennedy?"

"Oh sure. After Choate kicked me out, and they were despairing for my future, I told them. They were suitably horrified, but we agreed that it was best to keep it quiet."

"Was Kennedy still at Georgetown Academy at that point?"

"I have no idea."

"Was there any discussion of bringing in the authorities?"

"My father was on track to be the managing partner at Gerson Hobart," Chamberlain said. "That wouldn't do."

"Even though his son had been molested?" Kinsale asked. He was trying to break through to Chamberlain's real self, but the man had spent too many years reinforcing his defenses.

"Which one did you prefer?" he asked as if he were trying to remember. "Water under the bridge?"

They lapsed into a silence, and Chamberlain took advantage of the time to finish off his drink.

"You met with Kennedy on Wednesday?"

"Yeah."

"Where?"

"At some coffee place off of Wisconsin."

"The Laughing Dog?"

"Sounds familiar. Lowry would know."

"Who's Lowry?"

"Our chauffeur."

"What time did you meet Kennedy?"

"God awful early. Lowry could tell you."

Kinsale wondered why Lucy Thayer hadn't told him that Kennedy had been at The Laughing Dog earlier on Wednesday morning. He could understand her not paying him any attention at the time because she didn't know who he was but given that he'd died on her floor a few hours later, Kinsale didn't believe she wouldn't have remembered him.

"I'll need to speak with Lowry."

"Where the hell is White?" Chamberlain complained. He lifted his empty glass above his head as if they were in a crowded bar. "Usually, he'd be back by now."

Kinsale glanced toward the house just as White stepped out into the sunlight, carrying a tray with a sandwich and another Margarita.

"Took your time," Chamberlain said petulantly.

"Yes sir," White said. He placed the sandwich plate in front of Chamberlain and switched the full glass for the empty one. He turned to Kinsale. "More coffee, sir?"

"No thanks. I'm going to be heading out soon."

"Yes sir," he said and walked away.

Chamberlain was already two bites into his BLT. Kinsale noticed that Mrs. Wade had sliced off the crusts. "Is Lowry around?"

"He's driving my mother somewhere," Chamberlain said. "No telling when they'll be back."

"How can I reach him?"

"I haven't the faintest idea. He's always just there when I need him."

Kinsale pulled out two of his cards and set them side-by-side on the table. "Would you have him call me?" he asked and then tapped the second card. "And if you think of anything more based on our conversation, please give me a call."

"Will do," Chamberlain said, although they both knew he wouldn't.

"What did you and Kennedy talk about when you met?"

"He said he was having some legal trouble up in Michigan. He needed money to make a getaway."

"Did he threaten to expose what he did to you if you didn't give it to him?"

"And I thought I was special." He pretended to be disappointed. "Did he offer Larry the same deal?"

"And Chris Dowling."

"Chris Dowling?"

"Another of Kennedy's students at Georgetown. I think he was a couple of years behind you."

"Black kid?"

Kinsale nodded.

"I remember him. Small, a little effeminate. Jim would have liked him."

"Jesus!" Kinsale yelled before he could stop himself. "Are you really that dead inside?"

Kinsale's outburst jolted Chamberlain, and he sat up in his chair, but then a moment later, he oozed back down, and a look of smug satisfaction glinted in his eyes. Even as he felt pity for the man for what Kennedy and his parents had done to him, Kinsale was repelled by him and needed to collect himself. He asked, "What did you say to Kennedy after he threatened you?"

"I laughed him off. What do I care who he tells? I told him it would make me more interesting at parties."

"Just a moment ago, you said that your parents wanted to keep it quiet."

"That's when I was a kid. Since then, they've used it any number of times to explain to others why I've turned out to be such a disappointment."

"How did Kennedy react?"

"React? I didn't really notice. If I had to guess, I would say he was disappointed, maybe angry."

"Did he say he was going to go through with his threat?"

"Let me think," Chamberlain said, although Kinsale could see that the pause was merely an excuse to take a healthy sip of his drink. "I don't remember."

"Did you leave together?"

"Just to the sidewalk. He said he had another appointment in

Georgetown."

"That would have been with Farber," Kinsale said. "Did he mention Haslett at all?"

"No."

"He was trying to reach him."

"Ernie wouldn't have been too satisfying for him."

"Why is that?"

"Because he went to prison for the same shit that Jim did to him."

"He was molesting boys?"

"He was trying to. Looking at pictures on the web, hanging around schoolyards and playgrounds. I don't know what he eventually did, but he went to jail. Now he's a convicted sex offender who has to put himself on a list wherever he lives. Last I heard he was somewhere out west of Leesburg, practically in West By-God Virginia, but he has to keep moving. Parents in Virginia don't like having a sexual offender in the neighborhood."

"Parents anywhere."

"Virginia's the worst. Bunch of Bible-thumping, gun-toting hypocrites."

The tirade appeared to drain him, and he raised his glass and knocked back what remained.

"What do you do for a living, Randall?"

"Randy, please," he said, his eyes bobbing in a sea of alcohol. "We're best buds by this point."

"Okay, Randy, what do you do for a living?"

"Mostly this." He waved around the expansive terrace. "Sometimes I go to the club for lunch. My parents usually entertain on weekends, and I may crash if they get a decent caterer. There are a couple of bars in Bethesda that I like."

Seeing Kinsale's reaction, Chamberlain laughed bitterly. "Don't be so fucking puritanical. I don't have to work, so why should I? Everyone else works to have fun on the weekend. I have fun all the time."

"I wasn't being judgmental."

"If you won the lottery tomorrow, wouldn't you quit your job?" His smile was knowing. "Of course, you would. That day. That minute. And then you would start doing all the things you couldn't do because you have to work to pay your rent."

"Actually, over the past few months I had a pretty nice run of doing nothing but reading the books I've always wanted to read, and I think if it had gone on another week, I would have shot myself."

"Maybe you don't have enough of an imagination," Chamberlain suggested.

"Or maybe I have too much of one."

CHAPTER 15

As he drove back into the city, Kinsale kept circling back to the pain and devastation that Kennedy had left in his decades-long wake. In just the past two days, he'd talked to three men—and learned of a fourth—who had been broken by Kennedy. How many others had he hurt? How many other boys had he robbed of a future? At the Georgetown Academy? At the Midland Military Institute? Elsewhere?

He found a parking place just down from The Dog's front door and punched in the phone number that Chamberlain had given him for Ernie Haslett. After a half-dozen rings, a sleepy voice answered with a muttered "Who's this?"

"Detective Martin Kinsale with the Metropolitan Police Department."

"Wha . . ." Anxiety flooded into Haslett's tone. "What are you calling me for?"

"Did you know a James Kennedy?"

"No."

"Let me rephrase that," Kinsale said. "You knew James Kennedy. He was trying to reach you. I need to know if he did and what you talked about."

"He never . . . He didn't . . . Man, I haven't heard from him since I was a kid."

Kinsale flipped open his notebook to the page with the phone numbers and read off the second number that Kennedy had for Haslett. "Was that ever your phone number?"

"I don't know."

"Ernie!"

"Who knows their phone number?"

"Everybody."

"Not me."

Over his career, Kinsale had encountered uncounted lowlifes like Haslett, self-pitying and pathetic. Because of their addiction or the chaos of their lives, they were incapable of seeing beyond the tip of their nose. With Haslett, though, he needed to remember that this was Kennedy's doing. He took a long breath and read out the number again. "Think, Ernie."

"I don't know," Haslett whined. "I've had maybe ten numbers in the past two years. I don't even know what this number is."

"Then how did you give it to Randall Chamberlain?"

"Randy?"

"He gave it to me."

"I don't know," Haslett said. "Maybe he read it off his phone when I called him sometime."

"When did you last talk to him?"

Haslett didn't respond, so Kinsale prompted, "It has to have been since you got this phone number."

"I guess."

"When was that?"

"I don't know."

Kinsale struggled to tamp down his irritation. "Do you know Lee Simms?"

"Who?"

"Lee Simms. In Arlington."

"Arlington?" Haslett sounded confused.

"It's a simple question."

"Maybe?"

"What does that mean?"

"I don't know. Maybe I do. Who is he?"

"He—or she—has that phone number now. Maybe they helped you out with your phone . . . issues?"

"Nobody ever helps me," Haslett moaned, raw emotion flaring up. "Not ever."

Kinsale paused to let the edge come off the moment and then said, "I need to talk to you about Kennedy."

"Why?"

"Where do you live?"

Again, Haslett didn't answer, and this time Kinsale allowed some of his bubbling anger into his voice as he repeated the question.

Haslett let out a resigned sigh and said, "Near Hillsboro."

"Where's that?"

"West of Winchester."

"How far a drive is it from D.C.?"

"Not far enough," he grumbled.

"Where do you work?"

"I don't."

"Then I'll come to your house. Give me the address." Haslett struggled to recite it, so Kinsale repeated it twice to make sure he had it right.

"When are you coming?" Haslett asked.

Kinsale had dealt with enough "Hasletts" in his career to know that he wasn't asking to find out when he needed to be in his house, rather when he needed to be gone, so he said, "You'll know when I get there," and hung up.

Talking to Haslett had left a bad taste in his mouth, and he hoped some coffee would clear it. He was walking towards The Dog when his phone rang. Seeing it was the Second, he picked up. Before he could say anything, Captain Scott roared, "What the fuck game are you playing at, Kinsale?"

Kinsale didn't answer as his thoughts started racing through everything that he'd done in the past twenty-four hours to figure out where he had misstepped. Or had someone ratted him out to Scott? Duane Engler and Dontay Blalock were the two most likely suspects, but he couldn't believe either would do it. That left the various people he'd interviewed, but again he didn't see how that would get back to Scott. Getting nowhere, Kinsale asked, "Game?"

"Don't try that with me," Scott yelled. "Don't even think about trying that with me."

"Honestly, Captain, I'm trying to figure out what you're talking about."

"In my experience, Kinsale," Scott said, his voice quieter but still as hard as steel, "when someone says 'honestly,' they ain't being that."

"I am, Captain." Kinsale kept hunting for his mistake, but every possibility ended in a blank wall. "I have no idea what this is about."

"Where are you right now?"

"At The Laughing Dog."

"I can have a prowl car there in two minutes. I wouldn't want to have them show up, and you not be there."

"I'll stand outside on the sidewalk until they get here." Kinsale said, easing into the shadow of the building to escape the full force of the sun.

"You better not be bullshitting me."

"I'll be right here."

"Is that Post chick with you?"

That was the connection, and Kinsale breathed easier. "Come on, Captain, you know I wouldn't be so stupid as to talk to The Post."

"So, you do know what I'm talking about."

"She came by my place yesterday. Wanted to talk about why I'm not working any files. I told her I had nothing to say."

"Why didn't you tell me?"

"I figured that without my input, she had nothing. I didn't think she'd keep going."

"Did you tell her she was wrong? Or did you just say, 'no comment'."

"I told her I didn't know what she was talking about. Telling her 'no comment' would have been a green light to come after the Department."

Kinsale could tell that Scott wanted to believe him. The Captain knew that he wouldn't screw over the Department like that no matter what they did to him. But believing him went against all of Scott's institutional biases. "You could probably get a six-figure settlement at this point," he said. "Maybe even seven."

"If that's what I wanted, my lawyers would have been serving papers downtown weeks ago. You know me, Captain. I bleed blue. I don't want out. I want back in."

"That's not going to happen."

"Maybe," Kinsale said. "Maybe not. Regardless, I'm going to keep trying. And that's why talking to The Post is the last thing I would do."

"You bring in The Post and the Department would cut you off at the knees. Screw the consequences."

"I wouldn't blame them."

"You don't talk outside the lines."

"Never would," Kinsale said. "So, what did she have anyway?"

"She put in a request with the media people to talk to me about crime in the Second. They asked me to do it. She came in here this afternoon and the first question out of her mouth was that she'd gone through the arrest records for the past six months and wanted to know why you weren't on any of them."

"What did you say?"

"Told her you were working longer-term files that were more befitting your level of expertise."

Kinsale laughed at that. "Did she buy it?"

"Not a chance. And then she came at it from every angle she could think of, but it was always the same question: Why isn't Martin Fucking Kinsale working the street? She knew a lot about what's going on here. Too much to my way of thinking."

Occasionally—very occasionally—an idea would materialize fully formed for Kinsale, and he would marvel at its sudden appearance, like a father looking at his newborn baby. He was disappointed that these epiphanies appeared so rarely, but he'd also learned to embrace them when they did. So, he asked, "If I didn't talk to her, who did?"

"What are you saying?"

"It's what you said. She knows way too much. Someone must be feeding her information."

"Albert Gardner told me that you and her were an item."

Captain Albert Gardner commanded the Homicide Branch and hadn't liked Kinsale's relationship with Lewis. "For the blink of an eye and that was almost a year ago. Like I said, before she showed up last night, I hadn't talked to her since I came to the Second. But . . . somebody has."

The line went silent. Kinsale was still waiting for Scott when he heard a car door slam across the street. He turned and saw Lewis coming towards him from her British Racing Green MINI. Seeing that he'd spotted her, she smiled. He smiled back but held up a hand to keep her from coming too close.

"What about one of your friends on the force?" Scott asked. "They might have said something to her."

"I don't have any friends on the force anymore," Kinsale said. "No, Captain, it's someone in our shop."

"Why would they do that?"

"Because I still have a shield. That's got to be eating at the ulcers of more than one of the guys in the squad room."

Again, Scott went quiet, and again Kinsale waited him out. Lewis had stopped twenty feet away, and he mimed to her that he would be off in one minute. She nodded.

"I'm not totally buying it, Kinsale, but I'll look into it," Scott said. "In the meantime, I want you to stay away from here. And stay out of trouble." He hung up.

Seeing that the call was over, Lewis approached. "Who was that?"

"My boss. He called to tell me to stay out of trouble. I think he was talking about you."

She laughed. "I've been called worse."

"Buy you a coffee?"

"I was about to make you the same offer."

"I'll get this one. You get the next."

"Fair enough."

They headed towards the coffeehouse. "You're not very popular in your squad room," she said.

"Neither are you."

"I wouldn't be doing my job if I were."

"Me neither."

He held open the café door for her and guided her inside with a hand on her shoulder. It was a familiar gesture that raised a rush of fond memories that he was in no hurry to dispel.

Lucy Thayer was alone behind the counter, and she offered a resigned smile when she saw them. There were four other customers. Marnie, the musician, was at her table, and three high-school kids were at the table where Kennedy had met his demise. One was sitting and playing with a handheld electronic device while the other two hovered above him.

"What would you like?" he asked Lewis.

"Since you're buying, I'll have a large latte."

"That's my table." He pointed to the back of the café. "The last one."

She headed that way, and he went to the counter. "You decided to open?"

Thayer shrugged. "I didn't want to be home, and there was no point in me being here and not opening."

He gave her their order and then asked after Rennie Esposito.

"I don't think he's coming back to work," she said as she operated the espresso machine. "I've called a few times, but he hasn't picked up."

"He was a good kid. I liked him."

"Me too. He was working out well. Starting next week, I was going to give him a set of keys and let him open on his own."

"That would have made life easier for you."

She lifted her shoulders. "I've already put an ad on Craigslist."

"Is that how people get hired now? Off of Craigslist?"

"That's how I found Rennie."

He watched her pour the heated milk over the coffee. "It's going to be tough till then."

"It's been slow, and it's probably going to stay slow for a while," she said. "And Bill will help out when he can."

"People have a short memory," he said. "They'll forget about Kennedy soon enough."

She looked doubtful. "How's the investigation going?"

"I'm not on it anymore," he said. "Homicide has taken over."

"They were here yesterday. I'd feel better if you were still involved."

"I appreciate that."

She nodded towards Lewis. "Who's the lady?"

"She writes for The Post."

Thayer arched a quizzical eyebrow as she pushed the coffees across the counter. "Here you go."

Kinsale smiled as he put down a ten. "Keep the change."

He set Lewis' coffee on the table next to her reporter's notebook, which was open to a blank page. Sitting down, he asked, "What were we talking about?"

"We were trying to figure out which one of us is more unpopular with your colleagues."

"At this point, I don't think it's even a contest," he said.

"You don't sound too bothered by it."

"I am, but there's not much I can do."

"What's going to happen?"

"I hit my twenty late next year. Pension and benefits. I can hang on until then."

"And after that?"

"I've never really thought about life after the Department. I'd always assumed they'd wheel me out." He took a sip of his coffee. "I guess I'll hit the road and start knocking on some doors. Maybe find someplace where the summers are a little less humid."

"I'd miss you if you left," she said.

He felt the words in the pit of his stomach. She'd said them so simply and frankly, and he cursed himself for not being able to do the same. Even during their months apart, Lewis had never been far from his thoughts, and one solace in his impending departure from the Department was the possibility that they could rekindle what they'd had. He hadn't known—or dared ask—if she felt the same.

They eyed each other in a charged silence that continued to ratchet up until he didn't think he could he sit there another moment, but then she asked in a thick voice, "So, the old guy died here?"

Her question broke the spell, and Kinsale paused to let his breathing and heart rate return to normal before answering. "At that table where the kids are playing." He told her about Kennedy dying. He could have continued the story, telling her what he'd learned about Kennedy since then, but he wanted to keep that to himself for now.

"So, you're friends with the woman behind the counter and . . ."

"Hardly friends."

"You sought each other out when we came in," Lewis said. "And then the way she was checking me out."

"She's married."

"Like that makes a difference."

"I've been coming here for nearly six months," he said. "Naturally we became . . . friendly."

A spark flashed in her eyes, and she leaned across the small table. "I can't believe you're letting them do this to you."

"Who?" He raised his hands in mock defense. "Doing what?"

"Come on, Martin, the Department is blackballing you, and you're just rolling over."

"We're having a minor disagreement."

"Bullshit," she snapped. "They're done with you, and you're smart enough to know that."

"Maybe."

"So, fight back. If you don't, they're going to win," she said.

"Trish . . ."

"Let me help you," she pressed on. "One article about what they're doing, and they'll be tripping over themselves to bring you back into the fold."

"You don't know how cops think."

"Sure, I do."

"No, you don't. If I said anything, I'd be out for sure."

"More than you are now?"

"I have to sleep at night."

"Then on background. Give me a foothold, and I'll drag it out of them."

He considered her offer but then said, "There's no story here, Trish."

She flopped back in frustration. "Are you going to make me do this without you?"

"There's nothing to do."

"For old time's sake?"

"Well, when you put it that way," he said. "No."

She clicked her tongue in irritation and stood. Picking up her notebook, she made a point of closing the cover. "Well, thanks for the coffee."

"Can I ask you a question?"

Rather than respond, she sat down again.

"Scott said that you know way more about my . . . situation than he thinks you should. How come?"

"That's my job."

"Still . . ."

"I'm a damn good reporter."

"I'm not questioning that. I'm asking specifically, how you know so much?"

Her eyes flared. "I'm not going to tell you that."

"I'm not asking for names," he said, raising his hands to calm her. "I'm asking how you collected the information."

"Like I always do, by asking questions." She was still upset. "Let me tell you, any number of your . . . hmm . . . fellow officers are only too happy to shit on you. I ask what's the latest, and I can't get them to shut up."

"Alan—"

"You weren't asking for names, remember?"

"Right." He was satisfied. "Thanks."

"You're welcome."

"I'd still like to buy you a drink sometime."

She glared at him and then turned away. "I'd like that." Without looking back, she said, "Call me."

CHAPTER 16

Kinsale watched Lewis cross Chesapeake Street and disappear out of his sightline. Then he waited five more minutes. They may have had a shared history and might have something going forward, but professionally they remained antagonists. As she'd said, she was a damn good reporter, and if she thought he was holding out on her, he wouldn't put it past her to double back.

Once he was satisfied that she was gone, he walked over to Marnie the musician's table. He'd kept an eye on her while talking with Lewis. He could see that she was acutely aware of his presence while pretending not to be. Even at this point, as he approached, she didn't look up, ignoring him even harder and leaning into her yellow legal pad.

"Got a minute?" he asked.

She looked up. As so often happened when he was in an official capacity, a mix of anxiety and disappointment crossed her face. "Sure." she said, although she didn't sound like she was.

He sat down across from her. "I'm Martin Kinsale, by the way."

"Marnie Shea." She had a light twang in her voice, as if she were from the South but from a major city, like Charlotte or Atlanta. "It's nice to finally put a name to the face."

"Likewise," he said. "I don't think either of us were here to socialize."

"You and Lucy seem to get along."

"Every store owner likes to have a cop sitting in the back."

Shea looked to be in her mid-fifties. She had light brown hair that was thinning and graying, and the skin on her face was soft and powdery. Her eyes were a light blue behind rimless bifocals. She was wearing a black sleeveless blouse, black pants, and yellow espadrilles. A faint perfume floated across the table.

He said, "Lucy says you're a musician."

"Did she say that?" She looked pleased. "I had no idea that she knew. Yeah, I play, but mostly just with friends these days."

"What do you play?"

"Guitar, mandolin, tin whistle . . . whatever."

"Speaking as someone with no musical aptitude, that sounds amazing."

Again, she looked pleased. He pointed to the pad. "Are you writing music?"

"This?" She lifted the pad. "No, I'm trying to be a writer."

"Trying?"

"I'm retired," she said. "I was a graphic designer for forty years. I want to do something different."

He silently added a decade to his age estimate. "What are you writing about?"

"It's a blog about music."

"What about music?"

"Everything. Why I like it. Why other people like it. What makes it great."

"What's it called?"

She told him and he wrote it down in his notebook. "I'll check it out," he said. "I need to ask you a couple of questions about Wednesday?"

Shea turned somber. "I figured."

"You always seem to be here before me. Do you remember what time you arrived on Wednesday?"

"Around 8:30."

"Did you see Kennedy? That's the man who died. Did you see him in here earlier in the morning?"

"This place is busy in the morning. I can't say that I did, but I can't say that I didn't either. When I get going, I'm pretty focused."

"He would have been with a guy in his early thirties. Tall, languid, probably drunk."

"Drunk?"

"The younger guy would have arrived in a chocolate-brown, convertible—"

"Bentley," she blurted out. "How could I miss that? What a beautiful car."

"The man who got out of the car came here to talk to Kennedy."

She searched her memory but then shook her head. "To be honest, I didn't really notice the guy. I mean, I looked at the Bentley, drooled for a few seconds, and then got back to work."

"Do you remember what Kennedy looked like? I mean, when you saw him on the floor."

She thought about her answer before saying, "I think so."

"Do me a favor, then. Close your eyes, picture him in your mind, and try to remember if you saw him in here earlier on Wednesday."

She looked doubtful but complied. After about fifteen seconds, she opened her eyes and shook her head. "No, I'm sorry."

"No worries. Second question, do you know the name of the guy who usually sits at that table?" He pointed two tables behind her. "He's always talking into his headset."

"Tony Adkins."

"Was he here today?"

"I haven't seen him."

"Do you know how I could get in touch with him?"

"He lives in Silver Spring."

"Do you know where he works?"

"I think he works for a company in Minnesota or Wisconsin or somewhere out there. He does computer stuff."

"Do you know the name of the company?"

"No. He's probably mentioned it, but I guess I wasn't paying attention." She smiled coyly. "If you'd like, I could close my eyes and try to remember if he ever told me."

He laughed and stood. "One last question. That day, there was a third man. He was sitting between you and Tony. Do you know him?"

She turned to look at the empty table. "I guess I remember someone being there, but I didn't pay them any attention. People cycle through here pretty much all day long."

"Except for us regulars," he said. "Thanks for your help."

The afternoon sun was beating down out of a cloudless sky as he stepped outside, and he checked his pace to adjust to the heat. He hoped the car's AC system wasn't on the verge of one of its increasingly frequent breakdowns. Opening the car door, he gingerly sat inside to turn on the engine and get the air conditioning going. He then climbed out, sought the shade of a tree, and called Lee Simms.

"Hello?" a young girl answered carefully.

He introduced himself and asked, "Are you Lee Simms?"

"No." Her voice became smaller.

"What's your name?"

"Alecia Simms."

"Is Lee Simms your . . . father?"

"Yes."

"Is this your phone?"

"Yes."

"How long have you had this number?"

"Three months. My parents let me have a phone when I turned twelve."

"What does your father do for a living?"

"He works at Best Buy."

"Which one?"

"Tyson's."

"Thanks, Alecia," he said. "Do you know you haven't set up your voice mail on your phone yet?"

"Except for my mom and dad, I don't answer the phone."

"What about your friends?"

"We text."

"We're talking. Why did you pick up?"

"I saw it was a Washington area code. I thought it might be the government."

"Are you having an issue with the government?"

"No," she said. "Or I don't think I do."

"There's nothing to worry about on this end," Kinsale said. "Bye."

As he started back towards his car, the phone rang in his hand. He looked at the screen and saw it was Duane Engler. He stepped back under the shade of the tree.

"Duane," he said. "You've got the results on the glass pieces?"

"Nope, still working on that."

"Then to what do I owe this pleasure?"

"Thought you might be interested in something else about the old guy."

"Always."

"We ran through all of the prescription medicines in his hotel room," Engler said.

"He had a hotel room?"

"Right, you didn't know," Engler said sarcastically. "Turns out he was staying at the Hotel Windermere."

"Windermere Hotel."

"Yeah, that one. Anyway, the guy was a walking pharmacy."

"Most men his age are."

"Yeah, but not in a good way. For one, he was taking isosorbide mononitrate for his angina."

"Is that bad?"

"By itself, no, but combining it with the Viagra we found under the sink could cause a dangerous drop in blood pressure."

"Enough to cause a heart attack?"

"No doubt."

"What was Dr. Dunstag thinking?"

"That's the thing," Engler said. "Dunstag prescribed all of the medications except the Viagra."

"Who prescribed that?"

"No way of knowing. There was nothing on the bottle. My guess is that he bought the pills from someone else."

"Did he have Viagra in his system?"

"We don't have the toxicology from the ME yet."

"Will you drop me a line when you know?"

"Right after I tell Alan."

"Works for me," Kinsale said. "And the pieces of glass?"

"Why would I tell Alan about those? They're from a different case, right?" Engler said and hung up.

Kinsale walked to his car and opened the driver's side door. Leaning over, he felt the faintest breath of cool air. He figured that was as good as it was going to get, so he got in, shut both doors, and headed home.

He was climbing the stairs to his apartment when Manny Oturos opened his door and stepped out. He was wearing a pair of baggy cargo shorts and an old Pink Floyd concert T-shirt and was holding a blender in his right hand.

"I'm comparing a few recipes I found for Pina Coladas," Oturos said. "I need you to be a taste tester."

Kinsale hesitated, but it had been a long day and a long week. "How many recipes are you testing?"

"Eight."

"Sounds just about right."

CHAPTER 17

Kinsale was cleaning his Saturday morning breakfast dishes when his phone rang. Looking down at the screen, he saw it was the front door intercom and picked up.

"Hi Martin, it's Lucy."

He needed a moment to connect the voice and the name to his home, and another to wonder why Lucy Thayer would be outside his building on a weekend morning.

As if she were reading his mind, she said, "I was hoping to talk to you about Chris. Just for a minute."

"Sorry." He shook his head, as if that would disperse the brain fog. "I'll buzz you in. I'm upstairs"

He opened his door and waited for her. She was dressed casually, in a pale-yellow sundress, a red Washington Nationals ballcap, and mustard-yellow Nike running shoes. A small black leather bag hung from her right shoulder. As he stepped aside in the doorway, he caught a whiff of her rose-scented fragrance.

"Shouldn't you be at The Dog?" he asked.

"I really needed to get away, so I decided to close for the morning. I'll open this afternoon. Or maybe not."

"Are you doing okay?"

"Mm-hmm," she said as she looked around his space like a prospective buyer.

"Can I ask, then, how you knew where I live?"

She blushed. "That's one of the benefits of being married to a real estate attorney." She crossed over to the front window. "I like your street. Very quiet."

"You and Bill live in Chevy Chase, right?"

"Friendship Heights, really. On Jenifer Street, not too far from The Dog.

Speaking of which, do you have any coffee?"

"Yeah," he said and then hesitated.

"What?"

"Seeing as you get paid to make coffee, I'm worried mine won't pass muster."

"Bill makes the coffee at home. I don't know how he does it, considering I bring home the beans, but it always tastes like instant."

"Mine isn't that bad." He headed into the kitchen and started preparing the coffee. "So, Chris . . ."

"Chris," she repeated "Bill filled me in on your conversation at Starbucks."

"Is that where we were?" he asked lightly. "I hadn't noticed."

She tried to smile, but her concern won out. "I'm worried that you might get the wrong idea and . . ."

"Wrong idea?"

"About our decision not to report James Kennedy."

"What would the wrong idea about that be, exactly?"

"I'm not going to pretend that I wasn't involved in the process," she said. "And I'm not trying to make excuses. I was an adult at that point. My parents brought me into it from the first. In fact, that's when I met Bill."

"A tough time to start a courtship."

"In a strange way, the whole thing brought us closer together. Anyway, we made the decision as a family. Our family and Bernard Thayer and Bill."

"Okay," he said. "You were united in the decision, but why did you make it?"

"Chris had been through so much, too much. We were concerned about putting him through anything more."

"So, you let a man who had repeatedly raped your twelve-year-old brother walk away."

His blunt tone stunned her, and she turned towards the window to collect herself. "I know it's horrific, but all I can say is that it seemed like the best . . . only option for us. She faced him and crossed her arms over her chest. "You can't apply the sensibilities of today to back then. It was a different world for black people trying to move up. If you made one misstep, gave them one reason to close the door, you wouldn't get a second chance."

"I'm not going to argue that point with you, Lucy," he said. "You're right, I can never know what it was like. But as I told Bill and Chris, my problem is that you let Kennedy off the hook and gave him seventeen more years to do to other boys what he did to Chris."

With each word of his, she tensed, and her crossed arms tightened like a straitjacket. "At the time, that didn't occur to us."

"It should have."

"Maybe so, but it didn't," she protested. "And . . ." She paused and consciously lowered her arms. "I don't want to get into that. I just want you to know that in hindsight, all of us understand that we probably—no, we definitely know—made the wrong decision."

He wasn't ready to let it go. He wanted to drive home the point and make her see what an odious thing she and her family had done. He wanted her to . . . What? She'd admitted they knew they'd done the wrong thing. What more could she say? There was nothing anyone could do to change it now. Kennedy was dead. He wasn't going to destroy anyone else's life. Still, their naive selfishness stuck in his throat. Maybe bringing in the police would have destroyed Bernard Thayer's career, but Kennedy certainly would have gone to prison. Not only would he no longer have had easy access to young boys, but given what he'd done, his fellow inmates would likely have given him insight into the other end of homosexual rape.

Rather than continuing to pick at the open sore, he finished making the coffee. He rinsed out his cup and pulled a second one from the counter and filled them. He carried them to the coffee table and sat on the couch. "I talked to your father-in-law on the phone on Thursday," he said. "I'm meeting with him on Monday."

After a moment, she left her perch by the window and sat in the reading chair. She took a sip of her coffee. "That's really quite good," she said shyly.

"Thanks," he said, feeling absurdly proud.

They were silent for a while, and then she said, "He's quite a man and not just professionally. He raised Bill all by himself."

"Really?"

"Bill's mother died in a car crash when he was young. Bernard being able to raise him so well while having to deal with all the challenges of his career is really remarkable."

They started to settle into another silence, so Kinsale asked, "Why didn't you tell me about Kennedy on Wednesday?"

She dragged her gaze up to his, and he saw the hurt in her eyes. "I already told you."

"Tell me again."

Her face hardened as she put down her coffee. "I'd hated that man for so many years, more than anyone else in my entire life, but I'd never seen him. Then when I saw him hug Chris like they were long-lost friends, and I realized who he was, I was livid. If I'd had a gun . . ." She stopped, realizing what she'd just said. "Do you know what I mean?"

He nodded and she went on. "That man had destroyed Chris's life. I wasn't going to let him hurt him again."

"How would telling me the truth have hurt Chris?"

"I just wanted it to go away."

"I can hear what you're saying, but my problem is that you did the same thing seventeen years ago. You made a decision that wasn't yours to make."

He paused to let his point sink in. "It was never just going to go away. The man died. You didn't know why. You didn't know how. By not stepping forward and telling all you knew, you might have ruined any hope we have of learning the truth."

She frowned. "You don't understand. The bastard was dead. He was finally out of our lives. I didn't care why he died or how he died. I still don't."

"He died two feet from your brother. Your brother, whom you've just said had his life destroyed by Kennedy."

She understood the implication immediately. "Chris would never... Chris would not have killed that man. Or any man." Her voice climbed indignantly. "That is completely insane." She glared at him, her breath coming in short angry bursts. "How dare you. I—"

"Please, Lucy."

His calm tone checked her. She stared at him long enough to make her point. She reached for her coffee cup but put it back on the table without taking a sip.

He let her simmer, waiting for the edges of her emotions to dull. Then he said, "We're just starting the investigation, Lucy. At this point, we don't have any idea who—"

"Chris had nothing to do with it."

He put up his palms. "Calm down. I'm not making any accusations."

"That's exactly what you're doing?" she snapped. "And anyway, you don't even know for certain that he was murdered."

"Yes, we do."

The certainty in his voice scared her. "Why do you think he was murdered? He was an old man. He . . ."

"I can't tell you why."

"Can't or won't?"

"You're part of the investigation, Lucy. You, your brother, your husband, his father . . ."

She waved away his words. "How could Chris have done anything? They were having coffee in a public place. There was a cop sitting thirty feet away. What could he possibly do at that point to kill the man? What?"

"He could have given him two pills."

"Those were Alka-Seltzer," she scoffed. "Chris said Kennedy was feeling nauseous."

Kinsale shrugged. "They could have been something else."

"What?" she demanded. "I have poison pills handy in my kitchen for whenever someone I don't like comes into the Dog? If that's the case, maybe you should find another place to read your books."

Her words surprised her as much as they did him. She immediately looked sheepish, and he couldn't help laughing. After a moment, she laughed too.

"Maybe I've been pushing a little too hard," he said.

"Do you think?"

"Okay, definitely, but I have to. There are a lot of questions that we need answers to."

She nodded and then said, "Bill is going to start wondering where I am. I'd better be going."

He stood and grabbed her bag to give to her. "I'll walk you out."

Outside on the front stoop, he asked, "Did you know that Kennedy was in The Dog earlier that morning?"

"What?" She looked dumbfounded. "What do you mean?"

"He met with another one of his victims."

"What time was this?"

"Around 8:30."

"Are you sure?" she asked as she struggled to remember. "I don't recall seeing him."

"The other man arrived in a chocolate-brown Bentley. They had coffee and talked for quite a while. You really don't remember?"

"That's our busy period," she said. "I wouldn't notice an individual customer unless there was a specific reason."

"Like dying on your floor three hours later?"

"But I didn't know that was going to happen, did I?"

Kinsale nodded, but he was no longer so sure.

CHAPTER 18

Monday morning at his dining table, Kinsale was on the line with Geoffrey Lowry, the Chamberlains' chauffeur, when he got another call. He looked at the screen and saw that the Second was calling. He ignored it.

"What time did you arrive at the coffeehouse?" he asked Lowry.

"At 8:30." Like White, the butler, Lowry had a faint British accent, and Kinsale wondered if that was a job requirement.

"You're sure?"

"Yes sir."

"And you saw Randall Chamberlain go into the coffeehouse?"

"Yes, sir."

"Did you see what he did inside the coffeehouse?"

"No, sir."

"Did you try to?"

"No, sir."

"What did you do?"

"Mr. Chamberlain had instructed me to remain outside the establishment. He said he wouldn't be long."

"Was he?"

"No, sir."

"About how long?"

"Seventeen minutes."

"About seventeen minutes?"

"No, seventeen minutes."

"You're sure?"

"Yes, sir."

"Was he alone when he came out?"

"No, sir. An older gentleman exited with him."

"Blue blazer, gray flannel pants."

"Yes, sir."
"What happened then?"
"They shook hands and Mr. Chamberlain returned to the car."
"And the older man?'
"He walked down the sidewalk."
"How did they seem?"
"How do you mean, sir?"
"Were they angry with each other? Buddy-buddy?"
"Cordial would best describe it."
"Did you see where the other man went?"
"No, sir."
"What happened after that? What did you and Randall do?"
"We returned to the house."
"Did he go out after that? During the morning?"
"No, sir."
"You're sure."
"Yes, sir."

Kinsale didn't have any more questions, so he thanked Lowry and hung up. He hadn't thought Chamberlain was involved, and nothing Lowry said had changed his mind. The information that Kennedy left the Dog before nine that morning was new though. What did he do between 8:47 and his meeting with Farber at 10:00?

Next on his list was tracking down Tony Adkins, the other coffeehouse regular, but first he called into the station.

"I'll put you through to the Captain," Royale said, her voice was heavy with tension.

"Did you have a good weekend?"

"I'll put you through," she said.

Scott came on the line halfway through the first ring. "Where are you?"

"At my house."

"Come in. Now."

"On Friday, you told me to stay away."

"Now I'm ordering you to come in." Scott hung up.

What now? Kinsale stared at his phone, wondering what had crawled up Scott's ass. Besides his conversation with Lucy Thayer, it had been a quiet weekend.

Walking into the squad half-an-hour later, he only needed to look at Moon's face to know that he'd screwed up big-time. Her mouth was a tight line, and her eyes flashed a warning.

"What's up?" he asked.

"Watch yourself, Martin," she said under her breath. Her warning was superfluous, though, because as he walked past her desk, everyone in the squad room was already watching him.

Again, he raced through everything he'd done over the weekend to try to find his misstep, but again he came up empty. Just as he started to go through the mental list one more time, Brian Magner stepped into his path.

"I hope you didn't bother packing a lunch today, Kinsale." Magner's face twisted in a nasty grin. "Because you're going to be out on your ass within an hour."

"You'll be flat on your ass within a second if you don't get the fuck out of my way." Kinsale shouldered past him.

"Kinsale," Scott barked from his open office door. "Here. Now."

Kinsale had to turn around and walk past Magner again. The detective sneered evilly, but Kinsale paid him no attention. Stepping into the Captain's office, he closed the door behind him.

"Sit," Scott ordered. He was already behind his desk, his hands folded over a single sheet of paper on the desktop.

"I just spoke with the Chief." His voice vibrated with suppressed anger. "Put your shield and service weapon on my desk now. And she wants your resignation letter on her desk by the end of the shift. If that doesn't happen, you'll be up on departmental and criminal charges before the morning."

Kinsale was shaken but kept his face blank. "And what would those charges be, Captain?"

Scott pushed forward. "Don't give me that shit. You know exactly. Against my explicit orders, you've continued to conduct an unauthorized investigation. You illegally used departmental time and resources in pursuit of that investigation. You lied to a superior officer. Your failure to follow departmental procedures has seriously contaminated a crime scene and probably fatally undermined a murder investigation."

"How have I fatally undermined a murder investigation?"

"I'm not debating this with you."

"As for using departmental time, I've been sitting on my ass in a coffeehouse for the past half year, with the full knowledge of the Department. On the clock. Nobody got too upset then."

"Martin, this is not a discussion. You—"

"And exactly what departmental resources are you talking about? I've been driving my own car. Maybe it was the pen and paper I used to take notes?"

"It's not your time or your resources that I'm talking about," Scott said. He picked up the sheet from his desk and waved it in the air between them.

And seeing the familiar format, Kinsale understood.

"The Lab sent this report to Homicide this morning," Scott said. "Results from chem tests on several pieces of glass. Results were positive for a potentially indicative substance, which is a huge development in the case, except neither of the detectives working Kennedy had submitted the glass for analysis or even knew about it."

"Captain, I—"

"And then it turns out that the case number was wrong. The pieces had been logged in under a six-month-old vandalism case. White nationalist graffiti on the wall in the Whole Foods parking lot in Tenleytown."

"I—"

"Naturally, Homicide called me. Turns out it was your old partner, Alan Casey. And then I had to call the Lab. Talked to Duane Engler. Took a couple of minutes but got the whole mess cleared up. Turns out it wasn't a mistake. You were tampering with evidence and deliberately subverting a homicide investigation."

"That's hardly—"

"This discussion is over. Type up your resignation and give it to Royale on your way out. IAD will go through your desk and mail anything personal to you."

Kinsale leaned back in his chair. "Not going to happen, Captain."

Scott looked at Kinsale hard. "Don't do this, Martin. Don't do it to yourself. Don't do it to the Department."

"Fuck the Department."

Scott nodded as if Kinsale had said something profound. "I can understand you feeling that way but save it for someone who cares. We'll bury you. We'll bury you so deep, you won't be able to get a job as a crossing guard in Dubuque."

"I wasn't planning on moving to Iowa anyway."

"Always the smart ass, but that won't do you a bit of good once IAD gets hold of you. They've been aching to nail you to the wall."

"What was the name of that Post reporter again?"

Scott stiffened.

"You remember. The tall dish. Red hair. Cool as the other side of the pillow. Trish something, wasn't it?"

"You don't want to do that. You bring in The Post and you won't have a friend in the world."

"As opposed to my current situation."

"You play with that fire, and you'll get burned."

"Is that a threat?"

"Talking to her is not a good long-term strategy for you."

"I don't seem to have much of a long term right now."

"Don't do it. Resign and walk. You do that, and I'll do what I can to make it as clean a break as possible."

Kinsale hesitated. The Department very likely had a winnable case against him now. He'd screwed up with Engler, and maybe this was the price he had to pay. Except the Department had as much—or more—to lose by taking this to the mat. "I'm not doing anything until I talk to my lawyer," he said. "Maybe she'll tell me that you guys have got me by the short hairs and my best option is to hand in my papers. I don't think so, but she knows the law. Until I talk to her, though, I'm not doing a thing."

"You've got until five this afternoon."

Kinsale laughed. "Have you ever tried to get a same-day appointment with a lawyer?"

"That's your problem."

"No, it's your problem." Kinsale stood. "If the Department moves forward on this, a lot more is going to come out than my finding evidence that led to . . . What did you call it? A huge development in a murder case." Scott winced as he realized his mistake, and Kinsale pressed his advantage. "Maybe you'll make a case against me in the end, but it's going to look really bad when it comes out how the Department has handled my situation over the past six months."

Scott shook his head. "Memories are short in this town. The Department will be fine within a month. You'll be ruined for the rest of your life."

"I don't think so. If this gets to court, it will drag on for months, maybe even a year. It'll be your own little Watergate."

"Don't flatter yourself." Scott pointed to the door. "Get out of here. You've got until five."

Kinsale didn't budge, but Scott seemed to have decided he'd already left and turned toward his computer screen. After a moment, Kinsale took out his Glock and shield and laid them on top of the lab report. "You might as well start filing those charges right now, Captain, because these two are the only things you're going to get from me today."

He didn't think Scott would let him get to the door, let alone open it. As he stepped out into the squad room, he wondered if he'd played it wrong.

"Wait," Scott called.

Kinsale returned to the office, shut the door, and waited. The Captain studied him for a full minute. Kinsale stared back. Finally, Scott asked, "What do you want?"

What Kinsale wanted and what he could get were miles apart. "An extra day. That'll give me time to talk to my lawyer and weigh my options."

"Can't do that. The Chief said you have to be gone today."

"That's it then." Kinsale opened the door again and headed out.

He was halfway across the squad room this time before Scott called his name. He turned to see the Captain standing in his doorway. "You better make the right decision."

"Tomorrow then?"

Scott hesitated before nodding. "Tomorrow." His gaze passed over Kinsale's shoulder. "Detective Magner, please escort Mr. Kinsale directly out of the building."

Magner tossed aside the magazine he was reading and made a production of lifting his feet off his desktop and standing up. He sauntered over to

Kinsale.

"Didn't even make it to lunch time, did you, asshole?" Magner pointed to the door. "After you, MIS-ter Kinsale."

CHAPTER 19

Kinsale didn't call his lawyer because he didn't have one. He'd never had his own lawyer. Even in the depths of his tussle with the Department six months before, when he hadn't known if he would be out a job the next day, he couldn't bring himself to hire one. Instead, he'd relied on the lawyer that the Fraternal Order of Police assigned to his case. In the end, the FOP lawyer didn't have much to do because the Department kept everything unofficial. This time, even though the water was a lot deeper and a lot hotter, he still couldn't bring himself to reach for outside help.

Driving north towards Silver Spring and his appointment with Bernard Thayer, he called the FOP to tell them he would need some more legal assistance. The woman on the other end of the line took down his information and said she'd have someone call him.

Next, he turned to the call log in his notebook and found the number for Tony Adkins, the other coffeehouse regular. Adkins picked up on the first ring, and Kinsale introduced himself.

"You're calling about last week?" Adkins said. "I don't really know how I can help."

"I just have a single question. There was another man there that morning. He was sitting one table up from you, closer to the door."

"Yeah, he took off like a bat out of hell after the old man hit the floor."

"Do you know who he is? Had you ever seen him before?"

"Nope."

"You're sure."

"It was always just you, me, and Marnie."

"Yeah." Kinsale hadn't expected much from Adkins, but he was still disappointed that yet another trail had gone cold.

"Have you been back?" Adkins asked. "To The Dog?"

"Only in an official capacity."

"I think my days there are done," Adkins said. "I liked the vibe, but it's kind of a haul from my house. I've been trying some of the places around here."

"I think business is going to be tough for Lucy for a while."

"I always liked Lucy."

"Me too," Kinsale said.

His next call went to the Best Buy store in Tysons Corner. It took about five minutes for Lee Simms to come on the line, which was about four-and-a-half minutes longer than their conversation. Simms didn't know Ernest Haslett or James Kennedy and had gone to public school in South Boston. His thick accent backed up his story.

Finally, Kinsale called Trish Lewis's home number. She didn't pick up. When the call clicked over to her ancient answering machine, he left a quick message.

Thayer lived in Hawthorn, a sprawling senior community of a couple dozen mid- and high-rise buildings connected by enclosed walkways and skyways. The security guard at the gate called Thayer and then waved Kinsale through.

Opening his door, Thayer appeared to be in his late sixties or early seventies. He was small with light brown skin and gray hair. He looked to be dressed for church, with a pressed white shirt, a red-and-blue striped tie under a navy-blue cardigan, dark gray pants, and well-shined brown loafers. His skin sagged softly on his face, and his eyes were gentle behind a pair of wire-rimmed bifocals. "Detective Kinsale?"

"Good to meet you, Mr. Thayer," Kinsale said, extending his hand.

"It's Dr. Thayer actually. Please come in."

His apartment was small and tidy. The main space combined the dining and living rooms. On the left was a small, bright kitchen. There were four doors, all of them closed. The television was tuned to a news channel, but the sound was muted. On the coffee table in front of the green felt couch was a tray with a carafe, two cups, a sugar bowl and a small jug of milk. A gold-edged clock hung on the wall behind the couch, and to the right was a floor-to-ceiling arrangement of family photos.

"Would you like some coffee?" Thayer asked.

"If you're having some."

"Lucy and Bill bring me ground coffee from her shop whenever they visit." Thayer poured out two cups and gestured for Kinsale to add sugar or cream. "I'm sure I don't make it as well as she does, but it's better than what they serve in our dining room."

"Do you see them often?"

"Bill visits every weekend." He took a sip from his cup. "Lucy comes with him when she can. The shop takes a lot of her time."

"Did you see them this weekend?"

"Bill and I talked quite a bit, and of course I spoke with both Lucy and Chris, but no, they didn't come by this weekend. They had a lot more on their minds than visiting an old man."

"It's going to be a tough time for them. Especially Chris."

Thayer looked into his coffee cup. "Bill told me that Chris and he talked to you. He said that you didn't approve of the decision we made then. I couldn't agree with you more. It seemed like the right course at the time, but it has had consequences that I didn't anticipate and that I now have trouble living with."

The simplicity of Thayer's sadness struck Kinsale. Not dramatic or overt, it was just there, like an illness that he'd contracted years ago.

In the ensuing silence, Kinsale's gaze returned to the family photos. They were in two columns and appeared to be arranged chronologically top to bottom. At the top was a formal black-and-white family portrait of a much younger Thayer standing behind a seated woman who had a young boy on her lap. The photo next to it was in color and more relaxed. It was a few years later and taken outside. The father and son were tossing a baseball while the mother sat at a picnic table. The woman didn't appear in the photos below, which highlighted the key events in the Thayer men's lives.

"Were you surprised that Kennedy called you?"

Thayer had been gazing out the window and he turned to Kinsale. "I hadn't heard from Jim since he left the Academy."

"Were you surprised?"

"I'd hoped I'd never hear from him again."

"Yes, but were you surprised?"

Thayer appeared to finally hear the question. "Yes, I was surprised."

"You said he wanted to meet with you."

Thayer nodded.

"Did he say why?"

"No."

"Why do you think?"

"If I were to hazard a guess, I would say he wanted to extort money from me to facilitate his fleeing the country. Much like he did with Chris."

"Would you have given him the money?"

"No," Thayer said firmly. "I've waited a long time to try to make things right."

"If he'd followed through on his threat, it wouldn't have been good for you or the Academy or Chris."

Thayer shrugged.

"When did you retire from the Academy?"

"Four years ago."

"How long were you there?"

"Twenty-five years." He shifted on the couch and sat up taller.

"That's a long time."

"Longest tenure in the Academy's history."

"Very impressive."

Thayer accepted the compliment like it was owed.

"And at the same time, you raised Bill all by yourself."

He shook his head. "Not really." He gestured to the family photos that Kinsale had looked at earlier. "Pamela, my wife, died when Bill was twelve. He was a great boy, but I couldn't handle the loss, and raising him by myself and pursuing my career would have been an impossibility. He went to boarding school. In Canada."

"He said you were a model father."

"I guess that counts for something."

"How did your wife die?"

Thayer raised an eyebrow. "I don't see how that impacts your investigation."

"I don't either."

He hesitated and then said, "In a car crash."

"Where was this?"

"We were living outside Fredericksburg, Virginia at the time. She was driving on Route 4. She went off the road and hit a tree. This was before everyone wore seatbelts. She was thrown through the windshield."

"I apologize for dredging up old memories."

"That's all I have now." Thayer raised a sad smile. "Memories and regrets."

"Just a few more questions."

Thayer nodded.

"Do you know where Kennedy went after he left the Academy?"

"No."

"If he'd tried to work at another school, would they have contacted the Academy for a reference?"

"Yes, but my agreement with him stipulated that the Academy would not provide a reference per se. We would only provide the facts of his employment."

"Except for the really damning facts."

He stiffened. "You can't make me feel any worse than I already do."

"I keep trying, though, don't I?" Kinsale said with a half-apologetic smile. "Was Kennedy a good teacher?"

"In the classroom, yes, he was a very good teacher. He was passionate about his subject and interesting to his students."

"Did you like him? Before you found out what was going on?"

Thayer took his time answering. "As I recall, he was a likable person. Personable. He had, as I remember, a dry sense of humor."

"That's kind of incongruous, given what he was."

"I wouldn't know."

Kinsale stood. "I appreciate your taking the time to talk with me."

Thayer got up creakily and smoothed the front of his pants with his palms. "You're welcome, Detective Kinsale."

At the door, Kinsale handed over one of his business cards. "If something occurs to you, I'd appreciate your calling me. Call the cell number. I'm not in the office much."

"I've thought of little else the past few days, but if I did forget something, I will certainly call you."

As he was leaving Thayer's community, Kinsale realized he hadn't eaten any breakfast and was suddenly ravenous. When he reached downtown Silver Spring, he pulled into the first parking spot he found and went into the closest restaurant, which was a Chinese place that seemed to specialize in take-out. He took the table in the window, and after studying the menu, ordered the daily lunch special. Then he called Wingate in Midland.

"You're like a bad penny," Wingate said when he came on the line.

"I've been called worse."

"And recently," Wingate said with a snicker. "I talked to a couple of your Homicide detectives this morning. They've got a serious hard-on for you."

"We've had our differences."

"They said you're suspended."

"I—"

"And that you were probably going to call me again."

"And?"

"And that I should hang up and immediately inform them of your transgression."

"But?"

"But," Wingate paused, "that was just about the extent of our conversation. They didn't ask any questions about Kennedy beyond asking me to send over the file."

"Sounds about right," Kinsale said. He saw the waiter bringing his food, so he asked Wingate to wait for a few seconds. When the waiter had walked away, he said, "There has been a development in the case."

"What is it with your department? You're suspended but are more involved than Homicide."

"What can I tell you?"

"Okay," Wingate said. "What's the development?"

Kinsale told him about the lab finding an "indicative substance" on the glass shards.

"What substance?"

"I don't know," Kinsale said. "I'm suspended, remember?"

"Did your two homicide detectives know about this before they called me?"

"I was suspended afterwards."

"Fuckers," he muttered.

Kinsale's phone buzzed. He pulled it away from his ear and saw that Trish Lewis was calling. He smiled and tapped the "Call you soon" option on the screen.

Wingate asked, "So why'd you call?"

"I'd like to come out to see you."

"Why?"

"Because I need to know more about Kennedy."

"You're suspended."

"I'd still like to get a first-hand sense."

"My guys looked into the man for four months. What do you think you can find that we didn't?"

Kinsale had to tread carefully. Small-city cops often had inferiority complexes when it came to larger departments. They resented even the slightest implication that they weren't as smart or as technologically adept. "I'm certain that you have found all there is to learn about Kennedy, but you were looking at him as a sex offender. I'm looking at him as a murder victim. We can look at the same thing, see something different, and both still be right."

"Why shouldn't I just hang up and call your pals in Homicide? Get you out of my hair once and for all."

"That would be the easiest thing to do."

More than a minute passed before Wingate asked, "When are you going to get here?"

"I haven't made my reservations yet. I was thinking about flying out tomorrow afternoon. Would that work for you?"

"Give me a call when you know what time you're arriving. Someone from the department will meet you at the gate."

CHAPTER 20

Kinsale and Oturos were sitting side-by-side on the front steps of their building, enjoying the summer twilight. The shade from the street trees and a gentle northwesterly breeze moderated the heat and the humidity. They could have crossed 5th Street to the small park and sat on a bench, but they wanted to stay close to the rest of the six-pack of Corona chilling in Oturos's refrigerator.

"I can't believe he turned on you," Oturos said after Kinsale recounted how Engler's reporting of the lab results had led to his suspension. "I thought the guy was your friend."

"Duane is a friend, but I put him in an untenable position. I can't believe I didn't recognize that ahead of time."

"How so?"

"He had no choice. If he hadn't found anything on the glass pieces, then he could have called to let me know that I was wrong. No harm, no foul. But once he found something, it became evidence in an ongoing murder investigation. He couldn't do anything else but tell the investigating detectives right away."

"Still, he could have warned you."

"Yeah, he could have, but I don't think he should have," Kinsale said. "I put him in a bad place, but the Department really doesn't have anything on him. But, if he'd called me and they'd found out, he probably would have been out the door right after me."

"I think you're letting him off the hook too easy."

"That's not something I get accused of too often," Kinsale said and took a sip of his rapidly warming beer. "Anyway, I'm sure he and I will talk at some point in the next couple of days, and then I'll know what he found."

"So, what are you going to do?"

"Probably grab another beer."

"I meant about resigning. No way you're going to give in to the bastards?"

"No secret what you think I should do."

"They've been screwing you over for months. It's time you fought back."

Oturos was much angrier about Kinsale's situation than he was. In truth, Kinsale wasn't even angry anymore, having burned through all his righteous fury months ago. He was no longer thinking about working his way back into the Department. At this point, he just wanted to chart the course that would give him the best chance of closing the Kennedy file.

"I honestly don't know what I'm going to do. I'll wait until I call Captain Scott tomorrow afternoon and see what happens then."

"At least something good is happening now," Oturos said and gestured up the street. Kinsale looked and saw the jaunty, hair-bouncing walk of Trish Lewis.

"Isn't there an open-container law in D.C.?" she asked as she stopped in front of them.

"Is there?" Kinsale asked Oturos.

"If there were, you as a sworn officer of the Metropolitan Police Department would be enforcing it," Oturos said. "Since you're not, I guess there isn't one."

Kinsale turned back to Lewis. "Impeccable logic. Can we get you one?"

"Sounds good."

"I'll get it." Oturos jumped up and headed inside. "Time for refills anyway."

"To what do I owe the pleasure?" Kinsale asked as Lewis sat next to him on the step.

"When I called you today, you texted you would call me right back, but then, crickets. I figured I'd come by to see if I was getting ghosted again."

"I texted back."

"Yeah, but then you didn't call."

"Can I plead that it was a busy day?"

"Hardly, seeing as you're suspended?"

"How do you know that?"

His surprised look pleased her and he asked,

"Did Manny call you?" Kinsale asked.

"Why would I call her?" Oturos asked as he came out the door holding three open beer bottles between the splayed fingers on his left hand. "Unless you're no longer in the game, and then why wouldn't I call her."

"Even if Martin were still in the game, I'd pick up your call," she said, accepting the offered beer.

"If only." Oturos turned to Kinsale. "Why would I call her?"

"She already knows that I'm suspended."

"How could I have told her?" Oturos asked. "You only just told me about it when we were sitting here.

"Maybe I'm getting a little paranoid," Kinsale admitted.

"Maybe," Trish said, "but in this instance, they really are out to get you."

"Who is?"

She smiled. "I've got someone in the Second."

"Who reports to you on my situation?"

"That's what I ask them about."

"What else has he told you?" Kinsale asked.

"Did I say they're a he?".

"Are they a They?" Kinsale asked.

"I wouldn't imagine there are too many Theys in the MPD."

"Probably not," Kinsale said, although he knew of several. "What else did your source tell you?"

"Enough that I called your Captain Scott for confirmation."

"Jesus," Kinsale sat up. "Did he think that I put you up to it."

"I told him several times you weren't my source, but I don't know whether he believed me. He sounded pretty upset."

"You must have convinced him, though, because if you hadn't, he would have been all over me this afternoon."

Lewis took a sip of her beer and said conspiratorially, "Now that you're suspended, how about—"

"And they told him to resign," Oturos muttered.

Lewis looked from Oturos back to Kinsale, and he could see that she already knew that. Nevertheless, she said, "That's ridiculous."

"Not so ridiculous, if you knew what I did."

"What did you do?"

Kinsale smirked and drank some of his beer.

She asked, "So, you're resigning?"

"Not a chance."

"What are you going to do?"

"Tomorrow, I think I'll go for a drive in the country and then maybe climb on a plane and fly somewhere."

She perked up. "Where are you going?"

"Come on, Trish."

"But you're suspended."

"That doesn't mean I'm not still working."

"Working?" she asked, more to herself than him. After a moment, she asked, "The man who died at that coffeehouse up in Tenleytown last week?

When Kinsale didn't respond, she squinted her eyes to search her memory and then said, "But Casey and his partner pulled that."

"And two sorry excuses for detectives in the Second named Magner and

Collison."

"So, you are on it?"

"How could I be? I'm suspended."

"Come on, Martin, give me something. I'm only trying to help you here."

"Wouldn't hurt you too much either," he said.

He'd meant to be funny, but he saw that his words stung.

"Sure, it would," she said. "I'm already pretty much a pariah with the top brass and everyone in the Homicide Branch from Captain Gardner down to that bitch of a receptionist because of my relationship with you. Pursuing this story will shove me over the edge."

"I don't miss Jessica one bit," Kinsale said. "Anyway, that was wrong of me to say, but I still can't really tell you anything right now."

"Right now?" she repeated.

"Let's see how it all plays out. If I end up with something worthwhile, I'll give you a call."

She considered his offer as if there was a possibility she might refuse and then looked at her empty beer bottle. "Any chance a girl can get something to eat around here?

CHAPTER 21

At 8:00 the next morning, Kinsale headed out of the city. He was leaving about an hour later than he'd planned, because their happy hour the night before had gone into overtime. The three of them had headed inside, and Oturos had kept the Pina Coladas flowing while he'd prepared some black beans and rice. As the evening stretched deep into the night, Kinsale had entertained thoughts of Lewis staying over, but when she declared that she would call a taxi, he was just sober enough to recognize that was likely the most prudent decision.

Leaving late put him in the middle of the morning rush-hour traffic, and it was slow going for the first fifteen miles on I-66. After that, though, the west-bound lanes emptied out and the bright blue morning sky spread before him as it never could in the tight confines of the city. He set the cruise control to seventy-five and settled in for the drive.

Haslett lived on the other side of the Shenandoah River, which flows south-north about eighty miles west of D.C. After crossing the river valley, he climbed northwest into the foothills of the Appalachian Mountains on a succession of ever-narrower roads, until his GPS instructed him to turn left onto what looked like little more than an opening in the line of trees. He didn't trust the BMW to go off-road, but the GPS indicated that Haslett's house was only about a hundred yards away, so he turned onto the narrow track. Almost immediately, his old car was climbing at inclines better suited to a ski lift, and even in first gear he had to keep feathering the clutch to keep from stalling out. Bushes and branches brushed against both sides of the car as he bumped along over the deep ruts.

The short distance took him almost three minutes to cross, but then the driveway emptied onto a small clearing. A small, sway-backed mobile home sat off-kilter on cinderblocks in the center. The vinyl walls were rain-stained, and plastic trash bags covered the windows. The surrounding ground was worn down, with small weed patches amidst the packed dirt and loose stones. A rusted-out, red pick-up truck sat sullenly to the right of the trailer, and on the left were some weathered plastic lawn chairs and an overflowing burn barrel.

Kinsale climbed the three dry-stacked cinderblock front steps, pushed aside the meshless screen door hanging off its bottom hinge, and knocked on Haslett's front door. After about twenty seconds, he knocked again and then tried the door handle. It turned easily, but he hesitated to go in. After another twenty seconds, he pushed open the door, revealing a darkened interior that tilted away to his left. The sour stench of body odor and rotting food escaped through the doorway.

Remaining outside, he called, "Mr. Hasl—"

He sensed the shape hurtling out of the darkness before he saw it. Haslett's face was twisted in rage, and he was wielding an aluminum baseball bat above his head. Kinsale had no time to react as Haslett swung the bat downwards with enough force to drive it through his skull. But the man had started his swing too early. He hadn't yet cleared the interior of the house, and the bat traveled a couple of feet and then slammed into the top of the doorjamb.

Stopped by the sudden and solid resistance, Haslett's hands slid off the bat and he crashed headlong into Kinsale. Both of them tumbled off the small stoop and fell to the ground. Kinsale landed flat on his back, and Haslett flopped on top of him. Kinsale lay stunned and struggling for breath, but Haslett scrambled to his feet and stumbled to retrieve the bat, which lay just inside the trailer door. Recognizing the imminent danger, Kinsale pushed himself to his feet and backed away. He reached for his Glock, and then remembered that he'd turned over his service weapon to Scott.

Despite the upraised bat and venomous glare, Haslett didn't strike an imposing figure. He was small and bone-thin with scrawny arms and legs. He was breathing heavily, and his deep-set eyes darted around as if Kinsale might have brought reinforcements. Kinsale raised his arms with his palms facing Haslett, half as an appeal for calm and half to fend him off if he chose not to listen. "Ernie, I'm—"

Haslett let out a high-pitched atavistic scream, lifted the bat high, and came at Kinsale again. He was surprisingly quick, but also comically amateurish. Kinsale held his ground for an extra beat to let the attacker build up some momentum and then stepped to the side and stuck out his trailing leg. Haslett hadn't expected the feint and tried to change the direction of his charge, but he was moving too fast. Kinsale's leg caught his across the shins, and he let out an anguished cry as he went flying through the air. He landed with a heavy thud and the bat skittered away.

Kinsale stepped around the splayed and whimpering figure and picked up the bat. He hadn't held one in probably twenty-five years, yet it felt as if he'd just played a game over the weekend. He liked the heft. It sat well in his hands.

He went back to Haslett and used the bat-end to press him into the ground. "What the hell is wrong with you?" he demanded. The prone man didn't move. He just moaned a little louder. Kinsale pushed a little harder, and Haslett waved blindly at the bat with his right hand. Kinsale pulled it away so Haslett couldn't get hold of it.

After flailing at the empty air for a few seconds, Haslett dropped his arm. "You busted my leg," he complained. "I need a doctor."

Haslett was wearing filthy, yellow gym shorts and Kinsale didn't see any major damage to his legs. "You'll be fine, Ernie. Are you ready to play nice?"

"Go fuck yourself!"

Kinsale tapped the bat against the base of Haslett's skull. "I don't think you're in the position to be rude."

Haslett whipped around and clawed at Kinsale, raking his long and filthy fingernails across his pants legs. Kinsale stepped back out of reach and then surged forward, using the bat to shove Haslett to the ground and pin him on his back.

"Do that again and I'll break every single one of your fingers," Kinsale warned. "One at a time."

Haslett tried to muster a response, but it died behind his chapped and blistered lips.

"Are you ready to get up now?" Kinsale asked.

"I can't."

"Sure, you can." Kinsale took the pressure off the bat, grabbed Haslett by the collar of his soiled T-shirt, and lifted him into a sitting position.

"Ernie, I'm Detective Martin Kinsale of the Washington, D.C. Metropolitan Police Department. I spoke with you last Friday about coming out here to talk about James Kennedy. Now calm down before you hurt yourself."

"I already am hurt," he whined. "You broke my leg. I'm going to report you."

Kinsale leaned toward him but then rocked back from the stench of piss and sweat and infection. "You came at me with a baseball bat, Ernie. That's reason enough for me to snap your scrawny neck. If I didn't need to talk to you, I'd already be calling the County Coroner." He jostled the bat to drive home the point. "Now, get up!"

While Haslett struggled to rise to his feet, Kinsale retrieved two of the lawn chairs and brought them over. Both of them were caked with several seasons of dirt, and one looked like it was about to collapse on its own accord. He set that one in front of Haslett and sat on the edge of the other.

Haslett slid awkwardly onto the chair—which wavered but stayed upright—and then gripped his leg and started whimpering again.

"Cut the crap, Ernie. Answer my questions now and I'll leave you alone. Keep playing this stupid game and that leg is going to be the least of your problems."

Haslett kept his head down, his long and stringy hair draping onto his chest. His narrow shoulders were rolled inward and his knees were clamped together. He was wearing a pair of worn-out Nike running shoes with no socks. Kinsale brushed the head of the bat against the top of Haslett's right foot.

"First question. Why did you come at me with this bat?"

Haslett didn't respond, and Kinsale hit the inside of the man's right foot with the bat. Haslett yelped and pulled his foot under his chair. He closed into himself even more.

"I'm not fooling around here, Ernie." He nudged the bat against the inside of Haslett's right knee. "Why the bat?"

Haslett didn't hesitate this time. "How the hell was I supposed to know who you were?" He was talking to the ground. "You could have been one of them."

"One of who?"

"Assholes who won't leave me alone," he muttered sullenly. "Don't want me to live here. Don't want me to live anywhere. Up to them, I'd be strung up from one of them trees."

"Even if I were one of them, if you bash someone's head in, you'll have a lot bigger problems than you have now."

"Couldn't be any worse."

"It can always be worse," Kinsale said. "But I'm not here to talk about your neighbors. James Kennedy—did you speak to him last week?"

Haslett finally lifted his eyes to look at Kinsale. They were yellowed and bloodshot and crusty around the edges. The skin on his face was covered with dozens of tiny scabs, as if he had run through a rosebush a few days before. When he opened his mouth, his gums were raw, and he was missing several teeth. The man was a poster child for the downward spiral of a crystal meth addiction.

"Why are you asking me about him?"

"I'm asking the questions," Kinsale said, lifting the bat into Haslett's sightline to keep him focused. "Did he call you last week?"

"I already told you, man. No."

"Are you sure?"

"Man, he didn't call." He eyed the bat, afraid that his answers were disappointing Kinsale. "It's not my fault."

"Okay, Ernie, okay. Calm down." Kinsale paused to let him catch his breath. "When was the last time you talked to Kennedy."

"Not since I was a kid."

"Have you talked with him since you left the Academy?"

Haslett shook his head.

"Did he know what happened to you?"

"How could he?"

"Chamberlain might have told him."

"Randy?" Haslett smiled at the thought. "Do you think he did?"

"It would explain why Kennedy didn't call you. I know he planned to."

"Why do you keep talking about him in the . . ." Haslett's eyes widened and almost instantly tears formed. "Is he dead?"

Kinsale nodded. "He was murdered last week in Washington."

"What was he doing there?"

"That's what we're trying to ascertain."

Haslett became wistful. "I wish I could have talked to him. Maybe he would have understood what happened to me."

"When you were arrested and then in your trial, why didn't you turn in Kennedy? It might have gotten you some consideration."

"There's no consideration for men like me," he said. "Anyway, it never went to trial."

"Why not?"

"My parents, man. They couldn't bear the publicity of a trial. What would their friends think?" Haslett was angry but was so listless that it came across as pathetic. "They gave me a choice. Plead guilty and do the time, and they'd give me my trust money. Or go to trial and they would cut me off."

"Did they know about Kennedy?"

He nodded.

"And they still threatened to cut you off?"

"They didn't. They sent their lawyer. I haven't seen or talked to my parents in ten years."

Kinsale glanced around the dilapidated homestead. "But when they reneged, why didn't you say something then?"

Haslett looked confused, and then Kinsale understood. Haslett's parents were still paying. They were financing his addiction. Maybe they were even throwing a little bit more his way, in the hope of bringing forward that inevitable day when their son's heart burst or his brain melted.

Disgusted, Kinsale stood up. At the sudden movement, Haslett cowered deeper into the chair. Dropping the bat to the ground, Kinsale said, "I appreciate you taking the time to talk to me, Ernie. Take care.

CHAPTER 22

Kinsale called Captain Scott at 4:30 that afternoon from the glass-and steel Delta Airlines terminal at the Detroit International Airport. He hadn't flown into Detroit in twenty years or more, and back then, the terminal was a dingy, low-slung structure that required mile-long sprints between connecting flights. Now there was an elevated train that floated silently from one end of the terminal to the other. He would have liked to have waited until 4:59 to make the call, but his flight to Midland left at 5:00.

Scott blew past any pleasantries. "Faxing over your resignation now?"

"I need another twenty-four hours."

"Not possible. I told the Chief it would be on her desk by 5:00, or I would hand your file over to IAD."

"Come on, Captain. I'm just walking out of my lawyer's office right now. He said he won't have anything for me before—"

"Yesterday, your lawyer was a she."

"Really?" Kinsale said. "You would think I would have noticed."

"Kinsale, whatever game—"

"Like I was telling you, he said he won't have anything for me before noon tomorrow. Maybe I can push him to get it to me in the morning. How about that? We can compromise. Tomorrow at ten?"

"Not a chance in hell."

"Captain, I—"

"End of discussion." Scott hung up.

Kinsale stared out one of the huge terminal windows, disbelieving that Scott had refused. He'd been certain that he could squeeze another day out of him. In fact, he'd been confident that he could string the process along to the end of the week.

He wasn't too concerned about the charges, departmental or criminal. He was already out the door. Once the Department shut it behind him, all the charges would quietly disappear. No one on the Fifth Floor wanted this to reach the inside of a courtroom. All they wanted was for Kinsale to go. The charges would, however, complicate his life. Once the paperwork was filed, IAD would waste no time coming after him.

While in line to board the plane, he called the Fraternal Order of Police and updated the same woman as before about the situation. She said someone would call. He told her that she'd said that the last time, and it hadn't happened. She told him a third time and hung up.

The entire Midland airport would have fit into the Detroit terminal twenty times over. There were only four gates and no other planes on the ground. Kinsale had no trouble picking out the stocky guy in an ill-fitting gray suit and low-hanging red tie waiting at the gate. He was the only person waiting.

"Are you from Midland PD?" he asked.

"Wingate. Call me Ralph." He shook Kinsale's hand and then turned on his heel and headed towards the exit. On the sidewalk, he pointed to a black Malibu parked with flashing hazard lights. Within two minutes, they'd traded the airport for an empty two-lane road stretching dead straight in front of them and flat as a floor. On either side, it looked like the farmland stretched from Lake Huron to Lake Michigan.

"Nice country," Kinsale said.

"We like it," Wingate replied. He looked to be about Kinsale's age, maybe a few years older. He had heavy bags under his deep-set eyes, the skin around his neck was loose, and his hair had gone gray at the temples. He could probably stand to lose twenty pounds, but Kinsale had to admit, so could he.

"Flat."

"That's what most visitors say. Glaciers came through here at some point and scraped away everything. Highest point for twenty miles is the landfill. We'll pass it on the way into town."

"Don't want to miss that."

"I talked to one of your colleagues. Or should I say ex-colleagues?"

"Not quite yet."

"Guy named Magner."

Kinsale stayed quiet.

"I called your Captain yesterday after you said you were coming out and he handed me off to Magner."

That probably explained why Scott had hung up on Kinsale. "I'm surprised he didn't ask you not to help me."

Wingate let out a gruff laugh, "I didn't tell him you were coming out here. I just wanted to find out where they were on the case."

"And?"

"Can't say I was too impressed with Magner."

"He's even less impressive in person."

"I know that your Homicide guys have the lead, and those two seem to be at least putting in the effort, but Magner told me in no uncertain terms that he didn't see the investigation leading anywhere." He turned to Kinsale for a moment and smiled. "He said the previous investigating officer totally fucked up the case."

"That sounds like him."

"And then before we hung up, he added that the case wasn't a high priority for him because Kennedy was a . . . What did he say? A chicken-eater."

Kinsale laughed. "That's a new one on me."

"Does anyone in your department like you?"

"At this point, no."

They settled into an uncomfortable silence, and after a minute Kinsale said, "Look, I can see you're having second thoughts about my being here. I don't blame you. Honestly, I'd feel the same way."

Wingate's eyes stayed on the road ahead.

"I'm not here to cause you any trouble," Kinsale continued. "The second you feel like I've stepped over the line—"

"You're already over it. We both are."

"I'll still leave it to you. When we push past your comfort level, you let me know, and I'll back off."

"We're so far past my comfort level, I can't even see it my rearview." Wingate glanced in the mirror to drive home the point.

"If you want to call this off, just drop me off at the hotel. You won't hear from me again."

"You think I'm an idiot, Kinsale. Better for me to know where you are than let you run around like a free agent."

They passed over a four-lane highway. Wingate turned left onto the on-ramp, pressed hard on the accelerator, and headed west. "Why are you in such deep shit anyway?"

"This isn't my case."

Wingate flashed a derisive look. "I'm not talking about Kennedy. Your Captain Scott let me know in no uncertain terms that you're a rogue warrior."

"That's probably the nicest description you'll get about me."

"It can't be that you're just not a team player."

Kinsale was tempted to leave it at that, but Wingate was putting himself out for him, so Kinsale gave him the short version. Even so, they were well into the city of Midland when he finished. Wingate didn't say a word during the telling and stayed quiet afterward. Kinsale honored his silence and looked out the window at the passing houses. In D.C. right now it was rush hour, and the streets would be clogged like a fat man's arteries. Here, traffic flowed easily.

Wingate turned off the street into a small park. Two other cars were in the parking lot that bordered the curving edge of a children's playground. A couple of women were talking across a picnic table, but Kinsale didn't see any kids. Then a little boy popped out from inside a covered slide.

Wingate turned off the ignition. Looking straight ahead, he said, "As an outsider, I can't see what else you could have done. But if I were in your department, I'd do you the same way."

Kinsale stayed silent, knowing Wingate didn't need or want to hear any more from him.

"But Kennedy…" the Midland detective said eventually. "We'd been on him for four months. Out of all of them, he's the one I most wanted. He was at the center of the whole thing, the one who drove it. As long as you're working him, I'm willing to deal with you, but there's no leeway. First misstep, and I'm putting you on a plane."

"Fair enough."

Thirty seconds passed before Wingate said, "I was going to take you to the station to look at the file, but let's head over to Kennedy's place instead."

"Works for me."

Leaving the park, Wingate made several quick turns. At a light, he turned onto Eastman Avenue, which looked like a major thoroughfare. After a few blocks, the houses became noticeably bigger, and the landscaping required more than a lawnmower and weed whacker. They passed a golf course that came up to the edge of the sidewalk.

"This town is a lot more cosmopolitan than I would have thought," Kinsale said.

"Not really. Just a lot richer."

"Why's that?"

"Dow Chemical. This is their headquarters."

"Here?"

"Hmm. And they've got to compete with all those corporations based in New York or Dallas or L.A., so they spend a helluva lot of dough to make this place cultural and a good place to raise kids. We've got a symphony hall, probably the best-funded school district in the state—outside the ritzier suburbs around Detroit—and a police force that is about three times bigger than a town this size needs."

"Why's that?"

"Keep out the undesirable elements."

"You let me in."

"Not for long." Wingate wasn't yet ready to pull their relationship out of the deep freeze.

They entered a neighborhood of single-family homes along curving streets. Kinsale tried to follow the succession of turns, thinking that he might need to find his way back to Kennedy's house later, but he soon lost track.

THE MAN ON THE COFFEEHOUSE FLOOR

By the time Wingate pulled into the wide driveway of a large, two-story house on a corner lot, Kinsale couldn't even say which way was north.

"This is it?" Kinsale was surprised. The house had faded blue wood siding, a two-car garage, and a brick chimney. A small deck opened onto a large back yard. The grass had been recently cut. "It looks like a family would live here—Mom, dad, two kids, and a dog."

"He had a cat. Left it with a neighbor when he took off. Said he'd be back in a couple of days."

"Where is it now?"

"Pound," Wingate said and climbed out of the car.

Yellow crime-scene tape hung loosely across the sliding glass doors that led from the deck into the house. Wingate pushed aside the tape and slipped a key into the lock. Inside, the house was dark and too warm. Already, it smelled abandoned.

They entered into what would have been the family room, if a family had lived there. Kennedy evidently used it as his living room. The furniture was black and low-slung, the wood-floors were darkly stained, and dried grasses stood in vases on the hearth. Wingate dropped onto the sofa. "I'm going to make some calls," he said.

"I won't be long."

A counter separated the living room from the kitchen. The top was made out of patterned tiles and was bare except for a silver-wire bowl that held half-a-dozen apples and two bananas that were way past their use-by date. All of the appliances were top-of-the-line and sparklingly clean. The cabinets were sleek and European.

Kinsale went through a doorway into what would have been the dining room, except an upright piano against the far wall took up too much space to accommodate a table. To his left, a double-wide archway led into what would have been the living room, but it appeared to have been Kennedy's office. The long wall on the right was lined with floor-to-ceiling bookcases. At the far end of the room, Kennedy's hulking wood desk looked out through the bay window to the front yard.

Kinsale crossed to the desk. There was an empty space in the middle where Kennedy's computer likely had been. It was probably now sitting in the evidence room at the Midland Police Department headquarters. Remaining were a computer screen, laser printer, several short and neat piles of paper, and a cup holding an assortment of pens and a pair of scissors.

On the wall to the left of the desk hung a dozen-or-so color photos. Kinsale looked them over. They were all of the same type. In another teacher's office, they would have been uplifting, but here they were disturbing, because each showed Kennedy smiling with a different young boy.

"Wingate," Kinsale called. "Can you come in here for a minute?"

He heard the wood floor creak and moment later Wingate came into the office.

Kinsale asked, "Have you looked at these?"

His face tightened. "Yeah, we took two off the desk. They were kids from the Institute."

Kinsale tapped one near the middle of the top row. It was a young boy in a restaurant. He had a large Coca-Cola glass in front of him, and he was looking at the camera with bright eyes and a toothy smile. "That's Chris Dowling, undoubtedly before Kennedy got his hooks into him. It's probably the last time he looked happy."

"Maybe we should have taken all of them down, but we—"

"This one here is Chamberlain." Kinsale stepped back to take in the entirety of the display. He didn't see Farber or Haslett. "You should find out who all these other boys are."

"The state is handling that. They've got a couple vanloads of social workers up at the Institute 24/7," Wingate said. "I'm sure we'll get some testimony on Kennedy. With him dead, though, my team has to focus on building the cases against the others, and Kennedy's untimely demise isn't helping. Already, two of them have claimed that Kennedy was at the center of the whole thing, and they were barely involved. It won't take long for the others to start singing the same tune. It's going to be as if Kennedy was a ring of one."

"They'll turn on each other. They always do."

"Yeah, but we need to help them along."

Kinsale gestured towards the empty spot in the center of the desk. "You took his computer?"

"We had it before we knew he was gone. Same with the pictures."

Kinsale looked around. "I would have thought you'd have dusted the place."

"For what?"

"Kids' fingerprints. Or the guys in the ring."

"We have hundreds of hours of surveillance tapes placing all of them here. We don't need fingerprints. And anyway, it's not a crime to visit someone's house."

"Did you ever see the kids?"

"Twice."

"And you didn't move right in?"

Wingate faced up to him. "It was early in the game. We didn't know what we had yet."

Kinsale understood the reasoning. Stepping in too soon might have jeopardized their chances of winning convictions, leaving Kennedy and the others to continue their depravity elsewhere. Still, having seen the wreckage that Kennedy had left behind, he had to tamp down the visceral urge to attack the decision to not round up Kennedy and the others at the first indication. He gestured again towards the desk. "Mind if I go through it?"

"Be my guest." Wingate was still simmering. "Just clue me in if you find anything."

"Did you find anything on the computer?"

"Haven't even turned it on," Wingate said as he walked away.

Kinsale sifted through the paper piles on the desk. Two of them were students' papers, and the third stack contained paid bills going back several months. Each bill had a check number and date written in the same careful handwriting that he'd seen in the day planner.

Next, he went through the desk drawers. He took his time, not wanting to miss anything important, but found nothing until the last drawer. Lying flat on the drawer bottom was a large brown file folder. He lifted the two-inch thick file onto the desktop and opened it. Inside were a couple hundred dated pages from Kennedy's planner. He'd just started looking through them when Wingate returned. "How're you coming along?"

"Do you know about Kennedy's planner?"

"Planner?"

"He kept a pretty meticulous one. He wrote down all his appointments, phone calls, to-do lists—stuff like that. He brought it with him to the coffeehouse where he died. I turned over the original to Homicide, but I made a copy. Speaking of which . . ." Kinsale pulled his notebook out of his jacket pocket and flipped through the pages until he found what he was looking for. "Do you know a guy named Paul Portman?"

Wingate tensed. "Why?"

"Kennedy was supposed to have dinner with him last Wednesday night, before he did the runner."

Wingate relaxed. "He's one of the pervs. He's a lawyer in Bay City."

"Where's that?"

"About twenty miles east. You have the planner?"

"A copy. It's in my bag."

"I'd like to take a look at it."

"No problem." Kinsale picked up the stack of pages from the desk.

"Maybe you want to have someone go through these one-by-one. He might mention some of the other guys. Or the kids."

"Thanks for the suggestion," Wingate said derisively.

"No problem," Kinsale dead-panned and handed the file to Wingate. "I'm done here."

Kinsale went back through the kitchen and then out onto the deck. Even though it was early evening, the air was still heavy from the afternoon heat. Wingate locked the door, and they returned to the car. Grabbing his bag from the backseat, Kinsale pulled out the copy of the planner and handed it to Wingate.

Wingate slowly flipped through the pages and then returned to the one with the initials and phone numbers. "You've talked to all of these guys?"

"All of them."

"Do you like any of them for it?"

Kinsale shook his head.

"Not even a bit?" Wingate asked.

"Kennedy left a lot of damage in his wake. Top to bottom, those are some messed-up guys."

"Do you know if any of them actually met with Kennedy?"

"Farber and Chamberlain, earlier that morning. And then Dowling, of course."

"Couldn't one of those first two have slipped something in his drink," Wingate suggested. "Then a few hours later, when they're out of the frame, Kennedy catches the bus, and Dowling takes the fall."

"I just can't see it. That would take some level of planning and coordination. If you talked to these guys, you would . . ."

Kinsale's phone rang. Pulling it out of his pocket, he didn't recognize the D.C. number. He was tempted to let it go to voicemail, but instead signaled to Wingate that he needed to take it.

"Martin, it's Lucy." Her panic reverberated across the distance. "Bill and I are at the police station. They've arrested Chris. They're saying he killed Kennedy."

CHAPTER 23

Kinsale asked. "Who arrested him?"
"The police."
"Yes, but which ones?"
"Which ones? I don't understand what you're asking."
Thayer sounded like she was losing it, so Kinsale paused and then asked, "Where are you?"
"I already told you. At the police station?"
"Which one?"
"What does that—"
"Lucy," Kinsale cut her off. "Which one?"
"The one on Idaho Avenue."
They were at the Second, which meant Scott and Magner were likely involved. "Who have you talked to?"
"I don't know, a couple of detectives. That's why I called you. Can you come here and clear this all up? This isn't good for Chris."
"I would, Lucy, but I'm out of town right now."
"Out of town?" All the urgency drained out of her voice. "But I thought you were . . ."
"I'm working the case, Lucy. I'm in Michigan, digging deeper into Kennedy."
She was silent for a moment and then said, "They told me you've been suspended."
"Who did?"
"One of the detectives. He's fat and sneering and . . . He said you'd screwed up the investigation."
"Without me, Lucy, there wouldn't be an investigation. And I haven't

screwed up anything."

"I can't stand the thought of Chris being in here. You know how . . . fragile he is."

"I'll get back there as soon as I can," Kinsale said. "In the meantime, I'll see what I can find out."

"Please."

"Is this your number?"

"No, it's Bill's."

"What's your number?"

She recited it and he added both numbers to his call log. "Is there a vivacious woman at the front desk?"

"Yes. She's been very nice."

"Let me talk to her. And Lucy, this will work out. We know Chris didn't do this, and they'll know soon enough. Stay strong."

A moment later Royale Moon came on the line. "Martin?"

"Royale, those are good people. And Scott and Magner have this all wrong. Would—"

"It was Homicide that brought him in."

"Homicide? Who?"

"Detectives Casey and—"

"Harewood."

"Fine looking man."

"Well, they've got it wrong too. I'd appreciate whatever you can do for Lucy and Bill. I'll be in there tomorrow afternoon at the latest."

"I'll do what I can, but that boy won't be here too long. They're taking him down to Central tonight."

That was bad news. If a cell in the Second was hard on Dowling, the D.C. Jail would be hell. "Does his sister know?"

"Not yet."

"Let me talk to her."

When she came back on the line, Kinsale told her that Dowling was going to be moved to the D.C. jail. She broke down halfway through the telling and a moment later Bill Thayer came on the line.

"What's happening?" he demanded.

After repeating the news, Kinsale said, "It'll only be for tonight. I'll be—"

"This is fucking bullshit," Thayer growled and hung up.

Ignoring Wingate's inquisitive stare, Kinsale immediately redialed the number, but it rang through to voicemail. He hung up, and after consulting the call log, input the number again, one digit at a time. Again, it rang through. He wanted to hurl the phone out the window, but instead he just dropped it on his lap, leaned back against the headrest, and closed his eyes.

He needed to focus, but his anger was like a switch that kept tripping every time he tried to concentrate. He was angry at Bill Thayer for hanging up on him. He was angry at Casey and Harewood for jumping the gun and arresting Dowling. But mostly he was angry at himself. Being at the scene and having a motive had put Dowling at the top of the suspect list, but those reasons alone wouldn't have been enough to bring him in. Kinsale had handed Casey and Harewood what they needed with those pieces of the broken glass.

"They made an arrest," Wingate said after a minute.

"They made a case," Kinsale answered, his eyes still closed. "It's not a good case, and it's not the right case, but it's a case."

Wingate started up the car. "What happened?"

Kinsale recounted the events but when he mentioned the broken glass, Wingate cut him off.

"What the hell? You told me you were waiting on the results of the bloodwork for confirmation. Where did these glass pieces come from?"

"I thought Casey or Magner would have told you."

"They didn't see fit," he grumbled.

Kinsale gave him the details.

"That sounds pretty comprehensive to me."

"They're wrong."

Glancing at Kinsale, Wingate said. "You sound pretty certain. Based on . . ."

"Come on, Ralph, sometimes you just know. You can't really point to anything, but in your gut, you know."

"And you've never been wrong?"

"Not this time." Kinsale said, his voice rising with each word, and he wondered if that was to convince Wingate or himself.

Wingate looked doubtful but stayed quiet. He focused on driving, and four minutes later, they pulled into the parking lot behind a single-story, beige-brick building that had all the architectural styling of a shoebox.

Wingate punched in a code on the keypad by the back door and they walked down a long, empty hallway. He stopped in front of the last door on the left, punched in some more numbers on another keypad, and pushed open the door. Kinsale stepped into a space that was as big as the Second's bullpen but housed only half-a-dozen desks. On each desk was a computer with a large, flat screen monitor and a laser printer. Only one of the desks was occupied, by a young woman eating out of a yogurt container.

"Leslie, where are we?" Wingate called out to her.

"Quiet so far."

"Let's hope it stays that way. This is Martin Kinsale from Washington, D.C."

She smiled and waved with the plastic spoon. "You called about Kennedy last week."

"Seems like a long time ago."

Wingate continued across the room and opened the door of a large glass-fronted office. Kinsale let out an appreciative whistle.

"I used to work in Detroit PD," Wingate said as he went around his desk. "Greatest bunch of guys you'd ever want to meet, top to bottom, but every day we were sinking a little deeper in the shit. No funds, short-staffed, and out-gunned. By the time I heard about this job, I was up to my neck in it. I love that city and I loved working it, but I had to get out."

"That must have been a big change."

"This is a top-flight department." Wingate sat back in his leather office chair. "I'd put my guys up against anybody else in the country. We have all the same problems that they have in Detroit, or you have in D.C. The difference is we have a citizenry willing to pay to get the job done."

"No offense, Ralph, but I don't think we're talking the same scale here."

"I never said it was the same scale, but we're not some hayseed department like your friend Magner seems to think. We've got gangs here. We've got drugs. A lot of junk comes into this country through Canada. They bring it straight down I-75 to Detroit. Enough of it stops here, though, that things can get pretty lively sometimes."

"Point taken." Kinsale wanted to drop the subject because he needed to keep Wingate as an ally.

Apparently, Wingate felt the same way, because he asked, "You want some coffee?"

Kinsale glanced at the half-filled pot on Wingate's credenza. "How long has that stuff been stewing?"

"Since before I left to pick you up."

"I think I'll take a pass then."

"Suit yourself." Wingate opened the bottom right-hand desk drawer and pulled out a thick, reddish-brown file folder, which he dropped on the desktop. "Kennedy. This is just what we think might be relevant to your case."

Kinsale started to object, but Wingate waved him off. "Don't get your panties in a knot. We're not holding anything back. I just figured, given your time constraints, that you didn't need to see everything. There's easily five times more than this. And then there's the videos and the phone taps. If after you go through this, you want to see the rest, no problem."

Kinsale flipped open the folder and fingered through the first couple of pages. There were daily status reports. Despite the differences between their departments, Kinsale thought, at their core, they were essentially the same, running on paperwork and stale coffee.

"Where are you staying tonight?" Wingate asked.

Kinsale needed a moment to remember. "The Plaza Suites."

"MPD must have a generous per diem."

"This is on me, remember," Kinsale said. "I figured if I was coming all this way, I might as well get a decent night's sleep."

"How about this then? Your hotel isn't far from here. I could drop you there now. That'll give you time to read through this stuff. And then I'll pick you up at . . . How about 8:00? We'll start up again."

"I'm pretty beat, Ralph, so I don't think I'm going to get too far on the file tonight. I'll do better if I start on it first thing in the morning, so how about we make it 9:00?"

"What time is your flight out?"

"12:07."

Wingate worked out the timing. "That should work. Nine it is."

When he reached his hotel room, Kinsale tossed his overnight bag on one of the queen-sized beds and flopped onto his back on the other one. Immediately he felt the pull of sleep tugging him down, and he gave himself up to it, but it remained just out of reach. He could see it, almost touch it, but it wouldn't accept his surrender.

Prodding at him like an impatient two-year-old was the image of Wingate's squad room. He couldn't get past it. He saw the bright lights, the new technology, the clean floor. He could get a job in a place like Midland in a flash. Even now, Scott and the Chief would probably let him take his twenty years and give him a glowing recommendation if he would just walk away. It sounded easy and smart, but his soul shrank at the prospect.

He was self-aware enough to know that part of him didn't want to give Casey and Magner the satisfaction of running him out of town. Even more, though, he didn't want to come to work to someplace that was clean and orderly and simple. He didn't want to be watching the clock, counting down the minutes until lunch time or the end of the day. He didn't want to have all the advantages. If D.C. taxpayers were willing to pay a little more so the Second could get some new equipment or even a new coat of paint, he wouldn't turn them down, but that was ancillary. He wanted to be someplace where he could make a difference. Truth be told, if Magner were dropped into the Midland Police Department tomorrow, he would fit in fine. And for that reason, Kinsale wouldn't.

Finally, he sat up and called Trish Lewis' home phone. She didn't pick up, so he left her a quick voicemail. Thirty minutes later, he tried her cellphone. When she answered, he asked "Did you make it home all right last night?"

"Tucked in and snoring by one."

"You don't snore. It's more of a snuffle."

"I'm glad you remember. Are you at your apartment?"

"No, I'm out of town."

"That's right. I'd forgotten."

Because he was a cop and she was a reporter, he didn't truly believe that she'd forgotten. "I'll be back in town tomorrow afternoon."

"You're still not going to tell me where you are?"

"Hmm."

"Does it have to do with the Kennedy case?"

"I was taken off it, remember?"

"It's worked its way to the top of the pile here. Boy-wonder instructor at the city's most prestigious school arrested for killing man who molested him two decades earlier. I'm talking with Casey and Harewood first thing tomorrow."

"Captain Scott would probably be more insightful."

"I'd really like to get your thoughts."

"I don't have any thoughts."

"Sure, you do."

"Then none that I'm willing to share."

"Come on Martin. You're suspended. What are they going to do to you if you talk? Double-suspend you?"

"I don't think that's a thing."

"So, answer my questions."

"You can ask."

"Great. The young man they've arrested . . ."

"Chris Dowling."

"You know about that?"

"I'm suspended, not deaf, dumb, and blind."

"Okay, what was their relationship? Kennedy and Dowling?"

"What did he say it was?

"Come on Martin."

"Have you talked to him?"

"No."

"Then I can't say."

"Can't or won't?"

"It amounts to the same thing."

"Martin!"

He could feel her intensity through the phone, and he considered what to say next. He was getting comfortable with Lewis again, and he hoped to get more comfortable, but he still had to be careful. The smart thing to do would be to avoid answering her questions or—even better—to hang up. Instead, he said, "Here's what I can tell you. It didn't look like a homicide at first. It looked like an old man dying from a heart attack. We needed to wait for the forensics."

"What forensics?"

"I can't say."

"When were you on the case?"

"I was never on the case."

"If you were never on the case, how could they have taken you off it?"

He kept forgetting how good she was. "Okay, okay, Captain Scott asked me to shepherd Kennedy through the autopsy. Since we thought he'd died of natural causes, it seemed like a minor thing."

"Shepherding a heart attack victim through the autopsy," she said drily. "That doesn't sound like one of those important long-term cases that Scott said you were working on."

"Trish, are we talking about Kennedy or about me here?"

"Both. I think they're connected."

"How could that possibly be?"

"Mostly because you're insisting that they aren't."

"Instead of grilling me, why don't you talk to your snitch?"

"I have," she said. "They said you held back important forensic evidence, pieces of a broken glass with drug residue on them."

He was quiet for several seconds and then said with a little more venom than he intended, "You're both very well informed."

"You need to stand up for yourself, Martin. Or they'll take you down."

"They're going to take me down regardless."

"You are getting railroaded!" she protested.

Kinsale's fatigue came rushing back, and he finally accepted that he shouldn't be talking to her in this state. He would have liked to steer the conversation to less dangerous topics, like when they might have that drink, but he knew she would not be put off, so instead he just said, "Good night, Trish."

CHAPTER 24

Kinsale checked out of the hotel the next morning and carried his bag across the street to Café Déjà Vu. He ordered a large coffee at the counter and brought it over to a table that gave him a view onto the street. After a couple of minutes spent checking the headlines and his emails on his phone, he opened the Midland Police Department's file on James Kennedy.

Quickly, he was impressed with how comprehensive their case against Kennedy had been. They had transcripts of tapped phone calls, stills from video surveillance, daily reports, follow-ups on anyone Kennedy met with, and a history of his online activity. Any decent defense attorney would have advised Kennedy to plea bargain.

Still, working his way through the pile, he didn't find anything he could use. He already knew what Kennedy was. He didn't need proof of that. He needed an indication of why Kennedy was a murder victim. Still, he forced himself to peruse every sheet, knowing that relevance could hide in the smallest fact.

Three-quarters of the way down was a copy of Kennedy's personnel file from the Midland Military Institute. It showed that he had been a well-respected teacher. He'd been a member of the Parent/Teacher/Student Council for nine years, had written hundreds of college recommendations for students, and had earned two letters of commendation. Near the end of the file, he found Kennedy's resume from when he'd applied for the position. Wingate's team had checked the list of references, attaching Post-It notes to record the date they'd called each of them and the information they'd learned. Except for the Georgetown Academy, none of the other institutions had ever heard of Kennedy.

Kinsale sat back and gazed out the front window of the café. How could the Institute have hired Kennedy if he'd faked five of his six references. Wouldn't they have checked? Wouldn't they have at least confirmed his experience? Wouldn't they want to know what Kennedy's previous employers thought of him?

Returning to the file, he flipped to the next page and found the answer to all those questions. Reading the four-paragraph letter, the coffee in his stomach turned to acid. It extolled James Kennedy as a model teacher, mentor, and human being. It described him as "the finest instructor with whom I have ever worked," and hailed him as "a positive force in the life of our institution and all of our students." The letter closed by saying that "Jim's decision to relocate to Michigan is one of the greatest disappointments in my more than thirty years in education. We will miss him greatly. Your institution will only benefit from bringing him into your faculty."

Upon receiving such a letter, Kinsale could see how Commandant Shelvey, or whoever had led the Institute at the time, might have closed the application process right then and there. Not only was the letter unconditionally glowing, but it was signed by the headmaster of one of the most prestigious prep schools in the country, Bernard Thayer.

Kinsale slammed his open palm on top of the file, three times, in quick succession. The loud and angry noise pulled anxious glances from the pony-tailed barista and the three other customers in the café, but he ignored them. He couldn't believe what he'd just read, but he couldn't bring himself to read it again to confirm.

He knew enough to let his anger run its course, and after about two minutes, he started to read the letter again, but it was if a gauzy film covered his eyes and made the words unintelligible. Frustrated, he closed the file and returned to staring out the window. After a few minutes of fruitless reflection, he pulled out his phone and called Duane Engler.

"I was hoping you'd finally smartened up and wouldn't try to call me," Engler said.

"Hope springs eternal."

"Not with you it doesn't."

When Kinsale didn't respond, Engler said quietly, "You put me in a bad position. Once I'd analyzed the glass pieces, I—"

"I know, I know. I didn't think it through. It's all on me. You had no choice."

"Yeah, but I've got to admit that I didn't think it through either."

"I guess I really wasn't expecting you to find anything."

"You always underestimate me."

"So, what was it?"

"What was what?"

"What killed Kennedy?"

Engler didn't answer, and Kinsale could almost hear the scientist's mental calculations through the airwaves. Finally, he let out a long breath and said, "Orphenadrine Citrate."

"What's that?"

"It was originally developed for Parkinson's patients, but at some point, the suicide groups glommed onto it. Apparently, it's a fairly pleasant way to die, although I've never understood how they could confirm that."

"Kennedy didn't look like he was having a pleasant time."

"I don't know what to tell you. I found only trace amounts on the cup," Engler said. "This is more the M.E.'s territory, but the guy had several co-morbidities. Maybe it triggered the heart attack?"

"Have you talked to the M.E.?"

"Briefly. She said she would fast-track the bloodwork but won't make any determination until then."

"Trace amounts? How trace?"

"Since you were never the most technically minded detective in the Department, let's just say really trace."

"This stuff can't be that dangerous. It's a prescription drug, for Christ's sake."

"It's not dangerous at all in the prescribed amounts."

"So, there would have been more than trace amounts on the glass pieces, if that's how it was delivered."

"If you'd read my report, you would—"

"Alan isn't sharing the file with me."

"And who's fault is that?" Engler asked angrily. He paused to take a calming breath and then said, "If you'd read my report, you would know that's what I determined as well."

"So, the trace amounts?"

"They came from Kennedy's lips when he drank from the glass."

"The drug was already in his system."

"Definitely."

"What was Alan's reaction to this information?"

"Alan said that the higher concentration could be on the pieces that you didn't find."

"That's not going to hold up."

"Nope."

They were silent for a moment, and then Kinsale asked, "Did you take any heat for this? For the fake file number."

"Nah, I threw you under the bus so fast that I think they forgot I was even involved."

"Small favors."

"Speaking of which, would you do me one and maybe lose this number for a few weeks? I may be in the clear, but I know Alan, for one, is pissed at me. No point in poking him with a stick."

Kinsale saw Wingate's black Malibu pull to the curb in front of the hotel. "Deleting it now," he said, although he wasn't. "And I've got to go. I guess I won't be talking to you for a while."

"Hope springs eternal," Engler said and hung up.

Kinsale closed the Kennedy file, threw his bag over his shoulder, and headed out. He dropped the file on the front passenger seat as he stowed his bag in the back and then picked it up to sit down.

"What did you think?" Wingate asked.

"Your team put together quite a case," Kinsale said.

"We've done even better with the others," Wingate said. "Nothing is ever a slam dunk, but we're about as close as you can get. And once they start turning on each other . . ."

"Except, you said, they're turning on him."

"Yeah, that part is not going like we planned."

"At least it's not going like Kennedy planned either."

"Did you find anything that you can use?"

"One thing. The letter of recommendation for Kennedy from the Georgetown Academy."

"I remember seeing that. Struck me as a kind of weird, glowing like he was the second coming or something. So, the Institute?"

"Yeah, and I'd also like to talk to Kennedy's doctor, a guy named Dunstag. Do you think we have time to do both?"

"Shouldn't be a problem. We talked to Dunstag at his office last week. It's only five minutes away."

"Seems like everything in this town is only five minutes away."

"Except at rush hour," Wingate said as he pulled away from the curb. "Then it's six."

After a couple of quiet minutes of Wingate fixing his eyes on the road like he was traversing a narrow mountain track, Kinsale asked, "Having second thoughts again?"

"And third and fourth."

"You could just take me straight to the airport."

"Maybe I am." Wingate grinned nastily.

Dunstag's office was on the second floor of a three-story glass-and-steel building in the middle of the expansive and modern Mid-Michigan Medical Center campus.

"Dow?" Kinsale asked.

"Best medical care north of Ann Arbor. Maybe in the entire state."

Dunstag's waiting room was in marked contrast to its modern surroundings. The wall-to-wall carpeting was well-worn, the furniture was dark and heavy, and there was a framed print of the Norman Rockwell painting of the little red-headed boy getting ready for a vaccine.

Kinsale introduced himself to the elderly receptionist and said he needed to talk briefly with the doctor. She gestured them towards the sofa. A few minutes later, a young male nurse in bright red scrubs and a man-bun led them back. Dunstag's office kept up the 1950s' vibe, even down to the worn fedora hanging on the coat rack.

Dunstag was sitting behind his desk, surrounded by unruly piles of files, journals, and loose papers. He looked as Kinsale had imagined, a large man with a florid face and haphazard white hair. He was wearing a button-down shirt, black tie, and a black vest. He motioned them towards the visitor chairs. "A long way to come, Detective Kinsale."

"But necessary."

"How can I help?"

"Mostly, I wanted to come by and introduce myself. You were helpful with our investigation last week, and I wanted to say thanks."

Dunstag leaned back in his chair. The black leather was cracked and faded with age. He crossed his hands across his ample stomach, and an amused look settled on his face.

"Okay," Kinsale admitted. "I do have a few questions."

The doctor gestured for him to go ahead.

"Did Kennedy have Parkinson's Disease?"

The question surprised Dunstag. "No. Why do you ask?"

"Did he have any suicidal tendencies?"

"Are you asking me would Jim have killed himself?"

Kinsale nodded.

"I'll admit I hadn't considered that." He rubbed his chin. "No, I don't believe he would."

Kinsale flipped back a page in his notebook. "We found traces of Orphenadrine Citrate in his system." Out of the corner of his eye, Kinsale saw Wingate whip around, but he stayed on Dunstag. "We're trying to determine how it got there. Are you familiar with the drug?"

"I know of it."

"Did you know it's a popular suicide drug?"

"I believe I did, but again, from what I knew of Jim Kennedy, I would not say he was a suicidal person."

"From what you knew of him, would you have said he was a serial sexual predator?" Kinsale asked.

Dunstag studied the two detectives for a moment. "I had no idea," he said finally. "Jim never revealed any indication of the forces that were at war within him."

"He never even suggested anything?"

"No, and I suspect that's because he didn't think it was relevant."

"Why do you suspect that?" Kinsale pressed.

"I am speaking theoretically, of course, but I would think that Jim didn't see his sexual predilection as being anything pathological or wrong."

"If that were so, why did he and his friends creep around in the shadows?"

"Detective," Dunstag said, "Jim wasn't a fool. He understood that his appetites were illegal, and Detective Wingate here would put him away if they were discovered, but I am sure in his heart, he thought society was wrong."

"What do you think, doctor?" Wingate interrupted.

Dunstag turned to him. "About what?"

"Was he . . . pathological or wrong?"

Wingate's question was unmistakably accusatory, but Dunstag responded calmly. "I side with society on this issue."

Kinsale signaled to Wingate that he had what he needed, so they thanked the doctor and left. As they walked towards the car, Kinsale said, "You were turning the screw there."

"No one in Kennedy's circle gets a pass," Wingate said. "Just because we don't have video, it doesn't mean that Dunstag wasn't a player."

In the car, Wingate interrogated Kinsale about the Orphenadrine Citrate. Kinsale explained that he'd only just learned about it in the minutes before Wingate had picked him up that morning and hadn't had the opportunity to bring him up to speed. In no way, he stressed, was he holding out on him. Wingate wasn't inclined to accept the explanation, but before the exchange could get heated, they arrived at the Midland Military Institute.

As they walked up to the administration building, Wingate pointed to the expanse of farmland beyond the school's athletic fields. "The Institute abuts the city line," he said. "If it were on the other side, this would be the county's—or more likely the state's—headache."

"Come on, Ralph," Kinsale said, sensing a thaw. "This is what we live for."

Wingate glanced at Kinsale, and after a moment, acknowledged that truth with a tight nod.

They'd arrived between class periods and boys of all ages were marching purposefully among the buildings. Most of them wore the same uniform, dark blue pants, light blue shirt, a dark-gray officer's hat with red piping, and patent leather shoes. Others, in light blue T-shirts and dark blue shorts, were heading in small groups towards the athletic fields.

The double doors of the administration building opened onto a small reception area with a central desk and a seating arrangement of wood-framed furniture. When Kinsale introduced himself and explained to the receptionist that he wanted to talk to Commandant Shelvey, she said he was unavailable.

"I think he'll want to talk to us," Kinsale said. "Just let him know we're here."

Without waiting for a response, he turned away and joined Wingate on the couch. When he looked at her again, she was on the phone, and after a brief conversation, she told them that the Commandant would see them now.

Shelvey's office occupied one end of the building. In addition to a large desk backed by an expansive window, there were a suite of living room furniture, a conference table surrounded by a dozen chairs, and a wall with pictures of the school's past dozen-or-so graduating classes. On the credenza below the window was a long row of identically bound black leather books with the name of the school and a year inscribed on the spine.

Shelvey came around his desk. He was dressed in an identical uniform to the cadets, except for the large epaulettes on his shoulders. Even without the uniform, he would have looked like a soldier. Well into his fifties, he was tall and muscularly lean and stood like he had a titanium rod for a spine.

"How can I help you gentlemen?"

Despite the man's calm demeanor, Kinsale could hear the anxiety constricting his throat. Employing a sexual molester would do that to a school principal. "How are you dealing with the fallout from Kennedy?"

"Our first priority is determining the extent of his . . ." He paused, searching for the right word, and settled on "activities."

"He preyed on some of your students?"

"I have been advised by our attorneys not to say," he said, although by taking that advice, he was giving away the story.

"I really have just one question, Commandant," Kinsale said. "Did you speak with the headmaster of the Georgetown Academy prior to hiring James Kennedy?"

"That was quite a long time ago. Give me a moment." Shelvey's gaze shortened for several seconds and then he said, "Yes, I did. He'd written such a powerfully positive letter that I thought it might be a fabrication. I called Dr. . . ."

"Thayer."

"Yes, Dr. Thayer, that was it. I called him and he confirmed that he'd written the letter." Fresh angst arose in Shelvey's eyes. "Are there concerns about Kennedy's tenure at the Academy?"

"Did you check his other references?"

"I'm sure we did," he said but he didn't sound so sure. "But with such a powerful referral from one of the top schools in the country, I . . ."

"So, you didn't personally check?"

"No, that would have been handled by our human resources team."

Kinsale didn't bother to ask him to check with the HR team, because they obviously hadn't. "I read his personnel file," Kinsale said. "He appeared to be an exemplary teacher."

"Until last week, I would have agreed with you—one hundred percent. He was popular with the students, the parents, and his colleagues on the faculty." Shelvey stepped behind his desk and lifted the latest yearbook off the credenza. He turned it around on the desktop so Kinsale and Wingate could look at it and then flipped through the pages. Kennedy appeared early on and continued to feature regularly throughout the book. "We were well into the publication process on this year's book, but we've put a stop to it for now to cull any photos or mentions."

Kinsale didn't have any more questions, and when he looked over at his colleague, Wingate nodded towards the door, so they thanked Shelvey and left.

On the drive to the airport, Kinsale struggled to get his head around Bernard Thayer's duplicity. It was bad enough that he hadn't turned Kennedy over to the MPD when he learned what he'd done to Chris Dowling, but then he'd paved the way for Kennedy to continue his depravity on a new and unsuspecting community of boys.

"Did you get what you wanted?" Wingate asked as he pulled up to the curb at the airport. Theirs was the only vehicle.

"What I wanted?" Kinsale considered his answer. "No. But I think I have what I needed."

CHAPTER 25

Kinsale had two voice messages when he deplaned at Dulles International Airport. The first was from Lieutenant Douglas Dupree of the MPD's Internal Affairs Division, ordering him to meet at the Second at nine the next morning. The second call was from Austin Carroll, the attorney whom the Fraternal Order of Police had assigned to the case.

Kinsale called Carroll first. The lawyer didn't pick up, so he left a voice mail that the meeting with IAD had been pushed back to 1:00 in the afternoon. Next, he called Dupree to push back the meeting.

"It's not an invitation, detective," Dupree said. "Nine o'clock."

Kinsale was familiar with Dupree from his previous run-in with IAD. He'd spent a lot of time in their suite of offices during those weeks and had picked up a sense of who everyone was. Dupree was a fair-skinned African American in his late thirties, who—if Kinsale remembered right—had taken time off from the Department to go to law school.

"I'd be there if I could, but I'm in Michigan right now," he said as he stepped outside into the warm Virginia afternoon. "I'm not due to fly out until tomorrow morning."

"I'm not negotiating here. If you're not there—"

"Be reasonable, lieutenant," he said, trying to sound the same. "I only got your message ten minutes ago. That's less than a day's notice. With a little more warning, I would have rescheduled my flights, but it's too late now."

"I'll see you at 9:00 tomorrow morning at the Second."

"No, you won't. I was able to switch to a flight that gets me in at 10:40. But it lands at Dulles. Conceivably, I could get there by noon, but that would require that there be no traffic at all, and that hasn't happened in D.C. since the Hoover Administration. Sitting there and waiting for me doesn't seem like a good use of your time."

"Nine."

"Except I'm going to need to grab some lunch. Can we say 1:00?"

"Are you fucking deaf, Kinsale? I said nine."

"I've also got to pick up my FOP attorney, but hell, I'll skip lunch, so I should still be able to get there by 1:00."

"If you're not there at 9:00, I'll start without you."

"You've got to do what you've got to do, but like I've been trying to tell you, I won't even be in town until after that."

Kinsale reached the BMW in the daily lot across from the terminal. He dropped his bags and leaned back against the car.

"Get a flight out this evening," Dupree said.

"Don't you think I tried? The first available flight out is the one I'm on tomorrow morning, and I had to pay extra to switch to it."

"What are you doing in Michigan anyway?"

"Do you think the Department will cover the airline's change fee?" Kinsale asked. "I wouldn't be coming back so soon if it weren't for you."

"Why are you in Michigan?"

"I needed to get away for a couple of days."

"Wasn't the victim in this case from Michigan?"

"It's a big state."

"Are you still sticking your dick where it's not supposed to be?" Dupree growled.

"Can we say 1:00 then?"

"What happened to noon?"

"Come on, Dupree. I have to pick up my attorney."

"He doesn't have a car?"

"One o'clock?"

When the pause lengthened, Kinsale knew he had him.

"One," Dupree said and hung up.

Once he was on the highway, Kinsale called Lucy Thayer.

"Hey, Martin." She sounded forlorn.

"Where are you?"

"Working."

"After last night, you still opened this morning?"

"No, but I was feeling claustrophobic at the house. I had to get out. Right now, I'm up to my elbows cleaning the Marzocco."

"What's that?"

"Our espresso machine," she said. "Scrubbing is very therapeutic."

"Did they transfer Chris to the Jail?"

"Last night."

"Can you meet me there?"

"Why?"

"First, I'd like to talk to you about what happened yesterday. And then I'm going to need you to get me in to talk to him."

"I don't . . ."

"I'll be standing outside the jail in two hours, Lucy. I really need you there."

"Maybe, we . . ."

"Lucy. Today."

After a brief silence, she agreed, and then the line went dead.

When the D.C. Jail was built decades earlier, it was supposed to embrace socially enlightened principles about incarceration, looking imposing on the outside while providing a safe environment for the inmates. Those ideals had long since been crushed by the twin realities of rising crime rates and shrinking budgets. Now the jail was an ominous concrete behemoth that belched smoke into the outside air and bred desperation into anyone unfortunate enough to venture inside.

Lucy Thayer was standing outside on the sidewalk when Kinsale arrived. Her arms were clamped tightly across her chest, and her eyes were glued to the sidewalk, as if ignoring the jail building would somehow make it go away. He was almost upon her before she looked up. She managed a smile, but it took a lot of effort. He offered her a hug, and she fell into it. They stood that way until she eased away. "Thanks," she said. "I didn't realize how much I needed that."

"There's a diner around the corner. Why don't we get a cup of coffee before we go in?"

Except for the tall, black woman behind the counter, the Union Diner was empty. Kinsale guided Thayer to the first booth, and they sat across from each other. The woman arrived a moment later and placed two laminated menus on the table. Kinsale eased them away and ordered two coffees. They waited in silence until the woman came back with two cups and a bowl of creamers.

The coffee smelled like crankcase oil, but Kinsale took a sip anyway. Thayer watched as he then cut it by adding two packets of sugar and four creamers, but it was hopeless. Her coffee cup remained on the table.

"Chris won't survive in there," she said. "It's hard enough for him out here."

"We'll get him out. I don't know what they've got, but I don't see how it could be enough to hold him."

"They sounded pretty confident last night."

"Stupidity does that."

That cheered her a little. "No wonder they don't like you." She pushed her coffee to the side and leaned forward onto her elbows. "That Detective Casey told me to convince Chris to confess. He said any jury would go easy on him because of Kennedy's past."

"It would certainly make things easy for them. How much do they know about what Kennedy did to Chris?"

"Chris told them."

"Even about your father-in-law?"

She sat back, unable to hold his gaze. "No, we didn't get into that."

"They didn't ask why the school and your family kept it quiet."

"They did, but our lawyer said we wouldn't answer those questions. He said they weren't relevant to the case."

"Who's your lawyer?"

"Dennis Berns. He's a friend of Bill's. Do you know him?"

Kinsale didn't, but that wasn't surprising. Washington had more lawyers than manhole covers.

She asked, "When do you think Chris will get out of there?"

"Like I said, MPD has to convince the prosecutors that they have a winnable case. Those guys are often willing to stretch those limits to keep a good relationship with the Department, so they might take it."

"What are you saying?"

"That it's up to us to convince them not to."

"But the police aren't going to stop investigating?"

"No, but they'll take their foot off the gas and spend most of their time trying to reinforce their case against Chris."

"It doesn't help that he's a young black man," she said sullenly.

"No, it definitely doesn't, but he's from a good family, was working at the Academy, and has a lawyer for a brother-in-law. That should count for something."

"It should, but it won't."

Kinsale couldn't disagree, so he said, "The fact that Chris was sitting across the table from Kennedy when he died isn't enough to build a case. If it were, they could come after everyone in the place, including me. I was only thirty feet away."

She shut her eyes tightly and said, "There's more to it than that."

Kinsale felt a chill. "What?"

"They have someone who says that Chris was at the Dog earlier on Wednesday."

"How can that be?"

She winced. "Because he was."

His surprise was immediately swamped by a wave of anger and frustration, but he managed to hold it in check as she continued. "I told you Chris spent Tuesday night at our house because he was so upset about meeting with Kennedy. We have an extra bedroom, so it was easy enough. The next morning, Bill had to go to work early, so I drove Chris to the Academy. The Dog is on the way, so we stopped by to check in on Rennie and pick up a latte and a tea."

"Rennie told them about Chris?" Kinsale asked.

"I don't know for sure, but that would make sense."

"Last week, Bill told me that he drove Chris to work that day."

"We decided it was best to keep Chris out of it as much as we could."

That timeline didn't make sense to Kinsale. "But none of you knew what I knew when they came to see me. Chris had no need for an alibi at that point."

"We knew that if the police delved into Kennedy, Chris would be the easy target. We needed to protect him."

In lying to try to protect Dowling, they'd ended up doing the opposite, but Kinsale didn't see any value in hammering home that point. He signaled for the check and asked, "What time on Wednesday morning? When you went to The Dog?"

"Just after 8:00."

"How long were you there?"

"Only a couple of minutes. Chris needed to be at the Academy by 8:30."

"Did you make it on time?"

"Hmm."

The waitress arrived at the table with the check. If she noticed that both cups of coffee were still full, she didn't give it away. Kinsale left five dollars on the four-dollar tab, and they went to see Dowling.

Inside, the D.C. Jail gave the sense that it was falling down around them. The walls were dented, cracked, and holed, and the ceiling tiles either sagged or were stained brown from water leaks. Small piles of refuse huddled in the corners, as if the cleaning crew had brooms but no dustpans. Thayer seemed to pull within herself as they followed a corrections officer down the hall to the inmate interview area. Inside the room, he pointed to the long metal table lined with metal chairs on either side. Everything was bolted into the concrete floor.

They waited in silence. Like so many first-time visitors, Thayer had to work her way through the shock of realizing that society needed places like this and treated people like this. Kinsale tried to use the time to plan out his next steps in the case, but his thoughts kept spinning back to the drip, drip, drip of Thayer family secrets and wondering what they had yet to reveal.

After about ten minutes, Dowling came through the door from the cells. His sister gasped loudly and let out a whimper. Dwarfed by his over-sized orange jumpsuit, he looked like a broken child. He walked hunched-over and off-center, his hands and legs cuffed by lengths of wire to the belt around his waist. He struggled to sit down, and when he lifted his gaze, his eyes were glazed and blank.

"How're you doing, hon?" Her voice was soft and sad.

Dowling's eyes filled with tears. He dropped his head, and huge sobs wracked his frail body. Thayer turned helplessly to Kinsale, and he gestured for her to give her brother a little time.

After a few minutes, the crying slowed and then stopped altogether.

Eventually, Dowling looked up. His eyes brimmed with pain, but that was better than the vacant look he'd had before. Given his past and his size, the D.C. Jail had to seem like hell on earth but going catatonic would only make it worse.

"Can I ask you a couple of questions, Chris?" Kinsale asked.

Dowling looked to his sister for guidance. She nodded, and he turned to Kinsale and waited.

"First off, you'll be out of here in a couple of days, maybe even tomorrow. They don't have enough to hold you. They'll have to spring you."

Dowling nodded, but his expression didn't change. If he'd been in the young man's position, Kinsale would have reacted the same way. Until he'd actually walked out the front door, he wouldn't believe it would ever happen.

"Was last Wednesday the first time you'd seen Kennedy since you were a student?"

Dowling nodded solemnly.

"You didn't see him earlier in the day? When you went into The Dog with your sister?"

Confusion flickered in his eyes, but he shook his head.

"Did you know that Kennedy was also there that morning?"

"With me."

"No, he met with Randall Chamberlain there. At 8:30."

"Chamberlain?" It took him a moment, but then he understood the reason behind the meeting.

"Did you know Kennedy was going to be there?" Kinsale repeated.

Dowling shook his head. "Lucy had already dropped me off at school by then."

"What time was that?"

"8:25. I had an 8:30 class. I'm supposed to be at the school by 7:45, but I . . . I just didn't have it in me that day."

"Have you ever thought of committing suicide?" He asked the question as he'd asked the previous ones, calmly and quietly, hoping to draw a simple response.

It didn't work out that way. Thayer whipped around to look at him, and Dowling paled and looked down.

"Have you, Chris?" Kinsale asked in a low voice. "Have you ever thought about killing yourself?"

"Martin!" Fury climbed in Thayer's voice. "I can't let you—"

"You have to let me, Lucy. This is important." He turned back to Dowling and applied a little more pressure. "It's a simple question. Yes, or no?"

Dowling contorted himself in the chair like Houdini, but he had no hope of escape. To his credit, he recognized that, and after waiting a few seconds in the forlorn hope of divine intervention, he looked at Kinsale and said, "Every fucking day."

His sister groaned at the answer and gripped the edge of the table, but Kinsale ignored her. "How would you do it?"

Dowling didn't give his answer a second's thought. "Different ways, I guess."

"What ways? A gun? Jump in front of a train?"

"For Christ's sake, Martin," Thayer said. "What do you think you're accomplishing?"

Kinsale flashed her a look. "Better that I ask than one of the Homicide detectives or the U.S. attorney."

"Nothing so violent," Dowling said.

"Do you have a supply of anything?" Kinsale asked. "Something you've put away for a . . . rainy day?"

"I've never gotten that far."

"Have you gone far enough to decide which pills you would use?"

Dowling shook his head. "I think I would use a suicide bag. It's faster and less possibility of intervention."

The way he said it, Kinsale believed him. He didn't have anything more to ask, but he didn't want to end the interview on such a bleak note, so he asked Dowling about what he did during the morning before he met Kennedy. Then he suggested that Lucy sit with her brother for a few minutes alone. He would meet her at the front door. Thanking Dowling, he assured him again that he would be released soon and left.

At the front desk, he asked the uniformed officer if Ronnie O'Day was in. She took his name and picked up the phone. After a short conversation, she hung up and pointed to the secure door over her right shoulder. "I'll buzz you through."

O'Day was waiting on the other side of the door. He was a tall, heavy-set black man with barber-trimmed stubble. The two of them had gone through the Academy together, but after a few years working the street, O'Day had realized that he stood a better chance for advancement in the Department of Corrections. He'd spent a few years walking the cell blocks at the old Lorton Penitentiary and then moved into administration. Now he wore custom suits and kept his service weapon locked in a gun safe.

"How's the Second treating you?" O'Day asked in his bass-heavy voice.

"I'm suspended."

He laughed. "Some things never change."

"I could use some help, Hot Rod." From his first day at the Academy, O'Day had been "Hot Rod."

"Tell me something I don't know."

Kinsale had long made a point of stopping in to catch up with O'Day whenever he came to the D.C. Jail. As the top non-appointed official in the system, he was the one to talk to if something needed doing.

They went into O'Day's office. Kinsale dropped into the guest chair, which sagged and tilted to the left. "With the size of your budget," he said, trying to find equilibrium, "you'd think you could get a decent chair."

"Budget?" O'Day scoffed. "I had to buy that myself on Craigslist."

"This fucking city."

Again, O'Day laughed. It was a slow rumbling sound, like a tractor starting up in morning. "Same old Martin. So, how can I save your ass this time?"

"You've got a young guy in here waiting for arraignment. Chris Dowling."

"Okay."

"I'm working the case, unofficially. The short version is someone unknown put down the guy who molested Dowling when he was a kid and right now Dowling is the easiest choice for it." Kinsale paused. "I don't think he did it, and I'm working on proving that, but with his history and build, he's not going to do well in here."

"Nobody does well in here."

"I'd say there's a better than even chance that you're going to find him torn up and unconscious in a toilet stall by this time tomorrow."

"That won't happen," O'Day said but didn't sound convinced.

"You can make sure of that."

"You want me to segregate him?"

"Keep him out of the population. Put him in the disciplinary cells if you want. Wherever will be better."

O'Day weighed the request for less than a second before agreeing. He picked up his phone and ordered that Dowling be put in a transfer cell. He told Kinsale, "Once an inmate is designated for transfer, we immediately take them out of the population. We have a half-dozen cells where they stay until they leave."

"I appreciate this," Kinsale said as he stood. "I owe you one."

"Another one."

"Another one," Kinsale agreed.

Thayer was standing by the front door when Kinsale returned to the reception area. She turned and headed out of the building before he reached her. When he caught up with her on the sidewalk, he could almost feel the anger radiating from her.

"Are you okay?"

"Fine," she snapped.

"Listen, Lucy, I had—"

"I can't believe . . ." She stopped abruptly and turned on him. "In there. In the condition he is in. To ask him about . . . It's almost like you were trying to put the thought in his head."

"I'm sorry, but I had to ask."

She shook her head and started down the sidewalk at a brisk pace.

Again, he caught up with her and briefly recounted his conversation with O'Day. As she listened, she gradually slowed and then she stopped once more. This time, though, the anger was gone. She put a hand on his forearm and mouthed an apologetic "Thank-you."

When they reached her car, he said, "I'll call you when I hear anything."

"Anything at all," she urged. "We have to get him out of there."

"Chris is going to need a lot of help when this is over."

"He needed a lot of help a long time ago," she said. "We . . . I let him down. That's not going to happen again."

CHAPTER 26

Just short of six that evening, Kinsale returned home. Before heading up the stairs, he knocked on Manny Oturos' door. When he received no response, he knocked again, because he really wanted to decompress with a happy hour or two, but the door remained closed. Disappointed, he trudged up to his apartment. He took a shower to wash away the lingering remnants of the D.C. Jail and then carried a beer and his notebook to the dining table.

He opened the notebook to the call log, which now stretched to two pages. He remembered that his old colleague Raymond Johnson, who'd retired the year before when his wife became sick, had told him that a long call log was proof that the detective was really working the case. But he'd also said that when the numbers started to look familiar, the case was bogging down.

Bill Thayer's number looked depressingly familiar as he punched it in. When Thayer came on the line, Kinsale identified himself and apologized for calling after hours.

"It's no problem," Thayer said, although he sounded like it was. "What can I do for you?"

"I only need to take a minute of your time. Where did you father work before coming to the Georgetown Academy?

"Why?"

"I'm just trying to get a complete picture, Bill."

"Before he arrived at the Academy, he was the headmaster of the Montross School."

"Where's that?"

"Montross, Virginia. It's east of Fredericksburg."

"On the Northern Neck?"

"Yes."

Virginia's Northern Neck was the large peninsula between the Potomac River to the north and the Rappahannock River to the south, both flowing into the Chesapeake Bay to the east. It was bottom land, flat and agricultural, with a smattering of small towns. Kinsale had driven through the area about ten years earlier, on his way to Williamsburg for what was supposed to be a romantic weekend, but he didn't remember Montross.

"And before that?"

"He was the assistant headmaster at Fenton Prep, just outside New York City."

"Did you go to Fenton?"

"For a year."

"And Montross?"

"No, I'd already transferred to Upper Canada College?"

"Why is that?"

"My parents didn't think I would fit in at Montross?"

"Because you're black?"

"Yes."

"Even if you were the headmaster's son?"

"That would have made it worse," Thayer said.

"Was James Kennedy at Montross?"

"What?"

"Did Kennedy teach at the Montross School?"

"No," Thayer said. "Why would you think that?"

"Has your father ever said anything about knowing Kennedy before he came to the Georgetown Academy?"

"No."

"Are you certain?"

"Certain? No . . ." Thayer stopped. "Yes, I am certain. If my father had any knowledge of Kennedy, he would have said something when . . . when Chris told us what had happened."

"Not if he'd known about Kennedy's predilections and had hired him anyway. In which case, it would have suited him to keep quiet."

"How—" Thayer stopped. When he spoke again, it was in a measured tone, as if he were using a metronome. "What you're insinuating is despicable. My father dedicated his career to educating and nurturing young men. He made one error of judgment. An error for which he has suffered ever since. And now you are—"

Kinsale let the pause lengthen, waiting for Thayer to catch his breath and continue his rant. Only after the silence extended to fifteen seconds did he realize that Thayer had hung up. He put down his phone, walked over to the front window, and stared out into the twilight as he replayed the conversation in his head.

Based on the timeline of the case, Kinsale had been a cop for a little over a year when Kennedy started abusing Dowling. He was still in uniform at that point, assigned to the First District, so he wouldn't have been involved in the case even if Bernard Thayer had reported it. But he'd known of other, similar cases from around that time, and he wasn't so sure that it would have ended the way the Thayers believed, with the headmaster fired, Dowling forced out, and Kennedy walking away.

Certainly, there were times and places where that would have happened, but Washington D.C. wasn't one of those places and seventeen years ago wasn't one of those times. Kennedy would have ended up in prison, and Thayer would have been hailed for doing the right thing, even if it did tarnish the school's sterling reputation. And Dowling would have received the help that he needed, instead of having to fend for himself in the same environment where he'd been traumatized.

Kinsale went back to the dining table, found Bernard Thayer's number in the log, and called. After getting the pleasantries out of the way, Kinsale asked if he would be available the next morning for a quick interview.

"But Bill told me you're not on the case anymore."

"I'm trying to get Chris out of the D.C. Jail."

"I understand that, and we're very appreciative, but I don't see how I can be of any assistance."

"It won't take more than a few minutes."

"Perhaps we could do it now then?"

"I'd prefer a sit-down."

"But I don't see how I could help."

"Dr. Thayer, right now, Chris is on the hook for Kennedy's murder. Police departments being what they are, once they have somebody in custody, they tend to stop trying to find someone else. They devote their time and resources to strengthening their case against whoever they've got. Right now, the MPD is doing all it can to shore up its case against Chris. No one is trying to find the real killer. That's what I'm doing."

"As I said," Thayer let out an aggrieved sigh, "we truly appreciate your efforts, but I still don't see—"

"Five minutes, sir. Five minutes. I'll be in and out."

"I . . ."

Kinsale could tell that Thayer wanted to refuse in the worst way, but he had no reasonable way to do it, so Kinsale kept pushing and eventually they agreed to meet at nine the next morning. Thayer hung up without saying good-bye.

Kinsale's next call was to Randy Chamberlain, and he had to yell because the thumping background noise was so loud that Chamberlain kept asking who was calling.

"Hold on," Chamberlain yelled even louder, and after about a minute the thumping dissipated. "Is that better?" Chamberlain asked, still yelling.

"Hi Randy, it's Detective Kinsale."

"Detective," he slurred, sounding deeply inebriated. "I'm in the can here. It's the only quiet spot in the whole place."

"Where are you?"

"K2."

"Can't say I've ever heard of it. Sounds like a good time."

"This is just the pre-game."

"I need to follow up on our last conversation. Tomorrow morning?"

"Not too early. If you come by around noon, Mrs. Wade can whip us up some lunch."

"Tomorrow is tough for me. I have several other appointments tomorrow. It would work best if you come to meet me. How about The Laughing Dog, where you met Kennedy? At eleven?"

"That's kind of dark, don't you think?" He giggled. "Scene of the crime and all that."

"That's the whole point," Kinsale said. "I'll see you there at eleven."

Kinsale used the call log one more time to find Larry Farber's number. He phoned but the call went straight through to voice mail. He left a message telling him to call back as soon as possible, but by now he knew that Farber wouldn't.

A few minutes later, there was a knock on Kinsale's door. He opened it to find Oturos standing there with two unopened beer bottles in his left hand and a half-eaten sandwich in his right.

"It's getting harder and harder to find people willing to work," he grumbled as he came in and dropped onto the couch. Kinsale grabbed an opener and a plate from the kitchen and sat down across from him. "Shelly wanted to go to a rock concert tonight. She didn't tell me until she came in to work today. I said no, and she quit on the spot."

"Who's playing?"

"That's hardly the point."

"If it were somebody really good, back in the day, I probably would have done the same thing."

"It sounded like some DJ or something. How is that a concert anyway?"

They were quiet for a minute and then Kinsale said, "Well, the way things are going, I may be looking for a job soon."

"Forget it," Oturos said as he stretched out his legs on the coffee table. "You're a good friend, but you're a lousy employee."

CHAPTER 27

Bernard Thayer made no effort to pretend that he was pleased to see Kinsale when he opened his door the next morning. Without a word, he turned on his heel and walked into the living room. He gestured offhandedly toward the chair where Kinsale had sat on his previous visit and took his own place on the couch. And waited, his face pinched in annoyance.

Kinsale was unfazed, having faced similar attitudes hundreds of times over the years. "Just a few questions."

"You said five minutes," Thayer reminded him. Again, he was dressed to go out, in a light blue shirt, bow tie, blue blazer, tan slacks, and buff-shined loafers. "Which should be just about right. I have to be somewhere."

"Really? Where is that?"

"A meeting. The building's governing board. I'm the treasurer."

Kinsale didn't believe him but saw no reason to push it. The interview wasn't going to take too long. "I went to the Midland Military Institute this week and saw Kennedy's records at the school. Why did you give him such a glowing recommendation?"

Thayer hadn't expected the question, and he looked dumbfounded, his jaw slackening and his eyes going vacant. In the next instant, though, Kinsale saw the gears start to work behind those eyes, and Thayer said, "I made a mistake regarding Jim and Chris. And Jim made sure I continued to pay for it."

When Kinsale didn't respond, Thayer went on. "When I learned of his transgressions, I searched for the right response. I had to balance the punishment he deserved with the damage that meting out a punishment would have on the school's reputation. Jim and I reached an agreement. I would not report the incident, he would resign immediately, and the school would only provide the most basic information about his tenure. I believed this was sufficient because any school to which he applied would instantly recognize that our unwillingness to provide supporting information was a huge red flag. He would not be able to get a job anywhere."

"Yet . . ." Kinsale said.

"Jim was cleverer than I, or at least more devious. He understood the implications of the agreement. By not reporting the incident, I had inadvertently put myself and the school at his mercy. He recognized that we had much more to lose than he did, and he took advantage. But again, he was clever. He didn't blackmail me or do anything illegal. He had an instinctive feel of where the edge was and how far he could push."

"And that letter wasn't a bridge too far?" Kinsale asked, not bothering to keep the incredulity out of his voice. "Putting him back into a school?"

Thayer looked away. "It was the last thing I did. And I told him that. I said if he ever called on me again, I would go to the authorities, my reputation and the school's reputation be damned. And I didn't hear from him again until he called last week."

"You should have called his bluff from the first," Kinsale said. "There was no way he would have turned himself in."

"I couldn't take that chance."

"So instead, you loosed him on a group of innocent boys in Midland."

Thayer's eyes flared with anger. "I think we've already thoroughly plowed that ground, detective."

Kinsale wanted to tell Thayer they could plow that ground every day for the rest of his life, and it still wouldn't be enough, but the old man was way past hearing that. "Where did Kennedy teach before he came to Georgetown?"

"I don't know."

"I don't believe you, Dr. Thayer."

The old headmaster raised up as if he might reprimand Kinsale for his impertinence, but then he sagged back down. Likely when he was younger, he was a force to be reckoned with, but now he was old and guilt-wracked and had no staying power. "Wasn't it in his records at Midland?" he asked dully.

"The police department up there called all the schools where Kennedy claimed to have taught prior to coming to Georgetown. None had ever heard of him."

Thayer shrugged.

"He must have supplied some actual references when you hired him at the Academy."

He shook his head. "I'm afraid I can't help you."

"Can't or won't?"

"As headmaster, I wasn't responsible for hiring instructors. The faculty committee vetted all the candidates. My only role was to approve or reject their final recommendations, and I don't recall ever rejecting any."

"Would Kennedy's personnel records still be at the Academy?"

Thayer rubbed his chin as he considered the question. "I would imagine."

"Then that'll be my next stop." Kinsale stood.

"Would you like me to call to let them know you are coming? I still have some influence there."

"Thank you, but no."

He looked disappointed. "If that's what you prefer."

As he walked to the door, Kinsale asked, "How was it that you came to the Georgetown Academy, Dr. Thayer?"

"I'm not sure I understand."

Kinsale opened the door and turned around. "I mean, back then, it must have been a reach for a school of that caliber to hire an African American."

"I was the best qualified candidate."

"Even today, that wouldn't necessarily be enough," Kinsale pointed out.

Thayer thought about what he wanted to say. "The Academy was looking to hire minorities at the time. Perhaps not in the headmaster position, but they were open to the possibility."

"It must have been a tremendous coup for you."

"The high point of my career." Thayer reached out and grabbed the edge of the door and gestured with the other like he was herding an animal out of his apartment. "I hope I've answered all of your questions sufficiently."

"Time will tell." Kinsale turned away.

Just under an hour later, Kinsale pulled to a stop in front of the conical-roofed guard hut at the entrance to the Georgetown Academy. Over the years, he had driven past the large campus countless times, but this was the first time he'd ever had cause to enter the grounds. He identified himself to the uniformed guard, who gave him a visitor's pass and pointed up the long tree-lined drive.

The main building, four stories of aged red-brick and huge double-hung windows, exuded tradition and money. Each of the cars parked in the front circle probably cost more than Kinsale made in a year, and the surrounding athletic fields looked like they'd never suffered the indignity of a cleat, although on a far field he could see twenty or so boys in identical white T-shirts and dark-blue shorts playing soccer.

The office was to the right of the front door. Behind the waist-high counter, a woman who looked to be in her early fifties perched on the front edge of a stool. Her face was screwed in quiet concentration as she compared the two documents she was holding in her hands. When Kinsale came through the glass door, she put down the papers, removed her glasses, and asked how she could help.

"I'm Detective Martin Kinsale of the Metropolitan Police Department." He was getting used to the lie, and it rolled right off his tongue. "I'm investigating the murder of a former teacher here, James Kennedy."

Her face fell. "Oh, poor Chris. It's not possible. He would never have done such a thing. He is—"

"I would like to see Kennedy's personnel file," Kinsale interrupted. He didn't want to give her an opening to do anything officious, such as asking to see his shield. It was still sitting in Scott's desk drawer, and he doubted he would ever see it again.

"Oh, I don't think I can—"

"This is a murder investigation."

"Yes, I understand that. Of course, I do. But those records are confidential."

"I can get a search warrant. I'll have to speak to the judge, get him to sign it, and then bring it back here. To make sure it's worth all that effort, though, I'll have to make it broader than just Kennedy's records, and we'll need to bring a whole squad of officers."

He could see her picturing a dozen police cars with lights flashing in the front drive as the parents came to pick up their sons. She quickly decided the situation far exceeded her pay grade and reached for the phone. "Let me speak with the headmaster's assistant."

Kinsale nodded and turned away. Lining the long wall of the office were floor-to-ceiling photos of past Academy basketball teams. There were several dozen of them. The oldest picture dated back to 1938. It was a grainy black-and-white photo with the team standing under a wooden backboard in a dark gymnasium.

"Detective Kinsale," the woman said. "Headmaster McDaniel will be right over to see you."

Two minutes later, a tall man with tightly curled gray hair, a long and narrow face, and a prominent nose came through the doorway. He was wearing a heavy tweed jacket over a checked shirt, a thin wool tie, and gray slacks. He held a well-worn manila folder in his left hand. "Detective Kinsale?" he asked with a generous smile. "I'm Dr. Lamar McDaniel."

"I appreciate your cooperation on this."

"Dr. Thayer called earlier and said you might be coming by."

"That's odd. I specifically asked him not to do that."

"Really?" McDaniel cocked his head in surprise. "He said you were working diligently to help Chris Dowling, so anything we can do."

"Thank you." Kinsale pointed at the folder. "Is that Kennedy's file?"

"It is. Why don't you come into my conference room?" His eyes shifted over Kinsale's shoulder. "Beth, would you mind calling down to the kitchen and asking them to send up a pot of coffee?"

They walked across the marble-tiled entry hall and through an opposite door that opened onto a large executive office suite heavy with leather chairs and plush carpeting. Hunt prints and award plaques were interspersed on the walls. A woman stepped around a large desk that protected the open door to

McDaniel's inner sanctum. She was wearing a dark gray cigarette skirt with a sleeveless light-gray top.

"Detective Kinsale, this is Georgia Lancaster," McDaniel said, extending an arm towards her and lightly touching her shoulder. "If you need anything later on, and I'm not available, ask for Georgia. She's as fond of Chris as I am, and truth be told, she can probably get what you need faster than I could anyway."

"Nice to meet you, detective." Her voice was low and husky, and Kinsale caught himself staring. So did she, and she gave him a knowing smile.

McDaniel directed him to the left and into a small conference room. It was brightly lit and overly air-conditioned. In the center was a wood table with rounded corners and a dozen padded chairs. At the far end, a phone and silver water pitcher sat on a credenza, along with an impressively long line of yearbooks.

"We'll leave you to it," McDaniel said. "If you need anything, please let us know."

Kinsale sat down and opened the file. His typical approach would be to give Kennedy's paperwork a quick once-over before spending more time digging into the details, but there wasn't enough in his file to merit the method. It started with Kennedy's employment confirmation letter, signed by Bernard Thayer and Jerry Anderson, whose title was chairman of the Faculty Recruitment/Retention Committee. Next came a series of glowing annual reviews, again co-signed. Thayer's signature was a constant, but the Faculty Committee Chair changed each year. Finally, there was a double-sided sheet listing the students for whom he'd served as counselor. Kinsale skimmed over the names but didn't see Dowling, Chamberlain, or Farber.

That was it. There was nothing about Kennedy before he came to the Academy and no mention of when or why he left.

Kinsale closed the file, stood, and headed for the door. At that moment, it opened, and a young black man in a white waiter's jacket stepped in carrying a full coffee service. Kinsale and he looked at each other, unsure of the next step. Lancaster appeared behind the young man and said, "Please put it on the table, Tyrell." He did, and then with a quick bow to her, backed out and left.

"Finished already?" she asked.

"Not much in here" He handed the file to her. "At least not what I needed."

"I'm afraid I won't be of much help." She smiled sadly. "I arrived here with Headmaster McDaniel. We only overlapped Dr. Thayer for about a week."

"Headmaster McDaniel succeeded Dr. Thayer?"

She nodded. "Dr. Thayer recruited him personally from Saratoga Prep in New York."

"And you?"

"I was there as well. Headmaster McDaniel asked me to accompany him down here."

Kinsale wondered if her relationship with McDaniel was more than professional. He knew that if he worked in close proximity to Georgia Lancaster, he'd want something more. "You've been with him a long time?"

"Between the two schools, it's been twelve years, almost thirteen."

"Does Jerry Anderson still teach here?"

She shook her head. "I don't know the name."

"Would you mind looking him up? He was the chair of the Faculty Recruitment/Retention Committee when Kennedy was hired."

"Let me check." She walked around her desk, sat down, and typed into the computer. "Here he is. He retired to Bradenton, Florida."

"Do you have a contact number?"

She gave him another sad smile. "I'm sorry, but I really couldn't give that to you without his permission."

Kinsale smiled back. "Georgia, like I told Beth in the office, I'm going to get it one way or another. This is—"

"Okay, okay. I surrender."

She read it off, and Kinsale added it to the call log. "Thanks so much for the help."

"Do you want to have that cup of coffee before you go?" she asked.

"Nothing I would like more, but I'm actually going now to have coffee with one of your alumni."

"We call them old boys."

"I know that."

"Whom are you choosing over us?"

"Randall Chamberlain."

Her eyes widened in surprise. "Oh."

"Do you know him?"

"Not him. No."

"But . . ."

"His father is the chair of our Board of Governors."

"Big Man on Campus."

She laughed. "Yes. Very big."

"Good to know. Perhaps we could have that coffee another time?"

"Perhaps."

CHAPTER 28

When Kinsale walked into The Laughing Dog half an hour later, he was glad to see that business appeared to have returned to its pre-homicide level. At the front table, six high-school students were simultaneously talking and staring at their phones. Four of the tables along the wall were occupied, and the line reached almost to the door. Lucy Thayer was working the espresso machine, and a young black woman with blonde extensions reaching to the small of her back was serving customers at the counter.

The Bentley wasn't idling outside, so Kinsale figured that Chamberlain hadn't yet arrived. He doubted the young man had ever been early for anything in his life. He glanced down the line of tables to see if any of the regulars had returned. At the first two tables, two young women were tapping away on their laptops. A couple were talking closely across the next table. At the fourth one, an older man in a business suit was reading the Wall Street Journal. And the fifth table—his table—was empty. As he considered whether to get a cup of coffee now or to wait for Chamberlain to arrive, a group of high-school students came in and lengthened the line out the door. That decided him. He walked back to his table.

After about ten minutes, the older man stood up, wedged the folded newspaper under his arm, and walked toward the back of the café. He stopped in front of Kinsale.

"Mr. Kinsale?" he asked, his voice deep and authoritative.

Kinsale looked him up and down. The man was a couple of inches shorter and a couple of decades older than Kinsale, yet he had an aura of raw power and conspicuous wealth. His dark blue suit had a pinstripe that was ethereally subtle and fit his well-fed stomach sympathetically. "Detective Kinsale," he corrected.

"I think not," the man countered and sat down.

Kinsale was surprised and disappointed that Chamberlain had sent his lawyer in his stead. The young man had seemed happy to cooperate, but having his $500-per-hour attorney sit in a café and read the newspaper for ten minutes before confronting Kinsale suggested he'd changed his mind.

"You have the advantage on me." Kinsale leaned back in his chair. "I don't know who you are."

The man placed the folded newspaper on the table in front of him and interlaced his fingers on top of it. "Timothy Chamberlain. I'm Randall's father."

His wasn't a handsome face, and time and stress hadn't done him any favors, but his eyes were sharp and aggressive, and he was looking at Kinsale like he'd found him stuck to the sole of his shoe.

"Nice to meet you," Kinsale said.

"You will stop communicating with my son. Immediately."

Kinsale considered that for a few seconds and then asked, "You're a lawyer, aren't you, Tim?"

Chamberlain smiled stiffly at the familiarity. "Why do you ask?"

"Because normal people don't talk to police officers like that."

His smile morphed into a sneer. "But you're not a police officer anymore, are you, Mr. Kinsale?" He dragged out the "s" in mister.

"Unless you know something that I don't know."

"Come now, I spoke with Elizabeth this morning."

"Elizabeth?" Kinsale asked.

"Rooney." Chamberlain looked sad for Kinsale. "Chief Elizabeth Rooney. Your soon-to-be former boss."

"Well, she would know, and she should have told you that I am only on suspension. With pay. I'm still very much on the force."

"Not for long, she assured me."

That news was meant to rattle Kinsale, but he was well aware of the chief's antipathy. "That's not her call."

"Maybe not," Chamberlain conceded, "but it is her call whether you are involved in this investigation or not, and she said you are definitely not."

"I am pursuing independent lines of enquiry."

"I believe next time you open your email you will find an order from her telling you to stop."

"I don't get to my email too often."

"She said you had trouble with authority."

"Well, maybe if she asks nicely," Kinsale said.

Chamberlain leaned across the table and said in a quiet voice. "But I am not asking. I am telling. You will stop your . . . independent lines of enquiry."

"Are you threatening me, Tim?"

Again, the familiarity bit, and Chamberlain's eyes flashed. "Yes."

"At least we have that on the table."

"You seem to find this amusing. Let me assure you that it is not in any way. I am completely and morbidly serious."

"I guess I'm just wondering why you felt the need to be here, Tim. If Randy didn't want to talk to me, all he had to do was say so. As you've pointed out, I have no official standing in the case."

"As far as I am concerned, Randall has no involvement."

"Randy met with James Kennedy on the day he died at the location where he died," Kinsale said. "Your son has every reason to resent what Kennedy did to him. Frankly, Tim, I'm surprised he hasn't already been interviewed by the MPD."

"Elizabeth assures me that Randall is in no way implicated in this matter."

"Again, that's not her call."

"And neither is it yours."

"Did you tell the Chief that Kennedy sexually assaulted your son? Does she know about that?"

"That is a despicable accusation," Chamberlain responded, and Kinsale could tell that he'd prepared it. "I will sue you and the city for slander if you ever utter that in public."

"Your son told me that it happened."

"He didn't, and he never would. And as the only other person who could possibly corroborate your story is dead, you will be flying solo. That is not a course I would recommend."

"Why are you putting a blanket over this, Tim? Haven't you hurt your son en—"

Chamberlain erupted out of his chair, his face flushing with anger. "Don't talk to me about hurt. What that boy has done to . . ." And then just as quickly, he regained control. "Mister Kinsale, do not misunderstand my intention. If you attempt to contact Randall in any way, you will come to wish that you'd been in Kennedy's place last week." He gestured off-handedly toward the newspaper that he'd left on the table. "I'll leave that with you. You might want to check how your retirement funds are faring."

Kinsale watched Chamberlain walk out the door and disappear to the right. He thought that the man's heavy-handed threats were an overreaction. He was a lawyer. He probably made more in an hour than Kinsale earned in a week. He knew all his son had to do was refuse to talk, and Kinsale would have had no recourse. And maybe that was the problem. Chamberlain wasn't trying to stop Kinsale from talking to his son. He was trying to stop his son from talking to Kinsale. And for whatever reason, it was easier for him to try to close down the investigation than to keep his son in line.

"That didn't look like too much fun," Lucy Thayer said. She was standing a few feet away with a cup of coffee in her hand. He'd been so wrapped up in his thoughts that he hadn't seen her approach.

"It didn't go quite as I planned."

"Did it have to do with Chris?" She was nervous and set the cup on the tabletop to free her hands, which she then struggled to quiet.

He nodded. "He's the father of another one of Kennedy's victims from his days at the Academy. He was trying to scare me off."

"Trying?"

He gestured for her to sit, but she shook her head. "I have to get back. This is only Myra's second day of work." She jabbed her hands into her pockets. "I just wanted to find out how it's going. With Chris."

"It's going. More slowly than I hoped, but it's going our way."

"Like how?"

He didn't want to tell her about his growing concerns about her father-in-law, so he said, "I can't really say quite yet, but I'll let you know once I can."

She didn't like the answer but didn't push. She nodded sadly and turned away.

"Let me pay for the coffee." He reached for his wallet.

She waved him off. "You're doing so much for us. It's on the house."

Kinsale gave himself a few quiet minutes to enjoy the coffee and then headed off to the Second for his meeting with Internal Affairs. Traffic was light and he arrived a few minutes early. In the parking lot, he called Trish Lewis at home. She was out again, so he left another message. Then he opened his notebook to the call log to confirm that he had in fact memorized Larry Farber's number and punched it into his phone. Again, the call rang through to voicemail and again he left a message urging Farber to call him immediately. He couldn't imagine that Tim Chamberlain would fail to tie down such an obvious connection. He'd probably even sent someone out to talk to Ernie Haslett.

Near the bottom of the call log, he found the number for Jerry Anderson, who'd led the Georgetown Academy's Faculty Committee when Kennedy was hired. He doubted that Chamberlain had thought that far afield.

He called the number and a woman answered. Kinsale identified himself and asked for Anderson. She asked him to hold, and a few seconds later he came on the line. He hadn't heard about Kennedy's murder, so Kinsale gave him the short version.

"I never would have thought," Anderson said. "Jim always seemed so . . . I guess I don't know what he seemed, but not that certainly. And Chris Dowling. I remember him as a student. A really fine young man. To think that happened to him."

"He's an instructor at the Academy now."

"Really? Good for him."

"Yes, but things aren't looking too good for him right now."

"I can see that, but I don't really know how I can help."

"I'm calling about when Kennedy was hired at the Academy. You chaired the faculty committee at the time."

"I did."

"I want to talk to you about the hiring process. I'm trying to find out where Kennedy taught before he came to the Academy."

"I'm afraid I can't tell you."

"It's okay. The Academy gave me access to his personnel file."

"It's not that. I really can't tell you. We never saw his background."

"Didn't your committee vet his candidacy?"

"No, we didn't," Anderson said. "In the entire time I was on the committee, both as a member and then in my year as chair, that was the only instance in which the headmaster bypassed us."

"That would be Bernard Thayer."

"Yes. Dr. Thayer told us that he'd worked with Kennedy in the past and vouched for his being an excellent candidate for the position."

"I thought new faculty had to be approved by your committee."

"Had to be? I wouldn't say that. Ours was more of an advisory capacity. We would consider the candidates and then make a recommendation, and in almost every instance—maybe every instance—that person was hired. In truth, though, the headmaster had the final say in approving new instructors."

"Would you—"

"Dr. Thayer must be in anguish right now," Anderson said suddenly. "To think that Jim betrayed his trust like that. Well, that's really unthinkable, isn't it?"

CHAPTER 29

Kinsale and his FOP lawyer Austin Carroll met with Lieutenant Douglas Dupree in one of the interview rooms at the Second. Typically, when officers needed to meet at the stationhouse, they used the conference room on the first floor, but Dupree was making the point that to him, Kinsale was no better than a street dealer.

The lieutenant sat across from them and silently sifted through a six-inch-high pile of paperwork. Kinsale smiled to himself because the IAD detectives didn't seem to realize that the people whom they investigated used many of the same interrogation techniques. Dupree had probably pulled three-quarters of the pages from other files. The volume of paperwork was supposed to intimidate the suspect but having used the same ploy many times himself, Kinsale just sat back and waited. For his part, Carroll shuffled through his own pile of likely superfluous paper.

Dupree cleared his throat. "This is a preliminary interview to go over the charges arrayed against you. We have yet to file them officially. That will be the next step." He lifted a piece of paper off the top of the pile. "Unless, that is, you agree to resign today. In that instance, we will stop moving forward with the case."

"What exactly are the charges?" Carroll asked.

"We faxed them over last night, counselor." Dupree flipped through several sheets of paper before settling on one. "But I brought along another copy for you just in case you didn't get the fax."

Carroll didn't even glance at the paper that Dupree slid across the table. "We'll need time to review these before this goes any farther."

"Feel free," Dupree said with a generous smile, "but the offer to resign and walk away ends with this interview."

"I thought the offer expired at the end of the day on Monday when I didn't have my resignation on the Chief's desk," Kinsale said. "No, hold on, now I remember, it was extended to Tuesday. And now we find out it doesn't actually expire until a few minutes from now."

"Detective," Carroll said. "Let me handle this."

Carroll appeared to be in his mid-thirties. He tall and thin and had dark brown skin and sleepy eyes. He wore an off-the-rack suit and slouched low in his chair. It would be easy for Dupree to underestimate him, and Kinsale hoped that was what he was going for.

"That's not acceptable, Lieutenant," Carroll said. "I'll need time to go over our options with Detective Kinsale."

"It shouldn't take too long as he only has two options. Stay and go up on charges or resign."

"It's not for you to tell us what our options are," Carroll said. "I'll need both time and privacy to consult with my client."

Dupree shook his head definitively. "The resignation offer is non-procedural. My boss thinks it's a load of crap, but the Chief told him to make the offer in light of your client's many years of service." He turned to Kinsale. "We've got you dead to rights. We know it, and you know it. This is a favor that the Chief is offering. One time. Take it or leave it."

Halfway through Dupree's speech, Carroll had picked up a sheet from his pile of papers and had started reading it. He continued to read for another minute. Dupree waited, becoming increasingly irritated, although Kinsale didn't know if that was due to Carroll's stalling or to his having had to make the resignation offer in the first place. Not only did it go against IAD's desire to nail Kinsale to the wall, but it also exposed their hand. By offering to settle, the Department was all but admitting that its case against Kinsale wasn't as strong as it needed to be. In truth, it was probably still strong enough, but the Department would want to avoid any chance of losing, no matter how small.

"We're willing to consider your offer," Carroll said finally. "We're going to need—"

"No considering," Dupree snapped. "It's a one-time offer. If you haven't taken it by the time this meeting is over, we're filing the charges."

"No, you're not," Kinsale said. "You haven't got—"

"Detective," Carroll said. "I'll handle this."

"What's to handle, counselor?" Kinsale asked. "They don't have a fucking thing. Maybe I broke some two-bit regs?" He gave Dupree a quick glance. "Maybe? But if the Department goes public with that, it's going to have a public relations nightmare on its hands. They can't afford that, and that's why they're making such a bullshit offer. If they had any hope of taking me down, they'd be all in. That they're not says they're worried. He knows it. And I hope you know it."

Carroll eyed Kinsale for ten seconds after he'd finished, then asked, "Are you done?" When Kinsale didn't answer, he said, "If you're done, I'll get back to doing my job here." He waited until Kinsale nodded sullenly before turning back to Dupree.

The IAD detective didn't look happy. He was struggling to keep his face blank, but his eyes betrayed him. He knew that everything Kinsale said was true, and that Carroll was going to call his bluff. Still, Dupree had to go through with the charade, and Carroll understood that was how the game was played. They went back and forth for another twenty minutes before Dupree agreed to keep the offer open for one week and to let Kinsale retire early with full benefits rather than resign.

"So, that's it then, Lieutenant," Carroll said, picking up his briefcase from the floor and sliding his papers into it. "We'll get back to you in a week. Or sooner, if we reach a decision before then."

Seething in his seat, Dupree's eyes were locked on Kinsale in a death stare, but then he realized that only added to Kinsale's enjoyment of the moment, so he shifted his gaze to Carroll and nodded.

"Let's go, detective." Carroll pushed away from the table and headed out. Kinsale followed.

They were six feet out the open doorway when Dupree called out. "Kinsale. This isn't over. You're going to fuck up again, and when you do, I'll be there to catch you."

"Doug," Kinsale said over his shoulder, "the only thing you'll ever catch is your dick in your fly."

Carroll grabbed Kinsale by the arm and pulled him all the way to the elevators. He jabbed at the down button and said, "You like playing the edge, don't you detective?"

"It seems to suit me."

"Right now, we're in good shape on this thing. Lie low for the next week and you can retire with a pension. Then you can go work for some other department and double dip for the next fifteen or twenty years."

That was a deal Kinsale wouldn't have taken a few days ago, but he'd come around to accepting that was the best one he was going to get. Lying low, though, wasn't going to be in the cards.

CHAPTER 30

As he headed home, Kinsale tried to consider next steps, but the day had taken it out of him, and he had trouble concentrating. He'd expected to have made the breakthrough by this point to get Chris Dowling out of the D.C. Jail, but he hadn't come through. Dowling would certainly be spending the coming night in a cell and probably several more.

In his apartment, he fiddled around pointlessly for fifteen minutes and then lay down on the couch and closed his eyes.

The first knock on his door roused him but not enough to register what was happening. Only when the knock repeated with more intensity did he awaken.

"I'm coming," he called out as he got to his feet.

He expected to see Manny Oturos when he opened the door, but instead, Trish Lewis stood there with two opened Corona beers.

"Were you taking a nap?" she asked, looking pleased because she could tell that he had been. She pushed past him into the apartment, letting her bag drop off her shoulder onto the floor at the back of the sofa. "Feeling your age?"

"Did you call?" Still groggy, he looked around for his phone.

"I was going to, but Manny was taking out his trash and let me in." She dropped onto the couch and put the two beers on the coffee table. "He gave me these and said he'll be up in a minute."

"What's going on?"

"I came by to talk to you about something, but you know Manny. Any excuse to have a party."

Just then, Oturos came through the still-open door, carrying the rest of the six-pack in his left hand and balancing a bag of corn chips on top of a bowl of guacamole in the other. "Why would you need an excuse to have a party?"

Kinsale needed a few minutes to come out of his nap-daze, but then the combined effervescence of his two friends broke through, and they settled into the early happy hour.

"What did you want to talk to me about?" he asked Lewis when Oturos went to the refrigerator to get the remaining three beers.

"I heard that you met with Internal Affairs today at the Second," she said.

Kinsale blinked in disbelief. "How did you hear that?"

She gave him a sly smile. "My source."

"Who is this guy?"

Her smile widened.

"Then it's a woman?"

Before she could answer, Oturos returned with the bottles. "Who are you two talking about?"

"Trish's source inside the Second keeps feeding her information about my situation. She already knows about my meeting with Internal Affairs today."

"You met with Internal Affairs today?"

"Me and my lawyer."

"You have a lawyer?"

"He's with the FOP." Kinsale saw that the acronym meant nothing to Oturos, so he said, "Fraternal Order of Police."

"I don't get it," Oturos said. "The Department is trying to get rid of you, but they give you a lawyer to defend yourself?"

"He works for the police union not the Department."

"Yeah, but every cop in the union hates you too."

"Not every cop," Kinsale corrected. "Some of them don't know me yet."

"Small favors," Lewis said.

Kinsale flashed her a smile. "Anyway, this isn't really about me. It's about the contract between the Department and the union. The FOP fights anything that smacks of overreach, not just to protect the officer in a specific instance, but to keep it from becoming a precedent."

"The precedent in this case being an officer who willfully and repeatedly broke the rules?" Lewis asked.

"That's the one."

"Does your lawyer know you're a pariah?" Oturos asked.

"I don't know," Kinsale admitted. "I wouldn't be surprised, but I'm hoping he's a good enough lawyer not to let it affect him."

"How would you know that?"

"What do you mean?"

"That's he's actually working for you?" Oturos asked. "Maybe he's working against you behind the scenes."

The thought hadn't occurred to Kinsale, and he didn't think it likely, but he began to consider the possibility.

"Enough with these pointless suppositions," Lewis interrupted. "I'm on deadline and need some answers."

"We've been over this before, Trish. I'm not going to tell you anything."

"You don't even know what I'm going to ask."

"Of course, I do."

"Is that any way to treat a friend?" Oturos asked. "She's just asking for a favor."

"Yeah," Kinsale said. "A favor that will give the Department even more ammunition."

"I wouldn't do that," she protested.

"How would you not?"

"It would all be on background."

"Background wouldn't work in this instance," he said. "They'd know it was me."

"Have some faith. I'm good at what I do. I won't leave in anything that would possibly identify you as the source."

Kinsale didn't believe her. Not that she was lying. She likely believed her promise. But she was a reporter and operated in a different moral universe. He was certain that if she were hauled up in front of a judge, she would go to jail rather than give him up, but if she needed to reveal a little bit more about her source in order to make her article work better, he had no doubt that she would stretch and tug at her professional ethics until she could justify it. Nevertheless, he said, "Let's take it slow. See how it goes."

Surprise spread slowly across her face like she wasn't sure she'd heard correctly, but then she realized that she had her opening and needed to dive in before it closed. "Okay, okay," she said in a rush. "What happened after you brought down Chief Broughton?"

"I hardly brought him down," Kinsale said, although he definitely had. "The situation just sort of… It convinced him to accelerate his retirement plans."

"You said you would answer my questions."

"Ask me one I can answer."

"Why is the Department coming down so hard on you?"

"We had an unspoken deal," he said, trying to measure his words. "I would keep my head down at the Second, and they would let me ride out my time until I got my twenty."

"Come on, Martin. A second grader could have figured that out."

"Okay. Let's just say they took the deal more seriously than I did. I thought we'd agreed that I would not cause any trouble, and they thought I would sit on my hands for the next eighteen months."

"They don't know you very well."

"No, but it worked for a while."

"Until James Kennedy was killed."

"Until James Kennedy was killed, and I reneged on the deal."

"And what exactly did you do that's so pissed them off?"

Kinsale shook his head. "I've said enough," he said. "You'll have to rely on your snitch for the rest."

"Come on, Martin, we're so close." She smiled coquettishly. "You've taken me right to the edge."

"I can't go any farther."

"Just a little more, Martin" Oturos cajoled.

"Shouldn't you be on my side, Manny?"

"She's not asking so much."

Kinsale looked from one to the other. "I was trying to do my job despite their efforts to stop me," he said finally. "That required that I cut some corners and break some regs. I got caught and they've chosen to nail me to the cross over it." And then he mimed locking his lips and tossing the key over his shoulder.

Lewis turned to Oturos. "Every one of his answers raises three more questions," she complained.

"Martin?" Oturos pleaded, but Kinsale shook his head and gestured helplessly towards his compressed lips.

Lewis made a few more half-hearted efforts to get Kinsale to talk, but she recognized that he was done. "That's it, then," she said, putting her half-empty beer bottle on the coffee table and rising from the couch. "I'll be off then."

"What?" Oturos looked dismayed. "It's still early."

She shook her head. "Actually, it's late. I have to get to the office to write this up."

That shook Kinsale out of his silence. "You're writing your article tonight?"

"I told you when I arrived that I was on deadline."

"Yeah, but I figured that was just a figure of speech, like `kick the bucket' or `fly off the handle.'"

"Nope." She picked up her bag and headed for the door. "Look for my byline tomorrow. On the front page."

CHAPTER 31

At six the next morning, Kinsale awoke, threw on some clothes, and hurried down the block to the Rock Creek Market to pick up a copy of The Washington Post. He'd never gone to the market this early, because Manny and he used it solely for emergency beer runs, and he was surprised to find that it wouldn't open for another three hours. A rope-tied bundle of newspapers lay in front of the market's door. He could have easily taken one, but even at this early hour, he could see the irony if he were caught stealing a newspaper to read an article about his legal troubles. Instead, he walked the additional two blocks up to Georgia Avenue and bought a paper at the CVS drug store.

Lewis's article wasn't on the front page. He found he was oddly disappointed: For her, because she put so much of herself into writing the article; and for himself, because the editors didn't think his story was newsworthy.

On the walk back to the apartment, he flipped through the front section. He couldn't remember the last time he had read the paper version of The Post, and he struggled to peruse the pages while walking. When he reached page six, though, he stopped, because the headline across the top of the page read, D.C. Police Department Blackballs One of Its Finest.

The article filled more than half of page six and included small pictures of the facades of the Second District station and The Laughing Dog, as well as Kinsale's official Department photo, which was at least five years old.

He forced himself to read through it slowly, trying to absorb every word. By the end, he had to give credit to Lewis. He'd expected her to write a piece that portrayed him as a David battling the bureaucratic Goliath of the MPD, although in this instance, he was likely on the losing side. Instead, she'd written a well-researched, factual piece that told the story of how and why the Department had put him out to pasture. She'd included quotes from several members of the MPD, including Captain Scott, and Captain Albert Gardner, who headed Homicide. By including their uniformly negative comments about him, she'd highlighted that his treatment had as much to do with bruised feelings as legitimate performance concerns.

He folded the paper and headed back to his apartment. He took a shower, made some coffee, and then sat down at his dining table to read the article again. This time, he looked for any indication in the paragraphs that he'd talked with her. In a few places, he could see the shadows of his words, but that was only because he knew what he'd said. He was confident that the average reader would see no evidence of his involvement. At the same time, he had no doubt that the Department would have dozens of sets of eyes parsing every word to try to link him to the story in order to add it to the list of his transgressions.

And since that was the case, he finished his coffee, put on his gray suit, and headed out to transgress further.

He drove south out of the city into Virginia, merging onto I-95 at the southern edge of the Beltway. Forty minutes later, he exited the interstate at Fredericksburg and headed east on Route 3 into the farmland beyond. He practically had the road to himself and breezed through small towns with interesting names like King George and Office Hall, although he didn't see anything interesting about the towns themselves.

Coming around a long curve, he saw a Virginia State Police station on the left side of the road. It was a low-slung building with narrow smoked-glass windows and a gravel parking lot. He slowed and pulled in. A pair of dark gray Police Interceptor SUVs and a handful of civilian cars were clustered in the spaces near the front door. He parked in the closest open slot and went inside.

The uniformed officer at the front counter looked up as he approached. "Help you?" she asked.

"I hope so," Kinsale said with his winningest smile, but the officer, whose nameplate read M. George, looked back at him as if he were a cardboard cutout. He dropped the wattage by about half, introduced himself as an MPD detective, and set one of his business cards on the counter. "I'm heading over to Montross on a case, and I don't know if Montross is in this district, but I wanted to stop by as a courtesy call to let you know I was in the area."

She studied the card for a moment and then reached for the phone. "I'll tell Captain Samuels that you're here."

Two minutes later, Kinsale was sitting across the Kansas-sized desk from Captain James Samuels. The desk suited the expansive office, which spanned the back of the building and had a private bathroom, the door to which was wide open. Samuels needed a big office. He was a large man with a full-moon face and a belly that draped heavily over his belt. He breathed loudly through his mouth.

"What can we do for you, Detective Kinsale?" Samuels asked, holding the business card between his forefinger and thumb.

"Strictly a courtesy call, Captain. I'm on my way to Montross to talk to the folks at The Montross School about a former teacher who was murdered in the District last week. Just gathering information, but I didn't want to come through without letting you know."

"There's a town called Kinsale down this way."

"No relation," Kinsale said. He'd seen the town on a map many years ago but had never felt the urge to visit.

"I've met a few members of your department over the years at conventions and seminars. Maybe I know your boss."

"Maybe," Kinsale said. "I work out of the Second District. Captain Gregory Scott."

"Scott? Can't say I recall that name."

"He's the seminar type."

Samuels laughed. "Mostly I go to them to give the wife a change of scenery."

"Happy wife . . ."

"Hmm." Samuels tossed Kinsale's card on the desktop. "I appreciate you stopping, detective. Most of you boys from the big city just drive on by." He hefted his left arm and pointed vaguely eastward. "You got about eight miles to go up the road. The school is on the other side of town. Big stone entrance on the left side of the road. One of them historical markers out front. Can't miss it."

"Does Montross have its own law enforcement, or does your team cover it?"

"They got a police chief, plus a couple of part-time officers. Mostly for traffic stops. There's a long, straight stretch on this side of town. Lotsa people wait too long to slow down."

"I'll keep that in mind."

"We handle pretty much everything else."

"How long have you been here?"

Samuels thought for a moment. "Going on two years now."

"Where were you before that?"

"Martinsburg. Down in the southwest part of the state."

"Do you like it here?"

Samuels didn't seem to have anything better to do than talk with Kinsale. He leaned back in his chair, which groaned under the weight. "Yeah. My family is from down near Norfolk, so it's nice to be closer. It's quiet here. 'Cept for hunting season, when it can get a little hairy, but the rest of the time, it's the three Ds."

Kinsale hadn't heard that term and cocked his head.

"DUIs, domestic disturbances, and drugs."

"The human condition," Kinsale said.

"Not too many murders though," Samuels said. "Fact is, hasn't been one here since I arrived."

"Count yourself lucky," Kinsale said and stood up. "I won't take up any more of your time." With an effort, Samuels pushed himself up out of his chair, and they shook hands. Kinsale asked, "By the way, what's the name of the police chief in Montross. I should drop by and let him know I'm in his town."

"Chief Owens. Brad Owens. I can call him to let him know you're coming, if you'd like."

"I'd appreciate it. Where is the station?"

"Just on the other side of the Bend."

"The Bend?"

Samuels smiled broadly, revealing uneven teeth. A large gap on the right side looked like interrupted dental surgery. "Don't worry. You'll know it when you see it."

Kinsale nodded. "How long has Chief Owen been there?"

Samuels' eyes narrowed. "That's the second time you've asked that question, detective."

Kinsale held up his palms to defuse the sudden tension. "The victim worked at The Montross School around twenty years ago. I was just wondering if Chief Owens might have been around then. Whether he might even remember the man."

Samuels relaxed. "Chief Owens took office a couple of years 'fore me. 'Fore him, the chief was a fella named Doak Campbell. He was the man around here for a long time, busting heads way back in the civil-rights days."

"Is he still around?"

"I see him around every so often. He lives on Oak Row Road, south of the town. You need the phone number?"

"I may."

"I'll have Trooper George get it for you on your way out."

Kinsale soon found out what Samuels meant by the Bend. The town of Montross was literally a ninety-degree turn in the road. Whether the town had formed around the Bend, or the road had bent for the town, Kinsale couldn't discern.

He found the small red-brick police station easily. The door was locked. That suited him. He didn't really want to talk to Chief Owens, but neither did he want him to think that he'd been snubbed. Kinsale might need his help at some point. He scribbled a note on the back of one of his business cards and dropped it through the mail slot.

He continued east. About a mile past the town line, two stone columns stood tall on the left side of the road. He slowed and saw the historical marker that Samuels had mentioned. He turned into the lane between the columns.

About fifty feet ahead, a pair of open, black, wrought-iron gates hung from a hulking stone entry arch. Across the top of the gates, The Montross School was spelled out in gold metalwork.

The lane stretched straight in front him, mature trees lining its length as if they'd been planted a hundred years ago with the vision of looking just like this today. After a few hundred yards, he saw a large, white-painted stable on the right, flanked by two riding rings. Beyond, three dozen-or-so horses grazed in a large field bordered by a waist-high stone wall. And then in front of him rose the school itself, a classic colonial structure of red-brick with a large central door and uniformly spaced, double-hung windows on both the first and second floors. Attached at both ends were newer—but still classically designed—additions. The drive ended in a wide cobblestone circle. A broad, fan-shaped stairway led up to the central door. Above the door was the school crest: an outline of a colonial-era man on a horse, a half-dozen-or-so Greek words, and 1763.

Inside, the school didn't have the panache of the Georgetown Academy, but a sense of history and tradition weighed heavily in the air, which smelled of old wood and old money. Boys in burgundy blazers, striped ties, and gray flannel pants hurried about, some in groups, others alone. Here and there, adults in conservative suits walked with studied calm. None of the students paid Kinsale the slightest attention, but a tall, thin man wearing a herringbone sport coat stopped in front of him. Looking over the top of his reading glasses and speaking in a soft southern accent, he asked, "May I be of some service?"

"I'm looking for the office."

"Right over here." He led Kinsale to a door with a marbled glass insert. Opening the door, he stepped aside to let Kinsale pass. Kinsale nodded his thanks and went in.

Everyone Kinsale encountered in the office was unfailingly polite, until he'd worked his way up to Vice Headmaster Philip Bond, who was a small, soft man with a big, hard personality. Seated behind his desk, with a large oil painting of the school on the wall behind him, he listened impassively while Kinsale explained what he was seeking and then said, "That is private information, Detective Kinsale. We will not share it with you."

Kinsale nodded at hearing those familiar words. "The man is dead."

"School policy mandates not releasing information about any of our students or instructors." Bond was neither apologetic nor angry, merely stating a fact. "It is a policy that the parents of our students value highly."

"Why would the parents of your students possibly want the identities of past teachers to be kept secret?"

In a glance, Bond managed to convey that if Kinsale had to ask that question, he didn't deserve an answer. As little as Kinsale had liked him before, he liked the vice headmaster even less now. "This is a murder investigation."

Bond shook his head like Kinsale was asking for a better grade.

"I can get a warrant."

"I'm certain that you can."

"Then why put us both through that?"

"Policy. It is a rule."

"Rules are meant to be broken."

"No, they are not," he affirmed. "I would think that a police officer, above all others, would understand that."

Kinsale looked around the office for inspiration on how to breach Bond's defenses. The furnishings weren't too encouraging. They looked like they hadn't changed since Bond was in diapers: Solid, conservative furniture, a plush carpet, and heavy drapes that looked like they could stop a bullet. Every surface was clear, no papers, no framed pictures, no line of school yearbooks.

Kinsale raised his hands in mock surrender. "Okay, okay. Can you tell me if you have ever had a teacher here named James Kennedy? Not a specific James Kennedy. Just any James Kennedy. Going all the way back to before the American Revolution."

Bond considered the request for more than a minute, staring at Kinsale as if the answer were written on his forehead. "I cannot speak for the years before I came to the School," he said finally, "but during my tenure, we have not had a James Kennedy teaching here."

"How long have you been here?"

He sighed like he was running out of patience, but said, "Twenty-three years."

"Kennedy would have come and gone before that."

"I can't help you there."

"Why not? If you could help me with your time here, why not prior to that?"

"I acceded to your request, because I could see that you were desperate. It was a personal decision. I will not go any farther."

Kinsale wondered what Bond was like in his personal life, whether he took the stick out of his ass when he left for the day, but then his thoughts moved on to what his next steps might be. There was no way he could get a warrant, not even if he asked Dontay Blalock to front it for him. He was falling behind the curve and was running out of time to catch up.

"If there's nothing else, detective," Bond said, rising from his chair.

Still distracted, Kinsale stood. "Thanks for your time."

"I'll see you to your car."

The offer could have been due to Bond's inherent politeness, but more likely, he wanted to make sure Kinsale left the property. They walked in silence most of the way. Once outside, Kinsale said, "This school has certainly been around for a long time."

"Since 1763," Bond said, gesturing towards the school seal.

"After all that time, you must have some pretty impressive alumni."

Bond eyed Kinsale to determine if he was trying to wheedle some information out of him. Deciding that he wasn't, Bond nodded. "We like to think so."

"Anyone I might know?" Kinsale asked. "Maybe a U.S. President."

"We had two future Presidents of the United States apply for admission. Neither was accepted."

"Maybe you need to refine your admissions policy."

Bond smiled primly.

Reaching his car, Kinsale said, "Thanks for your help," hoping to inject just the right amount of sarcasm into his voice.

"Happy to be of assistance," Bond said, deadpanning it back in spades. He waited until Kinsale was driving down the lane before turning on his heel and going back inside.

When he reached Route 3, Kinsale stopped, pulled out his phone and call log, and dialed Doak Campbell's number. After explaining who he was and why he was in town, he invited the former Montross police chief to lunch. When Campbell accepted, Kinsale asked where they could meet. The old chief suggested the Inn at Montross and recited some directions, which were, essentially, that it was in Montross.

CHAPTER 32

Kinsale had no trouble finding the Inn. It was just before the Bend along a street that petered out into a gravel lane a few dozen yards past the parking lot entrance. The Inn was a broad, three-story Federal-style mansion with white-painted wood siding and black window shutters. Stepping into the high-ceilinged entry hallway, Kinsale felt a hollow silence that reminded him of a church. In front of him were a wide set of stairs up to the second floor and a carpeted hallway leading to the back of the inn. On his left, behind a pair of closed French doors, was a dark and empty dining room.

"Are you here for lunch?"

An athletic-looking young woman with blonde hair pulled into a ponytail came towards him down the hallway. She was wearing a faded Old Dominion University T-shirt and a pair of blue parachute pants with tie-strings at the ends. She was drying her hands with a cloth towel.

"Maybe." Kinsale said.

She extended a hand. "I'm Margie Rodriguez."

"Martin Kinsale."

"Kinsale? That's the name of a town not too far from here."

"I get that a lot. Are you the innkeeper?"

"Along with my husband Anton."

Kinsale nodded towards the dark dining room. "You don't do lunch?"

"We serve breakfast in there for our overnight guests. And then dinner on Friday and Saturday nights. And, of course, brunch on Sunday. We do lunch in the Snookery. It's in the basement."

"How do I get there?"

"The entrance is around back, but you can go this way." She pointed down the hall. "The stairs down to the Snookery are around to the right, just before the registration desk."

The Snookery lived up to its name, cozy and warm. The walls were fieldstone, and the wood-beamed ceiling was low. Several of the beams were charred, as if they'd been in a fire at some point. Against the far wall was a complete bar set-up, fronted by several stools. A half-dozen booths lined the opposite wall. The lighting was muted, and soft music floated out of hidden speakers.

Two of the booths were occupied: One by three men in casual business clothing chatting over half-eaten meals, and the other by an old guy wearing a checkered flannel shirt and a trucker's cap that looked like it had been used to clean up an oil spill. He was holding a Budweiser bottle wrapped in a paper napkin. Kinsale went over to him. "Chief Campbell?"

Campbell was thin but looked like he used to be heavy. He had tired eyes behind thick glasses, and close-cut hair under the cap. He smelled of beer and cigarettes. Gesturing toward the banquette across from him, he said, "They do a good beer here."

"Sounds good."

He called to the man behind the bar. "Anton, two more."

"Thanks for coming here to meet me," Kinsale said.

"I was already here when you called." He gestured toward an old cellphone on the table, next to a pack of Camels with a lighter tucked inside the cellophane and a small pile of paper napkins. "Spend most of my days here, don't I, Anton?"

Anton Rodriguez was holding two Budweiser bottles. A short man with thick arms and coarse black hair, he looked to be about ten years older than his wife. He smiled at Campbell. "Every day, Chief."

"'Cept Mondays," Campbell said. "They's closed on Mondays."

Rodriguez raised his hands in mock surrender. "Margie and me deserve one day off, don't we, Chief?" Without waiting for an answer, he turned to Kinsale. "Are you having lunch with us today?" Kinsale nodded, and Rodriguez went in search of menus.

"You won't get food like this anywhere else between Richmond and Washington," Campbell said as he picked up a paper napkin and carefully wrapped his new beer. "Anton and Margie really know what they're doing."

The menu backed him up. It wasn't anything Kinsale would have expected. There were lots of salads—one with pears—and all the sandwiches were on focaccia bread. There were enough balsamic vinegar, sun-dried tomatoes, and fennel to satisfy The Post's restaurant critic. Kinsale decided on the portobello mushroom sandwich with Belgian fries. Campbell ordered a cheeseburger—well-done—and another beer.

"Jim Samuels over at the Staties called me," Campbell said. "He told me you're down here looking into someone who taught at the School thirty years ago."

Kinsale gave him a quick rundown of the file, leaving out the part about his getting suspended. By the time he'd finished, their meals had arrived. Until that moment, he hadn't realized how hungry he was, and he immediately took a big bite of his sandwich. He chewed quickly, swallowed, and said, "This is phenomenal."

"Told ya," Campbell said, his mouth full of burger. "'Course folks down here don't appreciate good food. I don't give Anton and Margie another three months before the sheriff's putting a chain and padlock on their door."

Kinsale looked around. Rodriguez was talking to the other three customers. For the lunch hour on a weekday, the place was too empty.

"Same as the others went before them," Samuels continued. "Two from up your way and the last ones from . . . I think it was Colorado. Or someplace out there. Figured they could make Montross a place to come just by offering good food and a cozy bed. Truth is, there's nothing here but the School. Never has been. Never will be."

Kinsale relished his food as he listened to Campbell. The sandwich was damn good, maybe even better than that, but the old Chief was right. Montross was a long way to drive for a burger. After taking the edge off his hunger, Kinsale asked Campbell if he remembered James Kennedy.

"Can't say that I do," Campbell said after sifting through his memories for several seconds. "That don't mean much though. School pretty much keeps to themselves. Teachers live on the grounds or down towards the water. Kids don't come into town much. 'Course, why would they?"

"Did you know Bernard Thayer?"

"The headmaster?" Campbell asked and then nodded his head. "Black man made good. Never would have thought the School would let a Negro do much more down there than mow the grass."

"Times change."

"Not there, they don't. That's what those parents are paying for."

"What was your relationship with him?"

"Hardly call it a relationship, at least not until his wife died. And then he was gone a year or two after that."

"He told me about the accident."

"Didn't know her, 'course. She never came into town. Kept to herself. Always stayed in that nice big house they've got up there for the Big Dog. When I went up there to tell him, you could have pushed him over with a baby's breath. I'd say he turned white, but . . ."

"He's still a sad man."

"It'll take it out of you," Campbell said. "I lost my bride three years ago. Cancer."

Kinsale let the silence linger appropriately and then asked if Campbell knew of any legal issues at the Montross School.

Campbell finished his beer before asking, "Like what?"

"Sexual abuse? Anything like that?"

"This have to do with that fella . . . Kennedy?"

"There were allegations at other schools where he taught."

Campbell thought about his answer before saying, "Can't say I remember anything from back then. 'Course, if there was, they'd just have covered it up anyway."

"Nothing in the wind?"

"Small town like this, the wind's got a bullhorn. If there'd been something, everyone in town would know by evening. And I'd probably find out the next day."

"I get your point." Kinsale dropped his napkin on the tabletop. "That just about wraps it up for me here."

"Haven't finished your beer."

Kinsale glanced at the half-full bottle as he stood. "Got a long drive ahead of me."

"Leave it there, then," Campbell said. "I'm sure I can find some use for it."

Kinsale reached across the table to shake hands. "Appreciate your time."

"Can't really see how finding out about what your guy did at the School thirty years ago is going to help you," Campbell said.

"Right now, I can't see it either," Kinsale admitted. "I'll settle up with Anton."

Kinsale paid—after ordering another beer for Campbell—and left. The trip had been a harsh lesson in the dangers of getting one's hopes up. He'd anticipated making a breakthrough at the School, had almost tasted it, but now he was heading back to the city knowing that he'd wasted the day. Actually, it was worse than that because now he had to find a different angle, and he had no idea what that might be.

He backed out of the Inn's parking lot, pulled up to the stop sign at Route 3, and flicked on the right turn signal. He had to wait to let a classic red Mercedes convertible pass and saw Vice Headmaster Philip Bond behind the wheel. He was wearing a woolen brimmed hat and sporting brown leather driving gloves. Kinsale's earlier irritation with the man bubbled up but then morphed into what he hoped was another moment of inspiration. He pushed the turn signal down, confirmed that the road was empty now, and turned left towards The Montross School.

He asked the first student he encountered in the front hallway to direct him to the library. The young man pointed to the left and continued on his way to the right. Kinsale walked down the hall with a pace and purpose that suggested that he belonged there. Except for parting on either side of him like the Red Sea, the students ignored him.

The library was an impressively large space in the increasingly digital world. Six floor-to-ceiling stacks stretched towards the unseen back wall. In the front were several long tables and the librarian behind his desk. He was the same sport-coated man who'd earlier directed Kinsale to the office.

"How may I help you?" he asked.

"Thanks for helping me out earlier," Kinsale said. "I had a nice talk with Mr. Bond."

He'd started to stand, but at the mention of his boss, he eased back down into his seat. "Are you thinking of bringing your son here?"

"Two, actually. Twins. I thought I'd just take one more look around before heading home."

The librarian gestured towards Kinsale's chest. "All visitors need to wear a badge. Security. I'm sure you understand."

Kinsale looked down at his breast pocket. "Oh gosh, I forgot. I turned it in when we finished the tour. But then I mentioned that one of my boys is really into writing and wants to work on the yearbook. Philip didn't have any of the yearbooks in his office, but he said you had the entire set down here."

"I'll just call down to the office and have them bring your badge down." He lifted the receiver. "It won't take a moment."

"That would be great," Kinsale said. "Although I hate to put anyone to all that effort. I'm heading out right after this. I saw everything else, and I must say, I'm very impressed."

The man wavered, torn between his duty and not wanting to do anything that might jeopardize two potential applications. He put down the phone and pointed to the stack farthest from the door. "They take up three shelves now. We have quite a few yearbooks, as you can imagine."

"I'm just going to take a quick look," Kinsale said, "and then I'll be on my way."

Now he would find out if it truly had been a moment of inspiration. When he'd seen Bond drive past, he'd been puzzled at how the man's severe personality clashed with his driving a red convertible in a jaunty cap and driving gloves. That had led back to the man's spartan office, which, despite his obvious fealty to the School, didn't even allow for the customary line of yearbooks. And that thought had propelled Kinsale back to his visit with Commandant Shelvey, and how Kennedy had figured so prominently in Midland Military Institute yearbook.

Looking at these rows of yearbooks, it was easy to track the progression of time. On the top shelf, the books were thin, and the brown leather on the spines was cracked and dull. Moving downwards, the books became wider, and the leather took on the same burgundy hue as the boys' blazers.

Kinsale pulled out the yearbook from thirty years ago and flipped through the pages. Close to the front, he found a photo of a young Bernard Thayer smiling sincerely for the camera. Under the photo were several paragraphs. Kinsale started to read, but it was just a report on how successful the previous year had been, so he flipped to the next page.

And in the next moment, James Kennedy looked back at him. It was a casual photo on the right-hand page. He was standing in an English-style garden with his arms akimbo, holding open his black academic gown. His longish hair was pushed back from his forehead, and he had a bright smile. He'd been a handsome man, almost Hollywood handsome, although even across the decades, Kinsale thought he already could see Kennedy's dissolute character. Or maybe that's what he expected to see.

He was relieved to find Kennedy, but he wasn't surprised. He had to have been at The Montross School. The facts of the case only made sense if Thayer and Kennedy had a longer history together.

What did surprise him, though, was the name under the photo: Dr. James Nixon, PhD.

CHAPTER 33

Did Kennedy have a sense of humor, Kinsale wondered, upgrading his name from Nixon? Or had he hoped that a little of the sexual magic of the Kennedy name would rub off on him? Or maybe he'd just been a Democrat? Regardless, Kennedy and Thayer were connected long before their shared tenure at the Georgetown Academy. And though that by itself proved nothing, it was damning. Not only had the old headmaster lied about knowing Kennedy, which brought everything else he had said into question, but he was responsible for bringing the sexual predator into Chris Dowling's life.

Kinsale's phone rang as he pulled onto I-95 just west of Fredericksburg. He gunned the accelerator to slip between two eighteen-wheelers in the middle lane and slid over into the fast lane before answering the call. It was Ronnie O'Day at the D.C. Jail.

"Was about to hang up," he said. "Figured you were too busy to answer my call."

"Never too busy for you, Hot Rod. What's up?"

"Just calling to let you know your boy isn't doing too well. We found him on the floor of his transfer cell last night. Passed out cold."

"Was he alone?"

"From the time we put him in there?"

"So?"

"Doctor said he couldn't find anything specific. Said it seemed like the boy just collapsed. Was so overwrought that he… It's like he tripped a circuit, and his system shut down."

"Makes sense. Dowling is about as fragile as anyone I've ever met."

"Fragile don't work in this place."

"He shouldn't be there much longer," Kinsale said.

"You said that before, but I ain't seeing it. Alan Casey seems pretty confident."

"You talked with Alan."

"I called him to tell him about Dowling."

"What did he say?"

"Something along the lines of the boy better get used to it because he's going down."

"They've got the wrong guy."

O'Day let out an aggrieved sigh. "Maybe, maybe not. Either way, I hope this moves fast because that boy is more trouble than I need right now," he said and hung up.

Kinsale was nowhere near as confident about Dowling's future as he'd sounded. What he'd learned about Bernard Thayer and James Kennedy suggested something a lot darker and sinister than the cut-and-dried case that the MPD had put together against Dowling, but he still had nothing tangible.

He mulled over the situation, hoping for another moment of inspiration, but as he closed on D.C., he became increasingly anxious. Needing to do something to calm his thoughts, he called Duane Engler's cellphone.

"They can track this number too, you know," Engler said.

"Do you really think they'd go to those lengths?"

"To nail you, they'd call in the FBI, CIA, and NSA, if they could."

"It's nice to be wanted."

"Disturbingly, I don't think you're being as flippant as you think you are," Engler said. "Why are you calling me, Citizen Kinsale."

"I have a couple of questions about Orphena…"

"Orphenadrine Citrate."

"Right. How does it work? How much is fatal? Is it a common drug? I mean, could I pick it up over the counter, or would I need a prescription?"

"That's more than a couple of questions, but let me see what I can do." He paused to collect his thoughts. "How does it work? Essentially, it's a sedative and muscle relaxant. It reduces muscle spasms, quiets jerking nerves."

"It's prescription?"

"In the U.S., yes. You can get it over the counter in Mexico and in some places in Europe."

"What's a fatal dose?"

"Two or three grams."

"Is that a lot?"

"Depending on the prescription. If you had 100-milligram pills, you would need to take twenty or more, so in that instance, it's a lot, but if you had 200-milligram doses, you would need half that."

"Obviously, Kennedy didn't swallow twenty pills."

"Obviously," Engler agreed. "They were likely ground up into a powder and diluted in a liquid."

"Coffee?"

"Could be."

"Would there be any taste?"

"I have no idea," Engler said, and then added, "We need to hurry this along. I've just arrived at soccer practice."

"You play soccer?"

"No, my son does."

"But he's, what, two?"

"No, he's eight."

"No," Kinsale protested. "How is that possible?"

"Probably because the last time you asked about him, he was two."

"Oh." Chastened, Kinsale asked, "So, how's he doing?"

"Fine." Engler sounded annoyed. "Did I mention I'm his coach and practice starts in like... Now?"

"Right, just a couple more questions."

"That's how this conversation started five minutes ago."

"I guess what I'm wondering is first, how would the murderer know to use Orphenadrine Citrate and second, how would he know how to administer it?"

"Like I told you before, it's a fairly well-known suicide drug."

"I'd never heard of it."

"You're not the suicidal type."

"That's my point. Does it mean that the killer is the suicidal type? Not just to know about the drug but to have some on hand. After all, Kennedy only decided to come to D.C. the day before. That's hardly enough time to get a prescription or to FedEx the drug from Mexico or Europe."

"So?"

"So, Kennedy left some seriously damaged men in his wake. I wouldn't be surprised if one or two of them have contemplated suicide. In fact, I'd be surprised if they hadn't tried once or twice." Engler started to respond, but Kinsale spoke over him. "And at least two of them are on a first-name basis with drug use, so I think they'd be comfortable with something like this."

"That sounds pretty flimsy to me," Engler said.

"One more question?"

Engler laughed but stayed on the line.

"How long for the drug to take effect?"

"That would depend on the dose and the physical characteristics of the victim. On average, I would say if someone took a fatal dose, it would take somewhere between thirty minutes to an hour."

"But thirty minutes is the minimum?"

"I can't say for sure, and if it were a monster dose, it might start earlier, but yeah, it would take longer than that for the victim to start feeling the effects."

"Nausea, headaches?"

"Yeah," Engler said. "Sort of what I'm feeling right now."

"I appreciate the help, Duane. Now go and coach little… What's your son's name?" Kinsale asked, but Engler was already gone.

CHAPTER 34

For the first time in his adult life, the day of the week didn't matter to Kinsale. Being suspended from the Department, he didn't need to be anywhere for anyone at any time, and Saturday and Sunday were just two other days. Certainly, when he'd been on the job, he'd worked many weekends—probably worked more than he didn't—but he'd always been aware that that was what he was doing. Now, Saturday was just the day after Friday, and his only limitation was that others still thought of it as the weekend.

Having to accommodate that, he decided to spend the morning taking stock of his progress on the Kennedy file. First, though, doing what seemed to have become a pointless habit, he called Larry Farber. Yet again the call went to voicemail, and yet again he asked for a return call. He recognized that he needed to put some pressure on Farber because he'd met with Kennedy in those critical few hours before he died, but Kinsale just couldn't bring himself to believe that the pudgy accountant had the guile or the character to commit the crime.

With that task once more out of the way, he carried his notebook, phone, and a cup of coffee over to the couch, stretched out lengthwise, and let his mind wander over what he knew, what he suspected, and how he might merge the two.

First, he had to concede that Bernard Thayer may not have known about Kennedy's predilections while they were at The Montross School. The first reported instance of Kennedy's abuse didn't occur until after he'd arrived at the Georgetown Academy. It was possible that Thayer brought Kennedy there without any idea of the man's perversion.

While he had to account for that possibility, he didn't believe it. First, the fact that Kennedy changed his name after leaving Montross but before arriving at the Georgetown Academy pointed to some sort of run-in with the law. And second, the way that Thayer bypassed the selection process to hire Kennedy at Georgetown suggested he knew that the man's background wouldn't hold up under scrutiny.

If Kinsale were still in Homicide, he could have assigned some detectives to track down when and why Nixon had become Kennedy, but on his own, he had no hope. Likewise, he still wanted to identify the man who'd run out of The Laughing Dog moments after Kennedy died. He was likely just a secondary witness, perhaps only able to confirm that he'd been there and that Kennedy had died, but those types of interviews were integral to a complete investigation. He just didn't have the time or the manpower, so as much as he wanted to conduct an effective investigation, he had to admit to himself that it was going to be a challenge even getting to half-assed.

His phone rang, and he saw someone was at the front door. The thought that Trish Lewis was dropping by unannounced caused his stomach to flutter. He picked up.

"Martin. It's Greg Scott."

Surprised—and disappointed—Kinsale asked, "What can I do for you?"

"You can buzz me in."

"I'm on the second floor," he said and pressed nine.

He hung up, hid his notebook in a kitchen cabinet, and went to open the door. Scott had just topped the steps. He was wearing a light-blue polo shirt with an over-sized Ralph Lauren logo, a pair of tan slacks, and cordovan loafers without socks. He folded his sunglasses and hung them on his shirt placket.

"I served in the Fourth District right out of Academy," Scott said as he stepped past Kinsale into the apartment. "This neighborhood was a damn sight different back then."

"It's changed pretty dramatically in the few years I've lived here. Can I get you anything? Coffee?"

"Coffee sounds good."

Scott was sitting quietly in the reading chair when Kinsale brought two cups from the kitchen. He sat on the couch and put them on the table between them.

"You met with IAD?" Scott asked.

"You know I did."

"They want to strap you across a bullseye and use you for target practice."

Kinsale started to stand. "I've already played this out with Dupree, Captain. If they sent you down here to—"

Scott motioned for Kinsale to sit. "I'm not here about that," he said, reaching out and picking up his coffee cup off the table. "I already know you're too stupid or stubborn—or both—to do what's right for you and the

Department."

"Coming from you," Kinsale said as he sat back down, "I'll take that as a compliment."

Scott sipped at his coffee as he surveyed Kinsale's apartment like he was looking for the most likely place to find incriminating evidence. Kinsale let fifteen seconds pass before saying, "Okay, if you're not here to talk me off the force, then you're here to talk me off of Kennedy. You can save your breath. You know I'm not walking away. You know I'm not going to drop it. And you know that I don't like Chris Dowling for it."

"I don't like Dowling for it either."

Again, Scott had surprised Kinsale. "Then why is the poor kid sitting in a cell."

"You know how it works. We've got a decent case. Circumstantial, but decent. We'll hold him until someone better comes along."

Kinsale sneered. "I do know how it works and the only way someone better will come along is if they suddenly feel overwhelming remorse and turn themselves in."

Scott started to protest but thought better of it. "I'm not going to disagree with that one hundred percent." He was picking his words carefully. "We're working it, but maybe not as hard as we could."

"I worked with Alan Casey for a lot of years. You can bet he's already moved on to the next file."

"I can't speak for Homicide, but we're working it."

"Magner?" Kinsale sneered again. "The only thing he works is the system."

"It's hard to motivate everyone when the victim is an old perv. Who really cares that he caught the bus?"

"What about closing the file because if you don't, Dowling goes down for it?"

Scott brushed away the objection. "First off, you know that's not going to happen. We can hold him with what we've got, but we can't go to trial with it."

Scott certainly knew what Duane Engler had told Kinsale the day before, that it would take a minimum of thirty minutes between ingesting the drug and the bodily functions starting to shut down. That alone derailed the Department's case against Dowling.

"I need some traction on this, Martin," Scott said uneasily. "I need to know what you've got."

"That's rich," Kinsale said with a smile. "You do all you can to chase me away, and now you come to me for help."

"Regardless," Scott pressed ahead. "Are you going to give me something?"

"That depends."

He bridled. "On what?"

"On what you give me."

"What do you want?"

"I want you to spring Dowling tonight."

Scott appeared to have expected something else—maybe thinking Kinsale wanted him to lift the suspension—so he needed a few seconds to process the request, but then he shook his head decisively. "Can't do that."

Kinsale shrugged. "Then I guess it's no deal."

They negotiated in silence for more than a minute. Finally, Scott said, "If you give me something that I can act on, then, and only then, I will give the order. Without that, no can do."

"That's hardly a *quid pro quo*, Captain. I help you find the real agent, and then maybe you let Dowling go. You'd have to do that anyway."

Scott shrugged like that was Kinsale's problem. Kinsale shrugged back.

The silence settled over them again, but this time it didn't last even half as long. "Why don't you ever make anything easy, Martin?" Scott grumbled. "It's always got to be a fight with you."

"You call this a fight? This is a friendly discussion."

"I'm not feeling too friendly right now."

"This isn't about me, Captain. It's about Dowling."

"That's where you're wrong. It's always about you."

Kinsale started to reply but Scott cut him off with a wave of his hand. "You give me something to work with, and I'll cut Dowling loose tonight."

Kinsale was tempted to push for some sort of guarantee, but he held back. With anyone else in the Department—all the way up to the Chief—he would have wanted something in writing, but he trusted Scott. If he said he'd get Dowling out, he would. Knowing that, Kinsale felt bad that he was still going to hold back. "I've made a bit of progress."

"Let's hear it."

"I've been looking into Kennedy's three other local victims. He met with two of them on the day he died and was trying to connect with the third."

"That would be Chamberlain, Farber, and . . ."

"Haslett. Ernie Haslett."

"We haven't tracked him down yet."

"That shouldn't be too hard. He's a convicted sex offender and a tweaker. Chamberlain has his number."

"Fifth floor contacted me about Chamberlain. Said in no uncertain terms to lay off him."

Kinsale shook his head. "You can't do that. He met with Kennedy at the Laughing Dog that morning."

"Are you sure?"

"He told me so. Show Chamberlain's picture to a woman named Marnie Shea. She remembers Chamberlain's car. If she sees a photo, it might jog her memory."

"Who the hell is Marnie Shea?"

Kinsale spent the next five minutes giving Scott a highly redacted version of his investigation. He had to keep it as tight as he could because the Captain was sharp enough to pick out any inconsistencies. He completely omitted Bernard Thayer, but at the end, feeling like he hadn't offered enough, he threw in the secondary witness at the coffeehouse. He didn't think finding him would lead to anything, but it was red meat to Scott. If anyone could track him down, it would be Scott.

When he'd finished, Scott gave him an appraising look. "You've been busy."

"I've had the time."

"You didn't say anything about Midland. What did you learn up there?"

Scott may have thought that we would catch him off-guard, but Kinsale was ready for him, figuring that Dupree would have told him that Kinsale had been to Michigan. "Not enough to justify the money I spent on the airfare. Talk to Ralph Wingate up there about that end of the case. They've pretty much let Kennedy slip off their radar because they're working full-time on taking down the rest of them, but he'll give you the straight dope."

"And what about Montross?"

This time Scott had him. The Midland question had been a set-up, letting Kinsale get overconfident. Kinsale hadn't thought that Scott could know about Montross, so he wasn't prepared. He scrambled around for a good response but ended up asking, "How do you know about that?"

"Got a call yesterday morning from a Captain Samuels. He asked about a detective of mine being in his district."

"Really?" Kinsale remembered now how Samuels had casually coaxed Scott's name out of their conversation.

"He was just making sure everything was on the up-and-up."

"And what did you tell him?"

"I told him that you were following a line of enquiry."

In that instant, Scott changed the deal. He'd played Kinsale like a skilled fisherman, letting him run and think he was in control when all the time he was well and truly hooked. And it wasn't just that he'd known Kinsale was holding back on their deal. He'd covered for him with Samuels, which had to have been a difficult decision for him to make. And he hadn't handed IAD that final coffin nail, which must have been even more difficult.

Kinsale made a snap decision and hoped it was the right one. "When I was in Midland, I went to the Midland Military Institute, which is where Kennedy was teaching. I learned two interesting things. First, Wingate's team had checked Kennedy's job references and they found that, except for the Georgetown Academy, all of them were false. They stopped there. With Kennedy dead, they had no reason to pursue it further."

"Okay. And the second thing?"

"The reason why Kennedy was able to get the job despite all those false references was that there was a letter in his file from Bernard Thayer extolling his virtues as a teacher and a human being."

"And Bernard Thayer is…?"

"He is Bill Thayer's father, the husband of Lucy Thayer, who owns The Laughing Dog and is the sister of Chris Dowling. But, more importantly, Bernard Thayer was the headmaster of The Georgetown Academy when Kennedy abused Dowling and the others."

Scott looked confused as he tried to realign the chain of events to make sense of Kinsale's revelation.

"Weird, right?" Kinsale said.

"Disgusting and disturbing is more like it," Scott said.

"I wondered if there was some other connection between Thayer and Kennedy. When I got back to D.C., I went to the Georgetown Academy to find out how Kennedy came to be at the school, and I learned that Thayer hired him unilaterally, bypassing the normal channels."

"So, their connection went back farther than Georgetown."

"Bill Thayer told me that before coming to Georgetown, his father was the headmaster at The Montross School, which is—"

"In Montross," Scott said. "And?"

"I met with the vice headmaster, a stuffy prick by the name of Philip Bond. He wasn't inclined to help, and it was all I could do to get him to confirm that no one by the name of James Kennedy had taught at the School. That's what they call it down there, the School, with a capital "S.""

"No one by the name of?" Scott had picked up on Kinsale's wording.

"Exactly. I was pretty certain I was right, so I did a little extra digging, and I found that Kennedy had in fact taught at the School at the same time as Thayer, but under the name James Nixon."

"That puts a new spin on things," Scott said. "We haven't been looking at Bernard Thayer at all."

Kinsale could see Scott racing ahead, so he said, "You may want to hold off on tackling Thayer until the picture gets a little clearer. I've talked with the man a couple of times, and he has an answer for everything."

"That won't be so easy when he's in an interview room."

"Suit yourself, Captain," Kinsale said. "You do what you've got to do, but I'm just saying that this will work out a lot better if we have something tangible to drop on the table in front of him."

Kinsale had given Scott everything he had, and now he was requesting something in return. If he came right out and asked Scott to leave Thayer to him, the Captain would have had to say no. He couldn't take the chance that it might go wrong. But Scott was smart enough to see the lay of the land.

"We have to go after him. We don't have any choice. If I cut Dowling loose tonight, someone has to be lined up to take his place." Scott paused. "But I can see your point that maybe we want to put a little more in the file before we confront him. At the pace we're going, I'd say we'll move on him in about forty-eight hours, seventy-two at the outside."

Kinsale allowed a small smile of thanks to crease his lips. "That sounds just about right."

Scott left soon after, and Kinsale stretched out on the couch again and replayed the conversation, trying to measure how well he'd fared. He didn't like that he'd ended up giving Scott everything he had. Even when he was in the Department, he'd always held something back in his investigations. Primarily, it was a tactic for jumpstarting the team when their momentum stalled, but he had to admit there was also a measure of ego involved, knowing something that the others didn't. Yet, if that was what he'd needed to give up to get Dowling out of the D.C. Jail, he figured it was a fair exchange.

He reached for his phone and called Trish Lewis' home phone. He wasn't sure what he wanted to say and when the call clicked over to voicemail, he ended up leaving a long, rambling message.

She called back several hours later, as he was walking up Rock Creek Church Road to get an early dinner at the Caribbean restaurant on Georgia Avenue. He considered answering but decided not to.

CHAPTER 35

Trish Lewis didn't call again until early Monday morning. Kinsale was just making his first cup of coffee, and he turned on the gas burner with his left hand as he took the call with his right.

"You never called me back?" she said.

"It's been a busy weekend."

"Too busy to give me a quick call?" She sounded hurt.

"You're right. I should have called. I'm sorry."

"You're going to be sorrier."

A current of apprehension surged along his spine. "Why is that?"

"I had a long talk with my source over the weekend."

"Oh. What did he . . . they say?"

"You figured rather prominently in our discussion," she said.

"Why is that?"

He heard her take a deep breath, as if she were stealing herself for an ordeal. "They said that you've completely fucked up the Kennedy investigation."

"I guess that means your source could be just about anyone in the Department, with the possible exception of our squad secretary."

"That's not all. They said you have been intentionally sabotaging the investigation."

That got his attention. "Intentionally?"

"As good as," she said. "They said you've been tampering with evidence and intimidating witnesses. They provided details."

"Oh, is that all?"

Again, she paused too long. "Martin, this is serious."

"How serious?"

"You can decide for yourself. My article is on the front page this morning."

Now he needed a moment. "But you didn't give me a chance to rebut," he said finally.

"I called you on Saturday."

"I thought that was . . . He stopped himself. "What were you going to ask me?"

"I would have asked for your response to the assertion by an anonymous source inside the MPD that you are intentionally hampering the investigation into James Kennedy's murder."

Kinsale thought about what his response would have been, said "No comment," and hung up.

Kinsale threw on some jeans and a T-shirt and once again went up to Georgia Avenue to pick up a paper copy of The Post. As she'd told him, the article was on the front page, two short columns on the bottom right, and then a jump to page eight.

The casual reader would have no idea that Lewis had any feelings beyond contempt for Kinsale. By the time he'd finished the article, he wasn't so sure himself. Below the headline—Police Department Dissension Threatens Murder Investigation—Lewis flayed him from the first paragraph to the last. She began with her "anonymous, but highly placed" source saying that Kinsale was intentionally undermining the investigation, and it went downhill from there. Her source accused him of forcing the Saturday night release of Dowling, concealing witnesses, making a fool of Scott, and withholding vital information.

With the exception of making a fool of Scott, Kinsale couldn't really argue with the facts of the article. And he understood that Lewis and her editor didn't have that much to work with—their only source being an obviously biased member of the Department—so they'd had to resort to sensationalism. Still, he figured it would be best not to talk with her for a while.

Back in his apartment, he called the Second, and Royale Moon answered.

"I don't know how you do it, Martin," she said, a smile in her voice. "You keep getting more and more unpopular around here. I'd say you needed police protection, but . . ."

"As long as you still care, Royale."

"You know I do."

"Can I talk to the Captain?"

"I'll put you through."

When he came on the line, Scott said, "You're the last person I want to talk to today."

"Come on, Captain, you've got to know that wasn't me."

"I don't know that, Martin," he said. "Sometimes I think you're some sort of genius, playing four-dimensional chess or some other shit like that, and then other times you seem like you could give the village idiot a run for his money. Which one is it today?"

Kinsale's phone buzzed, and he looked at the screen. Lieutenant Dupree from Internal Affairs was calling. He declined the call. "Why would I do it?"

"It's not whether you would do it or not, Martin. It's that it's being done at all. I don't appreciate waking up to a call from the Chief telling me to clean up my shop. Or having to bring in the whole squad to say I won't tolerate leaks, and there'll be hell to pay when I find out who it was."

"I'm confident I can tell you who it was."

"I don't need your help, Martin," Scott said and hung up.

The conversation left a bad taste in his mouth. In fact, both conversations had. Figuring he might as well go for the trifecta, he put on a suit and headed out to Silver Spring to talk to Bernard Thayer.

On the way, he called Larry Farber again and got the same result. He pictured his voicemails lining up one after the other, ignored and unheard. Or maybe Farber listened to each one and then deleted it, cursing Kinsale under his breath. He preferred the second option because that meant he was getting under Farber's skin.

When Thayer opened his apartment door, he was once again impeccably dressed. He couldn't have done it in the time between the front gate guard's calling and Kinsale's arriving, so he must have just dressed that way every day. Today he had on blue slacks and an oxford-blue dress shirt under a tan cardigan. His bow tie was a mauve-and-yellow paisley.

"I hope I'm not intruding, Dr. Thayer," Kinsale said as he walked into the apartment.

"Unfortunately, I have to be going in a moment. I have a pressing engagement."

"You certainly are a busy man."

"I try."

"This won't take long."

"More questions?

"I always have more questions," Kinsale said. "It comes with the territory."

"Would you like some coffee? I have some made."

"That would be great. Do you mind if I use your restroom? It's quite a drive from the District."

Thayer pointed to a closed door. "Of course."

The bathroom was small and meticulously clean. The counter was bare, the towels folded as if they'd been pressed, and the shower door looked like it had been squeegeed clean. There was a second door that Kinsale surmised led to Thayer's bedroom.

He eased open the medicine cabinet. Prescription bottles were lined up on three shelves like curios. He started at the top and worked his way down. He was more hopeful than confident that he would find a bottle of Orphenadrine Citrate, but still he was disappointed when he didn't. Thayer could have put the pills in a different container, but Kinsale didn't have the time to check all of the dispensers. And he wouldn't be able to identify the pills anyway. That would take a search warrant and some of Engler's lab time, and that wasn't going to happen this morning.

He flushed the toilet and opened the door to the bedroom. A queen-sized bed stood against the wall to his right, flanked on both sides by small, nightstands. A light stood on the nightstand closer to him and a land-line telephone sat on the other. On the other side of the room were a long dresser and a matching mirror. Kinsale crossed the room and opened the top drawer of the dresser. He found a handful of carefully arranged personal items, including a stack of white handkerchiefs, matching fingernail and toenail clippers, and a single orange pill bottle. He picked up the bottle and shook it. It was empty. He read the label but didn't recognize the drug name. Figuring he was just about out of time, he dropped the bottle into his jacket pocket, shut the drawer, and opened the door that led into the living room.

Thayer was heading towards the closed bathroom door, and Kinsale's sudden appearance at the neighboring door startled him.

"I'm sorry about that," Kinsale said. "I got all turned around and went out the wrong door into your bedroom."

During his career in education, Thayer must have heard thousands of excuses from students, teachers, and even parents. Of those, Kinsale figured he'd just offered one of the lamest, but that didn't matter because the old man couldn't very well accuse him of lying. He was reduced to giving Kinsale a lengthy appraisal and then nodding. "It happens all the time. Why don't you sit down and have your coffee. As I mentioned, I don't have much time."

"A moment, I think you said."

"Yes. A moment."

They sat down across from each other. "Your questions?" Thayer asked.

"Right." Kinsale took a sip of coffee. "Why did you tell me that you didn't know Kennedy before he came to work for you at the Georgetown Academy?"

Thayer shuddered and looked down. He held his coffee cup with both hands like he was praying. "What are you saying?"

"What do you think I'm saying?"

Thayer made a ceremony of putting the cup on the coffee table. "You're saying that I knew James Kennedy before he came to Georgetown?"

Kinsale saw Thayer's gambit. At another time, he might have let it play out, but he'd lost patience with the old man's evasions. "Or James Nixon?"

Thayer seemed to deflate.

"Let's start at the beginning," Kinsale said. "Nixon taught at the Montross

School when you were headmaster."

Thayer didn't respond, looking down as if he could find a suitable answer on the floor.

"We can do this here or at the stationhouse. It's your choice."

"Based on the article I read in the paper this morning," Thayer said slowly, "I don't think you're in a position to make such threats."

"Don't fool yourself, doctor. That was a hatchet piece based on the petty grievances of one detective. The MPD is committed on this one. When an old white man is murdered in an Upper Northwest neighborhood, the powers-that-be get antsy. Next time it could be one of them. They want the case closed and an example made. One phone call from me, and MPD forensics people will be taking apart your couch and dissecting your search history."

The old man folded. "What was the question again?"

Kinsale repeated it, and Thayer, looking miserable, said, "Yes, he arrived about two years before I left for the Academy."

"Did you hire him?"

"The Board of Regents made the selection."

"Did you play any role in his hiring?"

"No."

"Did you know him before he came to Montross?" Before Thayer could answer, Kinsale added, "Under any name?"

Thayer gave him a grim look. "No."

"How soon after he arrived at Montross did Kennedy—Nixon—show his true colors?"

Thayer's eyes widened. "He never did."

Kinsale slammed his open hand onto the coffee table. "You're lying, doctor."

"I didn't know about him at Montross," Thayer protested, sinking into the couch. "Perhaps he . . . perhaps he did something. I hope to God that he didn't, but if he did, I knew nothing about it."

"How could you have not known about it?"

"That's my point." He spread his arms. "I would have known. And I didn't. So . . ." He pushed himself up, so he could perch on the edge of the couch. "Do you think I could have possibly brought him to the Academy if I knew he'd harmed one of the boys at Montross?"

"Yes," Kinsale said flatly. "After all, you gave him that glowing recommendation for the Midland Military Institute."

"I already explained that to you."

"If Nixon didn't get in trouble at Montross, why did he change his name to Kennedy?"

"Perhaps he did something after I left."

"And the school administration wouldn't have informed you? I find that hard to believe."

"I haven't spoken to anyone at the School since the day I left."

Kinsale waited for him to continue.

"I was hired during a brief moment of progressivism at the School. It died from almost the first instant I arrived. They regretted my tenure, oftentimes not too subtly, and they couldn't wait to see the back of me."

Having visited The Montross School, Kinsale had no trouble believing him. "That still doesn't explain why Nixon changed his name."

"He told me at the time that Kennedy was his mother's maiden name. He said that his father had abused him as a child, and he always hated carrying his name. He told me he changed it for therapeutic reasons."

"And you believed that bullshit?"

"I didn't see any reason not to."

"Do you believe it now?"

"No."

"Why do you think he did it?"

Thayer paused before admitting, "He was probably being sought by the authorities under his real name."

"How could that thought not have occurred to you at the time?" Kinsale demanded. "You had a responsibility to all those boys at the Academy."

"I knew him from Montross. I knew he was an excellent instructor."

"If you were so confident in his ability, why did you bypass the faculty committee at Georgetown?"

"What do you mean? I didn't—"

"I spoke to Jerry Anderson."

"Jerry Ander . . ."

"Why did you bypass the committee?"

Thayer went quiet, and Kinsale watched him consider and then discard various responses. Finally, he said, "If I hadn't, the committee would have looked into his background and discovered what it was that forced his name change."

"Doctor." Kinsale's frustration welled over. "You just told me that you thought he changed his name for, what was it, therapeutic reasons, and now you say you knew that he was a wanted man after all?"

"I know, I know." Thayer sounded tired. "It was all so difficult."

"You're not going to get any sympathy from me," Kinsale said. "Or likely from anyone else. Kennedy traumatized four boys that I know of at Georgetown and probably a whole lot more. And then there's what he and his fellow pervs were up to in Michigan."

"Kennedy was a homosexual," Thayer said. "He told me that he was a homosexual."

"I think we've already figured that out."

"Yes, but I didn't know it at the time."

"And?"

"He told me he'd left the School a few years after I did. He worked at various schools across the South. He was teaching in Nashville when he was caught in a police raid. It was a private party, but it was a huge scandal." Thayer mimed air quotes as he said, "Homosexual Teaching at Prestigious Prep School." He took a calming breath. "The police were going to throw the book at him. Unwilling to face potentially years in prison and an end to his career, he ran and changed his name."

"But why take him on at Georgetown?"

"As I said, he was an excellent instructor."

"There must have been hundreds of," now Kinsale mimed air quotes, "excellent instructors." He reached for his coffee but then changed his mind. "At a place like Georgetown, you could have had your pick. Why did you saddle yourself with one with potentially damaging legal issues?"

"A man's sexual orientation has no correlation to his skill as an instructor. Some of the best teachers I have ever known were homosexual."

"I'm not asking that," Kinsale said, frustrated by Thayer's constant deflections. "Why take on the legal risk?"

The old man looked at Kinsale, his eyes revealing a strength that had up-to-now lain dormant. "I know all too well what it is like to be discriminated against for something over which I had no control. For me, the color of my skin has been like a hundred-pound weight chained to my ankle, forcing me to work twice, three times, ten times harder than someone whose only advantage was where their ancestors were born. Jim Kennedy faced the same situation, and I could help, so I did."

Kinsale started to interrupt, but Thayer lifted a staying hand. "Before you raise what happened subsequently as evidence of my poor judgment, that is the hypocrisy of hindsight pure-and-simple. At the time, I didn't know of what he was capable, and I acted both in the best interests of the school and out of basic human decency."

They were quiet and Kinsale glanced at the clock above the couch. They'd been talking for more than twenty minutes. Thayer no longer appeared to be concerned about his pressing engagement. Kinsale asked, "How is your health, doctor?"

"Excuse me?" The new line of questioning unsettled him.

"Your health? You had a doctor's appointment on the morning that Kennedy was killed. How is your health?"

"It's fine."

"If it's fine, why did you go to the doctor?"

"That's what keeps it fine." Thayer offered a condescending smile. "When you get to be my age, you see your doctors more than you see your family. My son even created a calendar for me on my iPad so I can keep track of them all."

Kinsale's gaze followed Thayer's gesture towards the iPad on the side table. After considering it for several seconds, he said, "For someone who is fine, you certainly take a lot of prescription drugs."

Thayer needed a moment to understand and looked toward the bathroom door. "You didn't--"

"Just answer the question, doctor."

He shut his mouth. They faced each other down until Thayer gave in, saying stiffly "You didn't ask me a question."

"Okay, how's this? Will you give me permission to talk to your doctor about your health?"

Overflowing with indignation, Thayer asked, "What possible connection does my health have to Kennedy's death?"

"For one, I need to confirm that you actually did go to the doctor that morning."

"I told you I did."

"You've told me lots of things."

"You're not even officially on the police force any more. You have no official standing."

"As I told you, I'm working closely with—"

"Then have them do it. Get a warrant or a subpoena or whatever they need. If they can convince a judge that my medical history is somehow relevant, then I will gladly agree."

Kinsale stood and moved towards the door. "Once we get a warrant... or subpoena or whatever," he said, "we won't need your agreement."

CHAPTER 36

Kinsale checked his phone as he walked to his car. IAD's Dupree had sent him both a text and an email to go along with his earlier call, demanding that Kinsale respond immediately. He didn't, because he was feeling those tendrils of excitement that started to vibrate when an investigation picked up momentum, and he didn't want to let anything slow him down now.

Reaching the Tenleytown neighborhood, he stopped first in The Laughing Dog. Lucy Thayer was behind the counter, along with her new employee, and she gave Kinsale a tentative smile as he came through the door. Three people were in line ahead of him. By the time he reached the counter, she had his coffee ready.

She looked tired, her shoulders sagging and dark circles underlining the anxiety in her eyes. "Doing okay?" he asked.

"Did you see that article in The Post?"

"Ignore it," he instructed. "They don't know what they're talking about."

"It said that the police shouldn't have let Chris out."

"That's just some disgruntled cop who has nothing better to do than complain to the press."

"Wasn't it your friend who wrote it? Patricia Lewis?"

Kinsale nodded.

Thayer managed a wan smile, "With friends like that . . ."

"Journalists are a different breed."

Her eyes faltered, and she fiddled with the cash register to occupy her hands. "What she wrote . . . That you're intentionally sabotaging the investigation to get back at them?"

"She was just writing what her source said."

"But—"

He cut her off. "How's Chris doing?"

She was put off for a moment and then yielded. "He's staying with us right now. The Jail really took it out of him."

"The Department won't bother him anymore. The investigation is heading in a different direction."

Her eyes lit up and she asked, "What direction? Do you know who did it?"

"Need to know and all that," he said, shaking his head, "but Chris is in the clear." He laid three single bills on the countertop. "I've got to get going, but I have a quick question: Has your father-in-law been in here recently?"

"Recently? Not that I recall."

"You're sure? He didn't just drop by? On his way somewhere?"

"He doesn't get around much."

"Maybe with Bill then?"

Worry leached into her eyes. "Martin, what's this about?"

Needing to calm her concern, he said, "It's just when I last talked to him, he said he'd thought he'd seen me before. I wondered if it might have been here."

She relaxed. "I don't think so."

He turned to go. "See you around."

"I hope so," she replied.

He could have driven the short distance to his destination, but he decided to walk. The morning air was still cool, and there was a fresh breeze. He headed up to Wisconsin Avenue and then south for a block to Brandywine Street. He crossed at the light and then went halfway down the block to the three-story office building. He entered through the glass front door into a small elevator lobby. A set of stairs and the elevator were immediately in front of him, and there were glass office doors to both his left and right. A small display next to the elevator panel listed the building's tenants. Bill Thayer's office was on the second floor. Kinsale took the stairs.

The office door was open, and he stepped into a large well-lit space with three right-angle desks, piled high with light-blue legal sized file folders. Behind each desk sat a woman tapping away diligently on a computer. The shoulder-high beige filing cabinets that lined almost every inch of wall space were also stacked high with the blue folders.

"Can I help you?" asked the woman at the table closest to the door. She was a middle-aged black woman who had the air of someone who spent too much of her life sitting behind a computer.

"I'm here to see Bill Thayer."

She tilted her head toward an open door to the right and returned to her work. He crossed the room and stepped into the doorway. Thayer was surrounded on three sides by the blue file folders and typing rapidly on a laptop computer.

"Business must be good," Kinsale said.

Thayer looked up in in surprise, and then his eyes shaded to grim as he recognized Kinsale. "The real estate business is always good in D.C.," he said in a flat tone.

"As long as the federal government . . ."

"What can I do for you, Detec... Mr. Kinsale?"

Kinsale smiled. "Seems like everyone read their Post this morning."

"It really disturbed Lucy. And Chris."

"More so than him having to spend more nights in the D.C. Jail?"

The answer unsettled Thayer, and he stood to reassert himself. "I want you to stop meddling in the case and let the police do their work."

"Trust me," Kinsale said, crossing the room and sitting in one the visitor chairs. "That's the last thing you want."

"I don't see why I should trust you about anything," Thayer said, holding onto his anger.

"Because I'm Chris's best hope on this."

"The police have already exonerated him."

"As a lawyer, you should know that police departments don't exonerate," Kinsale said. "They cut him loose because they didn't have enough to hold him. That doesn't mean they're done with him."

"They don't have a case."

"They've made cases with less. A lot less."

Thayer was quiet then, and Kinsale said, "Why don't you sit down?"

The lawyer hesitated but then eased into his mesh-back chair.

"I saw your father this morning," Kinsale said.

"Yes, he called to tell me about it. He was quite upset."

"I seem to have that effect on people. Did you ever meet James Nixon?"

Thayer shook his head. "I don't think so. Who is he?"

"James Kennedy before he came to the Georgetown Academy. It was his name when he taught at Montross."

"Kennedy didn't teach at Montross," Thayer said.

"I guess your father didn't tell you that much about our conversation then, because Kennedy taught at Montross under his original name of James Nixon."

Thayer stared at Kinsale as if he were speaking a foreign language. "I don't understand."

"Kennedy, whose name was Nixon at the time, taught at the Montross School when your father was the headmaster. Your father knew Kennedy before he hired him on at the Georgetown Academy."

"My father wouldn't have . . . He never—"

"He did."

Thayer still struggled to get his head around it. "Are you saying that he knew about Kennedy's . . ."

"He claims he didn't, but frankly, I don't believe him."

Thayer came instantly to his father's defense. "If he told you—"

"Bill." Kinsale stopped him with a raised hand. "After all the lies your father has told since this started, he no longer has a shred of credibility."

"He wouldn't have brought Kennedy to his own school if he knew what he was capable of."

"I wouldn't have done it, and you probably wouldn't have done it, but I think your father did."

Thayer was distraught. "What you're saying would make my father a horrible man. It would mean that . . . Chris . . ."

"I'm sorry, but I just don't see any other explanation."

Thayer retreated into himself. Kinsale could see where his thoughts were heading, and it didn't take long. "You think my father killed Kennedy."

Kinsale didn't respond, but that was answer enough for Thayer. "I can't believe that. I refuse to believe it. And I don't see how you could believe it. My father is not that kind of man. Whatever you may think of him, he is not a murderer."

"If that's the case, help me prove that he's—"

"What do you mean prove. You're the only one who thinks this."

Kinsale shook his head. "Just the first one. The Department will get there eventually."

"We'll just wait for that then." He leaned back in his chair and folded his arms.

"Why put your father through that? The Department will get search warrants. They'll bring him down to the station. They'll question his friends." Kinsale paused to let the scene unfold in the son's head. "If you're so certain of his innocence, prove it to me."

A minute passed before Thayer said, "If you think I am going to implicate my father . . ."

"Just a few questions. If you don't want to answer any of them, don't."

Thayer was reluctant, but he nodded.

"Did you take him to see his doctor that Wednesday morning when Kennedy was killed?"

"Yes."

"How long were you with him?"

"I picked him up at Hawthorn around seven thirty. The appointment was at 8:30 and lasted about two hours. Afterwards we had an early lunch at the Clyde's in Friendship Heights. I dropped him back at his place around one."

"Did you bring him to The Laughing Dog that morning?"

Thayer shook his head.

"The night before?"

Again, he shook his head.

"When was the last time your father was at the coffeehouse?"

"I have no idea. A long time, though. He doesn't like to eat out. The main meal at Hawthorn is lunch, and he likes to make sure he gets it because he has to pay for it whether he eats it or not."

"Does he get rides from anyone else?"

"The community has a shuttle to take residents to the mall, the library, places like that."

"What about other residents?"

"It doesn't matter. He couldn't have been there because he was with me. And we were at his doctor's office."

"I need you to get me permission to see your father's medical records."

On firmer ground now, Thayer shook his head. "He told me that you wanted to see them. That's not possible."

"If he's not involved, then—"

"Exactly. He's not involved, so there's no need for you to see them."

"I said, if he's not—"

"It's a privacy issue. My father is a very private man."

"Has he ever tried to commit suicide?"

"What" Thayer demanded. "What are you . . ."

"Has your father ever talked about killing himself?'

"No," he snapped.

"Is he terminally ill?"

"I don't understand."

"Just answer the question."

A vein on the left side of Thayer's forehead began throbbing with his anger. "No," he said, clipping the word.

"You're certain?"

"Yes."

Kinsale paused and then asked, "Does your father suffer from Parkinson's Disease?"

Thayer's confusion trumped his anger. "What is this all about?"

"I'm trying to determine if your father could have gotten his hands on the drug that killed Kennedy."

"I've already told you that my father couldn't have been involved. He was with me."

"That doesn't mean he wasn't involved," Kinsale said and then added, "Or that you weren't."

Thayer's eyes flared. "What do you mean by that?"

Kinsale paused, letting the silence bridge to his next question, which was actually a statement, "When I was talking with your father this morning, he told me that you created a computerized planner for him to keep track of all of his medical appointments."

Thayer struggled to follow. "Excuse me?"

Kinsale started to repeat the words, but Thayer interrupted. "What does that have to do with anything?"

"Kennedy's day planner? The one you and Chris gave me when we were at the Starbucks?"

Thayer nodded uneasily.

"I made a copy, before I turned the original over to Homicide. An exact copy, down to the blank pages at the back. Did you take a look at it while you had it?"

"A quick glance."

"It ended on April 30." Kinsale said.

"That makes sense."

"I thought so too. But then when your father mentioned the planner that you created for him, I wondered why Kennedy's didn't have any May pages."

"Maybe he hadn't gotten around to putting them in."

Kinsale shook his head. "Months follow the constraints of the calendar, but our lives don't. Kennedy wrote down everything he had to do in his planner—appointments with students' parents, a call to a mechanic, dinner with a friend. Everything. Which makes it really strange that May wasn't in there. It's not like his life was going to end on April 30."

"Although," Thayer pointed out. "It did,"

"Yes, but he didn't know that."

"But he knew that he didn't have much of a future in Midland. There was a warrant out for his arrest."

"He only found that out on the 29th."

Thayer thought for a moment and then suggested, "Maybe he had two books, and he alternated them."

"That wouldn't make sense. He would have had to carry around two books all the time, and he only had one on him when he died. No, the May pages would have been in there as well."

"But you said yourself that they weren't."

"I think those pages were in his planner when he died, but when you gave it to me, they weren't."

"What are you saying?"

"You know what I'm saying."

"I wouldn't do that."

"If you didn't, then your brother-in-law did. You were the only ones who could have. Unless you showed it to someone else before you gave it to me. Lucy? Your father?"

"I didn't show it to either of them."

"That means we're back to you or Chris."

"Chris wouldn't . . ." He stopped himself, realizing he was cornered. "Okay. Okay. I pulled them out."

Kinsale pressed his advantage. "Where are they?"

"I threw them away."

"I don't believe you."

Thayer shrugged.

"Why did you take them out?"

Thayer looked over Kinsale's shoulder and out his open office door. Kinsale watched him, trying to discern what was going on in his lawyer brain, but he couldn't read his flat gaze.

"My father didn't meet with Kennedy before he died," Thayer said.

"That's what he told me."

"But they spoke on the phone."

"He told me that too."

"Kennedy wanted to meet, but my father refused. He knew exactly why Kennedy was calling and wasn't going to give him the satisfaction. He asked how much he wanted, and Kennedy said $100,000. My father is not a wealthy man. He has always been conservative with his finances, so he is comfortable, but he doesn't have that kind of money."

Kinsale waited for him to continue.

"He negotiated. Kennedy wasn't bargaining from a position of strength. There was a warrant for his arrest, and he needed to get something for his escape. Eventually, they settled on $20,000."

"And how is this relevant to the planner?"

"My father didn't have $20,000 in cash. He needed to liquidate some of his investments. They agreed that he would give the money to Kennedy on Monday. Kennedy wanted some sort of guarantee, so my father gave him his account number."

"And Kennedy wrote it down in his notebook for Monday," Kinsale said.

"When I saw it, I pulled out that page, but then I realized that it would look suspicious if one day in the month were missing, so I took out the entire month."

"But why throw it away? Why not hide it somewhere? Just in case."

"Keeping it would have been incriminating."

Kinsale was past hiding his annoyance. "What else was in there? Do you remember anything from the other pages?"

Thayer sighed in resignation. "Once I saw my father's name, I didn't pay attention to anything else."

"You're a lawyer, for Christ's sake. How could you be so stupid?"

"I wasn't thinking clearly. Everything was happening too fast," he said defensively "It's not my area of expertise. What can I say?"

"Not a damn thing," Kinsale said and walked out.

CHAPTER 37

Bernard Thayer's being at his doctor's office rather than his daughter-in-law's coffeehouse continued to undermine Kinsale's working theory. As much as the old man seemed to have been deeply embedded in every aspect of Kennedy's life for the past thirty years, it was unlikely that he could have managed to be in two places at once.

He walked back to the BMW and then continued on to The Laughing Dog. Lucy Thayer glanced sidelong as he came through the door for the second time in less than an hour. It was the pre-lunch lull at the coffeehouse, and only two of the tables were taken, both by singles staring at their phones, and no one was waiting in line. She was alone behind the counter. "Back so soon?"

"Just a short business meeting." His anger at her husband had largely dissipated during the walk, but he still had a sour taste in his mouth.

Uneasy, she asked, "With Bill?"

"Did he just call you?"

"No, I just figured with it being in the neighborhood. What did you want to see him about?"

Rather than answer her question, he asked, "Do you remember the leather planner on the table the day that Kennedy died?"

She nodded.

"Did you know at the time that it belonged to Kennedy?"

"I knew it didn't belong to Chris." She hiked her shoulders in apology. "But when he said it did, I . . . I didn't want to question him in front of you. Not after what had just happened."

"Did he tell you after?"

"Yes, and I told him to tell Bill. He would know what to do."

"Did you look inside?"

"No." And before he could ask another question, she asked again, "Why did you go to see Bill?"

"I had to ask him some questions."

"Had to?" Her voice trembled. "About what?"

"His father."

"Bernard? Why are you so interested in Bernard?"

"There were some issues that were bothering me. I wanted to clear them up."

"What issues?" Her concern was tumbling into panic.

He gestured for her to calm down. "How about I buy a coffee, we sit down at my table, and I take you through the conversation."

"Myra is on her break right now." She looked around anxiously. "I'll ask her to take the register and be right there."

He paid for the coffee and headed back to his familiar table. Just then a gaggle of high school girls came in. He watched them gather around the counter and begin ordering their drinks. Thayer stepped away from the counter to the kitchen door, pushed it open, and called back for Myra. A moment later, the young woman came through the still-swinging door and replaced her boss at the cash register. Thayer started working the espresso machine.

That sequence triggered a memory, and he got up and walked back up to the counter. He asked Thayer, "What do you know about Rennie?"

She was focused on the task at hand. "Like what?"

"What's his full name?"

"Rennie Esposito."

"Where he's from? Where he went to high school?"

"Why?"

"Lucy, would you please just answer my questions?"

She continued to make the drinks. "He's a junior at American, so that would put him at, what, twenty or twenty-one. He's from the Midwest somewhere. He's studying—"

"Where in the Midwest?" he demanded.

His urgency unsettled her. "I don't know. Why?"

"Do you have his number?"

The drink orders were lining up next to the machine and she was frustrated by the distraction, but she stopped, pulled her phone from her back pocket, and scrolled through her contacts until she found Esposito's number. She read it off. He jotted down the number, thanked her, and returned to his table.

Spinning his coffee cup between his thumb and forefinger on the tabletop, Kinsale pondered whether he'd failed all this time to consider the obvious. Esposito had been behind the counter that morning, giving him ample opportunity to tamper with Kennedy's drink. He'd been there when Chamberlain had met with Kennedy earlier, giving him time to put a plan into action. He was from the Midwest, perhaps Michigan. And he was of an age that fit into Kennedy's predatory timeline. Of course, there remained the issue of how he would have procured the Orphenadrine Citrate so quickly, but that was an open issue with everyone at this point, so Kinsale put it aside and dialed the number.

"Hey Detective," Esposito said after Kinsale identified himself. "What are you reading these days?"

"Do you have a moment to answer a couple of questions?"

"About the old guy who died?"

"Hmm."

"You know I don't work there anymore."

"Yeah. Sorry about that. If you need a reference . . ."

"Nah, it was my choice. I got a work-study gig at the library now. Much easier, although I do miss the coffee. The stuff here is crap."

"Lucy said you're from the Midwest. Where exactly?"

"Huh? What's that got to do with the old guy dying?"

"Background."

"Okay," he said, although he still sounded doubtful. "I'm from a town called Alvin in Illinois."

"Is that near Chicago?"

"It's not near anything." He laughed. "Or at least that's what it felt like growing up."

"Where did you go to high school?"

"Bismarck-Henning High. The Blue Devils."

"Did you ever attend a private school?"

He laughed again, but this time it sounded brittle. "My dad worked as a mechanic at Vermilion Chevrolet in Danville. Not exactly the income bracket for private school."

"American University can't be cheap."

"It isn't. I've got a scholarship and some loans. My mom has taken out some loans too. I do some tutoring. And I work."

"Your dad?"

"He died six years ago."

"I'm sorry."

"Yeah."

"Is Rennie a nickname?"

"Detective, I—"

"Is it a nickname?" Kinsale asked, putting some steel in his tone.

"Yes. My real name is Lawrence."

"Have you ever been to Midland, Michigan?"

"Where?"

"Thanks, those were my questions."

"Those were your questions? I thought they were back... Oh, never mind." He hung up.

Kinsale looked back at the counter and saw that the pre-lunch lull had ended. The line of high schoolers extended to the front door, and he knew from having sat in this spot for the past few months that the rush wouldn't abate for at least an hour. He also knew that while he'd been able to ignore the adolescent din while reading, it wasn't conducive to working the case or talking on the phone, so he finished his coffee and headed for the door. Thayer saw him going and gave him an apologetic look. He gestured to the crowd of customers, gave her a double thumbs up, and headed out.

He was hungry by the time he walked into his apartment, so he made himself a tuna salad sandwich, added some stale chips on the side, and carried the combo over to the dining table. Once he'd eaten enough to take the edge off his hunger, he called into the Second.

"You're the gift that keeps on giving, Martin," Royale Moon said.

"How so?"

"Captain took Magner and Collison into his office this morning. I could hear him from here. After a while, Magner came out and was searching all over his desk for a file. It must have taken him two minutes to find it and take it back into the Captain. When they were done, Magner looked like a puppy that got caught peeing on the carpet. Since then, he's been cursing you to anyone who will listen."

Kinsale couldn't have been happier. "Is the Captain still in?"

"Are you sure you want to talk to him? He's in a black mood."

"That'll be an improvement from our normal conversations."

She laughed. "I'll put you through."

Scott didn't bother with a greeting. "Homicide found an open sexual molestation charge from twenty-one years ago against a James Nixon in Athens, Georgia. That would be a year or so before Kennedy started at Georgetown."

"Sounds like our man."

"Definitely. Casey sent over the report. Athens PD tracked Nixon backwards to Montross, but then hit a dead-end going forward."

"Does it say who they talked to at the School?"

Scott was quiet as he looked. "Philip Bond."

"Figures. You'd have to waterboard the guy to get him to give up the lunch menu."

"It explains why Kennedy changed his name, but I don't see why the Georgetown Academy hired him."

"It all comes back to Bernard Thayer."

"Maybe it's time to pull him in."

"I can't get the timing to work," Kinsale said. "He was at his doctor's office, and I haven't been able to get even a whiff of him being at the coffeehouse that morning."

"You're not leaning away from him?"

"Not in the least, but I must be missing something. We need to find out if he really was at his doctor's. Can your team run that down?"

"We can handle it."

"That's not what I heard," Kinsale said with a chuckle. "Word is that Magner couldn't even find the case file this morning."

"God-damn Royale. She thinks she runs the place."

"She does."

"Hell, she does," Scott thundered. When he spoke again, he'd calmed down. "Anyway, I've pulled Magner off the case."

"You pulled Magner?"

"After that stunt with The Post."

"That was him?" Kinsale tried to sound surprised.

"What's wrong with that reporter? She didn't even talk to me. I could have put her straight. Instead, she let Magner rage."

"Magner was the rat." Kinsale failed to choke back a laugh.

"It's not so funny when you're sitting on this side of the desk."

"He admitted it."

"As good as."

"What happens now?"

"He tried to put up a fight, but the fight went out of him a long time ago. He agreed to retire and fade away nice and quiet."

"Can't say I'll be sorry to see him go."

"It'll be a close race to see which one of you goes first," Scott said. "But truth be told, I've wanted him gone since the day I got here."

"You know, Captain, I really don't get why you and I don't get along better."

"Because you're a self-important, obnoxious, disrespectful, anti-authority cocksucker."

Kinsale laughed. "That would explain it. Whose taking over the file?"

"Collison."

"Hardly an improvement."

"My best detective can't seem to keep from pissing off the Chief."

"She pisses off easily."

"Actually, Martin, she doesn't."

"What do you have Collison working on?"

"Tracking down whether Chamberlain or any of the others have tried to off themselves."

"You might have him look into Lawrence Esposito while he's at it."

"Who the hell is that?"

"He was working behind the counter at the coffeehouse when Kennedy died. It's a reach, but at this point . . ."

"Anything else we can do for you?" Scott asked sarcastically.

"Since you're asking, Collison should also look into whether any of them have Parkinson's in their families. It's not totally hereditary, but there is an increased risk."

"These guys are a little young to have Parkinson's, aren't they?"

"Michael J. Fox was 29."

"The *Back-to-the-Future* guy?"

"Hmm."

"He's got Parkinson's?"

"You didn't know that?"

"No reason I should," Scott said. "Is that it?"

"You've bled me dry."

"If only."

CHAPTER 38

Though it was difficult, Kinsale had to accept that the Department had taken over the case lead. He'd pushed as far as he could with his unofficial status, and now he needed the Department to throw around its weight to move things forward. He had no faith in Collison, but Scott appeared to have let the case get under his skin, and if he stayed on it, Kinsale felt they'd get there in the end.

Still, he wasn't going to while away the afternoon with a few beers and a nap. This was still his case, and he was going to stay on it until it was closed. If he couldn't work the streets to find new evidence, he could focus on what he already had.

He cleaned up his lunch dishes and made a pot of coffee, and then gathered all the pieces of the investigation together and laid them out on the dining table. It was a depressingly small haul. He just hadn't had the resources to collect all the information relevant to the case. Or, frankly, the inclination. Rather than investigate with a vacuum cleaner, hoovering up all the facts, he'd had to use tweezers, relying on his intuition to decide what to concentrate on. And the result was the modest mound of evidence in front of him.

He started on the pile chronologically, beginning with the report he'd written up for Scott on the first day. At the time, he'd tried to downplay the seriousness of the case in the hope that Scott would let him work it. He'd been successful in that effort, but the obfuscation essentially made the report useless. He put it aside. Next were his notes from the autopsy and then his meeting with Bill Thayer and Chris Dowling. He started to go through them, from when they were walking to the Starbucks . . .

He stopped. He wasn't really reading. Rather he was reading, but he wasn't absorbing anything. He was just going through the motions to satisfy . . . whom? There was no one to satisfy anymore. He no longer had to think about promotions or intra-department comity or the Fifth Floor. He would either nail the killer or he wouldn't. At this point, everything else was just superficial bullshit. So, he pushed away the papers, sat back in the chair, closed his eyes, and let his mind wander.

His instincts continued to insist that he was right about Bernard Thayer. The retired headmaster was too entangled in Kennedy's life to not have played a role in his death. And his incessant lying about their shared history suggested profound depths of guilt. Undermining Kinsale's confidence, though, was his inability to put Thayer at the scene of the crime. In fact, he didn't just claim not to be there; he had proof that he was somewhere else.

Or did he?

Both he and his son had steadfastly refused to provide that proof. It would have been easy enough. It was hardly a privacy issue to let the doctor confirm that he'd been at his appointment. Why hadn't they just cleared that up right away? Scott and Collison were going to pursue the issue, but who knew how long it might take to first get the name of the doctor and then get . . . But Kinsale already had the name of the doctor.

He got up and went over to the couch, where he'd draped the jacket that he'd worn that morning. He reached into the right-hand pocket and pulled out the empty pill bottle that he'd taken from Thayer's dresser drawer. He'd taken it to look up the medication on the Internet, but now he was only interested in the name of the prescribing doctor. There was no certainty that it was the same doctor with whom Thayer met that Wednesday morning, but Kinsale liked his odds.

The name on the pill bottle was Dr. A. Blevins. It took him fifteen seconds on his laptop to find a Dr. Andrew Blevins on Willard Avenue in Friendship Heights. He remembered that Bill Thayer had told him that he and his father had grabbed an early lunch after the appointment at Clyde's, which was at the intersection of Willard Avenue and Wisconsin Avenue.

He called Dontay Blalock in the Fifth District.

"What now?" Blalock asked.

"This is a quick one."

"But no doubt just as dangerous to my career."

"No doubt. I need you to run two driver's licenses for me."

"Whose?"

"Bernard Thayer. He used to live in the city, but now he's in Maryland. He doesn't drive anymore, so I'm betting he still has a D.C. license. And then William Thayer, his son. He lives on Jenifer Street."

"Give me a second."

As the sound of Blalock typing on his keyboard came through the phone, Kinsale asked, "How are you doing?"

"Be doing a whole lot better when you find someone else to do this shit for you."

"Most likely, this will be the last one. I'm hanging on by a thread."

"I got some scissors right here," Blalock said and then added, "You were right. Bernard Thayer. Address on 35th Street. Expiration date is just under two years from now."

"What's his birthdate?"

"His birthdate? What's that got to—"

"Dontay! Just give it to me."

Blalock waited several seconds before reading out the date. Kinsale wrote it down next to Doctor Blevins's phone number.

"And William?"

"Give me a minute. You know how slow this . . . Here you go. On Jenifer?"

"Hmm."

He read off the birthdate and Kinsale wrote it down.

"I appreciate it."

"Now you can do me a favor."

"What's that?"

"Lose my number."

"Don—," Kinsale started, but Blalock was already gone.

Kinsale wondered if he'd burned yet another bridge, but the smoke from all the others made it difficult to tell.

He called Dr. Blevins's number and said, "Hello, this is Bill Thayer. I'm Bernard Thayer's son."

"How can I help you?" asked the man on the other end of the line.

"He received an inquiry from his insurance company about his appointment two Wednesdays ago. They say he still owes the co-payment, but he insists he paid it. Could you check?"

"We—"

"I'm on the HIPAA Authorization Form."

"Let me just check," the man said. "The patient's name again?"

"Bernard Thayer."

"And his birthdate?"

Kinsale read it off.

"And your name?"

Kinsale told the lie again.

"And your birthdate?"

Kinsale recited it.

"Thank you. Let me see. Okay. We have the HIPAA. What was your question?"

"His appointment two Wednesdays ago? The co-pay?"

"That would be . . . April 30 at 8:30. And yes, we received the co-payment."

"Great," Kinsale said, although he didn't feel that way. "That's what I needed to know."

"Would you like me to email you a copy of the receipt?"

"No need," he said. "I can handle it from here. Thanks for your help."

He put down the phone and stared out the window for the best part of two minutes. If he were being honest with himself, he'd expected the confirmation. If Bernard Thayer were involved, he wouldn't offer an alibi that could be so easily overturned. And if he wasn't involved, there would have been no reason to lie about the medical appointment. Still, he hadn't fully prepared himself for the verification.

He needed to accept that he'd committed the cardinal sin for an investigator, doing exactly what he'd accused the Department of trying to do with Dowling. Early on, he'd formed a working hypothesis that fit the evidence. That, by itself, was reasonable and good detective work. But then, rather than keeping an open mind and accepting subsequent evidence that poked holes in that hypothesis, he'd focused solely on reinforcing it. So certain had he been of Bernard Thayer's guilt that he'd ignored any evidence that might have pointed at anyone else.

He pushed himself away from the table and went to the kitchen to make himself another cup of coffee. Returning to the dining table, he sat down and told himself that he needed to look again at every fact and detail in the case from a new perspective. No longer could he focus through the narrow aperture of proving Bernard Thayer's guilt. He had to broaden his field of vision and consider the motive and opportunity of everyone involved. It was a daunting task, and he had to accept that the window to finding the truth might have already closed, but what the hell else did he have to do.

The hours crawled by in a constant struggle to recognize and then dislodge each of his previous assumptions. He had to take them in turn—and there were so many—and to twist them first this way and then that in the hope that a new perspective would yield some clarity. The deeper he went into the file, however, the more holes he saw in his investigation. The leads he'd failed to chase. The calls he'd forgotten to make. The follow-ups he hadn't had the time to do. And as he neared the end, he became angry—with the Department and with himself--because he had to face the fact that these past two weeks had been a wasted effort. He was no closer to figuring out who killed Kennedy, and he had no idea of what his next line of inquiry might be.

All he had left were the photocopied pages of Kennedy's day planner. Before tackling them, he stood, stretched, and went into the kitchen. He considered making some more coffee, but his stomach was still sour from the last cup. He opened the refrigerator in the hopes of finding something more appealing. Behind a bunch of condiment bottles on the middle shelf, he found a single Sam Adams Pumpkin Ale. He'd bought two bottles last fall around Thanksgiving. He'd opened one, taken a sip, and then had immediately poured the rest down the drain. Now he considered the remaining bottle, wondering if the intervening six months might have improved the taste. Deciding to find out, he popped the top and took a small sip. If anything, it tasted worse than he remembered, but he was out of options, so he took it with him back to the table and sat down to read how Kennedy had spent the last month of his life.

He forced himself to go through every appointment and read every note. It was a slow and tedious process, but as he worked through the pages, he assembled a more detailed understanding of Kennedy. Judging by the large number of weekday dinners and weekend activities, he had a lot of friends in Midland. Kinsale could also confirm that Kennedy was meticulous and liked to be in control. Each Tuesday afternoon between 2:00 and 3:30, Beaver Trail Gardening worked on his yard. In the facing notes section, Kennedy would write down what they could have done better—"Edging on flagstone in backyard ragged"—and he had a scheduled call with them each Wednesday at 9:50, during which, Kinsale assumed, he would go over their failings.

The pages also painted a picture of a passionate educator. Kennedy devoted most of his weekdays to the Midland Military Institute, sitting on numerous committees, meeting with parents, counseling students, and overseeing the school's drama and debate programs. With the benefit of hindsight, though, Kinsale had no trouble seeing all those extra-curricular activities as part of a patient, but insatiable, search for new victims.

And so, he couldn't help feeling a sense of satisfaction when he came to the final page spread in the planner, knowing that this was the last full day of Kennedy's diseased life. He could see the panic in the suddenly changed handwriting, the fear in the scribbled notes, the frantic planning as he hastily recorded his victim's initials and their phone numbers, the frustration he would have felt that his predations had made the simple act of maintaining a working phone number too difficult for some of those whose lives he'd destroyed, and…

Kinsale saw his mistake.

The realization came in a flash. One moment he had nothing but the prospect of telling Lucy Thayer and Chris Dowling that he'd come up empty. And in the next, a door where none had been before cracked open, and a thin sliver of possibility shone through.

Maybe he'd been moving too fast in those first few days--or he'd been too confident in his investigative abilities—but the disconnect between the two phone numbers that Kennedy had for Ernie Haslett hadn't even raised a flicker. They should have.

Haslett's were the final two numbers on the list, one above the other.

BT 301-XXX-XXXX

CD 202-XXX-XXXX
LF 202-XXX-XXXX
RC 301-XXX-XXXX
EH 703-~~XXX-XXXX~~
XXX-XXXX

His first number had a Northern Virginia area code, but Kennedy had crossed it out and written the second number just below, seven digits, no area code. Kinsale had assumed that Kennedy had called the first number, and learning that Haslett's number had been changed, had crossed out the out-of-service number and written down the new number. He likely then called that number, but it would have just rung endlessly because Alecia Simms didn't answer random phone calls. Unless she thought it was the government.

Kinsale had gone through the same steps, although in the reverse order. He'd called the second number first, adding the Northern Virginia area code. When the call kept ringing, he'd hung up and called the crossed-out number. The recorded voice had come on the line after the first ring to inform him that the number was out-of-service and had been disconnected. That was it. There was no forwarding number.

So, where had Kennedy come up with that second number?

Looking at the list again, he realized that he'd connected the final number to Haslett because it followed the crossed-out number. There was a logic to that, but it was flawed, because it also followed all the other numbers. The only thing linking it to Haslett was Kinsale's assumption.

He pushed aside a few tendrils of doubt and decided it was logical that one of the five people in the list had given Kennedy the sixth number during that initial round of calls he made before climbing on a plane to come to D.C. Certainly there were other scenarios that would explain how he'd added the number to the bottom of the list, but Kinsale's options were limited, so he had to go with this one.

He immediately struck Haslett from contention because Kennedy never reached him. Chamberlain was unlikely. Given his drunken effusiveness, he would have shared that information with Kinsale when they'd discussed Haslett's phone troubles. Farber also felt wrong. He was too repressed and angry to share anything with Kennedy. Dowling was also out.

That left Bernard Thayer. Why did everything in this case keep coming back to him? And if it were Thayer, then whose number would he give to Kennedy. Kennedy had compiled all the other numbers on his own. Was it an unlisted number? Or . . . or was it just easier to get the number from Bernard Thayer?

Staring at that final number again, it began to look familiar. Identifying it with Thayer had joined two seemingly incongruous pieces of the puzzle. He reached for his phone and punched in the D.C. area code, and then the first three digits of the number. His phone auto-filled the rest. To confirm, he opened his notebook to the call log and ran his finger down the list. He found the number at the top of the second page.

In that first instant, he was surprised. But then he wasn't.

CHAPTER 39

Without thinking, Kinsale knocked back the last of his now warm and half-flat beer, but not even the beer's sweet, cloying taste—something like a boozy pumpkin pie—could puncture his good mood. It was too late in the day to act on what he'd learned, but it wasn't too late to celebrate. He picked up his phone to call Manny Oturos, but it rang in his hand. He looked down at the screen and it read, "Front Door."

He answered. "Hello."

"Hi," Trish Lewis said. "It's me."

"Hey," he said, thinking this was a better development. "Come on up."

"And me," a male voice said.

Kinsale stopped short. "Who're you?"

"Lieutenant Dupree."

"Dupree? What are you doing here?"

"You didn't answer my calls, texts, or emails."

"But why did you two came together?"

"We didn't," Lewis said. "We arrived at the same time, but definitely not together."

"Definitely not," Dupree confirmed.

"Okay." Kinsale glanced over at the papers on the dining table. He stood up and headed that way. "I'll buzz you in."

He gathered up the papers, carried them into his bedroom, and tossed them on the bed. As he came back into the living room, he heard a knock on his front door. He started that way but then saw his open laptop. He hurried over and shut it, then looked around to make sure he hadn't left anything else out. Satisfied, he went to let them in.

Both Lewis and Dupree looked uncomfortable when he opened the door, but not surprisingly, they were handling it differently. In a loose orange top that hung off one shoulder and her sunglasses pushed deep into her tangle of hair, Lewis saw the humor in their predicament, widening her green eyes cartoonishly as she cocked her head towards Dupree. The IAD detective, for his part, was standing ramrod straight, holding his leather briefcase tight against the front of his thighs and looking like he'd just shit his suit pants.

"Come in, come in," Kinsale said enthusiastically. "Welcome."

Lewis accepted the invitation, but Dupree remained in the hall. "This isn't a social call, Kinsale."

"Okay, then." Kinsale gestured to Lewis to give him a minute and then turned back to Dupree. "What is it?"

"You did not respond to my phone calls, texts, or emails, so you left me no choice."

"No choice about what."

Dupree looked pointedly at Lewis. "This needs to be a private conversation."

"Shouldn't my lawyer be here then?"

"No decisions need to be made tonight. This is purely informational."

"So . . . what do you suggest?"

"If Ms. Lewis will wait in your apartment, and promise not to listen at the door, we can discuss this out in the hall. It shouldn't take more than five minutes."

"Trish, does that work for you?" Kinsale asked.

"Sure, can I grab a beer?"

"None left."

"How about I go to the store and get some? That'll give Lieutenant Dupree and you ten minutes."

"How's that sound, Lieutenant?"

Dupree nodded, and Lewis slipped past both of them and headed down the stairs. Kinsale gestured for Dupree to come into his apartment. After a moment's hesitation, he stepped inside, but then immediately turned around, so when Kinsale closed the door, the two of them were standing two feet away from each other. Dupree said, "Her being here undermines your position."

"How so?"

"She works for The Post." Dupree said it as if that were enough, but then added, "She's the one who has written all of those articles."

"If you've read those articles, you would know that the last one was harsher on me than on the Department. And I've never been quoted in any of them."

"Background?" Dupree said, knowing how the game was played.

"I talked to her for the one last week—on background. She tried to call me last night about this morning's article, but we never spoke."

Dupree looked skeptical.

"We're just friends."

"Just like Siegfried was friends with that white tiger."

"Where did you pull that one from?" Kinsale resisted the pull of a smile. "Anyway, I'm pretty sure it was Roy, and it's not like that at all."

Dupree stepped back to put some space between them. Kinsale took advantage of the opening and maneuvered around him. "Can I get you anything? Water? Coffee?"

"I'm good."

"How about we sit down?"

"This won't take that long."

"Suit yourself." Kinsale crossed over to the reading chair and dropped into it. "So, why are you here?"

Dupree took a long, slow look around the room. "I talked to Captain Scott this afternoon."

"About me?"

"He told me he'd figured out who Ms. Lewis' source was in his squad."

"He told me that too."

That news caught Dupree by surprise, but he quickly reverted to form. "Because of you, a good cop is losing his job."

"If you're talking about Brian Magner, that he bitched to The Post is hardly my fault, and he was anything but a good cop."

"He served for 33 years."

"He filled a desk. Football players weren't wearing helmets the last time he closed a case."

Rather than argue the point, Dupree said, "Scott said you've been helping with the Kennedy case."

"Kind of undermines your accusation about those newspaper articles."

"It's not what was in the articles, Kinsale," Dupree said. "It's that they were written at all."

"Again, hardly my fault."

"Of course, it's your fault." Dupree's frustration bubbled over. He dropped his leather bag on the floor and leaned across the back of the couch. "Everybody I've talked to says you're a bright guy, whip smart, but all I see is a dumbass."

"Calm down, Doug."

If Dupree heard him, he gave no indication. His anger was untethered now, and he had no inclination to pull it back. "You're the reason those articles were written. If there were no Martin Kinsale, there would be no articles. Maybe you like to think that you're some sort of principled hero fighting against the Big Hats on the Fifth Floor, but what you really are is just some low-level worker bee who breaks things because it makes you feel like maybe you're important. But, man, you fuckin' ain't. You're no more important than the officer walking a beat or the crossing guard at my son's school. We all got a job to do, and if you're not willing to work with the rest of us to get it done—if instead you decide to undermine the rest of us every single minute of every single day—then you need to get gone."

Dupree stopped to take a breath. Kinsale waited for him to continue, but he was done. The anger and adrenaline that had fueled his outburst drained out of him, and within a few seconds, the button-down Dupree was back. "I apologize for that." He looked abashed. "That was un-called for."

"On the contrary," Kinsale said. "From the passion you put into it, I'd say it was totally called for."

Dupree looked quizzically at Kinsale for a moment and then reached down and picked up his briefcase. Holding it appeared to ground him. "Regardless of who is to blame for those articles, the Chief doesn't like them. They put the Department in a bad light."

"Maybe the Department puts the De—"

"Kinsale," Dupree interrupted. "I'm not here to debate this."

"Why are you here then?"

"The Chief wants you to leave."

Kinsale let out a cynical laugh. "I think we established that a long time ago."

Dupree took a deep breath. "If you agree to retire early, the Department will pay your salary until you reach your twenty as severance and then give you your full pension and benefits. And we will expunge everything from your record. You'll be able to work anywhere else in the country."

"But I like it here."

"No, you don't," Dupree said. "At this point, you're just staying on out of spite. That's not doing you any favors, and it only hurts the Department. It's lose-lose. Where's the sense in that?"

Kinsale knew he could drag out the conversation until Dupree gave up and left. And then, he could stretch out the disciplinary process for months. In the end, he might even win. But he also knew that Dupree was right. The final result was always going to be lose-lose, and he would eventually leave when his spite finally dried up and floated away in the breeze. Or the Department finally got enough to nail him. And it was a damn good offer.

"Okay. I'll go."

Dupree was already taking a deep breath to launch into his prepared rebuttal, and he had to stop short, when he realized that he'd won. He studied Kinsale for several seconds, and then his eyes soured with disappointment.

"What's wrong?" Kinsale laughed. "You got what you wanted."

"I got what the Chief wanted," he said. "What I want is to kick you out of the Department with nothing, and hopefully, have enough juice left over to bring criminal charges."

"That's never going to happen."

Dupree said grimly. "A man can dream, can't he?"

"So how do we do this?"

Dupree hesitated, as if he didn't believe or want to accept that Kinsale was truly acquiescing, but then set his briefcase on the back of the couch, opened it, and pulled out a beige file. "I almost didn't bring this because I thought there would be no point." He opened the file and removed several stapled pages. "All the relevant information is in the cover letter, which if you sign, has the power of a contract. The other pages are the legalese. You need to initial them and then sign the last page."

Kinsale stood and took the offered papers. Skimming the one-page letter, he was surprised to see the Chief's signature already on the bottom right, immediately next to an empty space for his. He flipped through the dense supporting pages. "You expect me to sign these without reading them? Or having my lawyer read them?"

"Do you read the user agreements on the Internet?"

"This is hardly equivalent to signing up for Spotify."

Dupree pointed at the cover letter. "Just read that and sign it. As you can see, it lays out the bones of the agreement. You leave and we pay. Have your lawyer go over the other pages and get those back to me by the end of the day tomorrow."

"I've got a heavy day tomorrow."

"Don't push it, Kinsale."

Kinsale so wanted to push it, but Dupree was right. "End of the day tomorrow."

He read the letter as he went to the kitchen to get a pen. It looked to be straightforward. He pulled away the supporting pages and set them aside on the counter. Then, he read the letter through one more time. Satisfied, he signed it and gave it to Dupree.

Taking the letter and slipping it into the beige folder, Dupree said, "That makes it final, Kinsale. You are now off the force. No comebacks."

"Got it."

"You're done with the investigation. No more telling people you're with the Department. You do that, and we'll come after you for impersonating an officer."

"Don't push it, Dupree."

Dupree scowled at Kinsale's sudden change of tone. He vacillated for a moment and then nodded to himself and tucked the folder into one of the pockets inside his briefcase. "End of the day tomorrow."

"Nice doing business with you."

Dupree turned on his heel, opened the door, and left. Kinsale reached out and closed the door. He hurried to the kitchen to pick up the retirement papers and then opened his bedroom door and tossed them on top of the Kennedy file. He made it back to open the apartment door just as Lewis topped the steps.

She breezed in like she had a running start, carrying an open Tecate can in one hand and the rest of the six-pack in the other.

"Cans?" he said.

"I figured it might take longer than fifteen minutes and I didn't have an opener." She made a beeline for the refrigerator. "Your Lieutenant Dupree didn't look very pleased."

"That seems to be his default setting." Kinsale went over to the couch.

She held up the beers. "Do you want one?"

"Definitely. Did he say anything to you?"

"Nope." She finished off her beer and brought two others into the living room. "He held the door open for me, though."

"If I'd done that, he would have accused me of cozying up to the press."

"Speaking of which," she said, flopping down next to him. "I can't believe you didn't call me this morning after the article came out."

"It was already out."

"Still, didn't it merit some reaction? Angry? Sad? Something?"

"I thought you did an amazing job of writing a few dozen paragraphs about the one-sentence complaint of a disgruntled detective."

"Thank you." She toasted him with her can. "That guy really doesn't like you."

"So, it is a guy."

She looked dismayed for a moment, but then shrugged. "You probably knew that anyway."

"I did."

"Was that why Internal Affairs was here?"

Since Dupree had left, Kinsale had gone back and forth about whether to tell her about taking the Department's offer. On the one hand, it could be big news for their relationship. On the other, it was news, and would be a good follow-up to her previous articles. He took a long, contemplative swig of his beer and said, "You're looking at a former MPD detective first class."

She needed a moment to process it, but when she did, her eyes ballooned, and she brought her left hand to her mouth. "Oh my God. They fired you? Because of my article?"

Her reaction warmed him. "No, no." He laid a calming hand on her arm. "I retired."

"You—?" She looked stunned. "But you've said over and over . . . Why?"

"Because they sweetened the package to about as good as it was ever going to get. And because I was eventually going to get pushed out, either because I finally stepped over some final, inviolate line, or they just kept ladling shit on top of me until I finally gave in. And because you were sitting out on my stoop wearing that orange top with your sunglasses keeping your confusion of red hair out of your magnetic green eyes."

She turned towards him, a smile blossoming on her face. "No more conflict of interest."

"None at all."

She leaned into him and kissed him hard. The beer cans quickly became an impediment, and they separated only to put them on the coffee table. They came together again, less frenzied but no less passionate, unleashing suppressed memories and reveling in their newfound freedom.

After a while, they paused long enough to take a breath and to slake their thirst with some short, quick sips of their beers. Then she took his hand and stood and moved towards the bedroom. He started to rise and then stopped, remembering the Kennedy case file lying on top of the bed. She looked confused by his reticence and stopped pulling.

In his charged state, sorting out the options was a challenge, but he quickly whittled his way down to two. Call a time-out while he went into the bedroom alone to scoop up the papers and hide them in the closet. Or keep up the momentum, go into the bedroom together, push the pages onto the floor, and deal with the consequences in the morning.

Spelled out like that, it was an easy decision.

CHAPTER 40

"It's hard to believe he was able to stay under the radar all those years," Lewis said as she put down the last page of the Kennedy file. It was the next morning, and she was sitting at his dining table. She'd gone through the papers as Kinsale had told her about Kennedy's predations.

"But that's the thing, isn't it?" he said. He was in the kitchen making a second pot of coffee. "He didn't really. Bernard Thayer knew. That school in Athens knew. I wouldn't be surprised if people at the schools in Montross and Midland also knew—or at least had an inkling." He carried the pot over to table and refilled their cups. "They knew but they didn't stop him. Whether for their own selfish reasons or because they just couldn't be bothered, they let him continue to prey on those boys."

"He really did some damage."

"And those are just the ones we know about, from a couple of years at the Georgetown Academy." He put the pot on the counter and sat next to her. "How many more are there out there?"

She shuddered at the thought and took a sip of her coffee. "What are you going to do? I'm guessing being off the force isn't going to deter you."

"No way. It might make it more difficult, but I feel like I'm really close."

"Really?"

"If it goes like I think it's going to go."

"And how is that?"

"Who would I be telling?" he asked. "Trish Lewis, intrepid reporter on the police beat for the city's dominant newspaper? Or Trish Lewis, with whom I hope to enter into a long and lustful relationship?"

"Enter into?"

"Continue?"

She smiled and draped a hand over his. It was still warm from holding the coffee, and he savored the sensation. "I won't write anything until you tell me it's okay," she said. "And if that happens to be before the Department releases any information, I'll just consider that yet another perk of our long and lustful relationship."

"That's good enough for me," he said and told her how he saw the day playing out.

When he finished, she asked, "And you think that—"

He stayed her with a raised hand. "All of that is just supposition. It's like I'm standing at the beginning of a long line of dominos. I think they're laid out right and that once the first one falls, they're all going to go down, one after the other, but I may be wrong. The first one might not topple, or it might fall sideways, or it might not trigger the chain reaction at all."

"Fair enough," she said, finishing off her coffee and standing. "I'll leave you to it. I've got to get home, grab a shower, and change. I can't really go to work looking like this."

He stayed at the table and sipped his coffee while watching her gather her things. It was a private and familiar moment, evoking memories of days passed, and he was both sad and grateful for it. When she was ready, he stood, pulled her close, and whispered in her ear, "I can't believe I let the past year go by without you."

"It got us to right here and right now." Her voice was thick and husky. She gave him a quick kiss and then eased away.

"See you tonight?" he asked.

"Definitely," she said and then was gone.

Kinsale waited until 10:00 to head out. It was a two-hour drive to Montross, putting him at the school around lunchtime, which he figured would be his best window. As he pulled up to the Montross School, he was relieved that Vice Headmaster Philip Bond's Mercedes convertible was not in its reserved space. He parked and climbed the steps into the school building.

In the office, he asked to see Bond. The receptionist informed him that he was at lunch and would return at 1:00 pm. Kinsale flashed an annoyed look. "I talked with him just yesterday about checking out the library here," he said. "I need to get a sense of your research facilities before making my final decision."

"It will only be an hour."

"My plane leaves in two hours. I came down here solely for the campus visit last week, but we had to skip the library."

"Of course," she said, her eyes brightening with recognition. "You spoke with Mr. Bond."

"I'm very impressed with the school."

"Let me see if I can have someone take you down there."

He waved off her suggestion. "I know where it is. We passed it on the tour, but we were running late so we didn't stop in. I can walk down there myself."

She was in a bind. As Bond had pointed out, rules were not meant to be broken at the Montross School, but she didn't want to take the chance of disappointing a prospective parent. Kinsale gave her a little push. "This is a big decision, for both of the twins."

She paled with his doubling of the stakes and reached for a visitor's badge. "If you could return this when you're finished." He gave her a smile that told her she'd made the right decision. He didn't envy her, dealing with Bond on the one hand and parents like him on the other.

The librarian was behind his desk, dressed in a slightly different tweedy jacket. He recognized Kinsale, and his eyes sought out the visitor's badge. Seeing it, he relaxed. "Back so soon?"

"Just taking one more look before we make the final decision."

"I can't say I blame you. It's one of the most important decisions you will make for your son. I assure you that you won't go wrong selecting The Montross School."

"Sons," Kinsale corrected, staying in character. "And I feel the same way. Do you mind if I glance at the yearbooks one more time?"

"Not at all. If I can be of any assistance, please don't hesitate to ask."

He started with the book from the year after Bernard Thayer left. He'd been replaced by Dr. Eugene Rollins, a patrician-looking man with the most pronounced widow's peak Kinsale had ever seen. He read through the new man's introductory letter. It made no mention of his predecessor. It could have been a case of "The King is dead, long live the King," but more likely they were just glad to be rid of the black man. Kennedy, or as he was known then, Nixon, appeared around a dozen pages later. He was leading a class, pointing with a yardstick at something he'd written on the blackboard in his pedantic handwriting.

Kinsale flipped through the following yearbooks and found Kennedy in the next two, but he was gone from the third. He checked the next two just to be sure, but Kennedy wasn't in either.

He considered two explanations for Kennedy's tenure extending beyond Bernard Thayer's departure. Either Thayer truly hadn't known about the man's predilections and had just moved on with his career. Or he had known and left without stopping the predation. Based on what he believed, Kinsale discarded the first option.

He checked the time on his phone and saw that he'd taken too much time nailing down the Kennedy timeline The receptionist had told him that Bond would be available at 1:00, but that didn't mean that he wouldn't return to the office earlier than that. If he did, Kinsale's time in the library would be short-lived.

He reversed the chronology and pulled out the book from the year before Thayer left. He forced himself to ignore the time pressures and scrutinized every photo, checking the faces and looking deep into the background. There were the requisite photos of Thayer and a couple of Kennedy, but Kinsale passed over them now. He reached the end without finding what he was looking for, so he put the book back on the shelf and pulled out the year-earlier volume.

The middle pages of each yearbook celebrated the School's athletic program. It fielded a lot of teams. The first four spreads featured team photos and an assortment of action shots for each of the major sports: Football, basketball, baseball, and—it appeared to Kinsale's untrained eye—polo. On the fifth and sixth spreads were team photos for the rest of the sports: Soccer, swimming, volleyball, rowing, track and field, cross country, and tennis.

That made for a lot of faces in the teams and in the crowds cheering them on, and Kinsale could feel his window closing as he worked his way through them. With the passing pages, doubts began to creep in. Maybe he'd once again jumped too soon. He already recognized that his investigation had a lot of holes in it. Was he just trying to make sense of what he had? Maybe it was time to—

And then there he was. In the cross-country team photo. At the end of the back row, standing half-a-pace away from his closest teammate, like he was the equipment manager or the scorekeeper. Kinsale wondered if that was his choice or the photographer's and decided it was probably a little of both. After all, he was the only black student that Kinsale had seen in the yearbooks. And he was the headmaster's son.

Bill Thayer had certainly seen his phone number in Kennedy's planner before he turned it over to Kinsale. He must have been horrified when he came upon it and probably agonized over what to do. As he'd admitted, he couldn't just pull out the single sheet. On the flip side of the April 29 notes was the hour-by-hour calendar for April 30, the day Kennedy died. Removing that sheet would have instantly raised suspicions. He and Dowling were the only ones with access to the notebook after the murder, and he couldn't afford to expose himself to that much scrutiny.

In the end, leaving the number made the most sense. It was well camouflaged, coming after Haslett's cancelled number and missing the area code. And it had almost worked. Casey and Harewood hadn't picked up on it, and Kinsale had probably looked at it a dozen times without making the connection. In the end, Thayer was only tripped up because his wife had used his phone to call Kinsale on the day that Dowling was arrested. Without that, Kinsale would never have recognized the number.

Once he'd connected the number to Bill Thayer, Kinsale reasoned that he had to have been a student at Montross. It was the only explanation for the almost inconceivable power that Kennedy had exerted over Bernard Thayer for so many years. Only something truly horrific could explain it—Kennedy's sexually abusing the son and the father doing nothing. That would make him Kennedy's for life, because the only thing worse than a child molester is a father who stays quiet about it. Kinsale already held the elder Thayer in profound disdain, but to choose his career over his son beggared belief.

Kinsale waved to the librarian as he walked out and headed down the long hall to the main doors. The lunch hour was ending, and dozens of students were milling around and talking before going into their classrooms. The population was still overwhelmingly white, although he saw several African American students, as well as one Latino and three Asians.

He didn't stop by the school office to return the visitor's pass. Instead, he went out the front door, started up his car, and drove off. He'd almost reached the highway when the red Mercedes turned onto the drive and came his way. The vice headmaster glanced over as they passed, and Kinsale saw the moment of recognition. He looked in his rearview mirror and saw the red flash of the Mercedes' brake lights, but then he was at the highway. He turned right and headed back to D.C.

He'd planned to drive straight through, but just before the Bend, he turned and parked in front of the Montross Inn. Margie Rodriguez was at the registration desk, a large check ledger and a pile of bills splayed in front of her.

"You're back," she said with a bright smile.

"I really like this place. I was thinking of coming down next weekend."

"We'd love to have you." Without even looking at the register, she added, "We have rooms available."

"Let me check with my friend. Can I have to the end of the day?"

"You can have to the end of the week."

"Great. Is Chief Campbell downstairs?"

"If the Snuggery is open, he's there."

Campbell was at the same table where Kinsale had left him the day before, with a napkin-wrapped bottle of Bud in front of him. Kinsale caught Anton Rodriguez's eye and signaled for two more.

"I thought I might find you here," Kinsale said.

"No might about it."

"Mind if I sit down for a moment."

Rodriguez appeared at Kinsale's side, and Campbell nodded at the two long-necked bottles he was carrying. "If one of those is for me, I don't mind a bit."

Kinsale waited for Rodriguez to put the bottles on the table and then sat down. Campbell finished off his current beer in one satisfied swallow and placed the bottle at the edge of the table. He pulled the new beer to him and applied a new napkin. "So, detective, what brings you back to our little town?"

Kinsale took a sip of his beer and savored it for a moment. "I had to visit the School again."

"I'll be honest with you. I'm hard-pressed to figure out why you're so interested in the time when that Thayer fella was the big dog up there. It's ancient history."

"Not so ancient. Can I ask you a few questions?"

He took a swig of his beer and wiped his mouth with the back of his hand. "Shoot."

"You were chief then, right?"

"Had been for a few years."

"And after Thayer left?"

"Still had a lot of good years left in me."

"I wonder if you could fill in some gaps then."

"Do what I can."

"After Thayer left, maybe about two or three years later, were there any whispers about sexual abuse up at the School?"

"Now you're asking about after Thayer left? I don't get it. What does that have to do with your case?"

"It might concern another individual who was at the school at that time. Was there anything?"

Campbell didn't respond. Kinsale waited. He'd watched these mental gymnastics uncounted times over his career. The individual had information but was trying to decide whether staying silent was the smarter move. And almost every time, the urge to show off eventually won. Kinsale just needed to let the process play out.

"I recall there might have been something around that time," Campbell said slowly, his Southern twang becoming even more pronounced.

"Did you investigate?"

He shook his head. "Not officially. I went up there and talked to the headmaster."

"Eugene Rollins."

Campbell raised an eyebrow. "You do your homework. Anyway, we had a little meeting."

"And?"

"And he said there was no problem."

"Did you believe him?"

Campbell laughed. "You don't know these people, do you?"

"I'm getting there."

"He might have been saying there was no problem, but what he was telling me was it was none of my business and to butt out."

"So, something did happen?"

Campbell shrugged.

"What did you do?"

"I butted out."

Kinsale slumped in his chair. He didn't need the confirmation that Kennedy had left the Montross School under a cloud, but it would have bolstered the investigation.

Kinsale's disappointment pleased Campbell, and he grinned. "But I did keep it at the back of my mind."

"And?" Kinsale sat up.

"Whenever the School hires a new teacher, they put a press release in the local paper." Campbell paused. "Usually, they include a paragraph about the teacher who left, thanking him for his years of service, blah, blah, blah . . . That time, because I was still curious, I paid attention and there was no mention of the one who left."

"Did you find out who it was?"

"Wasn't too hard. The School always sent me a faculty list at the start of each semester, with the addresses and phone numbers. Just had to compare."

"And?"

Campbell finished off his beer and moved it to the edge of the table. "Don't rightly recall his name."

"Was it Nixon? James Nixon?"

A light flickered at the back of Campbell's eyes. "Could be."

"He's the homicide victim. He changed his name at some point."

"'Cause of his, ah, peculiar habit?"

Rodriguez appeared at that moment, placed the new beer on the table, and took away the empties. Kinsale waited while the old chief wrapped the bottle and then asked, "Did you follow up on Nixon?"

Campbell took a drink before answering. "What was I supposed to do? Nobody down there was saying anything. I'm not going after a guy just for leaving his job."

"Why didn't you tell me this yesterday?"

"Because you asked about when that Thayer was here. This was after."

"You still should have said something, helped me out."

Campbell sneered. "Why the fuck would I help you out? You think buying me a couple of beers buys my soul. This town is here 'cause of the School. I may not like the way they look down their noses at us, but if you hurt the School, you hurt me, and you hurt Anton and Margie, and you hurt everybody around here."

"It's a murder investigation."

"Not down here it ain't. Anyway, the man was a kiddie-diddler. No loss there."

They faced off for a full minute. Campbell wasn't giving an inch, so Kinsale did. "Can I ask you about the car accident? The one in which Thayer's wife died."

"Already told you about it."

"I'm actually wondering about something you said."

"What's that?"

"You said you'd never seen her before that. You said she never left the School."

"Don't know about that, not for a fact, but I never saw her in town."

"Thayer was headmaster for four years, yet you never saw her?"

"Her people and my people—"

Kinsale pressed. "Not once?"

"As I recall, she had a condition."

"A condition?"

"Like I said, I never saw her, but people said she had trouble walking. Talk of a wheelchair."

Kinsale sat back and nodded.

Campbell eyed him. "But you knew that?"

"Not for sure, but I thought it was likely." Kinsale pushed his chair away from the table and stood up. "Got to get going. Thanks for your help, Chief."

He was almost to the door when Campbell called out. "Hey, don't forget to pay for the beers."

CHAPTER 41

Kinsale called Captain Scott immediately after he got back on the road. He told him what he'd found out about Bill Thayer and walked him through his thought process. Scott listened in silence and then asked, "Didn't we just do this a few days ago? Weren't you just as certain then that we should pull in this guy's father?"

"There is a bit of déjà vu here, but this time it's different. First, I told you we shouldn't pull in the old man because we didn't have enough. And second, I'm more than certain this time."

"I can't say I share your confidence. It's all circumstantial. In the end, when you scrape off all your suppositions, all you've really got is a man who didn't tell you that he was a student at the school where the murder victim once taught."

"And the Mona Lisa is just a picture of a smiling woman."

"You're not seriously comparing your half-assed work on this to the Mona Lisa?"

"Come on, I just laid the whole case on your desk, tied up with a pretty ribbon."

"Give me twenty minutes and I could lay out a completely different but equally plausible scenario putting it all on Chris Dowling."

"No, you couldn't, Captain. You're too married to the facts. I, on the other hand . . ."

"That's my point."

"What's the problem? You've got motive. You've got duplicity. You've got—"

"Opportunity?"

"Right, opportunity. I may be a little out on a limb on that."

"You go out any farther, and it's going to snap."

"Hear me out," Kinsale said. "Here's what we've got. Bill Thayer says he took his father to his 8:30 a.m. doctor's appointment, and Lucy Thayer says she stayed home and then she and Dowling stopped by The Dog for a coffee on the way to The Georgetown Academy."

"I don't see how that helps your argument."

"Who opened The Laughing Dog that morning?"

Scott was silent for a few seconds. "The barista. The kid from American University."

"Rennie Esposito," Kinsale said. "That would make sense except Lucy told me that Esposito was still new, and she hadn't let him open yet. She said he was going to start the following week."

Again, Scott was quiet. "Then what are you suggesting."

"We know that Bernard Thayer was at his doctor's office at 8:30 that morning."

"Yes."

"What we don't know is how he got there."

"His son . . ."

"Exactly," Kinsale said. "We have confirmation that old man Thayer was at his doctor's office, but we only have their word that Bill Thayer took him there."

"And if he didn't, he would have been the one to open the coffeehouse and . . . What?"

"Meet with Kennedy. Remember Bill Thayer's phone number was in the notebook. They were in touch. Thayer could have asked for an early meeting. That would be totally reasonable, not wanting to be seen with the man who assaulted him. They meet, he slips him the mickey, and then Kennedy leaves."

"And then?

"Bill helps out regularly at The Dog. I've seen him numerous times over the past months. I don't think it would have been weird for Esposito to show up to work and have Bill there. Easy thing for you to do would be to call Esposito and ask him."

"Finally," Scott said in an exaggerated tone. "Some real police work to do."

"Are you going to bring in Bill Thayer?"

"Let's see what Esposito says."

"Even without that, you have enough for an interview."

"Esposito first."

Kinsale stopped arguing because he knew Scott was right.

After some thought, Scott said, "Even if we put him at the scene, we can't prove motive. Only he knows whether Kennedy did anything to him. If he says nothing happened, we have nothing."

"We've got him lying about being at Montross."

"While that's indicative, it's hardly damning," Scott said. "Now if we could get his father—"

"Never going to happen."

"Then we're playing with fire here."

"I don't think so, Captain," Kinsale said. "I don't think Thayer will lie about what Kennedy did. He hid it for thirty years, and then he finally did something to purge it. I don't think he can shove it back down now. I don't think he wants to."

"That's pretty close to psycho-babble, Martin."

Kinsale let out a low chuckle. "I guess, but . . ."

"I'll talk to Esposito, then we'll see."

"Captain, I'm heading towards D.C. now. How about I come into the Second?"

"You're a civilian now, Martin. That's not going to happen."

"But—"

"You're at the top of the Chief's shitlist right now, and there's no one else even close. I let you near this, and I'll be right up there with you."

"I'm a material witness," Kinsale said. "I was there when Kennedy died. You could say that you brought me in to make sure that Thayer is telling you the truth."

Kinsale drove nearly a mile before Scott answered. "Depending on what the barista kid tells us, we may not even pull in Thayer."

"I'm certain you will."

Another half mile passed. "Okay," Scott said, sounding like he already regretted the decision. "I'll let Royale know you're coming in."

"See you in an hour."

Kinsale ran into heavy traffic just inside the Beltway and it was closer to ninety minutes before he arrived at the squad.

Royale Moon gave him a sad smile. "Sorry to see you go."

"Yeah, but at least I'm taking Magner with me."

"True. Normally I'd say that's a fair trade-off, but . . ."

"I appreciate that, Royale. You were my only sunshine these past six months."

She brightened. "I'd tell you don't be a stranger, but I can't think why you'd be coming back here."

"Just to see you," he said. "Is the Captain in?"

She nodded. "He's in Interview One."

Kinsale headed that way. It was the same room where Dupree, the FOP lawyer, and he had had their meeting. He opened the door to the adjacent observation area. It was a dark, narrow space with blank walls on three sides and a one-way mirror on the fourth. He wasn't alone. Paul Collison was standing at the glass. He reminded Kinsale of a younger Brian Magner, already going to seed and not caring enough to do anything about it. Collison looked over at Kinsale and grimaced like he'd just seen one of his ex-wives.

"Where's Homicide?" Kinsale asked quietly. The room was

soundproofed, but everyone tended to whisper. "They should be here."

Collison didn't respond at first, letting Kinsale know that he resented that he was there. "Captain called them last thing before going in. They told him two hours, and he told them he'd wait."

Kinsale nodded towards the mirror. "How far along are they?"

"Still going through the preliminaries."

"Did he ask for counsel?"

"Not yet."

"Idiot."

"They're all idiots."

Kinsale stepped to the one-way mirror and looked at Thayer. He was wearing a blue blazer and an open-collar white dress shirt. He was breathing easily, and his eyes were steady. Only his left thumb slowly rubbing the underside of his wedding band betrayed any sense of unease.

Scott's voice came through tinnily from the small square speaker attached to the ceiling above the mirror. "I'll be interested in your explanation."

Instead of answering, Thayer turned his head to the mirror, as if he'd sensed that Kinsale had arrived.

"As I said, we have a witness who places you at the crime scene," Scott went on.

Thayer turned back to Scott, but his expression didn't change, and he showed no inclination to respond.

Scott waited for about fifteen seconds and then said, "What James Kennedy did to you and to your brother-in-law was unforgivable. I'm not arguing that point. You may believe that what you did was understandable and righteous, and you may be thinking that a jury would sympathize with you, but let me tell you, that's not going to happen. You committed a capital offense. A jury couldn't rule anything else."

Again, he gave Thayer an opening to speak but got nothing. He went on. "We have motive and opportunity. We can also show that you have knowledge of Orphenadrine Citrate."

For the first time, Thayer looked uncertain, and Scott pushed into the opening. "That's the drug that was used to kill Kennedy. It's also used in the treatment of Parkinson's Disease. We have been reliably informed that your mother suffered from Parkinson's."

Kinsale had learned long ago that the art of interrogation was sensing flow. It could be as subtle as the breath of a breeze across the water on a dead-still afternoon. Turn away for a moment, and it would slip past unnoticed. And he would be the first to admit his own failings at it. Whenever he stepped into the interview room and closed the door behind him, the urge to assert control seemed to shut down the right side of his brain. He wanted to intimidate, scare, and sometimes punish. Often that worked despite itself, but never as well as a strategic approach. Scott appeared to have an innate feel for the flow. He was just sitting back, exuding calm and confidence. For a man in Thayer's position, nothing could be more worrisome. No screaming, threatening, or slamming of palms on the table. Scott left such theatrics to pikers like Kinsale.

"I take it too," Thayer said in a quiet voice.

"Excuse me, Mr. Thayer. What did you say?"

Louder he said, "I take Orphenadrine Citrate too."

"You take it too? You have Parkinson's?"

When Thayer nodded, Kinsale groaned so loudly that Collison glanced over. Kinsale couldn't believe he hadn't thought of that. He'd been so focused on the parent's health that he'd ignored the son's.

"I never would have guessed," Scott said.

Thayer smiled bitterly. "The wonders of modern science."

"Thank you for being so forthcoming, Mr. Thayer, but you should realize that this information is even more damaging to whatever defense you—"

"You can dispense with all that," Thayer said. "I'm not going to try to pretend that I didn't kill Kennedy."

Scott didn't react. He let a moment pass and then calmly said, "Mr. Thayer, please be careful about what you're saying. Are you certain you don't want to bring in a lawyer at this point?"

"What the hell is he doing?" Collison whispered angrily. "He's already read him up. It's on the tape. If he wants to dump, let him dump."

Kinsale ignored him. Collison had spent too much time rousting crackheads and other small-timers who didn't have the resources or the will to fight the system. They knew they were going to get rolled, so they just laid down. With someone like Bill Thayer, circumspection was critical. And a taped confession wasn't what it once was. Unless it was delivered in a manifesto or in court, juries assumed it was forcibly obtained.

Scott was taking every precaution. By giving Thayer yet another opportunity on tape to ask for his lawyer, even warning him that he was treading on dangerous ground, he hoped to short-circuit any future defense counsel's efforts to strike the confession.

"I understand," Thayer said dully.

"I want to make sure that you really do," Scott pressed. "What you say here is irrevocable. You are completely within your rights to refuse to say anything more and to request a lawyer."

"Jesus," Collison hissed.

Thayer shook his head.

"I'm sorry, Mr. Thayer, but I'll need you to respond verbally."

"No, I don't want my lawyer."

Scott nodded and eased back in his chair. "You're a lawyer yourself, aren't you, Mr. Thayer?"

Scott already knew the answer, but he was looking to reinforce the foundations under the confession. By highlighting that Thayer had a professional's knowledge of the law, Scott removed any way for him to later claim that he didn't understand his rights.

"I am," Thayer said.

"In that case, please take me through what happened on Wednesday the 30th of April."

Thayer didn't take the cue. He sat still, staring past Scott, past even the walls of the room. He was preternaturally still, not even appearing to breathe. After a minute of this, Collison gestured at the mirror and growled, "See, he's decided to clam up. Captain shouldn't have stopped him."

Kinsale looked over at his former colleague. He was likely fuming because now that he had the file in the Second, he had the most to gain when Thayer went down. Homicide would take the spotlight—they always did—but Collison was probably counting on a commendation, maybe even a bump in his pay grade.

Kinsale turned back to the war of wills in the interview room, although from the outside looking in, it looked more like two strangers sharing a table. Scott appeared to be completely relaxed, leaning back, his legs crossed, and his arms resting easily on his lap. For his part, Thayer might have been waiting for a bus.

"He was never going to go away," Thayer said at last.

"Who?"

"Kennedy. Nixon. Jim. He was never going to go away."

"How do you know that?"

"He threatened to come clean," Thayer spat out. "He used those exact words. Come clean. As if anything could wash that away."

"What was he going to come clean about?"

"About what he did to me and then what my father did. He said he'd turn himself in to the police unless we paid him."

"What do you mean about what your father did?"

"He tried to protect me. And our family. He made the decision not to go to the authorities about what Jim had done to me. He was willing to let him go free, but he didn't understand how that would make us vulnerable and how someone like Jim would seize on that vulnerability. That man was pure evil."

"Kennedy was blackmailing your father?"

"For the past thirty years. Whenever he got in trouble, he would show up at my father's door and threaten to destroy our lives. And he was going to do it again."

"How much did he want?"

"He demanded a $100,000. From me and my father. Each. He said he needed it to leave the country. He said if we gave it to him, we'd never hear from him again.

"When did he tell you this?"
"Wednesday morning."
"Where?"
"At The Dog."
"What time was this?"
"He arrived at 7:30."
"How long was he there?"
"It couldn't have been more than fifteen minutes. He wanted to stay because he was meeting someone there at 8:30, but I insisted that he leave because I needed him to be gone before Rennie showed up."
"Rennie Esposito?"
"He arrived just before eight."
"That's what he told us. He said you drove up a few minutes later."
"After Jim left, I locked up, parked a block away, and waited until I saw Rennie walk up. Then I pulled up like I was just arriving and opened the door for him. We'd done that a few times since he'd started, so I figured he wouldn't see anything unusual in it."
"Let's go back. Kennedy arrives at The Laughing Dog. Take me through it."
Thayer closed his eyes, as if he were picturing the scene. They were still closed when he said, "He parked right out front. I let him in the front door." He opened his eyes and looked at Scott. "He was an old man. The years and all that depravity had taken it out of him. But the malevolence was still there. He was oh-so-good at hiding it, but when he saw me and saw what I thought of him, he let it out."
"And."
Now Thayer pulled off his wedding ring, stared at it while he rubbed it with the fingers of his right hand, and then put it back on. "He came right out and demanded the money. He wanted it that day."
"What did you say?"
"It didn't matter because he was already a dead man."
"Already?"
"When he arrived, I asked him if he'd like a coffee. He asked for a latte. I'd already put the Orphenadrine in the cup."
"How much did you put in?"
"Just short of two grams. I'd crushed up eighteen pills the night before."
"The night before?"
Thayer looked confused by the question.
"You decided to kill him the night before?"
Thayer sneered. "I decided to kill him the moment I heard his voice on the telephone."
Scott paused for several seconds, letting Thayer's words hang in the air. "What if he hadn't wanted a coffee? What would you have done?"

"I would have beaten him to death with the cash register or stabbed him to death with a spoon," Thayer said calmly. "That wasn't going to be an issue, though. Jim was a man who always gave into his desires, and he would never have said no to a morning latte."

"So, what next? You expected him to leave and have a heart attack somewhere."

"That was the idea. No one would think anything of it. An old pervert's heart, black and diseased as it was, gives out under the pressure of being a fugitive. Case closed. Burn the body and toss his ashes in the landfill."

"But . . ."

"I didn't have enough Orphenadrine. He shouldn't have lasted long enough to meet with Chris. He should have been dead within a couple of hours." Thayer slapped his hands on the tabletop. "The man was a monster. Even in death, he had to destroy our lives."

Scott stayed quiet.

"And then that damn Kinsale was there. If he hadn't been . . ."

Collison bristled. Kinsale enjoyed that and liked that Thayer had said it on tape.

Sensing that Thayer had finished, Scott made a show of consulting his notes. In part, he was giving Thayer an opening to add something more, but he was also looking to fill in the blanks in the transcript. This would be his last best chance. The next time Thayer spoke on tape, he would have a lawyer who wouldn't let him be so forthcoming.

"What about your wife?"

"What about her?"

"She knew you were opening the café that morning. She never mentioned that."

Thayer looked unnerved. "Lucy knew nothing about this."

"She knew you were there."

"She knew I opened the door for Rennie," he insisted. "That's all. Like I said, we'd done it before. It would be nothing to her."

"What about Kennedy? Did she know you were meeting him?"

"She knows nothing about Jim and . . . and me. I never told her. I never told anyone."

"Except your father."

Thayer nodded.

"What about afterwards? Did you tell her anything?"

"Not a word."

Scott considered the response and returned to his notes.

Kinsale turned to Collison. "Give me your phone."

"Why?" Collison snapped. "Use your own damn phone."

"Just give it to me. You'll be glad you did."

Collison hesitated, trying to figure out what Kinsale was doing, but then shrugged and pulled out his phone.

Kinsale took it and called Scott. He heard the tinny ring through the speaker and watched Scott glance at his phone in annoyance. Then he looked up at Thayer. "Excuse me, I have to take this."

He answered, "What is it, Collison?"

"This is Martin. Keep pushing on his father."

"Why?"

"Because I think he was in on it."

"You think?"

"Ask him," Kinsale said and ended the call.

Scott put down the phone and went back to reading his notes for a minute or so. Then he said, "Mr. Thayer, we haven't yet talked about your father's involvement."

"My father?" Thayer looked from Scott to the mirror and then back. "He had no involvement."

"Sure, he did."

"No, he didn't. He didn't know anything about what I planned to do."

"I find that hard . . . very hard to believe."

"I can't speak to that."

"How did your father get to his doctor's appointment?"

"I arranged for a cab."

"Yet, he led us to believe—as did you—that you drove him there."

"Again, I can't control what you believe."

"You're splitting hairs here, Mr. Thayer."

Thayer shrugged. "I told him that I would meet him at the doctor's office. I was already there when he arrived."

"Did he know you were meeting with Kennedy that morning?" Scott asked.

Thayer hesitated and then reluctantly nodded. "Jim had told him. Turning the screws just a little more."

"Maybe he turned them too much. Maybe your father finally had had enough."

"My father had nothing to do with this."

"Kennedy… How did you put it? Destroyed your lives. Maybe you and your father decided to destroy his."

Thayer shook his head and jabbed at his chest with an index finger. "I decided to stop Jim from hurting my father anymore."

"The father who let Kennedy continue teaching after he molested you."

Thayer's cool finally broke. "You are… That's not… He would…"

"Mr. Thayer, this has gone on for too many years," Scott said in a quiet voice. "Please tell me what happened."

Thayer looked torn, and Kinsale struggled to understand why. A few minutes before, when he was confessing to murder and throwing his life away, he'd been placid and composed. Now, pressed for details about his father, he was tormented, wringing his hands like he was trying to strangle a snake. He was staring at Scott, pleading for a reprieve, but Scott gave him nothing except the expectation that Thayer would tell him what he wanted to know. Again, it was exactly the right strategy. Thayer had concealed the putrid truth from everyone for three decades. That effort must have been Herculean. Scott was giving him the chance to finally purge himself, and that must have seemed like a gift.

Thayer swallowed hard and deliberately separated his hands and placed them palm-down on the table. Sadness filled his red-rimmed eyes. "I think I would like to speak to my lawyer now," he said.

Scott didn't flinch, but Kinsale could see the surprise in his eyes. He hadn't expected that. Kinsale stole a glance at Collison. He looked dumbfounded. It had seemed that Scott had set up everything perfectly. The interview had proceeded like a bowling ball bearing down the center of the lane. Except now, at the last instant, the ball had careened to the side and tumbled into the gutter.

"That's within your rights, Mr. Thayer," Scott said, smart enough not to jeopardize everything that had come before by trying to get a little more. "Thank you for your assistance. I'll have an officer bring in a phone."

Scott closed and picked up the file. Slipping his phone into his pocket, he left the room. Collison and Kinsale hurried out of the observation room and met him in the hall. The three of them walked across the squad room and into Scott's office. Once the door was closed behind them, Collison started to speak, but Scott motioned for him to wait. He went around his desk, sat down, and called down to the duty officer to have someone take a phone into the interview room. That done, he leaned back into his chair, and asked, "Well?"

"You did real good, Captain," Collison said. He was sitting in one of the visitor chairs. "You played him like a fish. He's done for."

"Kinsale?"

Kinsale was standing by the door. "It's strange that he was willing to cop to everything but then wouldn't give up his father."

Ignoring Kinsale and speaking only to Scott, Collison said, "Maybe that's because his father wasn't involved."

"He was involved," Kinsale said.

Scott nodded. "I thought I had him. When he stepped back, there was nothing I could do."

"You did right," Kinsale said.

"We've got the killer," Collison protested. He didn't want to drag out the case any longer than necessary. He was like a relief pitcher who'd come into the game, thrown one pitch, and ended up getting the win. "We can't do anything to the father unless the son turns on him, and if he didn't do it in there, he's never going to do it. Let's not muddy the water."

Kinsale ignored Collison. "I think the old man finally found his balls and pulled in his son to kill Kennedy. Maybe Bill Thayer ground up the pills and put them in Kennedy's coffee, but his father gave him the push.

"And even now, after what his father did to him—and how it hurt all those other boys—he's still trying to protect him?" Scott asked.

"I'm never surprised at what a child will do for their parent," Kinsale said.

Scott nodded. "And I'm never surprised what a parent will do to their child."

CHAPTER 42

"It's after seven and the sun is only now going down," Kinsale said, for lack of anything else to say. He was sitting on his couch with his feet up on the table and a beer in his hand.

"Happens like that every year," Oturos twisted around in the reading chair and looked out the window. "Red sky at night, sailor's delight."

Kinsale only then noticed the pinkish hue to the evening sky. He finished off the last of his beer and tried to be delighted.

"Another?" Oturos asked. Kinsale nodded, and Oturos went and pulled two bottles out of the refrigerator. He gave one to Kinsale and dropped back into the chair "Maybe a few more of these and you'll start smiling. This is supposed to be a celebration, not a wake."

His friend was right. Kinsale should have been happy about closing the file on Kennedy. They'd nailed Bill Thayer. His confession gave them an airtight case. Kinsale doubted it would even make it to the jury. Given the sordid thirty-year history of the case, the U.S. Attorney would probably offer Thayer a reduced sentence in return for a guilty plea, but he was still going to do prison time.

Yet, that was what was eating at Kinsale. Thayer hadn't needed to confess. Without it, the case against him was entirely circumstantial. There were a lot of suppositions, but nothing that definitively proved he'd killed Kennedy. They couldn't even place the two of them together, and Thayer had a valid medical reason for having Orphenadrine Citrate. Collected in a file, the evidence looked damning, but if Thayer hadn't admitted to poisoning Kennedy, he'd have walked. And he was smart enough to have known that.

"So, are they going to give you your job back?"

"Not a chance," Kinsale said.

"Even after you broke the case for them?"

"Some things are more important."

"So, no gold watch."

"No," Kinsale laughed. "Although . . ." He reached into his pocket and pulled out his shield. "Scott slipped this to me before I left. For old times' sake, he said."

"Too bad he didn't give you your gun, too."

"It's much easier to get another one of those."

Kinsale's phone rang. He saw on the screen that it was the building entrance and he pressed nine. Getting up to open the door, he slipped the shield back into his pocket.

Trish Lewis came in wearing a white T-shirt and faded jeans with a torn left knee. Her hair was pulled back into as tight a bun as was possible, and her sunglasses were firmly in place. He asked, "Did you go to work in that?"

She glanced down. "After you called, I went home and put on my drinking clothes."

"You dressed right then." He gave her a quick kiss, and she pressed hard against him for an instant.

Seeing the two empty beer bottles on the coffee table, she said, "Looks like you two have started without me."

"We'd be a lot farther along except Martin's being a big downer. Now that you're here, maybe we can get this party started."

Kinsale grabbed a Corona for Lewis from the refrigerator, and she downed a catch-up swig. "Why the mopey face? You closed the case, and I get my exclusive."

"It's not over."

She looked leery. "It's over enough for my story, isn't it? I told my editor . . ."

"Don't worry about that."

"What do you mean then? You got Thayer? He killed Kennedy?"

"Yeah, but his father was in on it, and he's going to walk."

"His father?"

Kinsale nodded.

"Why can't you get him?"

"Because his son is willing to go down in order to protect him."

Oturos said, "But you got the guy who did the deed."

Lewis looked at Oturos. "That's not enough for Martin's sense of right and wrong."

"That does tend to get in the way," Oturos replied.

"Thayer's married to the woman who runs the coffeehouse, isn't she?" Lewis turned back to Kinsale. "I saw her that day when we had coffee there."

"Lucy."

"Have you talked to her?"

"No, and I don't think I will. At least not for a while. I've done enough damage to her family."

"Her husband did the damage," Oturos insisted. "All you did was catch him."

"Okay, quit your stalling," Lewis said, setting her beer on the coffee table and pulling her notebook, pen, and a mobile phone from her bag. "Start at the beginning and don't leave out a single detail. I have a Pulitzer to win."

So, that's what Kinsale did. This telling was different from his earlier debriefing with Scott because he told them everything. What he was thinking along the way. Where he'd stepped wrong. How he'd made the connections. When he finished, she turned off the recorder on her phone, and absentmindedly flipped through the notes she'd been taking. Oturos got up to fetch another round from the refrigerator. He gestured towards Kinsale, who waved him off.

"I see what you mean," she said. "The real criminal here is the father, and he's going to skip out of this unscathed."

"What kind of father lets his son go to jail for him?" Oturos said as he set a fresh bottle in front of Lewis and returned to his chair.

"It's not quite like that," Kinsale said. "No way I'm condoning what he's doing. The old man is a scumbag of the first order, but his son is going down regardless. That said, from what I've seen of Bernard Thayer, he's probably already rationalized that there's no point in both of them going to prison."

"It's grotesque," Lewis said, flipping back through her notes. "All the things that happened. All the people who have been hurt over all these years, probably many, many more than we know about. All because some school principal with a fancy title decided not to turn in the man who molested his son. It's really hard to believe."

It was hard to believe. And suddenly Kinsale no longer did. He didn't believe that Bernard Thayer would have kept putting boys at risk for all those years, or now let his son go to prison, just to protect his career and reputation. He didn't know what would drive a man to such despicable ends, but he knew that wouldn't.

"What?" Lewis asked.

Kinsale looked at her. "What do mean, what?"

"You're smiling."

"Am I?"

"You are. What's up?"

"I need to talk with Bernard Thayer."

"Why?" Oturos asked. "You said he's in the clear."

"For Kennedy, maybe, but maybe not for something else."

Lewis's eyes sparkled with surprise. "Something else? What?"

"I have no idea," Kinsale admitted. "That's why I'm going to see him. Convince him to tell me."

"Why would he tell you?" she asked.

"I can be very persuasive." He stood up. "I should be back in a couple of hours. Will you wait?"

"Will my story be better for it?"

"Immeasurably."

She settled into the cushions. "Then I'm staying. Manny is much better company than you are right now anyway."

Kinsale leaned over and kissed her. "When I get back, I'll be in a much better mood. I guarantee it."

He picked up his wallet, phone, and key ring and headed for the door. He was a pace short of it when Lewis said, "Brian Magner wasn't the snitch."

Kinsale's throat tightened, but he resisted the urge to clear it, as he stopped and turned around.

"I tracked him down today," she said, twisting on the couch so she could look at him. "The second that he opened his mouth, I knew it wasn't him, but I asked anyway. He nearly bit my head off."

"That's his default setting."

"But he deserves to be upset. The Department fired him over something he didn't do. And the snitch is still out there."

From the moment he'd first had that inspiration, Kinsale had known this conversation was inevitable. And he'd known what he'd have to do. "It would have to be someone who knows your home phone number," he said.

She shook her head. "Cops can get unlisted numb . . . How did you know he called my . . ." Her eyes widened and then her mouth fell open. "No. No. It was you."

He nodded and offered up a grin that he hoped was sheepish enough to earn him some forgiveness.

But Lewis wasn't in a forgiving mood, and she leaped off the couch, crossing the space between them in two long strides and cuffing him hard on the shoulder. "You bastard. How could you do that to me?"

As much as Kinsale didn't want to deal with the issue at that moment—itching to go after Thayer—he knew that it needed to be hashed out now. "I didn't do it to you," he said. "I did it for me."

"What the hell is that supposed to mean?"

"First off, when this started there was no us. There was just you and—"

"There was always an us." Hurt swamped her anger. "Life just kept getting in the way."

Her words grabbed at his solar plexus. "Then this was just another piece of life."

"But it wasn't, was it? You lied to me."

"I figured if you didn't know it was me feeding you the information, you would chase the story a lot harder."

"You let me run a piece that you knew was wrong," she said, her anger building again.

Kinsale glanced at Oturos, who appeared to be fascinated by the label on his beer bottle. Kinsale couldn't blame him. "It wasn't so much wrong as . . . incomplete. And if you remember, I warned you not to run the story. I told you it would come back to bite."

"After you gave me the red meat? You knew there was no way I wasn't going to go with it." She waved an annoyed hand. "Anyway, warning me like that was just a way to egg me on."

"Wait." He raised his hands to placate her. "Just wait. Let me tell you how it went down."

She was as angry as he'd ever seen her, but she managed to pull herself back from the edge. Still not trusting trust herself to speak, she gestured for him to go on.

He started slowly, feeling his way. "When I first got the idea, I was just trying to create some cover. I was going to be stepping on a lot of toes at the Second. I thought that by sowing some confusion, maybe even a little dissension, I could distract their attention."

"You could have told me."

"You wouldn't have been as believable if you knew. Scott would have seen right through you."

"Give me some credit."

"He's better than both of us put together."

"Better than you." She let out the smallest shadow of a smile and then to herself added, "And my home phone, I should have known."

"Should have known?"

"I figured he was calling that number to make it harder for the Department to connect him to me. Who even has a landline anymore?" Then she looked at him through narrowed eyes. "But you were just making sure we never talked."

"I was always a little anxious that you might pick up. That would have given the game away."

"The game," she repeated, her indignation regenerating.

"It got out of hand," he admitted. "Once I saw the spotlight moving toward Magner . . . Maybe I pushed harder than I should have because I saw a chance for a little payback."

"Payback?"

"You said it yourself. The guy is an asshole. And he was an even worse cop."

"Still," she said. "You put me in the crossfire."

"Yes, I did. And I'm really sorry. Truly. But, if you let me go and talk to Bernard Thayer right now, I'll see what I can do about getting you that Pulitzer as an apology gift."

"Apologift."

"What?"

"Apologift."

"That's a word? How is that a word?"

"Because of Neanderthals like you."

Throughout the conversation, they'd gradually moved closer to each other and now they were only a couple of inches apart. He tested a smile and asked quietly, "Pulitzer?"

She eyed him coolly and then, turning away, said. "Try to get some photos while you're at it."

CHAPTER 43

Kinsale waited until he was five minutes away from Hawthorn before making the call. Bernard Thayer answered on the third ring.

"I don't want to speak to you," Thayer said. "My son—"

"We're way past caring about what you want to do."

"Why are you hounding us?"

"Hounding? After what you've done for the past three decades?"

"What Bill did—"

"For Christ's sake, stop using your son as a shield," Kinsale yelled as he whipped around a slow-moving red Toyota pick-up and accelerated up Colesville Road.

"I don't—"

"I'll be at your house in a couple of minutes." He hung up.

He pulled into Hawthorn, stopped at the gate, and told the guard that he was Detective Martin Kinsale with the Metropolitan Police Department, and he was there to see Thayer. The guard picked up the phone, spoke briefly, and then hung up. "Dr. Thayer says to tell you that he can't see you this evening. He wants that you should come back tomorrow."

Kinsale pulled his shield out of his pocket and jabbed it out the window. "Raise the goddamned gate."

The words were barely out of his mouth before the bar started to rise.

When Thayer opened his apartment door, he was yet again dressed to impress. He was wearing a navy-blue sweater vest over a club tie with gray flannel pants and black oxford shoes, but he didn't look well. The skin around his eyes was pasty, as if he'd been crying.

Kinsale shouldered past him. The old man made a protesting sound but offered no resistance. Thayer shut the door and shuffled across the room, his eyes tracking the floor. When he reached the dining table, he put a hand on the back of one of the chairs for support and looked up.

"You don't seem surprised to see me," Kinsale said.

"I assumed you would get past the guard."

For the third time that night—and the second time illegally—Kinsale flashed his shield. "I've got a little more juice now."

"Congratulations."

"You're sweating, Dr. Thayer."

"Am I?" He rubbed a free hand across his forehead and looked down at it. "Maybe I should turn up the air conditioning."

"Why don't you sit down instead? I have a few questions."

Thayer moved stiffly to the couch and dropped onto the cushions. Kinsale remained standing.

"What did Kennedy have on you that you are willing to ruin your son's life . . . and have ruined the lives of so many other boys?"

Thayer squirmed in the couch like he was sitting on top of the truth, and it was trying to escape. "Bill already told you."

"You haven't told me a goddamned thing that was true." Kinsale crossed the space between them in two steps and towered over Thayer. "Every word out of your mouth since this whole thing started has been a lie."

Thayer was silent, except for the whisper of his shallow breathing. When he realized that his intimidation wasn't having any effect, Kinsale stepped back and let his blood come off the boil. In a measured voice, he said, "At this late date, after all you've done, and with your son facing a capital murder charge, isn't it time that you stood up and did the right thing?"

Thayer struggled to lift his head and then gave Kinsale a doleful look. In a choked voice, he said, "I don't know what the right thing is anymore."

"It's really not that hard."

"It seems to have become hard for me."

"Letting your son go to prison to protect you is not the right thing."

Thayer flinched at the words, so Kinsale pressed ahead. "You planned Kennedy's murder together, didn't you?"

The sadness slid off Thayer's face like rainwater down a windowpane, replaced by loathing and anger. "That man deserved to die. After everything he'd done, he deserved to die."

"Maybe, but that wasn't your call."

"If not ours, then whose?" He pushed himself up from the couch. It was an effort, and it quickly became too much, so he dropped back down onto the cushions. Catching his breath, he said, "Who better than the men whom he'd destroyed?"

"You've got it all wrong. He didn't destroy you. You did. When you decided to let his abuse go unpunished. You destroyed your own life and your son's and Chris's and . . . Do I need to go on?"

Thayer absorbed the words like body blows, one after another, and then closed his eyes. Kinsale waited, and finally the old man murmured, "I tried to stop him."

"Really?" Kinsale asked doubtfully. "How?"

"I told him that he had to leave the school at the end of the term, and that he would be stricken from any affiliation with The Montross School."

"That punishment hardly fits the crime."

Thayer looked up at Kinsale and there were still some embers burning in his eyes. "It was the most I could do. I couldn't bring the School into disrepute, and my position was always tenuous."

"The man had sexually abused your son."

"It was the most I could do," Thayer repeated miserably.

"But then you didn't even do that."

Thayer didn't respond.

"What happened? Why did you let Kennedy off the hook?"

Thayer remained quiet, but he stole the briefest of subconscious glances at the photos on the wall. If Kinsale had blinked at that moment, he would have missed it, but he didn't and now he looked there. He'd seen the two columns of photos on his other visits to the apartment. Top-to-bottom, the twelve pictures portrayed the history of the Thayer family. At the top were the two earliest photos side-by-side. On the left was the formal black-and-white shot of Thayer standing behind his seated wife, who had their young son on her lap. The photo on the left was taken several years later and showed Bill and Bernard Thayer tossing a baseball while his wife sat at a picnic table.

"What was your wife's name?" Kinsale asked.

Thayer winced at the question, and Kinsale knew he'd hit a mark. "Pamela."

"She died in a car crash, didn't she?"

Thayer began to breathe faster, sharp and shallow gasps, as if he couldn't pull enough air into his lungs. Kinsale took no small pleasure in seeing the guilt radiating off the man.

"She was going to report Kennedy to the police, wasn't she?"

Thayer looked up, his tortured eyes begging Kinsale to stop.

"And you tried to stop her." Kinsale was feeling his way as he talked. "What did you do?"

Thayer looked panicky now and reached out a supporting hand to the armrest even though he was seated. He closed his eyes again and sat still, trying to control his labored breathing. Sweat shimmered on his forehead. When he finally opened his eyes, he said simply. "Pamela had a mind of her own. We had agreed on what was best, for the school, for my career, and for Bill, but she changed her mind. She said she couldn't live with it. I had to stop her. I had to."

"How soon after you found out what Kennedy had done was this?"

"About a week. Bill was already on his way to Canada. I thought everything was going to work out, but she couldn't do it. It was eating away at her, worse than the Parkinson's."

"Of course, it was," Kinsale said harshly. "The man who molested her son was walking around free, her son had been exiled to Canada, and her husband was—"

"He was my son too."

"Then you should have protected him and fought for him, instead of trying to negotiate the best result for your career."

"What was I supposed to do? If I'd reported Kennedy, down there in Montross, he would have gotten away with it. That was just the way it was back then. They wouldn't believe a black boy. Not then, probably not now. But I would have lost my job, and Bill would have been kicked out. He had a chance to become something big. That's what he did. He became a lawyer."

"No," Kinsale said. "He became a murderer."

Thayer groaned. "I couldn't have known that."

The old man was fighting for breath now, but Kinsale didn't feel any sympathy. "So, what did you do to stop your wife from going to the police?"

"I just wanted to stop her. I needed some time to convince her that my way was better."

"What did you do?" Kinsale demanded.

He hesitated, not wanting to answer, but he'd already pushed his skis over the edge and gravity had taken over. "Every morning I gave her the medicine in her orange juice. That day I put in some extra. We'd been warned that exceeding the prescription could make her ill. That's all I wanted to do. I swear. I just wanted her to feel too sick to go. I was certain that once she'd had the time to calm down, she would see that I was right."

Kinsale waited until Thayer continued, "It seemed to work. She went back to bed, and I went to work, but like I said, she was a strong woman. She decided to drive herself. And instead of going to the town police, she wanted to go to the State Police."

"Because she knew Chief Campbell wouldn't do a damn thing."

"But as strong as she was mentally, she was weak physically and . . . Maybe she became more ill or maybe she fell asleep, but . . ."

Thayer let the sentence fade away, too weak to go on, and in that moment, Kinsale realized what the old man had done. So intent had Kinsale been on finding out what had happened thirty years in the past that he'd ignored the present. He crossed to the couch, pulled up Thayer, and shook him by the shoulders. "You've taken something, haven't you?"

Thayer managed a feeble smile. "Finally, I've done something brave."

"Brave?" Kinsale tossed him back onto the couch. He flopped like a rag doll. "You call this brave? You're taking the easy way out, leaving your son to face the music alone." He pulled his phone out of his pocket.

The old man weakly waved his hand. "Don't bother. I took half the bottle. They'll never get here in time."

"What did you take?"

Thayer pressed his lips together and settled back into the couch.

Kinsale started to make the call, but then thought better of it. If Thayer was going to die, he wasn't going to stand in his way. Letting Bernard Thayer leave this life would be a favor to everyone. He watched him for about half a minute. Sweat beaded on the old man's forehead, and his breathing became a brutal wheezing. His skin had the pallor of old potatoes.

"Did Bill know?" Kinsale asked.

Thayer tilted his head. "Know?"

"That you killed his mother."

"No!" The word drained him.

"But Kennedy knew, didn't he?"

"That man could find evil among the angels." He was slurring his words now, and a thin line of spittle rolled down his chin. "He honed right in on it. Within a day, he came and told me that he knew what had happened, but that he'd keep it a secret. He acted like he was doing me a favor, friend to friend, but we both knew he was just sinking in the hook."

"How did he know?"

"He told me that it was what he would have done. Maybe he and I weren't as different as I want to believe."

"And now you're both dead."

"Not quite," he whispered. "Give me a few more minutes."

"Well, you're going to die alone," Kinsale said and headed for the door.

"I did what I thought was right," Thayer protested faintly.

"But you couldn't have been more wrong," Kinsale said and headed out into the hallway, leaving the door ajar.

He stopped and called 911. When the operator came on the line, he identified himself as an MPD detective, recited the address, and told her that a man was dying of a drug overdose. She told him to stay on the line.

He walked to the elevator, holding the phone to his ear. He had just pushed the call button when she came back on the line and told him the paramedics would arrive in ten minutes.

The elevator door opened. He stood there, looking into the empty car and trying to make up his mind. When the door slid shut, he took that as a sign and headed back toward Thayer's apartment. Maybe this time, he could do CPR for ten minutes without passing out.

ABOUT THE AUTHOR

Gerry Donohue is a novelist and an author of books on tennis and cycling. He lives in the south of France.

Made in United States
Troutdale, OR
09/03/2023

12597988R00149